THE MYSTERIOUS BOOKSHOP
presents

THE BEST MYSTERY STORIES OF THE YEAR

2025

THE MYSTERIOUS BOOKSHOP
presents

THE BEST MYSTERY STORIES OF THE YEAR 2025

INTRODUCTION BY
JOHN GRISHAM

FOREWORD BY
OTTO PENZLER, SERIES EDITOR

**THE MYSTERIOUS PRESS
NEW YORK**

THE MYSTERIOUS BOOKSHOP PRESENTS
THE BEST MYSTERY STORIES OF THE YEAR 2025

Mysterious Press
An Imprint of Penzler Publishers
58 Warren Street
New York, NY 10007

Compilation copyright © 2025 by Penzler Publishers, LLC

Foreword copyright © 2025 by Otto Penzler

Introduction copyright © 2025 by John Grisham

"The Golden Road (To Unlimited Devotion)" by David Avallone. First published in *Friend of the Devil: Crime Fiction Inspired by the Songs of the Grateful Dead* (Down & Out Books). Copyright © 2024 by David Avallone. Reprinted by permission of the author.

"Home Game" by Craig Faustus Buck. First published in *Alfred Hitchcock Mystery Magazine* (July/August). Copyright © 2024 by Craig Faustus Book. Reprinted by permission of the author.

"Under the Blackjack Tree" by V. P. Chandler. First published in *Killer Nashville* (October). Copyright © 2024 by V. P. Chandler. Reprinted by permission of the author.

"Jamming at Jollies" by Tracy Falenwolfe. First published in *Black Cat Weekly* (#151). Copyright © 2024 by Tracy Falenwolfe. Reprinted by permission of the author.

"Totality" by James Hearn. First published in *Dark of the Day: Eclipse Stories*, ed. by Kaye George (Down & Out Books). Copyright © 2024 by James Hearn. Reprinted by permission of the author.

"The Art of Disappearance" by April Kelly. First published in *Dark Yonder* (Summer). Copyright © 2024 by April Kelly. Reprinted by permission of the author.

"Eat My Moose" by Erika Krouse. First published in *Conjunctions* (#82). Copyright © 2024 by Erika Krouse. Reprinted by permission of the author.

"The Other Brother" by Tom Larsen. First published in *Black Cat Weekly* (#162). Copyright © 2024 by Tom Larsen. Reprinted by permission of the author.

"Same Old Song" by Billie Livingston. First published in *Black Cat Weekly* (#146). Copyright © 2024 by Billie Livingston. Reprinted by permission of the author.

"Only a Story" by Kai Lovelace. First published in *Crimeucopia: Through the Past Darkly* (Murderous Ink Press). Copyright © 2024 by Kai Lovelace. Reprinted by permission of the author.

"The Secret Menu" by Sean McCluskey. First published in *Scattered, Smothered, Covered & Chunked: Crime Fiction Inspired by Waffle House*, ed. by Michael Bracken & Stacy Woodson (Down & Out Books). Copyright © 2024 by Sean McCluskey. Reprinted by permission of the author.

"Mister George" by Richard A. McMahan. First published in *Black Cat Weekly* (#137). Copyright © 2024 by Richard A. McMahan. Reprinted by permission of the author.

"Dream Stuff" by Lou Manfredo. First published in *A Dozen Ways to Die* (Genius Book Publishing). Copyright © 2024 by Lou Manfredo. Reprinted by permission of the author.

"Her Dangerously Clever Hands" by Karen Odden. First published in *Crimeucopia: Through the Past Darkly* (Murderous Ink Press). Copyright © 2024 by Karen Odden. Reprinted by permission of the author.

"A New Weariness" by Anna Scotti. First published in *Ellery Queen Mystery Magazine* (May/June). Copyright © 2024 by Anna Scotti. Reprinted by permission of the author.

"Snapshot" by Shelagh Smith. First published in *Devil's Snare: Best New England Crime Stories*, ed. by Susan Oleksiw, Ang Pompano, and Leslie Wheeler (Crime Spell Books). Copyright © 2024 by Shelagh Smith. Reprinted by permission of the author.

"Effie's Oasis" by Casey Stegman. First published in *Motel: An Anthology*, ed. by Barbara Byar (Cowboy Jamboree Press). Copyright © 2024 by Casey Stegman. Reprinted by permission of the author.

"The Lost and the Lonely" by Lamont A. Turner. First published in *All the Love You Can Buy for a Dollar* (Twelve House Books). Copyright © 2024 by Lamont A. Turner. Reprinted by permission of the author.

"Run and Gun" by Joseph S. Walker. First published in *Chop Shop: Season One, Volume 2* (Down & Out Books). Copyright © 2024 by Joseph S. Walker. Reprinted by permission of the author.

"Through Thick and Thin" by Andrew Welsh-Huggins. First published in *Ellery Queen Mystery Magazine* (September/October). Copyright © 2024 by Andrew Welsh-Huggins. Reprinted by permission of the author.

First edition

Interior design by Maria Fernandez

All rights reserved. No part of this book may be reproduced in whole or in part without written permission from the publisher, except by reviewers who may quote brief excerpts in connection with a review in a newspaper, magazine, or electronic publication; nor may any part of this book be reproduced, stored in a retrieval system, or transmitted in any form or by any means electronic, mechanical, photocopying, recording, or other, or used to train generative artificial intelligence (AI) technologies, without written permission from the publisher.

Library of Congress Control Number: 2025935473

Hardcover ISBN: 978-1-61316-683-3
Paperback ISBN: 978-1-61316-684-0
eBook ISBN: 978-1-61316-685-7

10 9 8 7 6 5 4 3 2 1

Printed in the United States of America

CONTENTS

Otto Penzler, Foreword — xi

John Grisham, Introduction — xv

David Avallone, The Golden Road (To Unlimited Devotion)
Friend of the Devil: Crime Fiction Inspired by the Songs of the Grateful Dead, ed. by Josh Pachter (Down & Out) — 1

Craig Faustus Buck, Home Game
Alfred Hitchcock Mystery Magazine (July/August) — 13

V. P. Chandler, Under the Blackjack Tree
Killer Nashville (October) — 31

Tracy Falenwolfe, Jamming at Jollies
Black Cat Weekly (Issue #151) — 49

James Hearn, Totality
Dark of the Day: Eclipse Stories, ed. by Kaye George (Down & Out) — 65

April Kelly, The Art of Disappearance
Dark Yonder (Summer) — 81

Erika Krouse, Eat My Moose
Conjunctions (Issue #82) — 95

Tom Larsen, The Other Brother
Black Cat Weekly (Issue #162)   113

Billie Livingston, Same Old Song
Black Cat Weekly (Issue #146)   143

Kai Lovelace, Only a Story
Crimeucopia: Through the Past Darkly
(Murderous Ink)   163

Sean McCluskey, The Secret Menu
Scattered, Smothered, Covered & Chunked: Crime Fiction Inspired by Waffle House, ed. by Michael Bracken & Stacy Woodson (Down & Out)   191

Richard A. McMahan, Mister George
Black Cat Weekly (Issue #137)   207

Lou Manfredo, Dream Stuff
A Dozen Ways to Die
(Genius Book Publishing)   229

Karen Odden, Her Dangerously Clever Hands
Crimeucopia: Through the Past Darkly
(Murderous Ink)   249

Anna Scotti, A New Weariness
Ellery Queen Mystery Magazine (May/June)   277

Shelagh Smith, Snapshot
Devil's Snare: Best New England Crime Stories, ed. by Susan Oleksiw, Ang Pompano, and Leslie Wheeler (Crime Spell)   303

Casey Stegman, Effie's Oasis
  Motel: An Anthology, ed. by Barbara Byar
  (Cowboy Jamboree)   319

Lamont A. Turner, The Lost and the Lonely
  All the Love You Can Buy for a Dollar
  (Twelve House)   335

Joseph S. Walker, Run and Gun
  Chop Shop: Season One, Volume 2 (Down & Out)   363

Andrew Welsh-Huggins, Through Thick and Thin
  Ellery Queen Mystery Magazine
  (September/October)   405

Bonus Story
Jacques Futrelle, The Problem of Cell 13   441

The Best Mystery Stories of 2025 Honor Roll
Additional outstanding stories published in 2024   479

FOREWORD

Welcome to the fifth annual edition of *The Mysterious Bookshop Presents the Best Mystery Stories of the Year*, which pays tribute to the large number of authors who set pen to paper (well, yes, mostly they sit in front of their computers) in an attempt to tell a story that captivates a reader's attention by being colorful, poetic, and original, compelling them to read it all the way through and inspiring a sense of awe or, at least, pleasure.

It is evident that crime fiction means a great deal to them. There can be no other explanation for deliberately choosing to engage in such a challenging form of literature. Heaven knows, it is not a certain, immediate path to wealth and fame

As has been true every year, this anthology (and its predecessor, *The Best American Mystery Stories of the Year*) is a wonderful collection of original fiction about extremes of human behavior caused by despair, hate, greed, fear, envy, insanity, or love—often in combination. Desperate people may consider desperate acts, and desperation is a fertile ground for poor choices. Many of the authors in this cornucopia of crime have described how antisocial solutions to difficult situations may occur, and why perpetrators felt that their violent responses to conflicts seemed appropriate to them.

The psychology of crime has become the dominant form of mystery fiction in recent years, while the classic detective tale of observation and deduction has somewhat faded into the background. Those tales of pure deduction may be the most difficult mystery stories to write, as it has become increasingly difficult to find original motivations for murder, a new murder method, or an original way to hide a vital clue until the detective unearths it.

The working definition of a mystery story for this series is any work of fiction in which a crime, or the threat of a crime, is central to the theme or the plot. The detective story is merely one subgenre in the literary form known as the mystery, just as are romantic suspense, espionage, legal legerdemain, medical thriller, political duplicity, and those told from the point of view of the villain.

To find the best of these stories is a year-long quest, largely enabled by my invaluable colleague, Michele Slung, who culls the mystery magazines, both in print and online, for suitable stories, along with short story collections (works by a single author) and anthologies (works by a variety of authors), popular magazines, and literary journals.

A fast and smart reader, she looks at somewhere between three thousand and four thousand stories a year, largely to determine if they are mysteries (you can't tell a story by its title), and then to determine if they are worth serious consideration. I then read the harvested crop, passing along the best to the guest editor, who collaborates with me to make the final selection of twenty stories, with another ten being listed on an honor roll. I also add a favorite story from the past as an example of a well-crafted mystery story from a hundred or so years ago.

When I began to search for contemporary crime fiction for *The Best of . . .* , literary journals were a particularly fertile field, where the authors were often surprised that their stories had been selected. Although they had written about crime, suspense, violence, and terror, their stories did not have detectives and so they didn't regard their work as fitting into the genre.

Although more than a hundred of these journals are still examined every year, there have been fewer and fewer stories suitable for this collection (although one of my favorite tales was originally published in *Conjunctions*, one of the greatest of all literary magazines). I don't know why this is so but hope it is happenstance rather than a trend.

While *Ellery Queen Mystery Magazine*, *Alfred Hitchcock Mystery Magazine*, and *The Strand Magazine* continue to publish outstanding stories, the popular consumer magazines that once upon a time proudly published detective and crime fiction have either stopped or gone out of business. Some extraordinary stories have appeared between the covers of *The Saturday Evening Post*, *The*

New Yorker, Playboy (which featured stories by Donald E. Westlake and Lawrence Block with regularity), *Redbook* (in which Dashiell Hammett's *The Thin Man* made its first appearance), and others, but it is very rare to discover a crime gem today.

Authors now mostly find a market (albeit not a lucrative one) in anthologies published by small presses or local groups. Five years ago, I had never heard of several of the publishing companies represented in this volume, including Cowboy Jamboree Press, Murderous Ink Press, Twelve House Books, and Genius Book Publishing.

Most are published electronically, with a print-on-demand option, and have modest circulations, so could not possibly pay their authors more than the price of a fast-food meal (though some are produced as fundraisers so neither editors nor writers earn even that much)—a tribute to the dedication of all those involved in the perpetuation of this most popular and successful form of literature.

In a slightly different context, the same could be said of the guest editors of *The Mysterious Bookshop Presents the Best Mystery Stories of the Year*—Lee Child, Sara Paretsky, Amor Towles, Anthony Horowitz, and, this year, John Grisham—all of whom took on the time-eating job of reading and writing for this collection. They took time away from their own work to selflessly help spread the word about these stories and authors, helping them reach a wider audience as (it is hoped) many avid mystery readers will discover them in this volume.

I lack the vocabulary to thank them adequately.

John Grisham is the author of more than fifty consecutive #1 bestsellers and has been translated into nearly fifty languages. That is not a typo. Over fifty consecutive #1 bestsellers which, I'm confident to say, is unequaled in the world of American literature.

His career began with *A Time to Kill* (1989) but it was his second book, *The Firm* (1991), that secured his position as the number one author of legal thrillers in the history of printed books with more than three hundred million copies sold. Of his more than fifty published books, nine have been made into films for theatrical release and another five were adapted for television.

Of course, by the time this book is released, all these numbers will probably have increased.

The work has been completed on this first-rate collection so the search has already begun for suitable stories for next year's edition. To qualify, a story must be–duh–a mystery and must have had its first English-language publication in the calendar year of 2025. If you are the author of such a work, or its editor, or any interested party (your credentials will not be reviewed), please feel free to submit it.

If the story was first published online, only hard copies will be read; these must include the name of the e-zine or anthology, the date on which it was published, and contact information. No unpublished stories are eligible, for what should be obvious reasons. Submitted material will not be returned. If you do not trust the US Postal Service to deliver the book, magazine, or tear sheets, please enclose a self-addressed post card to receive confirmation.

The earlier submissions are received, the less hurriedly they will be read. Please send submissions to Otto Penzler, The Mysterious Bookshop, 58 Warren Street, New York, NY 10007. If your story is one of the fifty or sixty or more customarily mailed by thoughtless dunderheads during Christmas week, it may not receive quite the same respectful reading as those submitted in less crowded months. If the story is published during the last week of the year, okay, fair enough. But if it was published in the spring and you just got around to sending it, I will view it as a personal affront and an attempt to ruin my Christmas celebrations; you will have had to write an extraordinary story for me to forgive you.

Because of the unforgiving deadlines necessarily imposed on a work of this nature, the absolute final date for receiving material is December 31. This is neither an arrogant nor whimsical decision but is essential in order for production schedules to be met. If it arrives on January 2, it will not be read. Seriously.

But, now, drop everything and enjoy this wonderful collection. If you are a reader, I hope you will enjoy it. If you are an author, I hope you will enjoy it *and* be inspired by it.

—Otto Penzler
February 2025

INTRODUCTION
Murderers I Have Known

The stories in this eclectic and varied collection all revolve around crime. As usual, the favorite is murder—the deliberate killing of another human. Murder was mankind's first crime, assuming we can discount Eve's disobedience and fibs. After she and Adam were banished from Eden, their sons settled a conflict when Cain killed Abel, probably with a primitive axe of some sort. It was the first murder on earth and is described in sparse detail in the Bible, the Torah, and the Quran. Thousands of years later, theologians are still arguing about it.

Why are we so fascinated by such barbarity? Why do so many readers who would never harm an animal, let alone another person, thrive on the blood and gore of a good murder mystery? Other crimes don't stand a chance. Who wants to read about an embezzlement, or a drug bust, or a sexual assault? Bank robberies have a certain romance about them, but a proper one usually involves a dead body or two.

In our violent culture, we read about so many murders and watch even more on-screen it's impossible not to become somewhat jaded by the violence. Still, we can't get enough. And when the identity of the killer is a mystery, we're hooked.

It's one thing to be entertained by make-believe murders, but how many people have actually met a real murderer? A person, who for whatever reason, took the life of another?

The first murderer I met was a young man wearing jailhouse overalls and handcuffed to a metal table. A judge had just appointed me to be his lawyer. We were in a cramped windowless room in the county jail. I was trying to appear confident as my stomach flipped, and I kept asking myself, "What am I doing here?" Seven months earlier I had been in law school. I tried to ignore the handcuffs but I was pleased that they were working.

Through my skillful questioning, I learned that my new client had pulled a snub-nosed .38 caliber pistol from his pocket and fired six shots into the head of the deceased, from point-blank range. One bullet went all the way though the skull, made a clean exit, and continued on about two feet until it hit the arm of a screaming young woman, shattering her elbow. She was the source of the conflict, the wife of my client, and the last lover of the deceased.

I was fascinated as to how a person would feel, emotionally, after having killed another human. It was a crime of passion, a reaction with little forethought, and he had not time to consider his actions until the deed was done. He was a tough guy, a kid from the streets who'd never had a chance, and he had known his victim for many years. I was surprised when his eyes moistened and he showed a moment of remorse.

However, the remorse did not last long. The killing was a violent end to a love triangle that went off the rails. My client claimed, and we later proved to the jury, that the deceased also had a pistol. It was a not so clear case of self-defense, and my client was quicker on the draw. The jury bought it and let him walk. The sheriff gave him his gun back.

A year later, the same judge reminded me that I had never lost a murder trial, then appointed me to another. The facts were different, there was no woman involved, but there was also a claim of self-defense. The victim was an old man sitting on his front porch, pistol in his rear pocket, waiting for my client to arrive so they could finish a festering argument. A witness said the old man fired first, but missed. My client got lucky when luck was sorely needed, and drilled the old guy in the heart, from forty feet away. Again, there was no remorse. Indeed, he was rather proud of his marksmanship. The jury let him walk too.

As a criminal defense lawyer who'd never lost a murder case, you might think my reputation spread and I was in demand. That never happened, not for murder, nor for any other crime. But I was in the room one time with a man who had killed at least three people and would soon go to trial for number four. He was a gangster who owned seedy bars and thrived in the underworld. He reveled in his reputation for violence and intimidation. Fortunately, I was not his lawyer and didn't stay in that room very long. But I watched his trial from the front row and was around him enough to realize he had no remorse. His killings were planned and purposeful. They enhanced his business opportunities. If properly analyzed, he might have been diagnosed as psychopathic, or even sociopathic. My analysis, one shared by the prosecution, was that he was just plain mean. He enjoyed killing.

I was relieved when the jury found him guilty and the judge sent him away for a long time.

Fortunately, I changed careers and managed to avoid meeting any more murderers. It's safer to simply write about them, and it's far more enjoyable to read about them. The enduring popularity of mysteries, police procedurals, and crime stories, real and fictional, attest to our endless fascination with the darker side of human nature.

We find them irresistible.

—John Grisham
March 1, 2025

David Avallone *is a writer of comic books, television, movies, role-playing games, and short stories. His ridiculous career in film can be followed on the IMDb. His comics work includes such iconic characters as Elvira: Mistress of the Dark, Bettie Page, Zorro, Vampirella, Red Sonja, The Shadow, Doc Savage, and John Carter (of Mars). His Kolchak comic won a Scribe Award from the International Alliance of Media Tie-In Writers. Most recently, he's been writing episodes of* Batwheels, *an animated series. He's only recently returned to writing prose after a thirty-year gap. He is the son of prolific novelist Michael Avallone and women's rights activist Fran Avallone. He lives in Hollywood with his delightful wife, Augusta, and three mischievous cats.*

THE GOLDEN ROAD (TO UNLIMITED DEVOTION)

David Avallone

Her name was Dawn, as far as I knew. Later I found out it wasn't: she had picked it, with great intention, for reasons both obvious and known only to herself.

In the summer of 1987, I was on my way to California when my beat-up '71 Chevy Impala convertible blew its engine in some desert nowhere and stranded me. I found a furnished dump and got a job in a furniture factory while a sweaty jackass named Reid worked very slowly on my car. Refurbishing the engine would eat up the humble stake I had saved to start my new life, which meant that, even after Reid the Snail finished, I'd have to stick around until I earned it back.

I spent a couple of months assembling the rails that hold cubicles together. It felt like working in one Dickensian workhouse to put together the cells for other poor suckers in some future workhouse. But the pay was fair, as was Dawn, my supervisor.

Even before I knew it was an alias, her name had a fanciful Ian Fleming feel. I clocked in at six every July and August morning and was greeted by a tall and gorgeous woman who called herself Dawn Summers. She had a sunny smile and an explosion of frizzy blond hair like a supernova. She whistled while she worked, and from her it was somehow sweet, rather than annoying. Her eyes were blue and kind, and as blue as they were, they were kinder than they were blue.

She was thirty-something and fun and charming. I was twenty-two and fresh out of school. I wasn't without some kind of rudimentary charm myself, but I'd never asked out an adult woman and was paralyzed by the prospect. Dawn was flirty, sure, but wasn't she at least a little flirty with everyone? There was something in her eyes when she looked at me that I was desperate to take personally, but should I? My confidence was still very much under construction, a fragile structure in need of more concrete and rebar.

By the first week of August, Reid had finally finished the Impala, and by the second week the sack of cash under my bed had almost hit my "time to move on" goal. On the one hand, I couldn't wait to get back on the road. On the other, there was Dawn, and the way she looked at me, which I was desperate to take personally.

One sun-blasted morning, a truck was late with a shipment of rails, and my section of the line shut down. Me and five other guys stood around the loading dock, killing time. Five other guys and Dawn.

I didn't socialize much at work. Our routine didn't allow for more than a few words with each other in the break room. The other guys had all gone to high school together. They called me "Hollywood," because I'd been dumb enough on Day One to explain where I was going. These guys would live and die within fifteen miles of the hospital they were born in, and my kind of dream—the kind you cross a continent for—seemed like a fantasy to them. At first, "Hollywood" was intended to needle me, but we'd grown on each other just enough that it didn't feel like a tease anymore. Just a nickname.

While we waited for the overdue truck, one of the other workers—a handsome dude whose name was probably John—asked Dawn, "What are you doing Saturday night?"

The rest of the boys made predictable noises of surprise and admiration at John's taking the big swing right there in front of us. That was the kind of boldness I didn't yet possess, and I was envious. Also, cliché or no cliché, my heart literally sank. It was a long time ago, but I can still remember my disappointment. Maybe she'd say yes, maybe she'd say no . . . but how could I ask her out now that John had made his move? It would seem like he'd given me the idea.

But something happened that was completely outside my life experience. Dawn gave him that big sunny smile and said, "I'm busy Saturday night." She took a dramatic pause, then looked directly at me with a shy conspiratorial grin. "David is taking me out."

I would love to report that I was smooth, but I can't imagine my face was clear of surprise. Lucky for both of us, this wasn't the most observant crowd in the world.

"That's right." I probably blushed. "We have a date. Saturday."

The boys made more sitcom-audience noises. (I say "boys," though they were all older than me, some by a decade. But that seventh-grade bio-class boy energy was still there.) Dawn blushed prettily in return, and my heart shot back from the bottom of my stomach, smashed its way through my brain, and shattered my skull on its way to the bright blue desert sky.

Before the situation became unbearably awkward, the truck showed up, and we returned to making partitions to keep future corporate drones separated and lonely.

At the end of the day, I found Dawn in the parking lot, leaning on her Volkswagen Bug. Waiting for me. For *me*. I went a little lightheaded at the sight of her.

"Surprised?" she said.

"Honestly? Yeah."

"Silly boy. I thought I was obvious."

If I'd had the self-awareness back then that I developed in the years that followed, I could have told her that my peer group had treated me like a homely weirdo for most of my life, and a couple of pretty girlfriends hadn't managed to drown out that childhood chorus. But the guy who could have said all that didn't exist yet.

"I wasn't sure. I figured . . . I'm just some guy passing through, you wouldn't be interested."

She laughed. "An attractive man who's not going to stick around and complicate my life? Baby boy, you're perfect."

From anyone else, I would have chafed like hell against that "baby boy," but I was new at this, and the prospect of a woman wanting to use me and let me go was startling and wonderful.

"There's a pretty good band Saturday night at Jerome's," she said. "Do you dance, David?"

She had never once called me "Hollywood." Another thing the older, wiser me might have taken note of.

Jerome's was a friendly dive bar in an abandoned mining camp just outside of town. Did I dance? After a fashion. I knew how to hold a woman and swing her around.

"I'll pick you up at eight," I said, and tried not to stammer.

Jerome's was hopping, and the band was surprisingly great. They played an impressive array of cover tunes from a wide spectrum of pop, and I felt a particular pang when they hit Steely Dan's "My Old School." But Annandale was over two thousand miles in my rearview mirror. They followed it with "Cream Puff War," and maybe I should have listened a little closer to the lyrics, like Bogart dancing with Bergman to "Perfidia" in *Casablanca*. Maybe you never notice those things while the story is in progress.

Freed from the confines of the furniture factory, Dawn was a revelation. Dancing with joyous abandon, eyes shining like diamonds in the neon light, singing along, kicking off her shoes and dancing barefoot on the sawdust. I was careful not to step on her pink-painted toes. I could tell she liked my arms around her, liked the gentle pressure on the lower back that telegraphs the upcoming swing. She was a little taller than me and giggled uncontrollably when I dipped her. I played into that a bit and dipped her almost to the floor. "Don't drop me!" she cried.

Dawn, radiating light and heat, uncontainable, captivated the crowd. Every eye in the place was on her, and that suited me just fine. I'd wondered, on the drive to pick her up, if the locals would resent seeing their resident supernova squired by the itinerant city boy... but she was more intoxicating than anything coming out of Jerome's taps, and her joy obliterated any jealousy that might have lingered in an observer's heart.

And then, during what turned out to be our last dance, she pulled me close and kissed me. If there *were* any jealous eyes watching, I was too delirious to notice. I might have started shaking—I was still young enough for that—but a couple of drinks had taken the edge off my nerves.

"Let's go look at the stars," she whispered in my ear.

And we did.

The Fair Grounds were a couple of miles farther out of town. At night, I couldn't tell what made them "Fair Grounds" and not just a patch of scrubby grass in the desert. The nowhere town didn't put out much in the way of light pollution, and I—growing up in New Jersey suburbs—had never seen so many stars.

The star-gazing part didn't last long. Despite our being grown adults who both had keys to rooms with doors that locked, the back seat of my convertible under the starry sky was where it happened. The supernova consumed me. At first with a flattering impatience, and then again with slow-motion intensity.

In between, we talked. I can be embarrassingly chatty in the afterglow, or mid-glow, or whatever you want to call it. I talked about where I was going, about my dreams. It didn't occur to me how that might strike her, but she was as kind as her blue, blue eyes.

I don't remember when we collapsed into unconsciousness.

I woke up entangled in her, in every sense you can imagine. The sun was just beginning to crack the sky and flood the desert plain with golden light. I sat up and watched it rise. I looked down at her and her eyes were open, and just that much bluer and kinder. She sat up with me and took in the view.

"This is my favorite. My favorite time," she said.

"Dawn's favorite time is dawn." I kidded. "That follows."

She smiled, but her mind had gone somewhere else, and she was still there.

"See the road?" she said. "The golden road?"

I followed her gaze to the lone country lane that ran from horizon to horizon. The daybreak had painted it with molten sunlight.

"It's like the Yellow Brick Road, but even more beautiful, more . . ."

She trailed off. Thoughtful.

"It's an invitation," I offered. "To go and keep going,"

She turned to me, nodding. "I knew you'd get it. You were following it, following the golden road, when you got shipwrecked."

I gestured to the Impala's endless black hood. "It took him a while, but Reid has repaired the mast and patched the hull."

I wouldn't say she frowned, but she got serious. I put my arms around her and kissed her. "That doesn't mean I'm going. Not—"

"—not right now," she interrupted me. "Not today. But you *are* going. You have to."

"You said that was part of the attraction."

"And it was. Is. You fall for a sailor, you can't be mad when he goes back to sea."

"Am I a sailor or the Scarecrow? We're mixing our myths."

She laughed, and she was so absolutely stunning I said a thing I hadn't expected to say. "It's a big car, Dawn. Seats two, with plenty of space left over. You could take the golden road, too. Take it all the way to the sea. With me."

"Oh, baby boy . . . you don't mean that. It's sweet, but don't confuse a girl."

I took a deep breath and looked out at her golden road. *Did* I mean it?

"Before yesterday," I said, "I had a clear path ahead. Another paycheck or two, and then westward I'd go. Things are less clear today. The boy is as confused as the girl."

We both looked back at the brightening desert plain, and I decided to change the subject. I looked at my watch. "The Red Fox is open. Nothing confusing about coffee and flapjacks."

So we ate breakfast and drank coffee and stared at each other with that comfort and bliss and affection completely unique to a "morning after" with no regrets. We spent the rest of the day in my furnished dump and continued to make up for lost time. We didn't talk about the future, or any yellow-brick or golden roads, or Odysseus and Calypso. . . .

On Monday and Tuesday and Wednesday, she spent the night with me, then slipped out while it was still dark to shower and dress for work at her own home. We kept it cool at the factory, but the boys on the floor knew. They teased me about it, but it wasn't mean. They were envious, sure, but they were also impressed. And they started asking me when I was planning to leave town, which was as charming as it was unsubtle.

Dawn and I made plans to go back to Jerome's on Saturday night.

"Farewell party?" she said, with a sad little smile.

"One-week anniversary," I said, and she laughed and beamed.

Thursday night, she didn't come over. I called her place, and she didn't pick up. I tried not to let my jealous, insecure twenty-two-year-old heart fry my brain. But I also didn't get any sleep.

Friday morning, she wasn't at work. Me and the boys got to it, assembling cubicle walls, but my heart was in my throat. Another cliché, but how else do you say it? My head was pounding. If you can't remember that kind of physical pain, then you don't remember your own fragile young self.

On my first break, I was picking up a payphone to try her at home when the cops walked in.

I hung up without dialing and watched them talk to the receptionist. Saw her point at me. My mind went to the worst thing, but I didn't guess right. There were other bad things it could have been, including at least one that never would have occurred to me.

They held up a picture of a woman with straight dark hair and sad eyes. Black and white, so you couldn't see the blue. But you could see the kindness. They asked the obvious question.

"Of course. That's Dawn, my supervisor. Did something happen to her?"

I got that smug-cop smirk. The "I know something you don't know" smirk. I kept my face blank and impassive.

"She didn't show up to work today. You know anything about that?"

"Nope. She seemed fine yesterday."

"What about last night?" His self-satisfaction was at its peak, but I didn't bite.

"In general, *yesterday* includes a full twenty-four hours. But I didn't see her after work, if that's what you're being cute about."

He didn't like that. He wanted a confession I'd been sleeping with her. "And the night before?"

"The night before, she was her usual happy self. What happened?"

"You her boyfriend?"

"You her mother?" I don't usually mouth off to cops. They have guns and limitless sadism and immunity from any consequences. But a bunch of folks from the floor had stopped work and were watching from a safe distance. I felt like my odds of getting beaten up or killed were slim.

"Listen, asshole. We know you've been sleeping with her. Did she ever tell you her real name's Alice Yvonne Bennett? And that she's a fugitive?"

"The one-armed man did it," I said. I couldn't help myself. This was a few years before the big movie, so the cop just got confused and angrier.

"The one-armed—what the fuck are you talking about?"

"Look," I said, taking a deep breath. "I'm sorry. It was a joke. I'm worried about her, and you two aren't making me less worried. What's she wanted for?"

The cops looked at each other. The silent one finally spoke. "Murder. Your girlfriend Dawn who's really Alice? Well, thing is, she murdered a man and ran away. Still worried about her?"

I played the part of shocked clown for a bit, and they calmed down. It wasn't entirely an act. I could think of reasons why a perfectly good person might run from a murder charge, but did I really want to start making excuses without hearing the story from her? Murder was hard to square with the woman I knew—but how well did I really know her? How well does anyone know anyone? Maybe for Dawn-who-was-Alice, the appeal of the golden road was just the appeal of escape.

THE GOLDEN ROAD (TO UNLIMITED DEVOTION)

I finished my day. I gave the front office the address of my old college buddy Bill in Los Angeles to send my last check to. With any luck, I could be on Bill's doorstep before the check hit his mailbox. I knew quitting now would look suspicious and leaving town only more so. Maybe those two cops and their buddies would chase me to the state line. Maybe they'd check to see if she was in my trunk.

Maybe it would take a little pressure off her if they wasted their time following me.

I didn't care. I hadn't killed anyone, and without Dawn I was done with this nowhere desert town.

I went back to my furnished dump and packed what little I had. I looked out the window and, sure enough, Tweedledum and Tweedledee had parked their cruiser across the street. Real subtle. Sterling police work.

I thought I was ready to roar off into the desert and leave Dawn behind me. In 1987, there were no cell phones and no internet. If I hit the road, the golden road, that would be it. I would never see her again, never know her story.

That didn't feel right, and I had a hard time accepting it.

Around dusk, I realized where she might be, if she wanted to see me one last time. If she wasn't already halfway to Mexico. First I had to lose the cops. I had an idea about that, too.

They watched me lug my duffel bag out to my car. They watched me leave the key to my dump in the mailbox. I'm sure they were excited. I got in the Impala and took a little tour of the nowhere town. They probably thought I was trying to lose them, but mostly I was trying to bore them.

After about a half hour of meandering, I drove into Reid's junkyard. The cops parked outside the entrance and waited.

Reid was surprised to see me. We didn't like each other. I was playing a hunch, though. His whole operation was shady, and there was no way in the world he liked cops. I told him these two were hassling me. I told him I'd noticed he had a back gate that led to a desert road. He stared at me in silence until I gave him a fifty. He took in the grim visage of President Grant, and said, "I'll open the gate. Let me pull my tow truck across the entrance, so they can't see you or follow you through the yard."

I spotted something helpful in his office and bought it for another twenty. Reid was having a big day.

He unlatched the back gate, then went around to fire up his truck. The sun had set. My lights were off. If I could keep off the brakes, they wouldn't see me driving into the desert. If I fought the impulse to speed, they wouldn't see a dust cloud. Reid rolled his tow truck to the front gate, and I pulled slowly out onto the dirt road. I took the time to get out and close the gate behind me, just in case.

The road was ruler-straight for miles. I didn't know how long it would take Tweedledee and Tweedledum to figure out what had happened, but I planned to be invisible long before they did.

A few miles down the road, I looked in the rearview and saw no signs of pursuit. Bless you, Reid. You overcharged for the engine block, but you came through in the end. I'd gambled on him loving a scam, any scam at all, more than he disliked me, and I'd been right.

With the help of a tattered map I'd picked up when I first hit town, I found the Fair Grounds. They were empty, of course. But I parked in roughly the spot I had a week ago, before the stargazing, and sat on the hood of my Impala. And waited.

The Milky Way wheeled slowly overhead. I tried to remember if I'd seen it before, but mostly I thought about the supernova whose name was Dawn or Alice. Dawn the explosion of life and joy, Alice the sad-eyed murderess.

I figured I'd give her until an hour or two after daybreak, then find my way to the closest thick horizontal line on the map and turn west.

It was still full dark when I saw headlights, small and close together. Not a cruiser. More like a VW Bug.

I got off the hood and watched her approach.

In spite of everything, her smile was still breathtaking, a supernova by starlight. We didn't embrace. She knew there had to be some talk first.

"I don't know if I'm surprised or not surprised," she said. "I wanted you to be here."

"I wasn't sure you'd want to see me again. But if you did . . ." She let it hang there, looked at her feet. "What did they tell you?"

"They told me you killed a man."

She looked up at me. "I did, David. I did that. I won't lie to you."

"There's a lot of reasons a woman kills a man. Which one was it?"

"Maybe not the first one that comes to mind."

I mulled that for a minute, then took a stab at it. "So it *wasn't* you? Then who was it? Mother, sister, niece . . . ?"

She looked at the horizon. The light had started to creep over. "You're smart," she said. "I always liked that about you."

"Go on."

She made eye contact again. "I have a sister. She had a husband. She showed up at my house one night, and her face . . . well, I barely recognized her past the bruises and the blood. I was washing out her wounds when he came pounding on the door and yelling for her." There was a pause. She bit her lip. "I kept a baseball bat by my front door."

"Did he threaten you?"

"He never got a chance to. Swinging the bat at his head was . . . it wasn't a hard decision. It was no decision at all. It felt good. Overdue. Even when I saw the blood, I didn't stop. I didn't want to stop."

She wasn't emotional about it. I wondered how long ago it had been. The girl in the photo with the dark straight hair looked maybe five years younger. But that didn't matter.

"Was there a trial? Or did you not stick around?"

"I didn't stick around. Her husband was a cop, David. I beat a *cop* to death. So it was another easy decision. I called an ambulance for my sister, kissed her on the forehead, and then—"

"—and then the golden road."

"Something like that," she said. We both looked over at the sunrise. Alice, not Dawn, but also Dawn. She gave a small laugh. "You kill anybody back in Jersey, David?"

"No. I'm one of those idiots who's running away from a perfectly fine life. There might have been an unpaid parking ticket or two." I took a breath. "You could leave the Bug here and get in the Impala."

She smiled again. "I couldn't. You're the sweetest boy, and your future is bright. I'd bring you down, and those dreams of yours . . . they wouldn't come true. They'd never have a chance."

"I'm tougher than I look. And smart, like you said."

"All that is true. But you didn't sign up for this. I know how you feel right now, but . . . we just met. Really. You don't owe me the things my troubles would take from you. You owe yourself a new life, like I did when I ran. Chase it. Give it your unlimited devotion and be happy. I'll be okay. I promise."

"Dawn," I started, but it was all I said.

"David." That was all *she* said. But it said everything.

I got my dusty Mets cap from my trunk and handed it to her. "Stuff your hair under that until you have time for a new dye job."

"Yes, sir," she said.

Then I went back into the trunk for the set of license plates I'd bought from Reid and a flathead screwdriver. I replaced the plates on the Bug, while she stared off at the golden road, stretching out to her next new life.

Last kisses are a lot like first kisses.

When editor Josh Pachter invited me to contribute to his anthology Friend of the Devil, Crime Fiction Inspired by the Songs of the Grateful Dead, *I was not a natural fit for the project. I enjoy the Dead, but I'm not what you would call a fan. Still, I like a challenge, and when Josh suggested the song "The Golden Road (to Ultimate Devotion)," my mind immediately went to a time in my life when I followed a kind of "golden road" and the story grew from there. To be honest, it's not so much a crime story as three autobiographical incidents hiding inside a crime story trench coat. Buy me a drink sometime and I'll delineate fact from fiction for you. For now, the crime element is fiction, but her name really was Dawn Summers.*

Craig Faustus Buck *was a journalist before he moved into nonfiction books, co-writing two* New York Times *#1 bestsellers—one pop-psychology, the other pop-gynecology. He transitioned into television drama, where he toiled for too many decades to admit. Now he's writing what he most loves to read: crime fiction. His short stories have won a Macavity Award and been nominated for many others, including two Anthonys, two Derringers, and the* Ellery Queen Mystery Magazine's *Readers' Choice Award.* Publishers Weekly *called his debut novel,* Go Down Hard, *"a solid romp through territory that Raymond Chandler first put on the map." Aside from writing short stories, he is currently shopping his next novel,* Go Down Screaming.

HOME GAME

Craig Faustus Buck

It sounded like a gunshot in her dream, but when Reni woke she realized she'd heard a bump from downstairs, as if someone's foot hit a chair in the dark. She poked her husband's shoulder.

"Teddy!" she whisper-shouted. "Wake up! I think somebody's in the house."

He groaned. "Go to sleep, baby. If it was anything, Cornelius would be barking."

"The dog's fifteen and going deaf. I'm telling you I heard something. Now's the time to practice your mindfulness. Be in the here and now."

"I'm mindful that it's time to sleep."

"Semper Fi, Teddy. What if there's a burglar downstairs? Get your ex-Marine ass in gear."

"You're an ex-cop. Take the ball and run with it."

She hated his sports analogies.

"I wasn't SWAT, I trained dogs."

"Take Papa's gun." He reached into his nightstand drawer and pulled out the Colt 1911 his grandfather used in France during World War II.

"Teddy!"

"Just in case, baby. But I'm sure you're imagining things." He laid the gun next to her on the bed, then rolled over and started snoring.

She was furious but not surprised that Teddy didn't sense her distress and rise to the occasion. If there was one thing she'd learned from the mindfulness course they'd attended in lieu of marriage counseling, it was that Teddy wasn't mindful. The training had never penetrated his thick skull, which only fed her simmering resentments no matter how many self-affirmations she expressed.

She tried one now: *Fear of failure does not control me.* She picked up the .45 and found comfort in its heft. This gun had fought the Nazis. What chance did some local punk prowler have? Before going to Veterinary school, she'd aced the LAPD Police Academy and spent three years in the K-9 unit. She should be able to take care of herself.

Reni crossed the carpeted room and silently stepped onto the hardwood floor of the hallway. After twelve years of nocturnal bathroom visits, she knew every creaking floorboard and so kept her feet next to the left wall to avoid making noise and to keep her right hand—her gun hand—unimpeded.

Likewise, she stayed close to the balusters as she crept down the stairs. At the bottom, she paused. The living room was pitch black, so she closed her eyes to concentrate on listening.

Was that movement behind her? Before she could react, her head exploded in pain. As she collapsed, she realized she was still conscious. She tried to raise the Colt but a scarred, silver-toed cowboy boot stepped on her right wrist. When the intruder bludgeoned her again, she felt a trickle of blood flow across her brow before blacking out.

Reni's head felt like someone was inside her cranium trying to break out with a sledgehammer. Her eyelids felt heavy, demanding an enormous effort to lift them. The light was blinding. As her eyes adjusted, a person came into focus. Teddy. Gray bands of duct tape wrapped his red flannel nightshirt like stripes, strapping his torso to his chair with his arms bound in back. His brown close-cropped hair was bed-headed at odd angles, and his hazel eyes looked angry.

Pain notwithstanding, she turned her head to follow his gaze. She saw a tall, rail-thin man sitting on their floral-print couch in worn jeans, a camo cargo vest, and cowboy boots, one of which she recognized as having stomped on her gun hand. He wore blue surgical gloves, and on his lap lay Teddy's grandfather's .45.

The man sported some sort of Mohawk-mullet combo in desperate need of shampoo, and his eyes were oddly close together, small, and a dark brown that looked almost black, like the saddle of the German Shepherd who sat expectantly at his feet.

The man extended his hand and the dog sniffed his glove, then gave it a lick. "Not much of a watchdog."

"He's old," said Reni. The retired police dog could have been helpful if he were ten years younger, but he was well past his prime.

"What do you want?" asked Teddy.

The man ignored him. "What's his name?" He reached into one of his cargo pockets and pulled out a cellophane wrapper containing a half-eaten Slim Jim.

"Cornelius," said Reni.

The man bit off a hunk of the meat stick and tossed the rest to Cornelius, who gobbled it down.

"Dumb name." The man ruffled the dog's ears. "You're a good boy. Yes, you are." He spoke in that silly voice people use on pets.

Reni never understood what made people think baby talk could bridge the language gap between species.

"Just take what you want and leave," she said.

Rather than answer, the man grabbed Teddy's vape pen from the coffee table and took a toke. The end of the device glowed blue. Reni had bought it for Teddy, even though she knew he hated to vape. He loved the ritual of rolling a joint, then firing it up and feeling the smoke go to his head. But, as with so many of his other joys—like cigars and fried pork rinds—Reni had put an end to it for health reasons. Teddy liked to say she made him go vapid. And now his vape pen was being defiled by their captor's disgusting spittle.

The man exhaled a faint wisp of marijuana as he eyed a collection of football trophies on the mantle, then looked at Teddy. "You play ball?"

"None of your goddamn business," said Teddy, who'd probably be big enough for the NFL if the weight in his belly were evenly distributed across his six four frame.

The man raised the Colt and pointed it at Teddy. "Beg yer pardon?"

"He coaches football at the high school," said Reni, wondering if the man was purposely torturing them with small talk or just slow on the uptake.

"I played in high school," said the man. "Tight end. Good hands too." Seemingly placated, he lowered the gun.

"We don't have any money in the house," said Teddy. "Only what we've got in our wallets."

"Don't make me no nevermind. House robbery don't earn out in the risk v. reward department."

If he wasn't here to rob them, why was he here? Reni's imagination reeled with frightening possibilities. Her heart sped up to a gallop. "Just tell us what you want!"

"I want to make me some real money by raisin' the stakes on what I was hired to do."

"What's that supposed to mean?" said Teddy.

"Now don't you go playin' Pollyanna on me." The man turned to Reni. "Your old man offered me five grand to murder you. Would you care to counter offer?"

Teddy's face blanched. "Baby, I swear to God! I never met this jerk before!"

She locked eyes with Teddy. He was unreadable. She didn't think he was capable of murder, but was bothered by her lack of confidence in that judgment. *You can be a success if no one else believes in you, but you will never succeed if you don't believe in yourself.*

"What do you expect him to say?" said the man. "I didn't get rid of you like he hired me to, so he's caught with his pants down, wiener-handed."

"He's lying," said Teddy. "Can't you see that? You know me. You know I'd never . . ."

The man interrupted. "Then why'd you leave the back door unlocked?"

"I didn't!" said Teddy.

The man looked at Reni. "It ain't jimmied or nothin'. If you wasn't taped up, you could see for yourself."

"We must have left it open by accident," said Teddy.

Reni shot him a glare. "I locked that door myself."

Teddy's face screwed up in frustration, whether with himself or with her was unclear.

"Bottom line," said the man, "I ain't riskin' no more prison time for five grand. So you two better spark up a little auction action. The highest bidder gets to live."

"Look, pal," said Teddy. "Why don't you take whatever you want and get out? Nobody dies, nobody loses. Slam dunk."

Despite her anxiety, Reni was irked that even begging for his life, he'd trotted out a sports reference.

"You better come up with some serious cash," said the man, "or I'll kill you both. Maybe Cornelius too." He took another toke. "Just kiddin'. I'd never hurt a dog."

"You're bluffing," said Reni. "You kill us and you'll walk away with nothing but a life sentence hanging over your head."

"You got quite a mouth on you."

It's not your job to like me—it's mine.

"All this talk is makin' me hungry," continued the man. "I'm gonna rummage me up some chow while you two work out this here bidding war."

And with that, he stood and left the room, tucking Teddy's .45 into the back of his waistband. His lizard boots left bloody footprints all over their antique Persian carpet. Reni assumed it was blood from her head wound.

"We've got to do something, Teddy," she said.

He squirmed around. "These chairs are pretty rickety. Maybe I can break myself free."

"And then what? He's got your gun."

"And then we'll punt." Teddy struggled to get all two hundred fifty pounds of himself upright and in some semblance of balance, which wasn't easy with a chair on his back and a fifty-pound beer belly messing with his center of gravity.

He swiveled his torso back and forth, reminding Reni of her father dancing the twist when she was a little girl. Without warning, Teddy's chair cracked. He froze, waiting to see if the man would respond to the sound.

Instead, they heard the clang of a cast iron skillet being tossed onto a burner grate. "Hey, Reni!" the man called out. "Where's your spatula at?"

"Hanging near the toaster!" she shouted.

She heard the sizzle of frying bacon followed by the loud rattle of their ancient exhaust fan. She'd been after Teddy to get that fixed, but now she welcomed the clatter that masked the sound of Teddy redoubling his awkward contortions. The smell of rendered bacon fat wafted into the living room, prompting Cornelius to get up and wander into the kitchen.

"Traitor," mumbled Teddy. His shimmying slowly broke down the chair until he was able to wrestle his bonds lose enough to work his arms out from behind his back. He was still wrapped in tape, and shards of chair legs and back slats hung at odd angles from his body, but his arms were no longer constrained by the shape of the chair. Mustering all of his strength, he was finally able to reach a tape end and rip it open to free one hand. It took him just a minute to free himself from the rest of his fetters. He looked around for a weapon.

"Teddy!" said Reni.

"What?"

Her eyes narrowed. "Theodore Murphy, I swear to God, I'm going to kill you myself if you don't get me out of this tape." *Focus on breathing.*

"We're in a hurry here, baby." But he ripped her bindings off nonetheless. She rubbed her arms where the duct tape left sticky red welts.

Teddy snatched up the fireplace poker. "That asshole is going to wish he was never born."

"I'm shakin' in my boots," said the man.

Teddy and Reni both turned to see their assailant standing in the kitchen doorway, a plate of what looked to be an entire pound of fried bacon in one gloved hand and Teddy's Colt in the other. He pointed the pistol at Teddy, who dropped the poker. Then the man motioned for them to sit in a pair of club chairs by the draped front window.

"You two got more pluck than I had you chalked up for."

With the man's attention on his two captives, some bacon fat dribbled from his plate. Cornelius eagerly lapped it off the floor.

"Here's the thing," he said. "If I kill one of you, the other knows I'm not afraid to commit murder, which is what, in my business, we call an insurance policy. If you think about goin' to the cops, you know I might just come back and finish you off. One plus one equals death. Therefore, I gotta kill at least one of you, just to know the other'll keep their mouth shut. If I don't, I got no insurance, capeesh?"

He set his plate on the small writing desk Reni used to pay the bills, then sat in her chair. He kept the gun leveled at Teddy as he picked up a piece of bacon.

"If you don't kill anybody," said Reni, "you won't need any insurance."

"Now that's where you're wrong, little lady." The man took a bite of bacon. Cornelius was riveted at the sight. "See, I done me some law schoolin' at the college of San Quentin, and what we have here is a kidnappin'. Don't matter none that I ain't took you nowhere. I held you right here against your will. And usin' a gun and all, that carries a good heavy load upstate. Could go up for life or worse. Nope. I got no percentage in letting both of you live. Not to mention I get me a sweet ass dog out of the deal."

He threw a piece of glistening bacon on the floor for Cornelius. The dog was in heaven as he wolfed it down.

"We'd prefer that you don't feed him people food," said Reni. "Gives him ideas."

"That so?" said the man, tossing Cornelius another strip. "I ain't got all night, so which of you is gonna make the ultimo sacrifice?"

Teddy's eyes burned with the sort of rage that Reni knew too well. It was the look he got when he was about to do something reckless and probably stupid, like try to go for the gun from across the room with no hope of accomplishing anything short of getting shot. She had to do something to diffuse him.

"How about we all calm down," she said, "and look at this from another perspective. Teddy and I don't want to die, and you don't want to walk out of here empty-handed, do you, mister . . ."

"You can call me Stuckey," said the man.

"You don't want to murder anybody if you don't have to, do you Mr. Stuckey? It's too risky. Murder is just a means to an end for you. And if you don't have to do it, if you can walk out of here with a ton of money and no worries about getting caught, you're golden, am I right?"

"I'm listening." Stuckey still held the gun, but she noticed he was allowing his hand to droop. His tension was easing.

"You can have your insurance without killing us. You just need some other kind of leverage."

"Like what?" said Stuckey.

"Like Teddy."

"Hey!" said Teddy.

"Hush," she said. "Why do you always have to interrupt? I hate it when you do that."

"I'm nobody's sacrificial lamb," said Teddy.

"I should have listened to your sister. You never care what I have to say. You just jump all over me before you even hear it."

"I hear you loud and clear. You're setting me up to get in the ring and take a dive."

"You going to let me finish, Teddy? Or would you rather die?"

"Hey!" shouted Stuckey. They both turned, startled. "If you don't stop bickerin', I'll just shoot the both of you right now and settle for the dog and a TV or two."

He waved the gun toward Reni as a signal for her to continue.

"As I was saying, you need a way to make sure we don't go to the police. Killing one of us could backfire. The cops might catch you anyway. DNA or whatever. So here's the deal. Teddy's got close to fifty thousand dollars in his IRA."

"Hey! That's for retirement!"

She glared at Teddy. "Be in the here and now, Teddy. This is our lives." He still looked angry but didn't argue as she turned back to Stuckey. "You claim he hired you to kill me. Well, let's do up a contract to that effect. Teddy signs it, we give you the money, and you go away forever. End of story. We can't go to the police because you could show them that contract and they'd arrest Teddy for conspiracy to murder."

"Won't work," said Stuckey. "That contract would incriminate me too."

"For what?" she said. "I'd still be alive so you obviously never did the thing. And if you do a good job of hiding the money, they won't know you ever took it. You could say you agreed to the contract to entrap Teddy so you could turn him in before he got me killed. No way could they prove otherwise."

Stuckey reached for another piece of bacon. "That might just work."

"Not for me," said Teddy. "He'd have blackmail power over us. What's to stop him from coming back and demanding more? We'd be screwed for the rest of our lives."

Stuckey froze at this thought, the rasher halfway to his mouth. In a flash, Cornelius leapt and snapped the bacon from his hand, shocking them all.

"I told you not to give him people food," said Reni.

Stuckey chuckled. "Not bad for an old-timer."

Cornelius licked his chops.

"Signing a contract like that would be signing away my freedom," said Teddy. "I won't do it."

Stuckey retrieved Teddy's vape pen and resumed his seat at the desk. He took a toke, then slowly exhaled.

"I guess we're back to you two deciding who dies," he said. "Now that we've established the minimum bid at fifty grand."

Teddy glared at Reni.

"We need mutually assured destruction," she said. "Like the arms race when the Soviet Union was around."

"Come again?" said Stuckey.

"The Russians couldn't destroy America without America destroying them back. We can do the same thing here. I sign a contract hiring you to kill Teddy. Teddy signs a contract hiring you to kill me. And you sign a contract hiring Teddy to kill whoever; it doesn't matter who because no one's going to kill anybody. But you walk away with fifty thousand dollars knowing Teddy and I can't go to the cops because, if we do, we'll go down with you. And we know you can't come back to blackmail us because we have your contract as insurance."

"That's pretty complicated," said Stuckey. "There's gotta be holes in there somewheres."

"Maybe," she said. "But who's going to risk going to the cops to find out?"

Stuckey took a rasher and held it out to Cornelius, but when the dog went to eat it, the man snatched it back and stuffed it in his mouth, taunting the dog by making a show of chewing it. Cornelius growled.

"I don't like it," said Teddy. "It's a Hail Mary play."

Stuckey dismissed Teddy's objection with a wave. "Okay, little lady. I think that just might work."

Teddy seemed uncharacteristically anxious, but he kept his mouth shut. She repressed the urge to ask him about it. *Ignore negative thought streams.*

"If you get out of my chair," she said, "I'll write up the contracts."

Stuckey stood and moved to the couch to allow her to work on her laptop.

"How do I know they'll be legally binding?" he asked.

"Who cares, as long as they're incriminating?" She opened a new Word file. "You'll have to take those gloves off. We'll need your prints on that contract as protection. And I'll need your full name."

"Benjamin Stuckey, like a stuck key, but only one k in the middle." He pulled off his surgical gloves. "And I want it set up for the coach here to whack a certain Walter A. Freemont. Esquire. If that dipshit didn't care so much about suckin' up to the DA, he coulda pled me out of two years upstate."

Reni whipped up a rudimentary murder-for-hire contract in short order. It was only one sentence long, but that's all they needed. She printed out three copies. Then she edited the file to change the names and printed out three of those. After one last change of names, she printed out the final batch.

"Teddy, take those out of the printer and give us each three copies of our own contract, the one with our name as the person doing the hiring."

Teddy reluctantly did as she asked.

"Just sign and put them on the coffee table." Reni continued. "We'll each get a set of executed contracts so we'll all have insurance against the others. Then it's just a matter of transferring the assets."

"Oh no you don't," said Stuckey. "Transfers leave paper trails. Cash only."

Reni couldn't stifle a laugh. "You expect us to walk into the bank and ask for fifty thousand in cash? They probably don't even keep that much on hand."

"Well, you'd better figure it out." Stuckey signed his last contract and dropped it on the table. "Because if the cops can prove I got paid that money, they're gonna pin an extortion rap on me, at the least."

"Let's see what our options are." She turned to her laptop to bring up the brokerage site where Teddy kept his retirement account.

"No!" cried Teddy, startling all three of them.

"I mean . . ." Teddy averted his eyes, then let out a sigh of resignation. "Don't bother. The money's not there anymore."

Reni stared at him, slack-jawed.

"Your wife says it is," said Stuckey.

"She's doesn't know." Teddy's eyes remained anchored to the floor.

Reni felt her heart falter. "What did you do, Teddy?"

"You promised me that money," said Stuckey.

Teddy finally found the courage to look Reni in the eye. "I'm so sorry, baby."

"You've been betting on football again." She spat the words out like spoiled fish.

Teddy's eyes teared up.

"How much did you lose?" she said.

"If the Rams win by six this weekend . . ."

"How much, Teddy!"

His stare was fixed on the floor. "All of it."

Her teeth clenched in anger.

Teddy buried his head in his hands. "Plus another ten grand I'm in the hole for."

Remi closed her eyes, forced her jaw to relax, and took two deep breaths, determined to prevent the magnitude of Teddy's recklessness from blocking up her chakras.

Stuckey, on the other hand, erupted. "That was *my* fifty grand."

Teddy looked up bitterly. "You'll never get a penny from me, you son of a bitch!"

Stuckey's face twisted into pure hate. "You can kiss my ass." He raised the gun at Teddy and fired. Reni screamed, horrified, as her husband grabbed his shoulder and fell to the ground.

Stuckey swung the gun toward her. She shouted, "Coco, take him!" Cornelius leapt as the second word left her mouth, clamping his fangs deep into the wrist of Stuckey's gun hand. The Colt went flying as the man screamed in pain, collapsing to his knees struggling to pry open the dog's unyielding jaws.

Reni snatched the gun from the floor. "Coco, give!"

Cornelius let go of Stuckey, but backed away only a few inches, growling softly, spring-loaded to pounce if the man posed the slightest threat. Stuckey froze in place, blood dripping from his hand, terrified of triggering the dog.

"Good boy," said Reni with no hint of a silly voice.

"Why the hell didn't you do that before?" said Teddy, trying to stanch his own bleeding.

"I wasn't sure Cornelius was up to it anymore," she said.

Stuckey moved and Cornelius snarled. The man resumed his frozen kneel.

"How could you, Teddy?" she said. "Everything we've saved for, everything we've slaved so many years for, everything we've dreamed of. Pfft." She flicked her fingers in the air to mime their future going up in smoke.

She turned back to Stuckey. "And you were going to take us for what you could then kill us both, weren't you?"

"And what if I was? You're not gonna shoot me? You don't have the balls." He reached in his boot and came up with a stiletto. The knife shot open with a clack. "So give me the gun, bitch and maybe I'll let you live."

She shuddered as the gleaming blade oversaturated her adrenaline level. *All progress takes place outside the comfort zone.* She shot him center mass.

Stuckey's eyes went wide, staring at her disbelievingly. She must have hit a lung because he was wheezing hard. He keeled over and coughed up blood.

Teddy gaped, thunderstruck.

"My God, baby! What did you do?"

Stuckey's wheezing suddenly stopped. As if pronouncing the man dead, Cornelius relaxed his vigilance and trotted over to Reni. "Good boy," she said, ruffling his ears.

She turned to Teddy and aimed the gun at his belly.

"And you . . . give me one reason why I shouldn't shoot you too."

"Baby, I get it," he said. "I fumbled the ball. But this isn't who you are. He had a knife. It was self-defense. I'm hurt and I'm helpless."

She let Cornelius lick her free hand as she considered.

"I'll make the money up to you," Teddy continued. "I'll get a second job. If nothing else, I'll drive Uber at night. I can't make up everything I lost, but it beats you being all alone. Or worse, you going to prison for life. Baby, you know I love you."

His expression evoked telethon faces of starving children.

"Right," she said, sarcasm dripping from the word like grease from a draining basket of hot fries. "I swear, Teddy, this is your last chance. You blow it and I'm done."

"Whatever you want."

"Here's the deal," she said. "I'm sick of you never listening to me. Like Stuckey showing up." She waved the gun toward Stuckey's corpse. "I told you I heard someone in the house and you blew me off."

"From now on, your words are gospel. Scout's honor."

"You say that, and you nod like you get it, but you never do."

"You're the quarterback. I'll run the plays just like you call 'em."

"And that's another thing. Your relentless sports metaphors are driving me crazy. Our marriage is not a game."

"I hear you loud and clear. Unsubscribe from the sports talk."

"And you've got to promise me, on your mother's grave: No more gambling. No football pools, no fantasy leagues, no online poker, no OTB, not even a scratcher."

"I promise. From my mouth to God's ear, I'll knock that one out of the park."

She sighed. "I knew you wouldn't listen."

She aimed at his chest.

"I'm listening! I am! I'm all ears."

"Then hear this, Teddy."

He started to speak, but she put her finger to her lips to shush him.

"I speak, you listen," she said. He nodded. "When Stuckey was in the kitchen, he yelled out a question. Remember what it was?"

"He asked for a spatula."

"What were his exact words?"

Teddy looked bewildered. "He said, 'Reni, where's your spatula?'"

"That's right. How did he know my name, Teddy? You always call me baby."

"Maybe he saw some old mail in the kitchen."

"It's all bills and ads, and they're all addressed to Renata, not Reni."

Teddy opened his mouth to answer, but no words came out.

"He knew because you told him my name when you hired him to murder me."

His eyes pleaded. "They threatened to kill the two of us *and* my sister if I didn't pay up. I had no choice. It was death to us all if I didn't cash in your life insurance."

"You have a policy too. Why kill me and not you?" she said. "You're the one who got us into this mess."

"I don't know. It just seemed . . . simpler."

"Do you think it's right that I should be the one to take the fall?"

Teddy hung his head. "No."

"Me neither." She shot him in the chest.

As Reni watched Teddy bleed to death, her mind was a whirlpool of thoughts and feelings. She needed to center herself. *I must push aside distractions to discover my real need in this moment.*

She closed her eyes and forced herself to be mindful of making adjustments to the crime scene before calling 911.

Reni stared at the video camera on the wall of the interrogation room. She wondered whether anyone was watching her as she waited for the detectives to return. There wasn't much else to look at. No two-way mirror like they always had on TV, no art on the dull green walls, no cushions on the gray steel chairs, no carpet on the concrete floor, and nothing but a thin file folder on the battle-scarred wooden table. Her only source of visual stimulation was the blinking red light on the camera.

She couldn't stop thinking about Teddy, bleeding out on the floor. Her decision to shoot him should have been a powerful self-actualization, but instead she felt diminished. As she pondered this, the door opened and Detectives Wanda Pharno and Carlo Minelli walked in.

Minelli had three Styrofoam cups of coffee. He set one in front of Reni, along with several packets of whitener and artificial sweeteners he pulled from his pocket. Pharno had a paper plate of Fig Newtons that she put in the center of the table.

The detectives settled into their seats across from Reni. Minelli took a sip of his coffee and winced as if he'd burned his tongue. Pharno tossed her head to swing her bleached blonde ponytail over her shoulder. She wasn't an unattractive woman, but Reni thought she could have done better for herself without the excessive eye makeup and the austere black blazer that was too narrowly tailored for her broad hips.

"Where were we?" said Pharno, grabbing a cookie.

"Mrs. Murphy woke up taped to a chair," said Minelli. "Saw her husband taped to a chair as well, and a man she says she never saw before holding her pistol."

"Teddy's pistol," said Reni.

"I stand corrected." Despite Minelli's military-style crew cut, there was a warmth in his pale blue eyes that put Reni at ease. "What happened next, Mrs. Murphy?"

"I've already gone through this twice."

"Indulge us," he said. "We want to make sure we get our facts straight."

"Do you usually pack a gun when you hear noises in the night?" Pharno reached for another Fig Newton, then had second thoughts and withdrew her hand.

"I can't remember ever hearing noises before. At least not the sort that make you afraid someone's broken into your house."

"Okay. So you were taped up and this gunman goes into the kitchen to find something to eat," prompted Minelli.

"He'd been vaping. Maybe he got the munchies. So, while he was out of the room, Teddy managed to break himself loose and free me as well. But this man . . . what did you say his name was?"

"Stuckey," said Pharno.

"Right. Stuckey. He blew up at Teddy for getting loose and he shot him. Twice! Then he just sat down and ate like it was nothing. And poor Teddy . . ." She closed her eyes to hide her pain as she imagined they'd expect a grieving widow to do.

"But you weren't taped up anymore," said Pharno.

"No, but he still had the gun. Then I got this idea that maybe the dog remembered his commands from his K-9 training. He's old and out of practice, so I wasn't sure, but I figured I had nothing to lose. So I sicced him on Stuckey and, sure enough, Cornelius disarmed him. When I grabbed the gun, Stuckey lunged and I had to shoot him. It was him or me."

"That's all consistent with the evidence so far," remarked Minelli. "But then things get a little fuzzy."

"Fuzzy?"

Pharno and Minelli exchanged a glance.

"Did your husband ever say or do anything to you that made you feel threatened, Mrs. Murphy?" asked Pharno.

"You mean, physically? Of course not. Teddy would never hurt me."

Pharno looked again to Minelli, then gave him a nod. He took that as a signal to pull a clear plastic evidence bag from the file folder in front of him. It contained a single piece of paper that was folded into a rectangle about the size of a playing card.

"Open it," said Pharno. "The lab's already processed it."

Reni nodded and pulled the paper out, then unfolded it to read. When she was through, she looked up at the detectives with a puzzled look. "What is this?"

"It's a contract, Mrs. Murphy," said Pharno. "We found it in Benjamin Stuckey's pocket. Your husband evidently hired him to murder you."

She did her best to look shocked. "Teddy would never do that."

"His fingerprints were on it, Mrs. Murphy," said Pharno. "As well as Stuckey's. And that appears to be your husband's signature."

She was pleased with herself for having had the presence of mind to ask Teddy to pull the contracts from the printer. She'd put on gloves before she'd planted this one on Stuckey, then burned the rest. *Life is not about finding yourself, but creating yourself.*

"It appears that your husband owed a lot of money to some dangerous people," said Minelli. "Maybe that's why Stuckey came by that night: to collect for your husband's bookie. When you came downstairs with a gun, Stuckey had to improvise and things got ugly."

In order to cry, Reni visualized a kitten she'd operated on two days earlier who'd died during surgery. It worked. Pharno pulled a Kleenex pocket pack from her blazer and offered it. Reni took a piece and blew her nose.

"Sorry," she said. "I'm just . . . I mean, poor Teddy. His death was so . . ." She struggled for the word. ". . . senseless. And this contract thing. I mean, why would he . . ." More tears flowed.

"Desperation," said Pharno. "People act out of character."

"If it's any consolation," said Minelli, "the facts seem to exonerate you of any wrongdoing. We'll recommend against the DA filing charges, so you shouldn't expect any complications with your funeral arrangements."

"Or with your life insurance claim," added Pharno.

"He had life insurance?" *I'm good*, she thought. *Maybe I should take up acting.*

"Five hundred thousand dollars. We found the policy when we searched the house."

"I had no idea. He must have bought it on the sly."

Just when the caterpillar thinks the world is ending, she turns into a butterfly. But Reni felt anything but fluttery. Shameful was closer to the truth. She remembered something her mindfulness coach had said about failed relationships: Revenge is only sweet if you're blameless. Something she'd have to meditate on.

---

*When I sat down to write "Home Game" I had a vague idea about the wife in a long-married couple hearing an intruder in the house in the middle of the night. Neither her husband nor her aged dog deigns to wake up, so she chooses to investigate on her own. That was all I had at the time and it was all I needed to start writing.

We writers often categorize ourselves as either outliners or "pantsers" (seat-of-the-pants writing without a storyline). I consider myself the latter. After too many years of detesting the writing of mandatory outlines (treatments) for producers, film studio honchos, and network executives, I joyously rid myself of the constricting task of outlining by turning to crime writing. The lack of adult supervision allowed me to let my characters, instead of some static blueprint, lead my tales to unexpected places.

In "Home Game," the wife needed the confidence to confront an intruder so she assumed the role of an ex-cop. Her dog became a retired police dog that she'd trained long ago. Her husband became a platitude-ridden football coach with whom she'd lost patience. The home invader became a double-crossing negotiator. And from there the characters took me on a wild ride. I hope you have as much fun reading this story as I did writing it.

V. P. Chandler *hails from a long line of Texas law enforcement—sheriffs, a pathologist, a forensic photographer, a parole officer, and a Criminal Justice professor—immersing her in a world of crime and justice from an early age. Fueled by a love of horror, fantasy, sci-fi, and westerns, it's no surprise that she crafts tales with genre-blending twists. Holding a BA in Literature from Southwestern University, Chandler has worked as a paralegal, a teacher, and a West Texas rancher. She draws from all these experiences to bring depth and authenticity to her stories.*

UNDER THE BLACKJACK TREE
V. P. Chandler

People say that sometimes it only takes a minute to change a life. I know it can happen in an instant. The first time my life changed was when my mama died giving birth to my baby sister, Mama's fifth child. I'm number three. I was only three when it happened, but I remember how our lives got turned upside down. Even when I saw her buried, I thought she'd come back. But she didn't. Then auntie Viola came and helped take care of us for a few years. I'm named after her. I'm Mary Viola. "Viola" like in "violet," not like the instrument.

Anyway, then my daddy married Cullie. She's now my stepmama and took us four children in like we were her own. She's the hardest worker I've ever seen. So, I guess that was the second time my life changed. Sometimes we call her "Mama" or "Cullie."

But I'm here to tell you about the third time. I should have known better. I was seven and it happened as fast as the pull of a trigger. My life'd never be the same.

"You sure you got that tray, Mary V?"

"Yes, ma'am." I take the tray from Mama and balance it with the two meals on it. This is one of my favorite things to do, giving the meals to our "guests" in the jailhouse. My daddy is sheriff here in Huntsville and the jail cells are on the second floor where we live. I like to do it because it makes me feel important. Of course, Daddy wouldn't let me do it if he ever thought it'd be dangerous. I carry the tray, careful to stay in the middle of the aisle, not getting too close to one side or the other. Mr. Bernard is on the right. He's a nice man but he drinks too much sometimes.

"Morning Miss Mary."

"Morning Mr. Bernard." His eyes dart to my daddy who's standing at the main door to the floor. Everyone else calls him "Bernard" and leaves out the "Mister" because he's dark. But he's always nice to me, so I like to add the "Mister." I place the tray on the floor and put his plate where my daddy told me to.

"Thank you, Miss Mary. You're an angel for sure."

I step back and smile at him as his shaking hands reach for the plate. Drink sure can make people nervous.

Then I get the second plate and walk it over to the cell where our new "guest" is in. And from what little I've heard him say, he doesn't sound like he's from around here. The morning sun pokes through the clouds. Sunbeams shine in the window and land on top of his head. His gold hair shines like a halo, and I almost suck in my breath. I've never seen hair like that. I mean, I've seen yellow hair before, but none so shiny. He flashes me a smile. Teeth almost perfect except the front two crisscross just a bit.

He stands up from his bunk. "Eggs and toast? Did you bake that just for me?"

I get a lump in my throat and my face turns red. His smile gets bigger.

"No. Mr. Wilson cooked it. I just deliver it." I place it on the floor in the right spot, trying not to drop it because I'm so nervous. I hurry away and walk toward my daddy. Daddy has his hands on his hips and kind of scowls at the man. I can tell he doesn't know what to make of him because Daddy gives me that same look when I do something like pull a frog from my pocket. Daddy puts his hand on my back as I walk by, and he locks the bar door and then the wooden door. When we get down to the first floor he says, "Don't be talking to him. We don't know anything about him."

I'm burning to know more and decide to push my luck. "What's his name?"

"He says his name is Joe Early but I sense he's not telling the truth. Stay clear."

"Yes, sir." I couldn't talk to him if I tried. He's so pretty, I wouldn't be able to get a word out anyways.

We go down to breakfast and Daddy turns on the radio and sits down with his paper. I don't know how he can do both at once and eat breakfast. But he likes to keep up with everything going on in our county and the whole world. I guess that's what a sheriff is supposed to do.

My brothers Roscoe and Augustus are snickering and giggling, like they always do. I don't know what they're up to half the time.

Mama says, "Now y'all sit down and behave. If you've got so much energy, I can think of a few more chores for you to do."

"Yes, ma'am," they say at the same time. Cynthia and I roll our eyes at each other. Boys.

I start wondering what those two are up to when I hear, "Miss Viola, you don't like my pancakes?"

"Huh?" I look over at Mr. Wilson who's standing at the stove minding the pancakes, bacon, and eggs. Whenever Daddy arrests Mr. Wilson, he helps Mama with the cooking for the "guests" and us too. Although Mama's a good cook, we're partial to his. But don't tell Mama I said so. I pick up my fork and give him a big smile.

"I love your pancakes!" I pour on the syrup and take a big bite and then show him my big cheeks while I chew. That makes him laugh but Mama says, "Mary V . . . behave." She wipes the corner of my mouth with a napkin.

The pancakes really are good, and I dig in some more.

Then an announcement comes over the radio. "Yesterday morning there was a bank robbery in Conroe . . ."

We all stop eating and Daddy lowers the paper.

The announcer continues, "The robbery occurred an hour after the bank opened, two men entered with guns and demanded money. The bank won't disclose exactly how much money was stolen, but we know that yesterday was payday for the oilfield workers in the area. Rumor is that they could possibly be connected to the infamous couple, Bonnie and Clyde. But our newsroom has not been able to confirm that."

Then the radio goes on to talk about Bonnie and Clyde. Of course, Daddy knows all about it, especially the escape from the prison farm just down the road aways. Even though I'm only seven, I know a lot of people got in trouble for that. The newsman starts talking about something else and Mama gets up and turns it off.

I look at my pancakes and take a bite. They still taste good but now the sugar seems too sweet and it's hard to swallow. It's quiet and all we hear is the last of the bacon sizzling in the pan.

We all watch Daddy, wondering if he's gonna say anything. He goes back to reading his paper.

I'm glad that the reporter didn't say anything about another lawman getting killed. I worry about Daddy. I've already lost my first mama. I can't lose him too. "Maybe you should start wearing a gun?"

Daddy puts down the paper. "No, Mary V. I've never had to wear one and I'm not starting now. Now y'all eat your breakfast before it gets cold. I'll be busy today making some phone calls."

Mama shakes her head. "What's the world coming to?"

Daddy says, "They'll be stopped. One way or another."

I finish my breakfast and take my plate to the sink. On the way out the door I try to remember my manners. "Thank you for the good breakfast, Mr. Wilson."

"You're welcome, Miss Mary. Maybe we'll come up with something special for lunch."

I go through the front door and wonder what to do next when I hear some scuffling and a woman talking in the alley next to our house. I decide to investigate and peek around the corner of the house.

There, standing in the gravel alleyway, is a movie star. Well, she could be. In fact, she looks a lot like that Myrna Loy who's coming out in that Skinny Man movie in a couple of weeks. Her dress is spotless and fresh, and her brown hair is shiny and perfect. Lots of people have ordinary brown hair. But not her. Somebody this fine and fancy in our town and I don't know about her?

I watch her pick up a small rock and toss it at the window. "Psst! Psst! Hey!" If she's trying to whisper, she's awfully loud.

I can't help myself. I step out and say, "Can I help you?"

"Oh!" She turns to me, and her mouth is in a perfect "O." She reminds me of a picture I saw of Shirley Temple. "My goodness! Well, hello there. And who might you be, young lady?"

I pretend to act grown up. "Why are you throwing rocks at my house?"

"Your house?"

"That's right. I live here. My daddy's the sheriff. You trying to talk to someone inside?"

Sometimes when people say they can "see the wheels turning" inside someone's head, it sounds like it can't be true. But I can see her wheels turning. "My name is Celia and I need to get a message to a man in the jail." She steps closer and I can smell her perfume. It reminds me of Mrs. Abel's gardenias.

"You mean the blond man, Mr. Early?" It's a guess but somehow, I don't think that she needs to talk to Mr. Bernard.

"Early? Um, yes. The blond man."

"If you wanna go in and talk to him, all you have to do is ask."

She hesitates. "Well, I'm hoping to avoid that."

"Why?"

"Well, it's a bit embarrassing. Let's just say that it's grown-up stuff. Would you be able to get a message to him?"

"Maybe. I don't know." No one's ever asked me to deliver a message before.

"Okay, okay." And then she starts muttering to herself. "This could work."

Now I'm wondering if she isn't a little bit crazy. And here I am, alone in an alley with a crazy woman. I might be in over my head, so I look around for help. I hear people in the square a block over. I hear Mama inside, clanking and washing dishes, and likely Cynthia's helping her. Daddy's probably on the telephone talking to all sorts of important people. Roscoe and Augustus are off doing what boys do now that school's out. And then I see a head poking out at the corner of a brick building. A dark-skinned girl is watching us. And now I don't know if I'm relieved that there'll be a witness to my demise or embarrassed that someone's watching me act high and mighty.

Then the Celia woman says, "I'll tell you what. I'll make it worth your while."

"Yeah?" This plan is already sounding better.

She reaches into her little purse and pulls out money. "How about a dollar?" She holds it in front of my face. A whole dollar!

"Sure!"

"Okay. Tell him I'm working on getting help. But I need to know where it is."

"Where what is?"

"He'll know what I'm talking about." She puts it back in her purse. "You'll get the dollar when I get my answer."

Now the wheels are turning in *my* head. I'm trying to size her up and figure out what her game is. And then I catch sight of her necklace and everything else goes out of my head. I can't take my eyes off the green stone on a silver chain. It's like a chunk of green ice just floating on her chest. I've never seen anything like it before.

"You like my necklace?"

Now I know I'm a girl that likes fishing and camping, but I also like girly things too. And that necklace is so elegant, just like the Celia lady. I nod.

She smiles and touches it. "He gave it to me. Bought it in Houston at a big, fancy store." She sighed. "So, you see why I need to get a message to him. His answer will help me get him out. I suppose I'll meet you here right after you deliver his lunch?'

"Sure."

Her face glows with a smile. "Swell. See you then." And with that she walks to the square and turns the corner.

"Whatcha doing?"

I almost jump out of my skin. It's the girl who was watching us. "You trying to kill me?"

"Sounds like you're trying to get into trouble."

I finally get a good look at her. She's about my age, in a spotless blue and white dress, bright white socks, and shiny black shoes. She's a good five inches taller than me but I feel smaller since I'm wearing my "play clothes" that won't get messed up if they get dirty. And in her hands, she's holding the fluffiest orange and white kitten. "Can I pet your cat?"

"Sure. His mama rejected him since he was the runt so I'm his mama now. I take him everywhere with me." He's asleep but she holds him up for me to touch. He's the softest kitten ever. Soft like a bunny.

"He's sweet." I keep looking at the kitten when I say, "I'm not trying to get into trouble. Just helping that nice lady."

"What's that guy in jail for?"

I shrug. "Dunno." A few more strokes. "I think he was drunk and unruly. It was Saturday night so that's not unusual."

"I'm Lottie."

"I'm Mary Viola. Mary V."

"And your daddy's the sheriff. My daddy works in the prison and my mamma's a teacher at the school." With a tilt of her head she motions back toward Rogersville that's a couple of blocks over.

I look back at the kitten and ask, "So why do you think I'll get into trouble?"

"If she was on the up and up, she'd go see him herself."

I stop petting the kitten and go sit on a big rock in our yard. She sits beside me.

"Yeah. I suppose you're right. But I could get a dollar out of it."

"I suppose it depends on what you want more. The dollar or to stay out of trouble."

"That's a stumper." I'd really like that dollar.

After helping Mama with some chores, I sneak upstairs to the two doors that lead to the cells. I listen to the house. Daddy's still on the phone and Mama's outside hanging clothes. I open the first door, the solid one, and stick my face in between the bars of the second one. I don't dare get the keys. "Psssst! Mister!"

Mr. Bernard looks at me with a scared face. "Child, what are you doing?"

I whisper as loud as I can, "I need to talk to Mr. Early."

"He's no good. You leave him be. He's trouble."

Then the blond man says, "Who's that whispering?"

"Ssssh, it's me. Mary V. I brought you your breakfast." I see him through the bars, and he stands up and smiles at me. I swear the sun is coming through the window and shining on him again and giving him a halo.

"Whatcha want, darlin'?"

Darling? My knees just about give out. Glad I'm holding on to the bars. "I got a message for you."

"Oh?" I can see that really catches his attention.

"A certain pretty lady says she's working on trying to help you. But she needs some info." This is exciting. I feel like I'm in a spy movie.

"I was wondering why she hadn't visited yet."

"She wants to know—"

"Mary? You around? I need your help," Mama calls.

I whisper to Mr. Early. "I'll tell you at lunch."

I close the big metal door as quietly as I can. I tiptoe down the stairs when it occurs to me that maybe I should have asked *him* for a dollar. Maybe I could make a business of this!

Lunchtime came quicker than I thought it would, but it also took forever. I volunteer to take the food again. It's hard holding on to the tray without dropping it because I'm so excited. Daddy unlocks the barred door and I walk in and give Mr. Bernard his food.

He whispers as he reaches for his dish, "You're courting trouble. Leave that man alone."

I don't say anything and walk over to Mr. Early and whisper while I put the plate down, but out of his reach.

"She wants to know where it is."

Mr. Wilson's apple pie was smelling really good. I hope that teasing him with pie will make him answer faster.

But his face gets red, and he squeezes his lips. "She doesn't need to know that."

"She says she needs it to get you out." And I need that dollar.

The phone rings downstairs and I glance at Daddy. He looks toward the stairwell then back at me. "Hurry up, Mary V. That's an important call."

"Yes, sir." Then I drop the man's fork and "accidentally" step on it. "Oh, shoot. I need another."

Daddy's irritated. He yells downstairs, "Cullie! We need another fork up here!" Then to me, "Come on out of there. I need to get that call," and he goes.

Mr. Early says, "Smart girl." But he doesn't sound happy.

"Tell me what she needs to know."

He eyes his food and nods. "Might as well. My other plan ain't panning out." He leans closer and whispers so as Mr. Bernard can't hear. "Tell her to go on the road to Trinity. Stop at the Burns farm. Tell her not to worry about them. They're currently . . . preoccupied. Behind the house is a blue barn. Behind the barn is a blackjack tree, a really big one. She'll find it there. And you tell her to hurry. I'm tired of being in here."

I nod. "Got it." I scooch the plate to where he can reach it.

He bends down to pick up his plate and looks up at me. "Hey, kid."

And now his eyes are different. I've never seen eyes like that, except once. And now I'm not in the jail anymore. I'm back where we used to live in town where we had the big tree in the backyard and Daddy had a slew of hunting dogs. We weren't supposed to play on the fence, but I was five and wanted to show my brothers that I could walk on the fence like on a tightrope at the circus. But I couldn't and fell into the yard. I had the wind knocked out of me and was lying there when Daddy's lead fox-hunting dog growled and stared down at me. I could tell that he was deciding whether to eat me or let me go. The other dogs started gathering around, waiting for his decision. Daddy came out and saved me and wanted to tan my hide. He hugged me and yelled at me. But he didn't need to. I remember those black eyes and never got close to the hunting dogs again.

Mr. Early's eyes are blue, but they look at me the same. He says, "Don't tell anyone else what I've said. Or you'll be sorry."

I pick up the tray and dirty fork as Mama walks through the door.

She smiles at me as we pass each other. I walk down the stairs and hear her lock the bar door behind me. I try not to think about what he said. Instead, I think about what I'll do with my dollar.

I drop off the tray and dirty fork in the kitchen and go outside to the alley. Sure enough, Miss Celia is there. I nod at her.

"Good girl." She reaches into her purse and holds up the dollar. "What'd he say?"

"Go on the road toward Trinity, stop at the Burns farm. Behind the house is a big blue barn. Behind the barn is a big blackjack tree. You'll find it there. He said not to worry about the farmers, they're per—peroccupied."

She hands me the dollar like she's giving me an award at school. I see her eyes glance across to the street that's catty-corner to us. There's a man sitting in a car. I'm confused. I thought Mr. Early was her love. Who's that hard-looking man behind the wheel? Miss Celia gently pulls on my chin to make my look at her. She smells like fresh face powder. Her eyes are almost as green as the stone on her necklace. "You're a good girl, so I'll also give you some advice. Women have it harder in this world than men do. Therefore, we must use our brains to survive. Stay smart. Now, do us both a favor and forget that we ever had this conversation. And don't spend that dollar for a long time. Hide it away for a rainy day. Good luck, honey."

And with that she heads toward the man in the car. I'm confused and don't know what to do. Then I decide that I don't care since I have my dollar. They're grown-ups, let them work it out. She gets in the car with the hard man. He frowns and looks at me. I don't know what he's saying, but I don't like it. She looks at me and smiles. Whatever she said seems to be okay with him and they drive away.

Glad that's done. I've got a whole dollar! I look at it again before putting it in my pocket. Maybe I can make a business of delivering messages?

"You really did it."

I turn around and Lottie's there, holding that cute kitten again.

"You spying on me? Don't you have somewhere else to be?"

"Maybe to the first, and no to the second."

I want to enjoy my dollar in private. "Leave me alone."

"Okay. But I'm telling you, don't mess with convicts. My daddy works in the prison and tells us all sorts of horrible things. If you knew, you'd stay clear."

"Oh, you don't know nothing." I walk over and touch the kitten on the head. He's awake now and just looks at me. "What's his name?"

"Butterbean."

We talk about cats and all sorts of stuff for about twenty minutes then a black car pulls up in front of the house and a man gets out and goes inside. I've never seen him before. He doesn't look like a lawman. I don't know how to explain the difference. But when you've been around a bunch of them a lot, they have a certain way that they look and walk and talk. This man reminds me of a gangster film. Maybe 'cause of the tilt of his fancy hat? Now I'm scared for Daddy. Could this man be one of Bonnie and Clyde's bunch? They've killed lawmen all over the state. Would they kill a sheriff in his own house?

I sneak up to the corner of the house. I can hear that Lottie is right behind me. As irritated as I was before, I'm glad she's with me. I motion for us to hide behind the front bushes. We hear the scraping of the metal door upstairs in the jail.

After a couple of minutes, I hear voices from inside in Daddy's office. They aren't yells, so that's good. I hear Daddy like he's giving instructions. I hear him say something about "bail" or "receipt."

Mr. Early and the gangster man walk out the front door and it closes behind them. They don't see us at first. Before Mr. Early gets into the car he stops, looks in our direction, and smiles. "Hey there, kiddo."

That smile. He's golden again. Maybe I was wrong.

"I can see your legs. I recognize your shoes."

The gangster man turns around.

I come out from the bushes and stand by the front walk.

Early says in a quieter voice, "I've got a proposition for you. If you want another dollar, meet me at . . ." He looks around and sees a sign for the cemetery down the road. "Meet me at the cemetery in five minutes. I have another message that you can deliver. You're such a smart kid, you're raking in the dough."

The other man makes noises like he doesn't like this, but Mr. Early holds up his hand for quiet. "Okay, Mary V? You'll get a dollar for just a few minutes of your time. Trust me." They get in the car and drive toward the cemetery.

Lottie comes out from the bushes. "That man is crazy."

I don't say anything. I'm thinking about how I can get another dollar.

"You aren't thinking about meeting him?"

"It's just a few of blocks away. I can get there and be back before anyone misses me. I've been there lots of times visiting my mama's grave. There are also lots of big trees that a person can hide behind. You could go with me."

"You've lost your mind."

"It'll be okay."

"And what am I supposed to do if anything happens? Supposing they steal you, or hurt you?"

"It'll be fine. I'm just a kid. They wouldn't hurt a kid."

She's shaking her head and looking at me.

"Fine. Then I'll go by myself. Time's awasting." And with that I take off like one of Daddy's dogs after a fox. I'm down the street before she even has a chance to say anything.

I run the three blocks over and one block up and enter the cemetery out of breath. I'm sweating and gulping for air. Where am I supposed to meet them? I listen for voices but only hear birds singing and smell pine sap in the warm sunshine. I figure while I'm here I might as well visit my first mama.

I find her, kneel at the grave, and brush off the pine needles. I've done a lot of crying here. I've talked to her a lot and missed her a lot. I've told her all about Cullie and how she's nice and taking care of us. I know Mama would like that. I trace my finger over her name. I don't know why but it sometimes makes me feel better. I hear leaves crunching and see the men walking toward me. The gangster man is wearing a coat which I think is odd since it's almost the end of May. But Mr. Early seems to be the one in charge, so I don't pay much attention to the other man.

When they're about five rows over I stand up and Mr. Early says, "Good girl. You're a smart cookie." And he shows me that movie star smile.

"So, what's the message and who do you want me to tell?"

Neither one says anything. I'm getting the feeling that Lottie was right. I stand taller and demand, "So what's the message? If you don't have one, I'm leaving."

Mr. Early smiles wider, and his eyes get cold again.

I'm confused.

The other man pulls out a shotgun. At least I think it's a shotgun, but it's shorter. Why do they have a shotgun? Are they hunting birds? Why would they hunt birds in the cemetery?

And then I see the flash, hear the boom, and I feel the hot pellets in my face. I don't know what's happened and all I can think about is my mama. I'm crying for her.

Mr. Early gets close to me and says, "If you live, keep your mouth shut or I'll kill the rest of your family. Not a word." Then I think I hear them running away, their car skidding out, and the engine disappearing.

But I don't know.

All I know is that I can't see anything, and my face is on fire. All I can smell and taste is metal. I'm trying to find my mama's headstone and I'm wondering if I'll finally get to see her again. I think I'm crying too but I can't tell because blood is in my eyes and everywhere.

"Mary V!" I hear my daddy. "Oh, Lord. Please don't die." He picks me up and starts running.

And then it all goes dark.

Three years later

Lottie and I are sitting on the tall sidewalk in front of Daddy's store. He's not a sheriff now but runs a grocery and hardware store. Lottie and I are good friends. Such good friends that we don't always have to talk. Which is good because I don't talk much these days. And sometimes it's good to just be in the company of a friend. Butterbean is grown and sits with us too.

What happened after I was shot is a blur, and I don't recall much of it. Which Mama and Daddy say is a blessing. The biggest miracle was that not one pellet of birdshot hit my eyes. I still have a pellet stuck in the corner of my left eye where my tears come out and three are stuck in my gums. A couple more are in my shoulder. The doc said that if they don't bother me, they're fine where they are. To dig them out might cause more problems.

I remember thinking I was dying. I remember the pain. People kept asking me who did it. I didn't say anything. Lottie told them what she could. There was a manhunt and roads were closed and all of that. But they never found Early. We also found out that the man with the fancy hat had tied up the Burns family and hid out in their house for a few days while Early was in jail.

Then about a month later, a hunter found a body in the woods. They said it had a fancy hat like one worn by one of the men who robbed that bank in Conroe. I heard Daddy talking about some kind of "double cross." I guess that meant fighting over the money.

And in the mix of all of that, Bonnie and Clyde were shot down a couple of days after I was shot. I remember Daddy and Mama saying that maybe people would start coming to their senses. But it just reminded me that there are lots of bad men out there. And one who said he'd kill me and my family.

Almost every night for a year I had bad dreams about Early. I'd dream that he'd sneak into the house and stand over my bed and then pry my mouth open to cut my tongue out. I'd wake up screaming and crying. Then Daddy would come and comfort me. He'd say, "Nobody wants to break *into* a jail." And then he'd sit by my bed until I fell asleep again.

The fear never really went away. I just got better at hiding it.

My shooting made big news and a people from all over sent me gifts and toys. There were so many that Mama told me to give some to the "less fortunate."

But there was one gift that I wouldn't give away. A small package that came from California. No name, no return address. It was the necklace with the green stone. Miss Celia's necklace. Of course, Mama and Daddy were confused, but I knew exactly what it meant. It meant that Early had gotten hold of her and killed her, and it was a message for me to keep my mouth shut.

Early's never been found so I'm still not taking any chances. If he could kill beautiful Miss Celia, get me shot in the face, and kill his buddy who got him out of jail, he could be anywhere any time and kill everyone I love.

Over the weeks and months people were nice to me. Even Cynthia, Roscoe, and Augustus were nice. I could tell that it shook them. Lottie would come and visit and bring Butterbean. Sometimes we'd just sit and I'd cry and pet the cat. Then she got to bringing books and reading to me. She's a really good reader. And then we got to sharing books from the library. And now we talk about everything. We both want to be teachers. I'll probably be a math teacher since I've found I'm good with numbers.

But today we're sitting in front of Daddy's store. I turn to Lottie to ask her what kind of book we should get from the library when Daddy comes up to me and says, "I've got to take the wagon and get some produce. Want to come with me?"

Lottie stands up and brushes off her dress. Butterbean stands up too.

Daddy says, "You're welcome to come too, Lottie."

"No thank you, Mr. Mitchell. I have to get back home and do some schoolwork. Y'all take care." And with that she and Butterbean head home.

Daddy smiles down at me. "Looks like it's just you and me."

"Fine by me."

We get in the wagon and head out of town. We don't get many chances for just the two of us to be together. With a house full of kids and him running the store, there're always people about. I often wish that I had more time with him. But now that we're alone, I can't think of anything to say. So, we sit in silence and enjoy the ride.

He turns the wagon into the drive of a farm and on the mailbox, it says "Burns."

"Daddy, is this—?"

"Yes, it is. Time's passed. And they're fine. I thought it'd do you some good to see that."

My heart races and I'm looking around for some kind of danger. Daddy goes around back of the house to the barn where a fat man in overalls is waiting for us. Daddy's talking loud like the man can't hear. They say hellos and start chatting about weather and the garden and the vegetables. I smile and wave hello and want to get some distance.

I see the blue barn. The color is faded but I can tell that it's blue. Burns. Blue barn. The big tree. A blackjack tree?

I leave the men and go behind the barn and see a large tree with rough bark. Its branches look like arms reaching out to grab me. I look around the base and see that on the other side it looks different at the roots. I spot a shovel leaning against the barn. I grab it and start digging. Surely if there was something worth killing for, it would have been taken away three years ago. I'm afraid of what I'll find and afraid of finding nothing. Then all the years of being afraid come over me and I'm mad. I start digging harder and harder and I'm crying. I'm so angry because I've been afraid for so long. Every creak in the house at night, every sudden noise makes me jump. I'm so mad of holding on to the fear. I want to find something even if it hurts me.

The shovel scrapes something solid. Probably a tree root. I stop and kneel in the fresh dirt.

"Mary? What are you doing?"

I ignore Daddy and brush away the musty dirt. I hope it's buried treasure. But I fear it'll be the skeleton of Miss Celia, that I'll see those horrible empty eye sockets and forget how green hers were and how kind she was to me.

I keep digging and I see yellow. And even though the hair is matted and dirty, I'd recognize it anywhere. Early. The golden man.

It smells horrible but I can't stop. I dig faster with my hands and now Daddy is beside me and he gasps. I'm scooping away the dirt faster and faster, like a hound dog after a rat.

He's saying things but I don't hear him. He pulls me away and steps in front of me. I let him take over.

I'm standing there, wondering, *How can this be? What about the necklace?*

And then I fall back and sit hard on the ground and start thinking. Who sent me the necklace? Miss Celia. She must have heard about what happened to me and felt bad. Maybe the necklace was a gift to say she's sorry.

Then I start smiling and laughing. Poor Daddy probably thinks I'm for the looney bin. No more worrying about Early coming to get my family. No more looking over my shoulder. I feel like my throat has been clogged for years and now it's unstopped, and I can breathe. I want to shout.

Miss Celia made it out all right and the devil man is gone.

I hug my knees and look up at the blackjack tree with its branches reaching up to the sky. We're both happy to let go of our secrets.

---

*Most of "Under the Blackjack Tree" is pure fiction. But it was inspired by some factual events and circumstances. The spark of inspiration came when my mother told me that her grandfather had been sheriff and that she got to help feed the inmates when she was a small child, circa 1940. I thought that image was so strong that I had to write some kind of story about that.

My great-grandfather also was sheriff in Huntsville, Texas, in 1934 at the time when Bonnie and Clyde were wreaking havoc in Texas. The family lived in the jailhouse, as was common in small towns in America.

And for the final item: When Mary was young, maybe about ten, they lived in the country. An older brother was practicing or shooting at a bird with a shotgun, and he pulled the trigger just when my grandmother came around the corner of the house. She got a face and shoulder full of birdshot. Thank goodness he was pretty far away and not closer. They thought she was going to die. The doctor was sent for. And of course, it being about 1915 and in a remote area, the doctor was on a horse. I've heard that it had been rainy, and the mud made it difficult to travel. My grandmother made a full recovery, and by some miracle, she never had scars. It was indeed truly miraculous that she didn't lose her sight. When we were little, the grandchildren would ask Grandmother to tell us the story and then she'd show us the pellet in the corner of her eye, near her tear duct, and the ones in her gums. Sometimes she'd move them around a little and we'd squeal in horror and then laugh.

Since winning the Bethlehem Writers Roundtable Short Story Award in 2014, **Tracy Falenwolfe***'s stories have appeared in over a dozen publications including* Woman's World, Black Cat Mystery Magazine, Black Cat Weekly, Mystery Magazine, Spinetingler Magazine, Flash Bang Mysteries, Crimson Streets, *and several* Chicken Soup for the Soul *volumes. A former human resource manager, retail manager, and bank teller, she decided writing fiction was more fun. Falenwolfe lives in Pennsylvania's Lehigh Valley with her husband and sons. She is a member of Sisters in Crime, Mystery Writers of America, and the Short Mystery Fiction Society. Find her at tracyfalenwolfe.com.*

JAMMING AT JOLLIES
Tracy Falenwolfe

"So," the drunk slurred. "What time do you get off?"

"Not soon enough." Zee wiped up the beer he'd spilled and palmed his keys in the process. He'd be face-down in the Corn Nuts before her shift was over, and it was a shame, because he was a nice guy, and she wouldn't have minded some companionship. But she didn't date guys who didn't know their limit.

Unfortunately, he didn't realize that yet. "I like your tattoos."

Zee just snorted at him.

Pretty Boy waved at her from the end of the bar. She'd tracked him from the moment he'd walked in the door. His date looked uncomfortable. Not uncomfortable like she didn't want to be with him. Uncomfortable like Jollies wasn't her kind of place.

Good for her.

Jollies was admittedly a dive bar. People came in to drink and shoot pool and shake off the day. The lone television in the joint was mounted behind the bar, and tuned to whatever Sugar, the owner, was in the mood for. The spot in the corner was reserved for whichever local band or musician Sugar fancied at the moment, for as long as they played what she wanted to hear—anything by The Eagles, .38 Special, Thin Lizzy, or Lynyrd Skynyrd except for

"Free Bird." Tonight, it was all jukebox, and Sugar was in a mood. She'd been upstairs in her office since she arrived.

That was fine. So far, Zee had been handling the crowd on her own. She made her way down the bar to where Pretty Boy had planted both elbows on the mahogany. She lifted her chin.

"Yeah," Pretty Boy said to her. "Let me get a beer and a slippery nipple."

Zee eyed him and his date, Miss Priss. "You have ID?"

Pretty Boy grabbed his chest. "Are you kidding me?"

Miss Priss dug her ID out of her purse and handed it over.

It checked out. Zee handed it back and looked at Pretty Boy. His face was red, but he passed Zee his driver's license. She took her time with it before handing it back. He'd turned twenty-one the day before. Made him legal, even if he was an ass about it.

She rattled off the list of beers they had on tap, and he picked one. He flashed his cash while sliding his license back inside the little plastic window in his wallet, then put the wallet in his back pocket. Easy pickins. Strictly pay-as-you-go for him. If she ran him a tab, there was a good chance he'd have lost his cash by the time he was ready to settle up. A real good chance.

She pulled the beer and let it set while she layered the shot. That's when she started getting the feeling. She glanced into the mirror behind the bar and scanned the room. Her heart raced as she caught a glimpse of a guy who was the right height and build milling around in the corner near the jukebox. Was it him? She'd been on high alert for the past three days, and the suspense was killing her. The guy's back was to her, and her stomach bottomed out waiting for him to turn around.

"What's the word, Zima?" Randy flipped open the bar flap, drawing her attention away from the boogeyman in the mirror. Randy was the size of a rhino and served as barback, bouncer, and boy toy at Jollies. He squeezed past Zee and emptied a tub of ice into the trough.

"Slow night, Randy." Her tips wouldn't come close to covering the trip to the grocery store she'd planned. Especially after she gave him his cut. Not that she was complaining. He was worth every penny.

Even though she could handle herself, she felt safer with Randy around. She was smart and wiry, but he was a wall. His black T-shirt strained at the biceps and across his massive shoulders. He wore V-necks because his neck was so thick it didn't fit through the hole of a crew neck shirt.

Thankfully, she didn't think she'd need him tonight. When she'd turned and looked, she saw the guy at the jukebox was one of the regulars shooting pool. Probably just looking to play his favorite song. At least she thought it was one of those guys. He was the only one in the place wearing the same color sweatshirt as whoever she'd seen. But the guy at the jukebox had been wearing a hat, hadn't he? And the pool player was not. Doubt started creeping in.

"Zima." The drunk caught his second wind and picked his head up off the bar. "Zima." He squinted. "That sounds familiar. Have we met before?"

They hadn't. It sounded familiar because her parents had been stupid kids in the '90s and thought naming their kid after an alcoholic beverage that had played a huge part in her conception would be cool. So, Zima Melissa Pawlowski was born. Her parents finished high school before splitting up and dumped baby Zima on her father's mother, who'd done the best she could before dropping dead at forty-nine.

Zima went by Zee now, and usually inflicted punishment on anyone who called her otherwise, but Randy was different. Randy had her back.

Zee served a second beer and a third martini to two guys who were talking sports and edging closer to each other. She topped off three glasses of wine for the desperate housewives she'd overheard plotting murders they'd never work up the nerve to commit. How many times could one person work the word hypothetically into a conversation, anyway?

She closed out a tab for a regular and accepted a generous tip. "Thanks, Paul." She slid the cash into her front pocket. Maybe she'd eat this week after all.

Paul played pool Mondays, Wednesdays, and Fridays with Marcus and Bateman and Sanders. Some weeks, the four of them were the only thing holding her head above water. Sanders was the one she'd mistaken for trouble earlier. But now that she glanced at him again, there was no way he could have passed for who she thought he was. The build was wrong, and he was definitely not wearing a hat. There wasn't even one hanging on the coat rack where the pool players usually kept their stuff.

"See ya, Zee." Paul gave her a two-fingered wave on his way to the door.

Zee said goodbye but kept her eye on the end of the bar near the drunk, where a middle-aged couple had been parked for an hour or so. First date, she guessed, but not strangers. The Frump and The Suit. Trying to decide if they were going to take whatever they had going any further. Maybe they were cheating on their spouses. Maybe they were coworkers forbidden from fraternizing. Maybe they were something else. But Zee had the feeling that whatever they were to each other was going to change tonight.

"Zima." The drunk raised his head. "Hit me again."

"Sorry," she said. "You're cut off."

"Seriously?" he slurred. "I'm not even drunk."

"You're sloshed. I'm not serving you anymore. Time to settle up and head home."

"Zimaaaa," he whined.

"Don't call me that. Now come on. Pay up and get out."

He reached into his shirt pocket and threw a wad of cash on the bar. Then he called her a word that, if he'd been sober, would have had her rearranging his gonads. He twisted around and patted his pockets. "Where are my keys?" He kept patting and twisting, patting and twisting.

It wouldn't do him any good. His keys were in the box under the cash drawer, where they would stay until he came back for them when she was sure he could pass a breathalyzer. Of course, most people never knew their keys had been swiped. They assumed they'd left them somewhere, or lost them, or dropped them down a sewer grate in their stupor. That's why there were fourteen other sets of keys in the box, along with a handgun, two tasers, and a couple of bags of psychedelics. Zee liked to avert trouble when she saw it coming. She said, "Call yourself an Uber."

"You don't have much of a bedside manner," he slurred.

"We're not in bed."

"But we could be." He had trouble focusing on her.

"Not a chance." At least not anymore.

While he was arguing with her, The Frump slid off her stool and headed toward the ladies' room. The Suit watched her until she rounded the corner, then pulled a clear vial out of his breast pocket. He looked up and down the bar, discounting Zee and the drunk. As he began to uncap the vial, Zee grabbed his wrist and pinned it to the bar.

"Son of a bitch." He tried to pry her fingers away with his other hand. "That hurts."

Zee divested him of the vial and slipped it into her pocket with her tips. "Don't try to tell me those were eye drops."

A vein bulged in his neck. He twisted, and Zee heard his shoulder pop. "I'm going to fucking sue you if you don't let go of me."

"Randy," Zee called.

Randy appeared. "You need some help taking out the trash?"

Marcus and Bateman and Sanders all looked up from their game of Cutthroat, ready to lend a hand if Zee or Randy needed one. She knew Bateman and Sanders carried. The flannel shirts they always wore didn't do much to hide that fact. She wasn't sure about Marcus, but she knew she didn't want the situation to escalate.

Zee let go of The Suit's wrist. He stumbled backward and rotated his shoulder, then rubbed it with his opposite hand.

"You need to leave," Zee said.

The bar quieted.

The suit opened his mouth to argue, but Randy took a step toward him, convincing the guy to turn and flee instead.

Conversations resumed. The guys went back to their game. The drunk took out his phone and called a ride, but not before giving her a glad-I-dodged-that-bullet glance.

The excitement was all over by the time The Frump returned from the ladies' room. She'd made her decision. Zee could see it on her face. Whatever she'd been thinking of doing with the

Suit, she'd decided not to. Maybe he knew she was headed there, and that's why he'd decided he had to drug her. Or maybe he was just a scumbag.

The Frump looked around. Caught Zee's eye. She pointed to The Suit's empty stool. "Have you seen my friend?"

Zee wiped the bar. "He skedaddled when you went to the bathroom."

"He left?"

"I'm sorry," Zee said. "But he also stuck you with the tab."

Out of the corner of her eye, she caught the guy she'd seen hanging around the jukebox slip out the door and tamped down her urge to vomit.

A couple of hours later, Sugar came downstairs to help close up. Sugar was a six-foot blonde. Most of that was legs. She was of indeterminate age but had enough life experience to be a hundred and ten. Over the years, she'd worked the pole, turned tricks, and starred in some soft-core internet porn. She'd also made some shrewd investments. When she'd had enough of the life, she bought Jollies and ripped out the poles and the private booths. She kept the name, the liquor license, and Randy, and had hired Zee when no one else would.

Sugar was an astute businesswoman. She still dressed like a dancer, though, right down to her five-inch fuck-me-pumps. But it suited her. "Until tomorrow," she said to Zee as she sauntered out the back door, hips swaying to a beat only she could hear.

Zee and Randy left through the front. Randy locked the door with his key. "You walking tonight, Zee?"

"Yeah. You?" Sometimes they walked the first few blocks together, and then Randy took the train the rest of the way home. Tonight, though, before he even answered her, a red Lamborghini turned the corner, engine purring. Sugar.

She rolled up next to Randy and lifted an eyebrow. He folded himself into the low-slung car and pulled the vertical door shut. Zee guessed he was still on the clock tonight. She put her hood up and started for home. She looked back twice, because her senses had been pinging ever since she'd seen whoever she'd seen in the bar, but she had the street to herself.

Or so she thought. Three blocks in, while she was walking past the burned-out shell that used to be a social security office, someone grabbed her from behind.

She bent at the waist and thrust her elbows back, but her attacker was ready for her. She stomped on his instep, but he dodged. He knew that was coming, too. His arm was tight around her head, pinning her chin to her chest. She chomped down on his flesh, and when all the bells and whistles in her head cleared, she heard his voice close to her ear. "Zee! Zee goddammit. It's me."

He eased his grip enough for her to turn and face him. "Chance." She took a step back. No more anticipation. Her worst fears had come true. "It *was* you in the bar tonight."

He didn't deny it. "We gotta talk, Zee."

She knew it. Her gut was never wrong.

"Come on, let's go somewhere."

She'd known this day was coming. She'd been dreading it for five years. Waiting for it since he got out three days ago. Now that it was here, she mostly felt numb. "I can't have any contact with you, Chance. It's part of my parole."

"Part of your parole." He snorted. "Who's watching?"

"Chance, I can't."

"You even see your PO more than once since you've been out? Most of them are crooked. Pay him off and you can do whatever you want."

Her parole officer was not crooked. "I can't be seen with you."

"Take me to your place then."

"No."

"I'm not taking no for an answer. Come on. One drink."

When she wouldn't agree, he snorted. "Tell me you didn't go straight. You find God on the inside, or what?"

"Fine." She looked around. "One drink."

He dragged her to a hole in the wall across the street named Charlie's. It made Jollies look swanky. They served flat beer in dirty glasses, and if you complained, you'd find part of that glass embedded in your forehead.

"When'd you get out?" Zee asked.

"Monday."

Zee nodded. She'd known that, of course, but she didn't want him to think she cared or that she'd been keeping tabs.

"I served the full nickel, Zee. Every damn day of it. You didn't even serve a year."

"It was your third strike."

"Think I don't know that?" After he yelled, he motioned like he was going to backhand her. Nobody in the bar cared. He could have set fire to her, and no one would have cared. They all knew who he was, and who he ran with.

Zee knew who he was, too, and had been careful not to flinch when he raised his hand to her.

"I guess you've toughened up." Chance looked at her with something that might have been respect. "Prison does that."

It wasn't prison that made her strong, but she kept her mouth shut.

"You look good, though." He raked his gaze over her.

She felt nothing at all.

"How'd you end up working in a bar, anyway. Isn't that a violation of your parole, too?"

"No. It isn't. And if you must know, my PO helped me get the job."

Chance drank the beer like it was good. "Ruthie sends her regards." Ruthie was Chance's sister. The ringleader of their family operation. "Even though she still figures you're the reason we got busted."

Zee was careful not to be baited. She was not the reason they got caught. Chance was. God knew what he'd told his sister about the night they got busted, but it probably wasn't that he'd been confounded while trying to come up with exact change to get out of the parking garage. "I'm sorry she thinks that."

Chance shrugged. "She said she'll call it even if we get the band back together."

Zee wanted nothing to do with Chance, or the operation, and even less to do with Ruthie. Ruthie was a psychopath. "I don't do that anymore."

Truth is, she hadn't done much in the first place. Swiped a few sets of keys. Caused a few distractions. Chance had boosted the cars, and Ruthie ran the chop shop.

"She said you'd say that." Chance's eyes twinkled. They were a brilliant blue, and he used them to his advantage. They used to make her melt, but she was immune now.

"I gotta get going."

Chance grabbed her wrist. "I'm not done with you yet."

She could have broken his arm, but this was his crowd, not hers, and she couldn't take them all on. Knowing when you were outgunned was just as much of a skill as being able to take someone down.

"Ruthie knows you're working in that bar." He leaned close enough for her to smell the funky beer on his breath. "She says all you gotta do is call out the marks. Detain them until you get the all-clear. You can do that, can't you?"

"No, Chance. I can't."

He tightened his grip. "Why not?"

"It's a small place. Most of the customers are regulars, and they don't drive anything worth taking."

"Ruthie said you'd say that, too."

"Because it's true."

"Fine then." He let go of her wrist and drained his beer, unconcerned with what was floating in it. "She really only wants the Lambo."

Zee's stomach turned. "That's my boss's car." Sugar's pride and joy.

"I know."

"Come on, Chance. You boost that car, and she'll know I had something to do with it. I need that job. You know how hard it is to get hired anywhere when you've been inside."

"Oh, boo-hoo. Don't you think you owe me?"

Now she was the one to raise her voice. "Owe you for what?"

He leaned closer and got right up in her face. "I know about the baby."

Her insides liquified and turned ice cold. Bells clanged in her ears, and she stopped breathing. If she'd had a knife, she would have cut his tongue out for even mentioning the baby, no matter whose turf they were on. But she was unarmed.

Chance leaned back in his chair. "When were you going to tell me?"

"Never," she said.

His blue eyes bored into hers. "Was it mine?"

She looked away. "I'm not sure."

"Ruthie said it was."

"How would she know?"

"She said you wouldn't have cheated on me back then. She said you were like a lovesick puppy."

Zee turned her glass around on the table in an effort to look bored, or amused, or anything other than terrified. "What else did she say?"

"She said the kid was born in prison."

Zee nodded. "Yeah."

"And that you gave it up for adoption."

"I did."

"We should find it."

"It?" She pushed her glass away.

"Our kid. It would be like almost four years old now, right?"

She reminded herself to breathe. "Right."

"You ever think about what our kids would be like?"

"No. It was a closed adoption, Chance. I don't know who got the baby, and I don't want to know."

"Ruthie could find out."

Her heart thumped. "What would be the point?"

"She's already started looking."

"She what? Why?"

"She says I could get the kid back no problem since you gave it away without telling me I was the father."

"No." Zee shook her head. "I told you I don't know if it was yours."

"Ruthie knows."

Ruthie. The psychopath.

"Think about it," Chance said. "We could get that one back and have a couple more. Raise them right, turn them loose on the street and be rolling in it. We'd be like, who is that guy in the movie?"

"You mean Fagin? From Oliver Twist?"

"Yeah, him."

Interesting choice for movie night in the joint. "Your sister lost her kids for doing that," she reminded him. Ruthie had three children she'd trained to be thieves until child protective services had removed them from her home.

"We'd be smarter than she was about it."

Chance wasn't smarter than anyone about anything. "I'm not having any more kids."

"Fine. Be that way. We're taking the Lambo, and you're going to help. If you don't, Ruthie is going to find some other way for you to pay your debt."

She rubbed the bridge of her nose. "I don't have a debt, Chance."

"Well, Ruthie says you have one, so you do. It's going down Friday. That's your busiest time, right?"

"Yeah, I guess."

"All you gotta do is keep the boss lady away from the car and the back door until we're all clear."

On Friday, the bar was hopping. Sugar and Randy both had to step in to help Zee. When they were at their busiest, Chance walked in. He sat at the end of the bar and ordered a draft.

Sugar's band du jour was playing "Take it Easy," and the regulars were shooting pool. Randy's black shirt was stained with sweat. He was working hard. He filled a glass with water for himself, drank half, and set it on the back of the bar next to the cash register.

Chance tracked Zee's every move. She considered telling him to go to hell, until Ruthie walked in and sat next to him. Her sly smile warned Zee she was being watched, and that she'd better not think about being uncooperative. A cold finger of fear traced Zee's spine. Unlike her brother, Ruthie was smart and calculating. She ordered a bourbon, neat, and threw a twenty on the bar.

Picking it up made Zee feel like a failure. Like Ruthie was still calling the shots. In prison, Zee's cellmate had warned her that falling back into the life was easier than anybody knew. And she was living proof—she'd been a guest of the state for the third time by then. The only way to break free, she'd told Zee, was to cut everybody from the past out of your life. And sometimes even that wouldn't be enough.

Zee waited on the next few customers in a daze.

Sugar slid past her to pull a draft. "Everything okay?"

"Yeah," Zee lied. "Why?"

"Two of your customers are waiting on refills."

"Sorry." She'd meant Chance and Ruthie, and Zee had been trying her hardest to avoid them.

Sugar was watching, so Zee made her way down the bar and poured Ruthie another bourbon. When she offered Chance another beer, he got up and left.

Showtime.

Ruthie smiled around her bourbon glass. She was there to make sure Zee didn't warn anyone about what was going to happen. To make sure Zee was complicit in another crime. One that would ruin her life and send her back to prison, if they got caught, or keep her in a stranglehold if they didn't. And there wasn't a whole lot she could do about it.

While she was closing out a tab, she slid the vial of roofies she'd taken off The Suit the other night, and dosed Randy's drink. Since Randy was such a big guy, she dumped in the whole vial. There was a lump in her throat the size of a brick, and she had to fight back tears. She hated what she had to do. Hated it. Less than a minute later, Randy gulped down every last drop.

Seconds after that, he got a strange look on his face, then crashed to the ground. She hadn't expected it to work that quickly. Or that completely. Maybe she'd given him too much. Or maybe there was something other than roofies in the vial. "Can I get some help here?" Zee called. "Is there a doctor in the house?"

There was not.

"Call nine-one-one," Zee told Sugar.

Sugar did.

Bateman, one of the regular pool players, was an off-duty police officer. He came over to offer his help. "What happened?"

"I saw her put something in his drink." Zee pointed to Ruthie. "And he drank it before I could stop him."

Ruthie's face turned purple. "I did no such thing."

Zee continued to point. "She put the vial back in her purse."

"That's ridiculous." Ruthie stood and grabbed her purse off the bar.

She was so mad it took Zee's breath away, but she couldn't stop now. "I saw her. Check for yourself."

"Ma'am." Bateman showed Ruthie his badge. "Would you mind turning out your purse?"

"I'll do no such thing."

"Fine," Bateman said. "Then please sit down while I get a warrant."

"Fine." Ruthie glared at Zee. "Look for yourself." She dumped the contents of her purse onto the bar. The clear vial rolled out, along with a handgun, wallets from two other patrons, and Sugar's Lambo keys.

Ruthie was horrified.

Bateman was already on the phone calling the station. "Do you have a permit for that weapon, Ma'am?"

"That's not mine. I didn't put that there."

"How's he doing?" Bateman called to Sugar.

Sugar was on the floor with Randy. "He has a pulse and he's breathing. He just won't wake up."

Bateman turned back to Ruthie. "Ma'am—"

"Lawyer." Ruthie was smart enough not to say another word. She knew what Zee had done, but she didn't accuse her of anything. Her cold hard stare promised retribution, though.

The paramedics arrived to help Randy. Two uniformed officers followed. They spoke to Bateman before they arrested Ruthie.

Outside, as they were putting her in the cruiser, the other regulars from the pool game—Bateman's partner Sanders, and Marcus, Zee's parole officer—led Chance around from the back of the building in cuffs.

"Ruthie," he yelled when he saw his sister being put in the back seat. "She double-crossed us. That bitch double-crossed us."

"Shut up, Chance." Ruthie looked like the top of her head was about to blow off. "Don't say a word."

"Freakin' Zee. I'm telling you she ratted us out."

On Sunday, Zee lit four candles on top of a unicorn-shaped birthday cake decorated with gold and silver glitter. Pink and purple streamers hung from the light above the table in her tiny kitchen.

Zee's parole officer Marcus and his two pool buddies, Bateman and Sanders, leaned against the sink. Randy, Sugar, and Zee's mother sat at the table around Zee's daughter, Angel.

Finding out she was three months pregnant less than a month after she got to prison had sparked Zee to get in touch with her birth mother, who agreed to adopt Zee's baby, especially since she regretted not raising her own. They found a lawyer who would record it as a closed adoption, so that if anyone tried to search for Zee's child, they wouldn't have much luck.

That hadn't stopped Ruthie. Zee's mother told them Ruthie had been to the house on Friday morning, claiming to be collecting donations for the church. Zee's mother had shut the door on her, but not before Ruthie got a look at Angel.

They sang happy birthday, and Angel blew out the candles. "Can I open my presents, Mommy?" Angel looked up at Zee with brilliant blue eyes.

They celebrated not on the day Angel was born, but on the day Zee came home and they were able to be together. Someday, Zee would explain it to Angel.

"Open mine first, Honey." Sugar handed her an elaborately wrapped package. Angel tore through it and came up with a crystal-studded denim jacket that she loved. "I invested some money for her too, of course."

She always did.

"Mine next." Randy gave her a gift bag filled with books. Angel was already reading on her own, and since Zee wasn't home for her bedtime, she read to her every morning. It was precious mother daughter time.

"The books are great." Zee pulled Randy aside. "But you already gave her the biggest gift she'll ever get."

Randy shrugged one massive shoulder. "I'm glad I could help."

Marcus, Zee's parole officer and champion, clapped him on the back. "I'm sorry there wasn't an easier way, but for the charges to stick, the drug had to be in your bloodstream."

"I'd do anything for the little princess," Randy said. "For Zee, too."

Zee had made the decision to go to Marcus immediately after Chance tried to suck her back into the life. It might have made her a narc, but it gave her today.

Zee's mother helped Angel open the next gift. Zee leaned back against the sink with Sanders and Bateman. "Did it work?"

"Chance is looking at twenty years," Bateman said.

"Ruthie's got herself a good lawyer," Sanders added. "But she'll do five years for drugging Randy no matter what."

Five years. Zee watched Angel open her last gift. They'd be safe for five years. After that, they'd be coming for her and her little Angel again. And she'd be ready.

When I set out to write Zee's story, I knew she was a criminal and that she'd be back to doing what got her into trouble in the first place. I didn't want her to be a victim of circumstance, or any other kind of victim. So why would she slip back into her old ways? I could only think of one reason. That reason has Zee using her skills to become the heroine of her own story. And I don't think she's done yet. Life's a struggle, but I'm rooting for Zee to keep coming out on top.

James A. Hearn *(jamesahearn.com) is an Edgar Award nominee for Best Short Story. His work has appeared in* Best American Mystery and Suspense, Alfred Hitchcock's Mystery Magazine, Black Cat Mystery Magazine, *and numerous anthologies, including* Monsters, Movies & Mayhem *and* The Eyes of Texas. *Hearn is a two-time finalist for Writers of the Future, a contest honoring new authors in science fiction and fantasy. He and his wife reside in Texas with a boisterous Labrador retriever who keeps life interesting.*

TOTALITY
James A. Hearn

It's been ten years since a date stood me up, and longer still since I've spent Valentine's Day alone. Tonight, I was doing both. Dressed to the nines in a black dress and high heels, at least I was striking out in style.

I raised my Maiden-No-More cocktail—trying not to take my drink as a metaphor for my life—and silently toasted myself. Denise Marie Fletcher, here's to you. Fifty years old, twice divorced, and waiting for a man who's passed you over for a younger woman.

I took a sip, then idly twirled my drink and thought about Vanessa Towers. My rival was everything I wasn't: natural blond curls to my auburn split ends, slim to my down-to-earth curves, stunning to my ordinary. But our most pronounced difference made it difficult for me to hate her, despite her hypnotic hold on my missing man: Vanessa Anne Towers, wife of esteemed neurosurgeon, Dr. Clayton Towers, was very dead.

I downed the rest of my drink in one go, raising some eyebrows from other diners. The Vince Young Steakhouse was jam-packed for a Wednesday, mostly couples squeezed together on the same side of their booths, hands clasped. Amid the University of Texas burnt-orange décor, the pink flowers of kalanchoe succulents were opened for the day, as if inviting an early spring.

The romantic imagery was spoiled by a middle-aged man making eyes at me from the bar. He wore an expensive brown suit with a garish yellow tie bisecting it like a line of mustard down a hot dog. A lawyer, I guessed, and I suspected he could tell lies just as easily in the bedroom as he did in court. My withering glare told Mustard Tie to keep nursing his margarita.

Love and lust were in the air this Valentine's, like the pollen exploding daily from the millions of cedar trees across central Texas. I gave an unladylike sneeze and dabbed at my watery eyes with a napkin. Love might've been in the air, but love wasn't sitting across from me, complimenting me on my black satin dress. Love wasn't playing footsie with me under the table or drowning in my blue eyes.

No. Private detective Charles "Trip" Allison III, my missing date, was in his office three blocks away, no doubt poring over Vanessa Towers's Murder Book. Three months ago, a "friend" at APD had given him a copy, and I'd given up asking how Trip had pulled the Book from his bag of tricks. When it came to cashing in favors, he was Felix the Cat.

Calling it a "book" was like calling Everest a mountain; it was closer to a small library of crime scene photographs, forensic reports, transcripts of detectives' notes, and witness statements. I had visions of pouring something over that damn book.

Like gasoline.

I took out my phone and, against my better judgment, texted Trip. I was angry and a little drunk, so I corrected the autocorrect that refused my cowgirl-themed curses. There. Now, if I had some rope and a branding iron, I could make good on my threats.

"Trip," I said to his empty chair, "you're going to catch hell when I've sobered up enough to drive."

I've never been good at sharing, and for years I've shared Trip with the entire state. I suppose he's known from the Panhandle to the Piney Woods as Texas's most famous private detective. I'm no slouch when it comes to sleuthing, but I was never in Trip's league. While Trip worked for governors, I made my bones catching cheating husbands for divorce lawyers. (It's funny how I was great at catching cheaters for clients, but was always the last to know in my personal life.)

Trip and I met in the Hill Country, among the bluebonnets, and wound up joining forces on the same case. But for all his fame, Trip didn't find the gold mine that day. I did. Trip didn't save his nephew from cartel hitmen. That was me. By the end of our first day together, Trip and I were millionaires, and he'd fallen hopelessly in love with me.

So why was he spending Valentine's with a dead girl?

As I waited for Trip to arrive, I found myself dredging up headlines of Vanessa's murder. Austin Socialite Murdered in Mansion. And: APD Seeks Man in Black. Ending with: Dr. Clayton Towers Cleared in Wife's Murder. On August 18, 2017, a mysterious figure in black broke into the Towerses' mansion and strangled Vanessa in full view of a state-of-the-art security system . . . the very system Trip had installed for her.

In the beginning, APD focused on Dr. Clayton Towers, the victim's husband, and tabloids wallowed in their troubled marriage like pigs in a sty. The Towerses' impending divorce was going to be expensive and messy. Jurors don't take kindly to cheating spouses, especially ones who need temporary restraining orders to keep the objects of their "affections" safe.

Towers had millions of motives, but also a rock-solid alibi. How could he be the man in black, his lawyers claimed, when he was two thousand miles away in Pacific City, Oregon, with his mistress? There was a mountain of exculpatory evidence: plane tickets, witness statements, phone GPS records, credit card expenditures, airport surveillance videos, and hundreds of photos chronicling their trip to Towers's seaside condominium.

When APD announced Towers was no longer a suspect, the doctor and his mistress, Molly Peach, celebrated by jetting off to Tahiti and tying the knot, scandals be damned. Back in Austin, the months passed, and Vanessa's case went cold. A year after her murder, APD declared her death a botched burglary and closed their investigation.

"Horseshit," I said to my absent dinner companion. Surprised burglars didn't dawdle to strangle homeowners; they ran like hell.

No, Vanessa's murder was a crime of passion, and the only suspect in Trip's mind was still Clayton Towers.

But Texas's greatest detective was stumped: How could the good doctor be in two places at once? The answer was in the Murder Book, Trip was certain, and he was setting everything aside until he cracked the case. Including me.

I polished off another Maiden-No-More, relishing the burn as Gunpowder Irish Gin reared its redhead above the triple sec, brandy, and lemon juice. I motioned the waiter for another, then ordered dinner: shrimp cocktails, Caesar salads, prime porterhouse, lobster, and two pecan fudge tarts.

The minutes ticked by, and the kalanchoe flowers around the restaurant closed their petals with the setting sun. That fit my mood. The increasingly nervous waiter brought out waves of food, but knew better than to question a lady dressed to kill with an expression to match the outfit.

I ate in silence, feeling the swell of my stomach within the form-fitting dress, while Trip's meal grew cold. When I finished dessert, I resolved to leave his meal here, along with a very generous tip on Trip's running tab. He was going to pay for this night, in more ways than one.

As I rose to leave, Mustard Tie got up from his barstool and approached me. He glanced nervously at the empty chair and said, "Whoever is missing is a damn fool."

"No argument," I said. But Trip was my fool.

"Mind if I—"

I cut him off. "I do mind, and so would your wife."

Mustard Tie's right hand involuntarily went to his left, perhaps in an effort to cover the small band of whiter skin where his missing wedding band should be. Like the now-closed kalanchoe flowers, the poor man was folding in on himself, seeming to shrink before my eyes.

I put a hand on his arm. "It's very sweet of you to come over. Another me would've invited you to sit down, out of spite. Another me would've asked you home, again out of spite. But not this me. Go home to your wife."

Without a word, Mustard Tie bobbed his head and hurried from the dining room with a thoughtful look. Not long after, I stalked to the parking lot and drove home to change. If I was going to kick Trip's ass, I needed cowboy boots, not high heels.

I found Trip in his office, fast asleep in an overstuffed wingback chair and his booted feet on the desk. The Old West motif—cowhide furniture, historical Texas maps, and Louis L'Amour novels on the bookshelf—was a touch on the nose, but it was a true reflection of the occupant. Like a locomotive, you could see and hear Trip coming from miles away. And like a locomotive, he was essentially unstoppable once he got started.

On the wall facing Trip was his most prized possession: painter Frederic Remington's masterpiece, *A Dash for the Timber*. The Amon Carter Museum of American Art had gifted it to Trip when we solved an art heist. As his "associate," I got a firm handshake from the museum director and a pat on the rear from Trip. In fairness, my name isn't on the office door, so I don't mind playing second fiddle to a legend. Most of the time.

As I suspected, the Murder Book was open on Trip's desk, and stacks of photos, phone records, and witness statements were strewn everywhere.

I glanced at Trip. His Stetson was pulled over his face, covering the zigzagging bridge of his broken nose, and he was snoring. This was his first good sleep in three months. Quiet as a church mouse, I stood over the desk and gazed longingly at the evidence, my hand inches from some photos. Trip had guarded these secrets from me. Ostensibly, this was to maintain his source's anonymity; I had other theories.

Biting my lips, I pulled my hand away from the photos and sat down. Trip stirred, but didn't lift up his hat. Was he watching me beneath his bushy eyebrows and his Stetson?

My curiosity got the better of me and I found myself thumbing through a stack of pictures of Dr. Clayton Towers and his mistress. It was their vacation to Oregon, taken while Vanessa was busy getting murdered. Unlike photos from a digital camera or phone, these pictures didn't have timestamps. According to an investigator's notes, they'd been taken with a traditional 35mm camera, with real film. That struck me as odd, and I filed the detail away.

In the photos, Towers was a lean, blond-haired man with a constant smirk no matter the occasion. In a dinner jacket, on the beach, or reading his daily *New York Times* in his clifftop condominium, his white teeth gleamed. Molly Peach—a younger but not prettier version of Vanessa—was either behind the camera or posing for selfies with her sugar daddy.

These photos from August of 2017 were the core of Towers's alibi. He was a cheater, but he couldn't be the man in black strangling the life from poor Vanessa, that was certain. Here he was, the day of the murder, calmly reading an edition of *The New York Times* with the Pacific Ocean stretching away to nothing behind him, his gold Rolex sparkling on his wrist . . . as he'd done every day during the vacation.

I separated out these "newspaper" photos from the rest, my mind wandering as I reexamined them. Were those hibiscus flowers blooming on the balcony behind Towers? They were such pretty flowers, opening and closing with the rising and setting of the sun. On the day of the murder, as Towers read his newspaper dated August 18, 2017, two prominent stars were peeking into a purplish sky. Or were those planets?

I tapped a forefinger to my chin. It was extremely convenient of Towers's floozy to take these photos of him reading his newspapers; it was the Rock of Gibraltar of alibis, the kind to make police detectives quickly dismiss someone from further investigation. Out of hundreds of photos, there were seven of Towers and his newspapers, ranging from August 16, 2017, to August 22, 2017, including the day Vanessa was murdered.

Trip never believed in Towers's alibi. And all photographic evidence to the contrary, neither did I. Truth be told, I've never trusted a man who smiles too much, and Towers had the predatory leer I've encountered all too often as a private investigator.

My gut told me Dr. Clayton Towers, respected surgeon and a pillar of the community, was a killer. Men can be different at home, and good men can turn bad. Even a life-giving surgeon might decide he's tipped the karmic scales so far in his favor that he can take a life. Just one. In the photos, Towers's smirk seemed to say, I've earned that right.

"Are you going to say something," Trip asked beneath his hat, "or just sit there looking pretty?"

Damn you. I didn't look up from the photos.

Trip removed his Stetson, took his boots off the desk, and stretched. "Well?"

"Trip, do you know what day it is?"

"It's Tuesday."

"Guess again."

Trip stood up so fast he nearly knocked over his chair. His craggy, careworn face had the look of a man who knows he's stepped into a pile of fresh manure and tracked it all over the house.

Good.

"Honey, I'm sorry I forgot our date."

I continued looking through the photos.

"I got caught up in the Murder Book, and I put my head down for just a minute. Jesus, why didn't you call me?"

My eyes blazed. "Don't put this back on me. You're an adult, and you can keep track of the time."

Trip sat down, head bowed.

"I've been very patient with you since this book arrived." I gestured to the desk and the piles of evidence. "What happened to Vanessa isn't your fault."

"But it is, Denise. When Towers and his hussy took off for Oregon, I let my guard down. I went on a fishing trip, thinking she'd be safe. If I'd stayed—"

I held up a hand, and his teeth clicked shut. I said, one word at a time, "Not. Your. Fault."

"Not my fault," he repeated half-heartedly.

I stood up and faced him squarely. "Trip, I've been thrown over before, but never for a dead girl. That's hurtful."

"Now wait a minute," Trip said with a spark of anger. "I admit, I've been distracted lately, but I haven't thrown you over. You know I'd marry you tomorrow, if you'd give the word."

He would, but that was beside the point. I said, "I need to know one thing. Just one, and don't lie to me. Were you in love with Vanessa Towers?"

His eyes darted away, and I felt a genuine flutter in my heart. "Are you in love with her?"

Those broad shoulders shrank a fraction. He said to an empty corner of the room, "No."

"Liar."

Trip crossed the distance between us and took me in his arms. I took a step backward, but I didn't try very hard to evade him; I wanted those arms around me.

"I could've loved her," Trip admitted. "I would've, if fate had given us more time. But I'm not in love with her now, Denise. There's only you, and that's God's truth."

I looked deep into his brown eyes, and the needle on my bullshit meter didn't wiggle. He bent down to kiss me, and I melted like butter in a hot skillet. That kiss told me he loved me, and I felt all was right with the world again.

Then Trip ruined the moment by saying, "After I bring Vanessa's killer to justice, things will go back to the way they were, I promise."

Vanessa! I stepped out of Trip's arms. "You're done with this case, or we're done."

"Denise, please . . ."

"This isn't a negotiation, Trip. You're neglecting your health and our relationship for a case that a team of detectives worked on for a year and couldn't find one suspect."

Trip pounded his desk. "Dr. Clayton Towers murdered Vanessa. That bastard told her he'd kill her, and my cameras caught all the action."

He was in anguish, but so was I. "And Molly's camera caught Towers in Oregon on the day in question." I gathered up the photos and held up the one with Towers reading his newspaper the day Vanessa was killed. "Trip, this case is going nowhere. Just like us."

Trip returned to his chair and sat down, defeated. In that moment, he seemed so much older than his sixty years that it broke my heart. He said, "I can't give this up. If I don't solve this case, no one will. No one but me can solve it."

I sensed a challenge, and my pride rose up and quashed whatever tender sentiments I felt. "I can solve it."

Trip smiled deprecatingly, his dimples deepening. "You?"

"Why not me? Give me this Murder Book, and I'll solve it."

Trip burst out laughing. Oh, how that got my goat!

"Denise, no offense, but I've been thinking about this case for nearly seven years. I've practically memorized APD's Murder Book, and I've followed up dozens of leads with no luck."

I took a seat across from him and our eyes locked. We were two poker players going head-to-head in a winner-takes-all showdown. "Let's make it interesting. A wager."

Trip's eyebrows threatened to leave his head. "This isn't a competition, Denise, and it isn't about us."

"Au contraire, mon amour. This is about you and me, in every way that matters. You're a detective; I'm a detective. We solve the cases, but you take all the credit. Well, I'm tired of living in your shadow, Trip."

"Denise..."

"Make me a copy of every piece of evidence, and I'll solve this case before you. Say no, and I'm walking out the door and out of your life." I stuck out my hand, waiting to seal our bargain in true Texas fashion.

I could feel our relationship hanging in the balance, and the palm of my extended hand was damp with sweat. After what seemed an eternity, Trip took my hand and squeezed it.

Thank God.

"The stakes?" Trip asked.

I grinned a shit-eating grin. "If I win, you take me to Paris."

"Paris? Sure, I'll take you to Paris." His smile matched my own.

"Nice try, Trip. Not Paris, Texas. Paris, France."

Trip's entire body tensed. He probably had visions of escargot crawling across a plate and a snooty waiter insulting him in French.

"Okay. France."

I nodded. "And London. And Rome. In fact, for three months, you take me everywhere I want to go and do everything I want to do. Without complaint."

"Those are high stakes," Trip said, his eyes flashing. "So I'm upping the ante. If I win, we get married. No ifs, ands, or buts."

Married? My self-control cracked, and I swallowed hard. Two failed marriages was enough for one life, and I'd sworn never to try for thirds. Trip had me over a barrel, and he damn well knew it.

"I'm waiting," Trip said. "Do you fold?"

"Deal."

Two days later, five bankers' boxes of evidence showed up at my door with a handwritten note that said, Good luck. I unpacked them and set to work.

The weeks passed, with no word from Trip. I feared any second he'd phone and lay down his royal flush, the case solved. As for me, I had something between jack and squat, like a gambler with a two-seven off-suit hand.

One Friday night in early April, I was close to giving up. My only company was a bottle of Crown Royal Vanilla, a country music playlist, and wounded pride that prevented me from calling Trip to offer a truce.

"Don't think about him," I said. "Think about Vanessa Anne Towers. On August 18, 2017, a man clad head-to-toe in black broke into her mansion and strangled her." I'd watched the footage dozens of times, but I forced myself to watch it again. The man had the same sinuous build as Dr. Clayton Towers and the same long-fingered surgeon's hands that could give life or take it. He was in and out of the mansion in five minutes.

"He killed her," I said aloud. "Start with that."

I took a sheet of paper and wrote at the top:

DR. CLAYTON TOWERS MURDERED
HIS WIFE ON 08/18/2017.

Underneath this, I wrote:

1. Molly Peach, his alibi, is an accessory to murder.
2. Clayton and Molly were not in Oregon on the day of the murder.

But their plane tickets, airport surveillance videos, and statements of airline employees placed them at Austin-Bergstrom Airport and Portland Airport, a round trip from August 16th to August 22nd.

They didn't fly back to Austin, that was certain. Could they make the trip by car? I got out my laptop and pulled up a map between Austin and Pacific City. It would take thirty-three hours, driving the speed limit, to go 2,150 miles. Driving in shifts and stopping only for gas and bathroom breaks, it could be done.

3. Clayton and Molly took their plane trips, just as witnesses said. When they arrived in Oregon, they immediately took a vehicle back to Austin.

I checked the cellular GPS records. Sure enough, both phones registered as being in Oregon during the times in question. Specifically, they registered as never moving from the condo's address. Therefore . . .

4. They left their phones in Oregon, turned on to register their GPS locations.
5. If Clayton and Molly went for strolls on the beach and out to eat, as the pictures indicated, they took a 35 mm camera but not their phones.

That was certainly suspicious, but it was hardly a smoking gun. What about the photos from the condo? I thumbed through the pictures of Towers reading his daily newspaper.

6. The photo with the August 18th edition was not taken that day. It was taken after the murder and their drive back from Austin, possibly on August 21st.

That meant . . .

7. The photos documenting their trip were taken on the same day. Towers and Molly changed clothes,

once for each day of their fake trip, to make it appear the photos were on different days.

I allowed myself a sip of whiskey and studied the newspaper photos more closely. APD would've detected if it had been Photoshopped, so the picture wasn't fake.

In his "alibi" photo, Towers was sitting at a table with his *New York Times*, the date of the murder clearly visible above the headlines. He looked so smug, dressed in his smoking jacket and his sparkling Rolex, that I wanted to slap him. Beyond the sliding glass door to his balcony, the Pacific Ocean churned beneath a darkling sky, the potted hibiscus flowers closed in reproach.

On a whim, I blew up a digital copy and examined the face of Clayton's watch. It read 10:16. But was it morning or night?

Outside, the sky seemed much too dark to be morning, with several stars clearly visible. It must be night, as the shut hibiscus flowers indicated. But that didn't look right, either. The sky, though purplish, was much too bright, and surely there should be more stars visible in a dark sky location like Pacific City? What were these two stars, anyway?

When Bonnie Tyler's "Total Eclipse of the Heart" came on my playlist, the answer hit me like a freight train. The closed flowers on Towers's balcony, the darkling sky behind him, with stars visible during the day . . .

My fingers danced across my laptop, and a quick online search verified my suspicions. Clayton and Molly were so busy taking their photos, they were completely unaware that a total solar eclipse was happening outside . . . on August 21, 2017.

"Hot damn!" I said aloud. I picked up my phone to call Trip and announce my triumph, but then stopped. I'd won the wager, but what would I really win? Would it be Trip's gratitude for proving Towers's alibi was a lie, or Trip's resentment that I'd done what he couldn't?

Was there a way to save Trip's pride and salvage our relationship? The answer was already on my laptop, among my search results. In three days, another total solar eclipse would pass through Texas on April 8, 2024.

I laughed for the first time in weeks, then picked up my phone and called my nephew. "Nick, Aunt Denise here. Do you still own that fancy telescope?"

"This is the Celestron 925 CPC Deluxe telescope." My nerdish nephew, Nick, patted his instrument like a proud father.

Trip stood to one side, looking less than thrilled that I'd brought Nick to Trip's ranch for the solar eclipse. Trip listened with a bored expression as Nick rattled off facts about the optical tube, U-shaped motorized fork, and computerized tripod. With the telescope's cords, cameras, and gears, it looked like something from a science fiction movie.

It was a perfect day, with an inviting spring breeze. Above us, the moon and sun were converging in a cloudless morning sky.

"Let's get this party started," Nick said. His fingers played across his phone, and the telescope began to move.

Trip stepped back. "What's it doing?"

"Moving toward the sun."

"How does it know where the sun is?"

Nick pointed to a camera mounted along the axis of the main scope. "With this. You see, the telescope knows exactly when and where it is, through my phone's GPS, and an astronomy app knows what the sky should look like based on our time and location."

"So, the camera in this . . ." Trip's voice trailed off.

"Finderscope," Nick supplied.

". . . finderscope takes pictures of the sky and aligns the telescope with the sky's movements?"

"Exactly."

When the telescope stopped moving, Trip bent over the eyepiece. "What am I looking at?"

"The moon's beginning its transit in front of the sun," Nick said. "When the sun's completely hidden, we call that totality. The sky darkens to twilight, and shadows disappear. It'll last for about two minutes."

"What happens during totality?" I asked.

Nick warmed to his subject. "As the sky darkens, the brightest stars and planets become briefly visible."

I looked up. "Like what?"

Nick consulted his phone. "Venus for certain. Maybe the stars Capella, Rigel, and Betelgeuse."

Trip raised up from the telescope, a faraway look in his eyes. "What happens to plants during a solar eclipse?"

Nick consulted his phone. "Nyctinastic plants are fooled into thinking it's night and close their flowers."

I took a turn over the eyepiece. The moon was slowly eating the sun, as if it were a giant lemon pie. What could I say to prod Trip toward the solution? "I'm amazed your telescope can find celestial objects, based on the time and location."

I could almost see the wheels turning in Trip's head. He said, "Does it work in reverse? Can your astronomy app tell you when you are, based on where you are and what's in the sky?"

Nick furrowed his brow. "Theoretically."

Trip was bouncing in his boots. "Nick, I want you to look at a photo that may solve a murder."

We made Trip wait until after the eclipse to show us the Murder Book. In his study, he gave Nick the "alibi" picture of Towers and his newspaper, supposedly taken the day of the murder.

Trip said, "The watch and the newspaper say it's 10:16 on August 18, 2017. See those two stars behind Towers? I want to know what they are. I want to know if they correspond to the where and the when."

Nick did an online search of Towers's condo to find the address, then opened his astronomy app. "I've input the condo's latitude, longitude, and the time and date."

"Is it morning or night?" Trip asked.

Nick played with his app. "Great question. It's morning, even though we see Venus at roughly 70 degrees"—he pointed to the brightest object in the sky behind Towers—"and the star, Sirius. Is this Photoshopped?"

"I don't know much about astronomy," I said. "But stars aren't visible when the sun's up. Something's screwy."

Trip said, "Nick, what's the date?"

Nick shrugged. "I can only guess at the celestial coordinates of Venus and Sirius. Based on their positions, they fit the where."

"What about the when?" Trip asked.

"It's morning, around the day of the murder. Beyond that, we can't say for certain."

"Actually," Trip said, "I think we can. Look at the hibiscus flowers on the balcony."

I stepped closer. "What about them?"

"The blooms are closed," Trip said. He'd moved to his laptop and began typing furiously. When he finished, tears sprang to his eyes. "Towers's photo was taken during an eclipse."

Nick had his astronomy app out. "Of course! On August 21, 2017, at 10:16 A.M., Pacific City was in the path of totality for a solar eclipse. Look."

Nick showed us his screen, where the moon clearly covered the sun, as viewed from Pacific City on the day in question. To one side, Venus and Sirius sat like pearls in a twilit sky.

My jaw dropped. "And the hibiscus flowers . . ."

". . . would be closed during totality," Nick finished. "The brightest stars and planets, such as Venus and Sirius, become visible."

Trip grabbed Nick in a bear hug. "God bless you and your telescope!"

I held up my left hand, ring finger extended. "Congratulations, Trip. You win the prize."

Trip shook his head. "I'm winning you back, but not like that. Nick, can you mind my ranch for a few months? Your aunt and I are taking a vacation, after I visit with Austin PD."

"You bet!" Nick said. "Where are you going?"

"Paris," Trip said with a wink.

"Nick," I said. "Shouldn't you say thanks to Uncle Trip?"

My nephew raised an eyebrow. "Uncle Trip? But you're not married."

I smiled. "Not yet."

*My interest in astronomy is rooted in my childhood love of science fiction. At night, I'd go outside with my binoculars and look up at the sky where these future adventures would occur. I learned the constellations, the names of the brightest stars, and the motions of the planets as they performed their seasonal dance. My real hope during these excursions was always to spot some mysterious visitor, like a comet. Or better yet, a flying saucer. For a time, I was on a path to astronomy as a career, but the pragmatic part of me opted for a more earthly—and perhaps less rewarding—career in law. As an adult, my telescopes got bigger, and so did my imagination. I turned to writing to flesh out what I was seeing in my scopes and in my brain.

When I met editor and writer extraordinaire Michael Bracken at a science fiction convention, I got turned on to writing mysteries and crime stories. In fact, the private detectives in "Totality" appeared in my first professional sale to Michael's excellent anthology, The Eyes of Texas. More crime fiction sales followed, and with childlike wonder I discovered a passion for new genres, such as mysteries, suspense, thrillers, and noir. It was like a brand-new night sky had opened up before my eyes.

In 2023, Michael recommended me to Kaye George, editor of Dark of the Day: Eclipse Stories. "Totality" was a chance to combine my loves of astronomy and mystery together, and I hope you enjoy it.*

April Kelly *was born on Long Island to parents who would have much preferred a new dinette set. Overcoming that inauspicious beginning, she went on to graduate, in 1991, from the oldest homeopathic college in the UK, making her eminently qualified to treat your scrofula, your goiters, and your leprosy. While that skill set didn't help Kelly in her decades-long career as a TV comedy writer and producer, neither did it hurt.*

These days, she writes crime fiction that has appeared multiple times in Mystery Magazine, Tough Crime, *and* Shotgun Honey, *with one-offs in* Punk Noir, Down & Out Magazine, Dark Yonder, *and* Mysterical-E. *Kelly's work has twice made the final five for a Shamus and once for a Derringer.*

Her speculative novel, Winged, *won First Place/General Fiction in Kindle Book Promos' 2014 International Contest, and was a* Writer's Digest *indie book awards Honorable Mention. The* Kirkus *review for Kelly's humorous PI novel* Valentine's Day *called it "first-rate escapist reading."*

THE ART OF DISAPPEARANCE
April Kelly

If this were Namibia, that rapid popping sound might be the tongue clicks of a Khoekhoe patriarch admonishing his grandson not to urinate so close to the family hut, but this is the Everglades, and the more prosaic source of the hollow clatter is a wind chime strung with a dozen baby 'gator skulls set to dancing by a hot, humid gust. Never meant to be decorative, the gruesome display hangs from a corner of the porch eave as a warning to the larger kin of those long dead reptilian hatchlings. True, it's unlikely the apex predators inhabiting the surrounding waterways accurately interpret this metaphorical *No Trespassers* sign; however, it is a fact that in eleven years, not one adult alligator has come closer to the ramshackle, wooden structure than the end of its dock.

The brief puff of heavy air succumbs to inertia; the skulls cease their dry chitter; and the man rocking languidly on the porch continues listening for the flatboat's arrival. Garlen Driscoll, known in certain circles as "The Magician," specializes in making people disappear. Through clandestine channels spiderwebbing across the country, his services are discreetly made known to women's shelters, empathetic pastors, and social workers disgusted with systemic failures in an impotent safety net.

Here, so deeply hidden within South Florida's one and a half million acres of wetlands formerly known as a swamp, Gar's rustic hideaway contains—in addition to his own spartan bedroom—an office housing the technology of his unique trade, and a large, cheerful space with rainbow wallpaper, children's toys, a crib, two cots, and a twin bed offering rest and security to weary women who often still bear visible proof of their abusers' fury.

The double tap of Milo's barge pole against the low-riding hull of his flatboat alerts Gar to an imminent arrival, so he vacates his rocking chair and walks to the end of the dock, clicking awake the lantern and gathering up the tie rope.

Tonight's client is not a battered woman fleeing for her life; nor did he find Gar through the network of compassionate clergy, social workers, and samaritans facilitating survival through disappearance. No, this evening Gar will host a criminal running two steps ahead of the mobsters from whom he has embezzled four million dollars, a lowlife who found Gar's particulars on the darknet. The unassuming listing touts the skill of an experienced magician to teach the art of disappearance. Worded obliquely, the offer is not likely to attract the notice of a soccer mom looking to book entertainment for a five-year-old's birthday party. Plus, kindergarteners rarely need to fake their own death.

"Arthur," Gar says, extending a hand to the beefy man lumbering up onto the dock.

"Huh?"

"Your new name, Arthur Benedict. Best if you start getting used to it immediately to avoid future slip-ups."

"Right. Smart. I guess that's why you get the tall coin."

As they shake hands, Gar notes the fresh Band-Aid on the man's thumb. This means "Arthur" has followed instructions, although he did question the necessity of cutting himself and leaving a smear of blood on the rental car's steering wheel. Gar knows anyone tracking his client, whether law enforcement or the thugs he robbed, will deduce their man was snatched by his other pursuers somewhere between Orlando's airport and the theme-park-adjacent hotel where he booked a room, but never showed. That's the first in a long list of precautions designed to sever the ties that bind him to his old life.

Milo hefts a leather valise and a large box of groceries onto the dock, carefully tucking in a tissue-wrapped bunch of flowers among the comestibles. He nods at Gar, then pushes off into the darkness. Arthur slaps at a mosquito scouting locations in his sweaty neck creases, then takes a look at the weathered cabin.

"This the shithole where I'm spending the night?"

"I assure you, Mr. Benedict, your villa in Algarve will more than make up for a few hours of roughing it."

When a light splash catches Arthur's attention, he whips his head around to peer into the murk, seeing no line of demarcation between sweltering air and sluggishly moving water.

"Relax. It's only a frisky fish. The alligators don't come around unless I send them an engraved invitation."

His host's disarming chuckle reassures Arthur, so he picks up his valise and follows Gar down the dock and up five steps to the porch. Once inside the sprawling cabin, Gar sets the box of food on the kitchen counter and leads Arthur to the spartan bedroom, where a folded white jumpsuit lies on the bed alongside a pair of spa slippers.

"Strip off everything," Gar says, as he pulls a black, plastic garbage bag from the night stand's single drawer. "Put it all into this for disposal. When my associate returns in the morning, he'll bring your new wardrobe and luggage."

"You ordered the suits from my Italian tailor, though, right?"

Gar wonders how a so-called criminal mastermind can be this clueless.

"Traceable, Arthur. If you left so much as a crumpled receipt in the back of a drawer, or were ever overheard by a co-worker when you placed an order, that information becomes a lead that could jeopardize my entire organization and cost you your life."

Arthur grunts a sheepish acknowledgment.

"This is not my first rodeo. Follow the instructions that have worked for all my previous clients and I guarantee you will never be found by anyone pursuing you. So get changed while I put away the groceries."

Gar asks if he would like something to eat before getting to work, but Arthur declines.

"Your guy had sandwiches in a cooler when he picked me up, so I'm good. Wouldn't mind a Scotch, though."

"Of course. Macallan okay?"

"Hey, my brand," Arthur says, perking up. "What are you, psychic?"

No, Gar thinks. *I just do more research than you.* He smiles and leaves the room.

Arthur knows there are four million reasons for Big Frank Lomino's crew to track him to the ends of the earth. He briefly considered accepting an offer from the feds, but turning state's evidence meant giving up the money and spending the rest of his life in a crappy tract house in some version of Scottsdale, Arizona. And what if a weighty bribe to a clerk with file access was able to breach the so-called impenetrable wall of witness protection? No, Garlen Driscoll is his best option, so Arthur shifts into full-cooperation mode.

Once he has put on the jumpsuit and been handed his requested beverage, he joins his host in the tech room. Three computer monitors display floating bubble screen savers for the moment, while Gar passes hard copies of several documents to his client. There is a social security card, a passport in the name of Arthur Benedict showing travel stamps going back for years, and a printout of an impressive—totally fabricated—forty-year business career.

"You'll have ample time on the flight to get familiar with your new work history."

Gar does not rush his client through the realtor's glossy information packet for the lavish villa perched on a Portuguese hillside overlooking the sparkling water of the Atlantic and only a half mile from a world-class golf resort.

Invariably, men who seek out and can afford his specialized services are hardwired to be guarded, suspicious of the motives of others, perhaps a reflection of how untrustworthy they are themselves. Gar needs Arthur to feel completely secure before moving on to the part of the evening where the real magic will be performed, and so he has, as always, done his homework.

Turning to the keyboard, he brings up a slideshow of the villa's amenities on the middle screen—the one directly in front of his chair—and is not even a little surprised when the man sitting next to him interrupts.

"Hey, stop. Go back to that shot of the entryway."

Gar does, sending the image to the left-side monitor in front of Arthur's seat.

"Can you go tighter on that?"

The bag of golf clubs fills Arthur's screen.

"Holy crap! Do you know what those are?"

"Well, you mentioned you're a golfer and I thought you might want a set of clubs waiting for you. I don't play," Gar says disingenuously, "so I asked the resort's pro to pick out something decent. Did I get hosed?"

"Are you kidding me? You're looking at some of the finest clubs on the planet."

When Arthur quietly slipped away from his house two nights earlier, it very nearly broke his heart to abandon his set of Callaway Stratas, certainly more so than leaving behind his wife of thirty years as she snuffled through her CPAP mask. Drinking in the beauty of the custom golf bag full of Bentley clubs, he forgets all about his old reliables. The space-age Japanese technology that goes into the manufacturing of these pricey sticks is reputed to add distance and increase accuracy, while the fifteen-degree heads on the woods dangle a tantalizing promise of shaving points off Arthur's handicap, perhaps someday putting him within reach of scratch.

The clubs vanish from Arthur's screen, replaced by an image of a beautiful young woman in a maid's uniform.

"And this is Mafalda, a local girl who is available to perform housekeeping services for a modest salary."

Arthur's eyes shine with lust.

"Oh, *hell* no. I can always hire some old bag to clean the toilets, pal; this one's talents would be better utilized in the boudoir, if you catch my drift."

Gar does, indeed, catch Arthur's drift, but masks his distaste as he always must, reminding himself that men like this unwittingly fund the more noble branch of his work.

"That's a negotiation you'll have to take up directly with Mafalda," Gar says, matching his client's smarmy grin with one of his own. "Now, since my associate will be back at sunrise, I suggest we get our business arrangement out of the way so we can enjoy a nightcap before you hit the rack."

Fingers flying over the keyboard in front of the central monitor, Gar pulls up bank records while Arthur continues his eye-ravage of the Portuguese beauty.

"All right," Gar says. "Here's your four million parked in the offshore."

"Huh?" Arthur reluctantly tears his gaze from Mafalda's chest and turns it to his Cayman Islands bank statement.

"Before I break it up into smaller amounts and move them to less cliché financial institutions around the world, where hackers hired by Uncle Sam or your former employers won't be able to sniff them out, let's get your bills paid."

Arthur's eyes dart back to the shadowed valley hinted at by the open vee of the unbuttoned maid's uniform top, until Gar taps him on the shoulder and points to the third monitor, the farthest one from the client's seat. Columns of numbers crowd the screen.

"This is an accounting of my out-of-pocket, so, with your permission, I'd like to pull four hundred thousand from the offshore and send it to my own bank."

"Jesus H. Christ! You said your fee was twenty-five grand."

"It is. And *here* it is," Gar replies smoothly, touching his fingertip to the top row of numbers.

Arthur reluctantly leans away from Mafalda and squints toward the screen on the other side of his host, obviously agitated by the thought of losing ten percent of the money for which he has killed a man.

"And *this*," Gar continues, "is the cash price I paid outright to buy your new villa."

As he slides his finger down the rows of numbers, Gar blandly recites the expenditures.

"New passport, forty-year paper trail of IRS filings for your new identity, first-class airfare to Portugal, three custom business suits, thirteen-club set of Bentleys—"

"Okay, okay, I get it," Arthur snaps, cutting him off. "Apparently, it takes a goddamn village to disappear."

Gar lets the man's irritation subside for a moment. They never like parting with a penny, so it's his job to ease their suspicion they are being bilked. He waits till Arthur throws back the remaining swig of Scotch, then flashes his best, twinkly-eyed smile.

"I also laid out a substantial sum to Mafalda to ensure her *immediate* availability on your arrival, if you catch my drift."

After a message-received nod and one last glance at his future playmate, Arthur willingly gives up his user name and password, allowing Gar to gain access to the four million and relocate it, piecemeal, all around the globe.

Poising an index finger over the keypad, Gar holds off on the final stroke.

"Before I make this irrevocable, I have to ask one last question and I don't mean it to be indelicate. Would you like to direct any funds to your wife?"

"Sheila?" Arthur scoffs. "Nah, she's been bellied up to the money trough for three decades. Let her drag her fat can out of bed and get a job. Pay for her own manicures and fur coats for a change."

"No judgment here, dude. I just wanted to be sure."

With a flourish, Gar taps a final key and announces, "Done."

"About time. I'm sweating like a whore in a confessional and I need another drink."

"This time I'll join you."

Gar leads his client back to the main living space of the cabin, where Arthur flops heavily onto the couch, grumbling about the stifling heat and humidity. Gar crosses to the wet bar and takes out two clean glasses. Though his back is to Arthur, he can hear rustling as the man shifts his meaty shoulders in the coveralls.

"What is this thing made out of? Paper?"

"Close. It biodegrades in water in less than an hour. After you change into your new bespoke apparel tomorrow morning, that monkey suit will go into the Everglades ecosystem, severing any scent trail that could be followed by a persistent dog, whether four-legged or two."

Gar hands Arthur a fresh glass with an extra-heavy pour of Macallan, then sits in one of the armchairs with his own skimpy tipple.

"You should be a bartender," Arthur jokes, carefully holding the glass level so as not to spill a drop when he takes his first sip. "You'd go broke, but your customers would nominate you for sainthood."

Gar smiles, raising his own glass in acknowledgment, as Arthur slurps another warming dram of Scottish excellence over his fleshy bottom lip and onto his tongue.

"So, how does this work? I mean all those accounts you set up for me?"

"When my associate returns to pick you up, I'll give you a manila envelope with everything you need for your new life: keys to the villa, Mafalda's phone number, and all documentation including bank locations, account numbers, and access info. I had to create new passwords to establish the scattered financial hidey-holes, but once you get to your destination, use the on-site computer to reset them so no one else can get at your nest egg. Including me."

"Man, you think of everything," Arthur replies, genuinely impressed by Gar's thoroughness.

They are not always this easy to fool, some of them insisting Gar leave the room while they enter the initial access information privately. Not that it matters. In addition to the software collecting every keystroke of the entire transaction, there are two well-hidden cameras recording images of the central keyboard.

Had the corpulent crook done his own embezzling, he might've whiffed to the sleight of hand Gar employed, but his lazy-ass approach had been to "delegate" the thieving to a mid-level accounting guy. Using both carrot and stick, Arthur had promised two things to the poor schmuck: one, that he would earn a twenty-five percent fee for doing the dirty work, and two, that Mrs. Schmuck would learn of her husband's ongoing affair with a barista named Cheyenne if he opened his mouth about their illegal venture.

Once Arthur confirmed the stolen money had reached his offshore stash, he contacted Gar and arranged to be in the wind right before the stooge he'd coerced died in a suspicious, single-car crash, thus staying ahead of any in-house auditing triggered by one death, one disappearance, and a shit-ton of missing mob earnings.

"By the way, the envelope I give you will also contain a few hundred bucks in euros and US currency to cover the cab from the airport to the villa, and any incidentals you need before setting up a bank account nearby."

"Keep it," Arthur says magnanimously. "I got twenty large in my valise."

One of Milo's favorite phrases, reflective of his rural upbringing, pops into Gar's mind: *dumber than a hay rake.*

"It's a violation of federal law to transport undeclared cash out of the US in an amount greater than ten thousand dollars. You want to risk a routine TSA search finding cause to detain and question the freshly minted Arthur Benedict?"

"Yeah, I guess that wouldn't be too swift," an embarrassed Arthur admits. "So, what should I do with it?"

"Leave it on the night stand and I'll deposit it in one of your accounts tomorrow, before you land in Portugal and lock me out of them," says Gar, struggling to maintain patience with the cretinous creep. "Look, no disrespect, but I've done this dozens of times without a hiccup."

Arthur drains his glass, then shakes his head no when Gar points to it with a questioning look.

"Before I turn in, I'm curious about one thing. Was the legendary Shank Torres a client of yours?"

Gar clearly recalls the shaved head and obscene tattoos of the Rojas cartel's brutal lieutenant, a nasty piece of work who wormed his way into old man Rojas's good graces in record time for a non-family member, mostly by savagely murdering anyone his boss considered a potential threat.

Gar gives Arthur a noncommittal shrug, saying, "Confidentiality is the keystone of my business."

Taking that as a yes, Arthur smirks.

"Rumor has it he and two pallets of cartel cocaine went missing at the same time. Everything pointed to Shank getting ambushed and killed during the transport to the States, but Rojas searched for months without picking up a trail or a body. Impressive."

Torres had converted the coke to cash before reaching out to the darknet's disappearance expert, Gar knows, but still, it's always interesting to learn what others have heard and believe.

"And then, maybe a year or so later, a handwritten letter arrives from Rio de Janeiro, Torres giving Rojas a middle-finger salute, bragging about stealing the shipment and murdering the other four cartel soldiers who accompanied it. At least, that's the story on the street."

After reading the incendiary letter, the furious drug lord spent millions trying to locate his former protégé, coming up with nada. That incident had burnished the credibility of Gar's online alter ego and brought in even more lucrative business. It had been easy to goad Torres into writing the letter for Gar to post more than a year later. His psycho client was so entranced by the picture on Gar's computer screen he would have done pretty much anything his host requested. The image that inked pervert devoured was of a sloe-eyed Latino boy around ten years old, dangling his coltish legs in a sparkling swimming pool behind a million-dollar hacienda.

"Well, Arthur, as a rule, when I help people become dead"—and here he sketches a pair of quotation marks in the air—"I prefer them to *stay* dead."

"Don't worry," Arthur says, yawning, "I won't risk mailing out any postcards from paradise."

An hour later, as his client snores loudly, Gar rocks in his chair and considers the human garbage he has worked with over the years. Shank Torres wasn't even the worst of them. That crown belongs to a trust fund baby named Atticus Noel Coventry III, an entitled scumbag who absconded from his Ivy League college while bonded out on multiple rape charges, after his billionaire daddy's extravagant cash offers failed to convince four young women to retract their accusations. The cocky little bastard sat right here on this porch and arrogantly assured Gar he would return to his privileged position back home as soon as all the fuss died down. Two years, tops, he confidently predicted, till his father's powerful connections had quieted the women, one way or another.

Taking money from vermin like Atticus Noel Coventry III to finance better lives for women and children in desperate need of rescue gave Gar a sense of satisfaction, justifying in his own mind the necessity of catering to the depraved desires of his morally bankrupt clientele for the brief duration of his in-person interactions with them.

On some level, he suspects, he is still trying to atone for his inability to save his own mother from her abusive boyfriend, "Uncle" Darien. As a terrified preschooler, Garlen wasn't articulate enough to explain to the investigating detective that Thomas the Train could not have done it. Thomas was in Gar's hands when his mother went down the stairs headfirst.

He had heard the scuffle, the shouting—not unusual occurrences after Darien moved in—but his mother's cut-off shriek, followed by a series of ominous thuds, drew the boy from his bed. For security, he hugged his favorite toy to his chest as he crept to the open doorway. His mother lay unmoving at the bottom of the stairs, while Darien glared at her from above, chest still heaving from the effort of hurling Sharon Driscoll to her death.

"Mommy?"

The boy's whimper caught Darien by surprise and, in a heartbeat, Thomas was ripped from Gar's hands and chucked down the stairs, not only to break apart as it smashed into step after step, but to be blamed for causing the fatal fall.

Darien got off, four-year-old Garlen went into the foster care system, and Sharon became, officially and forever, a sloppy drunk who had tripped on her son's toy train and snapped her cervical spine on the nonstop somersault to the first floor.

Gar's memory is haunted by the visuals of his mother's bruises, black eyes, plaster casts and, ultimately, her undignified sprawl, but he pragmatically accepts those disturbing pictures are not what drove him into his current line of work. It was a young Afghan woman who triggered his ongoing efforts to level the playing field, or rather, her assault by two of his men.

Gar reported the incident up the chain of command, and Milo, youngest of the soldiers for which he was responsible, volunteered to testify about the bragging the two perpetrators had done, the copper bracelet trophy they had shown off to others in the squad. Word came down from the brass that the incident was to be swept under the proverbial rug, so as not to further destabilize an already volatile local situation. Those on high assumed the family would never speak of the attack, for fear of diminishing the seventeen-year-old's marriage prospects, and that a hush-hush transfer of the guilty soldiers would erase the incident like blown sand over a decomposing corpse. They were wrong.

A week later the girl was dead at the hands of her father and two brothers, victim of an honor killing because she had wantonly allowed herself to be ambushed and defiled while walking the half mile from the market to her village with food for the family's evening meal. Accepting the harsh reality that the deck would always be stacked against the innocent and the helpless, Gar decided what was needed was a different way to deal the cards.

He did not re-up when his tour of duty ended.

Movement at the end of the dock draws his attention: tonight's client is waking from his Scotch and chloral hydrate nap. While Arthur sluggishly hauls his bulk upright, Gar grabs the glass bottle of kerosene from the small table next to his rocking chair, steps over to the porch railing, then pours the fuel into the concrete firepit on the ground below. Shaking off his stupor, the man on the dock notices his ankles are secured by loops of rope tied to a steel ring set into the weathered planking, and clumsily bends to untie the simple knots. This is Gar's cue to strike a match and drop it into the firepit.

The whooshing column of flame shoots seven feet into the night for a few seconds, then settles into a more compact feeding frenzy, red-orange tongues licking hungrily at clothes, valise, passport, and every piece of documentation supporting the existence of a man named Arthur Benedict, along with a stock photo of some random Portuguese girl dressed as a sexy maid.

Gar sits back down to enjoy the show. The towering fire geyser and subsequent jittering flames are not a *literal* engraved invitation, but they might as well be. The two eyes that rise to float on the surface of the brackish water glitter with reflected golden movement. Gar can't be positive, but the wide separation between those glowing orbs suggests to him they belong to the one he has nicknamed Grandpa, a fourteen-footer who is a regular customer at Gar's dockside all-you-can-eat buffet.

Cursing loudly, the porky slob in the paper suit fumbles open the loops that hold his ankles, stepping free of them and straightening up. He barely has time to register the presence of his host twenty feet away, rocking languidly and giving Arthur a Miss America wave, before a flicking splash catches his attention, causing him to spin around in fear and stare into the gloom. A single, braying complaint from a wood stork hiding among the cypress trees pierces the night, then all goes deathly still. Not understanding the significance of the ominous pall that silences birds, mammals, and a million insects, Arthur releases the breath he has been holding and allows his tension to ebb away.

Grandpa explodes from the water like a nine-hundred-pound rocket, seizing the horrified man as he turns to escape. Monstrous jaws clamp around the prey at its midsection, multiple punctures misting the air with blood. Arthur's scream cuts off when the massive beast crashes down into the river, serrated teeth sinking deeper into soft flesh and crunchy bone to forcibly pincer Arthur in place for his dizzying tilt-a-whirl ride to Hell.

With a flash of gray-green belly and a foamy churn of water, the reptilian dervish begins its death roll, twirling crazily while the flailing arms on one side of its Oligocene-epoch snout and thrashing legs on the other side flop more and more limply with each violent spin of their interspecies pas de deux.

The disturbance abruptly subsides when Grandpa sinks below the surface to consume his well-marbled entrée in peace. Other floating eyes appear, awaiting chunks or scraps that might escape Grandpa's attention and bob to the surface. Gar has no fear they will approach the dock, too many years of having bullets sprayed all around them if they try. Their portal of opportunity opens only when the column of flame signals a meal has been left for the fastest among them.

He turns his thoughts to the next arrival, a young mother with two sons, three and five, who will be ferried by Milo to this remote haven tomorrow night. They will spend a few days recovering from their perilous domestic situation and desperate flight to safety, before leaving for the snug home Gar purchased for them in Costa Rica. A legitimate trust, generously endowed through the years by degenerates like Shank Torres, Atticus Noel Coventry III, and the worthless pig being consumed a short distance away, will issue a check every month to the young mother, in an amount bountiful enough to provide for all her own and her two boys' needs. Those electronic deposits now go to more than one hundred women and an even larger number of children.

The man in the rocker rises and stretches, eager to get some sleep after his long evening. He has three beds to make up in the morning, welcoming flowers to arrange in the vase on the nightstand by the twin bed, stuffed toys to put on the two cots, and several meals to plan.

Unlike alligators, who don't differentiate between the taste of murderers, rapists, and drug dealers, children can be very picky about what they eat. Tomorrow he'll put up a pot of marinara sauce to simmer all day while he makes kid-size meatballs. A chilled pinot grigio and broiled chicken breast with Caesar salad will do for Mom, and if the boys don't want spaghetti, he'll have grilled cheese sandwiches and PB&Js for backup.

Everyone dines well on Gar Driscoll's watch.

---

*Since reading Hamlet *in the tenth grade, I have been fascinated by the concept of a decent man trying to deal with an indecent situation. I'm not talking about some merry, modern-day Robin Hood "redistributing" wealth to level the playing field in an unfair economic paradigm. No, I'm interested in darker, more complex characters who are capable of realizing that the cost of balancing the scales might just be their own morality but are willing to pay that price.*

In my story "The Art of Disappearance," Garlen Driscoll is haunted by the injustice of his mother's murder, but would have, without further provocation, grown up to be a normal (albeit brooding, Hamlet-like) guy. When an incident in Afghanistan proves he is as helpless an adult as he was a preschooler to right a fatal wrong, he embarks on a path of protecting the Davids, while engineering the fall of the Goliaths.

Erika Krouse *is the author of four books of fiction and nonfiction, including a collection of short stories,* Save Me, Stranger. *Krouse's memoir,* Tell Me Everything: The Story of a Private Investigation, *was a* New York Times *Editors' Choice and winner of the Edgar Award, the Colorado Book Award, and the Housatonic Book Award. Her short fiction has appeared in* The New Yorker, The Atlantic, Esquire.com, *and other places. Krouse mentors for the Book Project at Lighthouse Writers Workshop, where she won the Beacon Award for Teaching Excellence.*

EAT MY MOOSE

Erika Krouse

Who knows what a euthanizer is supposed to look like, but judging from my clients' expressions when they answer their doors, they don't expect a sweat-sopped middle-aged guy in overalls, nauseated from a bumpy flight or a long truck drive on a chip-seal highway. Sometimes I'm greeted by a lady with a walker or an entire family dressed in springtime colors to cheer their soon-to-be-departed loved one. Either way, they're always relieved to see me, even me. It doesn't matter what death looks like, acts like, smells like. It only matters that I'm there.

I've assisted 221 suicides all over Alaska. My job: I get a name and address, go there, help them die, and then travel to the next address. I source the materials, maintain the planes, trucks, and helo, and do most of the jobs. When Bonnie was working, she dealt with the clients and money, and she vetted every job to make sure it was euthanasia and not murder.

Bonnie loved subterfuge and never gave me an assignment by phone. Instead, she'd write the time, date, and GPS coordinates on a cigarette using a micro-tip felt pen, replace it in the pack, and hand it to me when we met for coffee and muffins. There were usually two or three cigarettes in the pack, and if she wanted to add a stop to a bump run, especially north of the Arctic Circle, she'd Express Mail another pack to me up there. After the job, I would smoke the evidence under that pearly sky, thinking of her. We'd both started smoking again, once we achieved temporary immortality.

There are three reasons people hire me:

1. Life insurance policies don't always pay out for suicide, even if you're terminal.
2. The stigma. Some sick clients fear judgment from loved ones who expect them to endure the pain. Pain is easy to understand until it's yours.
3. Some clients have nobody. They're afraid to die alone.

Although we usually serve families, a number of my clients are lonely subsistence hunters and fisherfolk, hours from roads or towns or other people, scared and sick enough to let a stranger help them die in the agreed-upon manner. Even after Bonnie quit, they still find my number somehow. Some of their cabins are so remote and clotted with forest that I doubt even a bush rat like me can fly back out without bending metal. Some of them change their minds once they see me, their first person in months or years. Then I just fly them back to Anchorage and drop them off at a bar or a hospital so they can live their remaining days surrounded by the humans they didn't know they needed.

But most folks go through with it and die. I provide the chamber, which is a plastic bag to fit over their head, like a turkey bag with elastic on it. Tubing to funnel the gas in there. A tank of helium, or nitrogen for an extra fee. They work the same and neither one shows up on your general autopsy, but some people like to be expensive.

I don't:

- Pull the bag over their head or snake the tube in there. They have to do that.
- Turn on the gas. I usually have to loosen the knob, however. These are very sick people.
- Hold them down.

- Tell them my name. They only know my alias, Clyde, a name Bonnie used to give them for humorous reasons. My real name is Colum.

I do:

- Give them instructions.
- Wear gloves.
- Hold their hands. Tightly, if they ask, if they're worried they'll struggle.

After they're dead, I check the carotid pulse with one hand and bag up the kit with the other. Bonnie always said, "Get out of there before the magnitude hits anyone, especially you." I keep my coat and boots on to make leaving faster. I'm gone inside a minute, lighting Bonnie's telltale cigarette inside my truck or plane or helo. It's like flying away from a bomb site. Which I've also done. But with these jobs, I feel ephemeral, anonymous, once I'm in the air or down the road. Under the roof of clouds, I check my body for pain and find none. Oftentimes I forget the client's name within miles. Sometimes I sing.

It's not uncommon for clients to offer me whatever they're leaving behind: a truck, a plane, a shack, jewelry, food. In a ten-by-ten, poorly chinked log cabin in the Interior, one man's last words were, "Eat my moose." A whole winter's supply of butchered bull moose hung in his shed; he thought he'd live long enough to eat it all. It became a joke for Bonnie and me. "Eat my moose," she'd boom randomly and I never knew what she meant, only that it made her laugh.

But I never take anything clients offer, not even the untraceables like meat or money, not even if they beg. I leave it there with the body, for someone else to find, or never find. I don't like to take my work home with me.

I first met Bonnie at an Anchorage VA cancer support group four years ago. The group was for terminal patients, Stage 4 with months or weeks to live, many of them combat vets like me and

Bonnie. Bonnie had deployed five times to Afghanistan, and I was air force with four deployments to Iraq and three to Afghanistan. We only talked about it via our cancers, the chemicals we had inhaled in theater, the nightmares we still got.

My cancer was pancreatic, Bonnie's a brain tumor, both inoperable. We were in our fifties, a couple of years apart, retired from service. Everyone in the VA support group had quit their civilian jobs. I had been flying for the Postal Service. Four out of five Alaska towns are only reachable by plane or boat, no roads in or out; bush carriers like me kept them connected to the world, even as we floated above it. Bonnie had been running a high-stakes underground poker game that sent her back and forth between Anchorage and Fairbanks until she began to forget where she was.

Bonnie's chemo did squat besides steal her hair. Without eyelashes or eyebrows, she always looked like she had been crying—almost funny given her hard-edged character. Her nose was continually pink, chafed from the oxygen tubes, with little red lines veining the thin skin under her nostrils. She sometimes forgot her last name but never forgot to bring doughnuts. Even with the monster eating her brain, she said things like, "The only reason we need this shitty support group is because no one else can love killers like us." It's like the things inside my head came out of her mouth. I had three ex-wives I had shredded on the altar of my viciousness, my drunkenness. Bonnie had the foresight never to marry at all. "And now I'm too bald to wear the veil," she said.

By the first time Bonnie asked me to kill someone, I too was on oxygen and Bonnie had stopped chemo. I was at home trying to decide between Raisin Bran and stale bread, knowing I'd barf up either one, when I heard her knock on my door. Bonnie wore a green dress soiled at the hem and pulled her own oxygen tank in a trolley behind her. She stood at the bottom of my steps and said, "Wyatt needs a spot of help."

Wyatt was the other vet I liked at the support group. Stubborn like me and Bonnie, an old sourdough. Leukemia. Bonnie said, "He wants to go out on his own terms." She explained the mechanics he wanted, the gas and the chamber and everything.

"It's kind of cool, actually. No pain, just a little panic. Et voilà, it's over!"

I have to explain something special about Bonnie: she always gets her way. Bonnie ran that underground poker game for six years and it was the most peaceable business in all of Alaska, because you don't say no to Bonnie. You can only try, and grumble, and fail.

"Why doesn't he just take pills or something?" I asked, but I already knew the answer. Wyatt was twenty years sober. And why shouldn't a man die any old way he wanted? How you die should be up to you. How you live is usually up to everyone else.

It was not a small favor. Bonnie and I were likely weeks from death ourselves, and could barely go a few hours without a nap. Bonnie used a cane because her balance was fucked, plus both of us had our oxygen trolleys. It was spring, with snow and rain and snow and rain, and it all added up to sticky, half-frozen mud. I still had the same damn pain that had alerted me to the cancer in the first place, a bizarre burning that radiated outward from my belly and back, like a pulsar inside me. It got so it made me stop drinking, and even three wives couldn't make me do that.

So we drove to Wyatt's cabin and hobbled inside. He showed us how he wanted it done, but he was too weak to turn on the gas himself, so Bonnie twisted the knob. It took a couple of tries, but we finally got him dead. It wasn't nearly as horrible as anything we'd seen or done in theater, me or Bonnie. The only really bad part was that we were next and we knew it and so had Wyatt, so fuck him for asking us. But who else did he have? He barely had us, and now he was just a bunch of cells beginning to decompose. Nevertheless, when we pulled the bag off his head, his face bore the smirk of a man who had gotten his way.

"He's lucky we're still around to help," Bonnie said, staring at Wyatt's empty body. "Maybe we should consider going out this way." But nobody would ever help us besides each other. Which meant one of us would be left alone in the end, literally and figuratively holding the bag.

We called 911 and left the phone off the hook by Wyatt's hand. Then we drove away in silence. At a Fred Meyer, we parked to wipe down the tank and plastics and dump them out back. Bonnie walked inside the store without even using her cane, and emerged a few minutes later with a bag of apples and wrapped tuna sandwiches. We sat on the bumper of my truck and ate like healthy people.

"Are we going to hell now?" Bonnie asked.

I thought we were already in hell. Except at that particular moment, pain had hit a miraculous pause. That pulsar was gone from my abdomen, my head. None of the shakes, none of the nausea.

"You know what?" Bonnie said. "I feel kind of amazing. I'm not even dizzy right now."

"Adrenaline? Or maybe we're rallying," I said. They called it "terminal lucidity" in our support group and I had come to anticipate it, that last flame before death, like the fire of maples in autumn.

"The end is nigh," Bonnie said.

We smoked and ate apples, and then I drove Bonnie to her place and went home alone to recover from what we'd done. But the sickness didn't return. I spent the next days and then weeks cleaning my house, scrubbing all the grime that had accumulated while I was feeling so damn awful, airing out the old man smell. I rose early each day, packed all my belongings into boxes, and scribbled "For Goodwill" on the side. There was nothing worth sending to my ex-wives. They wanted to forget me. Anything that remained of my life was best left for strangers.

Three weeks after Bonnie and I helped Wyatt die, my place was all packed up and I still felt tremendous. I even started running five klicks a day like I used to. I waited for the crash, and waited. Finally, I visited my doctor, who gave me blood tests, ultrasounds, X-rays, and a CT scan, and then said, "I'm sorry, but you still have Stage 4 cancer. Your tumor is the same size. The good news is that it hasn't grown as of late."

"Aren't I supposed to be dead by now? Or at least sick?" The doctor began to explain terminal lucidity, but I cut him off. "All this time, though? A month ago I was on oxygen. And now?"

Like a dork, I dropped to the floor and did some rapid push-ups. "Explain that, Doc."

He said, "I'm glad you feel good. We'll schedule a follow-up in seven days." He hesitated, hand on the doorknob. "Just . . . what comes up must come down. Have a good week." The way he said it made it sound like a week was all I had.

I didn't think so, though. I knew what dying felt like. This sure wasn't it.

I only wanted to talk to one person. But how do you explain your good luck to someone with such bad luck? I had stopped going to the support group after Wyatt, and I waited to call Bonnie for so long, I worried there wasn't a Bonnie to call anymore. When I finally dialed her number, she answered on the first ring. "You're still alive!" she exclaimed.

"I'm feeling better. Like . . . all the way better." At her silence, I said, "Ever since we did Wyatt. The cancer's there. I'm just not sick."

I winced, waiting. Bonnie's laugh bubbled. "What the everlasting fuck."

"I'm sorry. I feel funny—"

"No. I'm saying, I haven't been sick since Wyatt either."

"You're better?"

"Well, I probably couldn't parachute out of a helo. But I did just clean my gutters and eat most of a pizza. Meat lover's."

I don't know why relief feels so damn funny, but we were like kids, laughing until tears, until urine threatened, until we felt empty and scared. I stared at the Goodwill boxes stacked against the wall. "How much longer do you think it'll last?"

Her voice was dryly amused. "A day, forever, who knows? You and I defy science."

"But we're assholes. People like us don't deserve miracles."

"This is no miracle. We still have cancer," Bonnie said. "It's a stay of execution. We're on loan to God."

"Okay, so what does God want us to do with the rest of our lives?"

"It's obvious, dummy," Bonnie said. "He wants us to kill people."

I said no, and then no again the next time Bonnie asked, and no the next two times we saw each other. I couldn't make a vocation out of killing again, not after Iraq and Afghanistan. That was a hole with no bottom, and this time, I had a choice. At a coffee shop, Bonnie pressed my sleeve, and it had been so long since anyone but a doctor had touched me, my skin quaked under my flannel shirt.

"Not real killing," she said. "This time, we'd just help them kill themselves."

"How would we even find people for that?"

"Dying people are everywhere. We could start with our support group. Word of mouth is everything."

"Dead people don't make referrals."

"Don't worry about advertising. I'm a wizard." Bonnie's underground poker games ran for years, and everyone knew about them except the cops. "We could make some real money. My doctor's bills are fucked. Anyway, you've got to do it; it's too much for me alone. We're already trained for it. It's like we were talent-scouted by God."

"Or the devil," I mumbled.

"The devil is us. Come on, Colum. How else do you explain you and me getting better at the same time, directly after we offed Wyatt?"

I admitted it did feel like a sign.

"Not a sign," she said. "A signing bonus. Our lives."

Someone once told me Buddhists don't believe in suicide, not even assisted suicide. Karma comes in the form of pain, and if you avoid that pain, you lose your big chance for enlightenment. So what Bonnie was proposing wasn't just illegal; it might be cosmically cruel, setting humanity back lifetimes. But I'm no Buddhist. I couldn't imagine it was good karma to watch someone suffer without trying to end it.

"We both know the suffering side too," Bonnie said, reading my thoughts the way she did. "We could actually help people."

When I was about eight, I found a rat whose spine had been broken, probably by a dog or cat or hawk. Its back legs were paralyzed and it could only drag itself forward in an army crawl. I offered it water and my bologna sandwich, which it refused. I sat with it in the forest, sang to it to make it feel better. My parents didn't allow rats in the house, so I had to leave it alone at dinnertime. When I came back, the rat had slipped into the underbrush and I couldn't find it. I felt like I failed that rat, that instead of singing to it, maybe I should have run it over with my bike or stomped it to death. In my mind even now, fifty years later, it's dead but also alive and still suffering, Schrödinger's rat.

When you do bad things in the military, you tell yourself they're not bad because you're on the good side. You might kill people but only to protect the innocent. That's how you lose your own innocence.

And suddenly, *you're* not worth saving anymore.

"Okay," I told Bonnie. "What the hell. Let's kill some sick people."

Those four years Bonnie and I worked together, our tumors slept. No pain and no gain. Bonnie's hair grew back, dull silver and yellow, and she put on some muscle in her shoulders, legs, arms. She was always beautiful to me but now she was pretty too. The doctors finally conceded we were in remission. They wanted to do tests to find out why, chemo, radiation, but we said no, no. We knew how to survive. Just do the work. And I had Bonnie, who became my reason to survive at all.

Bonnie and I were both used to teams from the military but this was different, because nobody else told us what to do. Bonnie worked locally and I took most of the distant jobs so she could rest her leg, which had throbbed on flights ever since her chemo. Even alone in the air or in the forest or on the tundra, I felt like she was there with me.

But I never asked her on a date, not once. What would we even do? Everything we had in common was death. Bonnie moved back to Juneau, where she was from. "No roads in, no roads out," she said. It was an odd choice to headquarter an illegal death operation but she liked the rainforest and marine lifestyle. "Don't get too comfortable," I told her but she did anyway, outfitting a cabin out the road that she had inherited from an uncle. My Goodwill boxes were long gone, and I lived in hotels.

Bonnie never invited me to stay over, shooed me off at night after dinner. Sometimes she touched my hand or booped my nose. She was a booper. But I wasn't allowed to boop back or touch her at all.

About a year into our new arrangement, it was raining that misty kind of rain that envelops, and we sat on her porch swing. Bonnie started talking about her high-school cannery jobs as a fish sorter and a gutter. It wasn't romantic talk but I went silent, sitting next to her. I leaned closer in gradual millimeters, like I was trying to catch a fly, and Bonnie talked faster and faster. When I reached out to turn her chin toward my face, she jumped in her seat and smacked my cheek hard.

My eyes watered. Because of the slap. It's just a physical response. She looked shocked, distressed, like she couldn't understand what had just happened.

"Bonnie, I'm so sorry," I said. "I don't—"

"I'll get you another iced tea," she said and walked inside.

I almost cried for real then, from relief that she wasn't kicking me off her porch and out of her life. So stupid, I was. It was a while before Bonnie came back with two bottles of iced tea and two scratchy wool blankets. She handed me one of each and said, "It's cold," tossing me an even, fake smile.

"Thank you, Bonnie. I really didn't—"

"Stop." Her face zipped up. And then, an uncustomary, "Please."

I shut up. Bonnie never talked about Afghanistan. I didn't try to touch her again.

I'm proud to say that there's scarcely a town in Alaska where I, like Death itself, haven't visited. Most of our work was in Juneau, Fairbanks, or Anchorage, but I also did jobs everywhere from Utqiaġvik to Chicken to Adak Island. I have flown the wetlands and deltas of the Alaskan Southwest, and landed on tiny volcanic islands to wait out gale-force winds. I have skimmed the rainforest and fjords of Southcentral and Southeast Alaska, the boreal forest and extreme tundra of the Interior, the barren ice fields of the Far North. I have watched the glaciers get smaller each year I continue to live.

Seems like every other person in Alaska is a pilot, so our comings and goings never drew suspicion. Bonnie used a sliding scale and some jobs we did for free, but somehow we still made fistfuls of money, too much to spend it all. I outfitted my high-wing Piper for the bush with a taildragger, skis, and tundra tires, and bought a dinged Cessna with floats. I was used to landing on empty roads, seawater, sandbars, fields, and even glaciers sometimes, but I needed more agility, so I also bought a used helicopter and rebuilt it myself. With that eggbeater, I could drop down anywhere, and then vanish again in minutes.

I'm originally from Missouri and only moved to Alaska after I served twenty-five years in the Air Force. It's what some soldiers do, disappear into the biggest state in America, capacious enough to absorb even our contamination. I can float over ranges upon ranges of mountains, like wrinkles on the face of a weathered god, ancient enough to withstand us all. I land, end a human life, and soon I'm back in the air again, flying for hours to make it on time for a sunset cigarette with Bonnie.

Times when things go wrong: when a client tears off the chamber but is too loopy to give consent to continue. When a client is too far gone to consent in the first place, and I discover that it's all a murder ploy for the relatives to get their inheritances. When the relatives accuse *me* of murder and I have to abort. When I arrive but the client changed their mind or checked into a hospital. When I finish the job and their healthy, bereaved spouse begs me to kill them too. Winter weeks when the cloud ceiling is too low to fly, while sick people wait in pain, sometimes for a month or more. When all I find is an open door to the tundra and I have to search for the body. When the client got tired of waiting for me and botched the job themselves, lying prone on the floor for who knows how long, in pain but incapacitated, dead but still alive.

The job that made Bonnie quit was this: a few months ago, her aunt Elspeth asked us to do her. Elspeth was the only relative who still spoke to Bonnie, and that was only because she had dementia. But the Alzheimer's killed Elspeth's resolve to die. She had waited too long before taking action against herself. It wasn't Bonnie's fault. Impossible to tell if Elspeth's body was rebelling against the gas or if she changed her mind, but Elspeth fought like a murder victim. Bonnie pushed me away and ripped off the chamber, but it was too late. She started CPR, pushing on that old chest until the ribs cracked, breathing into the dead mouth. Crying. Me pulling at her hands, but she wouldn't stop. "She didn't want to go!" Bonnie cried. "She changed her mind!" I had to half carry Bonnie back to the Piper, fly her home, and tuck her into bed cradling a fifth of rye.

She called the next day, slurring, still drunk from the night before. "Colum, I'm settling my debt with God. You can keep going. But I quit." She drawled the word into two syllables, stoppered by a hard *T*.

I didn't know if she was quitting the work, quitting me, or quitting life. I was scared. "But what if you get sick again?"

"Fuck you, buster," she said.

Bonnie didn't take my calls for days. I apologized on her voicemail over and over. I didn't really know what I was apologizing for.

The following week, she finally picked up the phone, said, "Hey sugar booger," and started talking about her geraniums. It was as if she had never hated me, as if there was nothing at all to hate in me.

Life is precious here, and it also isn't. We kill a lot, right? Even vegans own guns up north, but folks don't seem to like shooting themselves. With zero repeat clients or advertising, people nevertheless find my number and I always have work.

But it was hard for me after Bonnie quit. I missed her. I spent as much time as I could on her red plaid BarcaLounger circa 1975. We would eat and smoke until she yawned and I left, aflame. I could love her just as well from afar, maybe better that way. There's such a thing as a safe distance.

A month into my solo career, Bonnie's voice started sounding thin and distant, like dry twigs more likely to splinter than bend. She stopped inviting me over. I didn't see her for a few weeks, and then a few more. When I asked if she was all right, she snapped, "Get over yourself. I just don't want you around." Increasingly forlorn, I took more jobs in the Interior, sulking in Fairbanks hotels when I didn't have work, feeling stupid now

Bonnie didn't need me anymore. It was fair. She had told me back in our VA cancer support group: nobody can love a killer. Not even another killer.

One day I called to ask how she was, expecting her to blow me off again. But this time she said, "Party's over."

The world emptied. "Oh no."

"The tumor's begun to impair my facilities. Is that the word? No. My faculties." This time, her voice was clean and clear. "Colum, I need a favor. One I won't be able to return, I'm afraid."

I was crying already.

Bonnie said, "You have to eat the fucking moose now."

"I never know what that joke means. It's not a funny joke."

"Tomorrow's good. I'll make Danish. Put on your hero goggles and stop blubbering, you gigantic pussy." But she sounded like she was going to cry herself. Then she hung up on me.

I don't know if there's such a thing as redemption for someone like me. Not after what I did in Iraq and Afghanistan, who I was there, and how I came back from each deployment somebody else entirely, drowning my marriages one bottle at a time. Even now, in my late middle age, I don't know who I am. I only know how to smoke cigarettes with Bonnie.

Next morning, I flew to Juneau and drove straight to Bonnie's house. She lived out the road, past the St. Thérèse shrine with its whole island dedicated to murdered souls of the unborn. *My Bonnie lies over the ocean*, I sang on the way. When clients ask me to sing to them, this is the song I sing. When they hear my terrible voice, sometimes they interrupt their dying to tell me to stop, that I'm ruining it for them.

It was the kind of day I would've hated to leave behind: fog shrouding the mountains that stretch up from the water, petrichor surging from the earth, the whisper mist that coated my skin and XTRATUFs. Western and mountain hemlock, Sitka spruce, Alaska yellow cedar. Bonnie's place is remote, and animals roam everywhere: bears, porcupines, beavers, marmots, deer. You can smell them when you can't see them. Rain pushes life from every crevice.

So when Bonnie answered the door, her hair curled, wearing a freshly ironed yellow dress, I wanted to ask, *Are you sure you want to leave all this today?* But she was starting to look the way she had when I first met her. Blue-tinted fingers, shadows on her skin. I shoved my hands in my pockets and eyed her oxygen tank, the battalion of pills lined up on her coffee table, her pocketbook open and upside down on the floor. She had kept the suffering to herself. Soldiers don't complain.

Bonnie handed me coffee, asked, "How are you?" and then laughed. "It's weird, isn't it? I want to catch up, but why? Pretty soon there will be no me to remember anything you tell me. Might as well start."

We organized the plastic, the tank, the tubing. It all felt different this time, everything too slippery, cheap, and disposable for the permanent thing we were about to do. Bonnie said, "You're going to have to restrain me, just in case I fight the gas. I don't want to risk turning into a vegetable if I pull the bag off. I refuse to be a rutabaga for the rest of my short, painful life. Boop!" She booped me on the nose and I smiled, and then felt like an idiot. "Seriously, Colum. Finish the job."

"I promise."

"I know you're in love with me. But don't fuck this up."

My lips turned numb. I had never told her that. But of course she knew.

Bonnie said, "Oh, and once I'm gonzo, will you do the dishes? I didn't feel like it on my last day. But they shouldn't just sit in the sink like that."

"I'll do the dishes."

For the first time since I'd met her, I saw doubt skid across her hard-lined face. "We thought we were following the signs. We thought we did good. Helped people."

"We did help people, Bonnie."

"Did we, though? Were we right or wrong, how we used our second chances?" I struggled to say something comforting, but I had no answer for her. Finally, she shrugged. "Well, I guess I'll find out in a few minutes."

I offered the chamber, but she turned her face away.

"Don't mess up my hair," she said.

I fitted the chamber over her head, snaked the tube inside, cinched it all up around her neck, and turned on the gas.

Bonnie held out her arms. "It's hug time!" When I hesitated, Bonnie barked, "Fuck's sake, Colum! Hug me! Hug me!"

She had never let me touch her before. I reached for her timidly, like she was made of butterfly scales, and then just grabbed her and held her tight.

She flinched, tensed, and then relaxed. She still had residual strength from the military, gardens, snow-machine driving, shoveling, splitting wood, and firing her shotgun at the lynxes who tried to invade her henhouse. She was assigned to multiple special forces combat teams in Afghanistan, even though army women weren't technically allowed to fight yet, even though she was already thirty-five, even with her bum leg from a childhood chainsaw injury. She did a hundred push-ups a day until she got sick. She once faced down a bear who broke into her home and tried to eat her cupcakes. Now, the tense cables of Bonnie's muscles vibrated under my hands, in her mostly healthy body, run by her diseased brain. We were closer than we had ever been, close enough for me to kiss her if we hadn't also been separated by a dome of plastic, fogged by her breath, which quickened into panting. It had been everything I wanted, to hold her, but not like this, too late. The gas hissed and Bonnie caught my gaze with her green eyes that deepened into midnight at the edges. Her skin smelled of lavender. She gave me a shy smile. I already missed her.

"I love you too," she said through the clear plastic.

Then she began to gasp. Then she began to struggle.

I had watched this fight hundreds of times. But I had never felt it in my arms. Bonnie twisted away from me, her stubby nails reaching up to scrabble at my chest and face. I didn't know if she was already half rutabaga like she feared, and if she still wanted me to kill her, or save her, and what was which. It was a miniature revolution inside her—short gasps, tiny pants, growing softer. Her expression split in half, top and bottom. Her mouth pursed into an O, sucking air, but each breath only delivered more death. Above her mouth, Bonnie's face was perfectly blank, the way it never looked in life, forehead smooth, free of thought, despite the chaos of her mouth, her hands. It felt like her body stayed behind to fight, but her mind had already made its decision and left the room. But maybe I was just telling myself that.

How would I know if she changed her mind? I thought. I searched her closed eyes for answers. *I have to stop this. Ask her if she still wants to die.*

But instead, I tightened my grip as she tried to escape me. I couldn't fuck up. Bonnie needed me to be strong enough to kill her when her body still wanted to live. It's like we had been training for this all along, Bonnie and me, and I knew this was my last time. Now, instead of stopping, I wanted to hurry her death so she wasn't fighting herself any longer. *Should I break her neck?* I thought wretchedly.

Time bent itself into unrecognizable shapes, but it probably took only one more actual minute for Bonnie to sag heavily in my arms. She drew her last breaths, and then she wasn't breathing at all. I lowered her body to the ground and checked for a pulse, my fingers on her neck and my ear to her chest. Nothing moved inside her. Her body was the stillest thing I had ever known, like outer space must be, like the point between exhale and inhale, like the eternal present moment, like love.

I didn't leave within the minute like I usually did. This time, I stayed. I lifted Bonnie from the floor, tucked her into bed, and waited with her as her body cooled. I smoked her cigarettes. I talked to her. I sang in my terrible voice. I did her dishes, scrubbing them long after they were the cleanest dishes in all of dish doing. I vacuumed, dusted. When there was nothing left to do, I dialed 911, kissed Bonnie's cold face, and left the receiver tucked in her right hand. I didn't want her to rot there. Even though she wasn't my Bonnie anymore.

Driving away from the house, I grabbed my side. There it was, that fucker, just like I expected. As punctual as the military. Only one thing ever felt like that, a pulsar radiating pain from inside, shocking my nerves, thudding through my organs. My tumor had waited me out, and now my Bonnie lies over the ocean, it's come back for me.

It's a relief, you know. Nothing but. I've traveled alone over a frozen, white world longer than my due. I've eaten your fucking moose, Bonnie; now I've got to eat my own. And after, maybe I'll be able to answer your question: if we hurt more than we helped, if we bet on the wrong side of God, or if all our killing managed to save us enough so I can see you again.

Once during a creative writing class, a student unexpectedly confessed to a crime: she had restrained her struggling terminally ill friend during her (illegal) assisted suicide. My student would have gone down for murder. I pestered her to write that story for years until she said she never would, and that I should.

My first stab was called "ABCD." Not a good title, and not a good story. I revised it seven times but it still felt forced. I was about to chuck it when I suddenly remembered a detail: my student's friend had somehow arranged for a stranger to help her die. "He drove seven hours and showed up at the door, just some middle-aged guy in overalls," my student had said. They all got the job done, and then the stranger was gone in seconds. I realized that his was the interesting perspective, the man who drives fourteen hours to help kill strangers for a few minutes. Why did he do it? What was his past? What was his future? I fell in love with this character, and I hope I did the real euthanizer justice.

Tom Larsen *was born and raised in New Jersey and was awarded a degree in Civil Engineering from Rutgers University. He is the author of six novels in the crime genre. Larsen's short fiction has appeared in* Alfred Hitchcock Mystery Magazine, Mystery Tribune, Sherlock Holmes Mystery Magazine, Black Cat Mystery Magazine, *and* Black Cat Weekly. *His stories have appeared in the anthology* Best Mystery Stories of the Year *(2022 & 2023) from Mysterious Press.*

THE OTHER BROTHER: A WILSON SALINAS MYSTERY OF ECUADOR

Tom Larsen

In my hometown of Cuenca, Ecuador, the moon and the stars are usually obscured by the clouds that blanket the city at night. Up at 3,500 meters in *El Cajas* the moon shone big and bright against the black sky. I was driving my friend Emilio's taxi, making a few extra dollars to augment my meager earnings as a private detective. I was taking a fare on the three-hour trip to the airport in Guayaquil. It was a good gig—$125, of which I had to give Emilio twenty-five and fill his gas tank.

The interprovincial buses run all night and the trip costs about twelve dollars. I guess my passenger preferred the relative comfort of Emilio's Hyundai to the cramped seating, loud snoring, and body odors that came with an overnight bus trip.

"*Él es un alemán*," Emilio told me. A German, as if that explained it.

There is a particular spot on this mountain journey where the warm moist air coming up from the Pacific Ocean meets the cool night air of the high Andes. Along that stretch of two or three kilometers, a dense fog settles in. Day or night, summer or winter, visibility is less than a car length. I slowed to five kph, opened the windows and blasted the defroster. The wipers flung big droplets of water side to side as they struggled to keep the windshield clear.

As abruptly as we entered it, we were clear of the fog. The moon was especially bright at this point, so I could make out the craggy outline of what my mother would call *el hombre en la luna*. I turned off the defroster and was about to tromp down on the gas when I saw the man standing a few meters in front of us. He wore loose-fitting black trousers and a red poncho, and he held a shotgun diagonally across his chest.

I hit the brakes, drawing a grunt from my passenger. Out of the corner of my eye I saw a similarly dressed individual approaching from the side of the road. He was carrying a shotgun also, not a sawed off, short stock one like his partner, but an old-fashioned double-barrel model that a farmer might use to hunt rabbits or scare crows away from his crops. I wondered why, rather than extending the barrel out in front of him in my direction, he was leading with the butt end of the stock.

I didn't wonder for long. I felt the butt contact my forehead. I saw a flash of bright light and then only darkness. The last thing I heard was my passenger in the back seat screaming, "*Es war mein Bruder!*"

I woke up face down on a steep downhill slope, the smells of damp earth and vegetation assaulting my nose. I rolled over onto my back, touched my forehead gingerly, and wished that I hadn't. When I opened my eyes, I saw that a big rock outcropping was all that had saved me from plunging a thousand meters or more into the canyon below.

I heard the occasional swishing sounds from above—tires on damp pavement—and I realized that I was only twenty meters below the road. I got to my feet, feeling the impact of every rock or tree branch that I had encountered on the way down, and then scrambled up the slope. The sun was out now, and steam radiated from my rapidly drying clothes.

I'm not sure what I expected to find, but what I did find was nothing. Emilio's taxi was gone. There were no signs of either of the shotgun-wielding men or my German passenger. I walked thirty meters in either direction, finding nothing of significance. No expended shotgun shells, no breaks in the underbrush where a body might have been thrown over the embankment—other than the one made by me. There were plenty of footprints in the muddy shoulder, but as many of them were made by horses or mules as by people.

Somehow, despite the pounding in my head and the occasional flash of light that appeared before my eyes, I was able to form a few coherent thoughts. The first thing I had to do was call Emilio and tell him I had misplaced his taxi. Of course, my phone was in the taxi.

I don't wear a watch; I use my phone to tell me what time it is. I usually turn the taxi back over to Emilio just as the sun is coming up, so I was at least two hours late. I imagined my phone buzzing with increasingly frantic calls and texts from my friend.

I managed to flag down an old *campesino* in a battered Nissan pickup, hauling a load of pineapples up from the flatlands to the *mercados* in Cuenca. The engine was hitting on three out of its four cylinders as the truck labored up the grade. I leaned forward, willing the beast to go faster, drawing an amused smile from the driver. He wouldn't accept money for gas, but he wanted two dollars to use any of the precious minutes on his cell phone.

I don't memorize phone numbers anymore. Who does? I had them in my phone. Luckily, I was able to remember Ana's number and called her to assure her that I was okay. I got Emilio's number from her. I was in no mood to explain to my friend what had happened to his precious taxi, so I sent him a cryptic text and handed the phone back to the driver.

As we descended the hill, nearing the turnoff to Molleturo, I saw a commotion ahead. Black *polcía transito* pickups and white cars from the *policía nacional* were parked haphazardly on both sides of the road. A cluster of uniform-clad men gathered on the north side, peering down into the canyon.

"*Choque*," the driver said, unnecessarily.

"Yeah. Let me out here."

"*¿Aquí? Son solo treinta kilómetros a Cuenca.*"

"Yes. Here. Please." I handed him two dollars. He shrugged and added them to the pile of coins in the ashtray. I got out and the driver began the laborious task of pushing the old truck up the final grade before the road descended into Cuenca.

I shouldered my way into the crowd, which now included local farmers and a few schoolchildren. Before I reached the damaged guardrail, I saw what I expected. A car had come to rest a few hundred meters down the embankment. A yellow car with orange and black license plates that identified it as a taxi. A black-uniformed transit cop retrieved a pair of binoculars from his pickup and focused them on the wreckage below.

A heavy-set sergeant from the national police sidled up next to me. "What happened to your face?" I acted as if I hadn't heard him. It wouldn't be long before they identified Emilio as the owner of the cab, and he would identify me as the driver. It was common for drivers to abandon their vehicle after a crash, especially if anyone was injured. I would be subject to all kinds of uncomfortable questions, for which I had no satisfactory answers.

"*Uno... Cero... Tres... Ocho.*" The transit cop started calling out the numbers from the roof of the cab, momentarily distracting the suspicious cop. I slipped back through the crowd and hopped onto a blue and white *Flota Imbabura* bus that was waiting to be allowed to continue its journey. I took a seat near the back and the bus soon rumbled on its way. I watched from the window as the transit cop looked up the owner's information on his cell phone. The big sergeant watched over his shoulder, forgetting about me for the moment.

I got down from the bus in the center of Molleturo, about ten kilometers off the E528. Once a thriving trade hub on the old road that wound its way from Cuenca to the coast, the town suffered when the new highway was built in the early 1960s. Still, the small town with a population of about 5,000 souls seemed to be thriving on this midweek day. The town was nestled in a small depression in the mountains and served as a collection point for farmers and ranchers to bring their wares down out of the hills to be shipped on to Cuenca or Guayaquil for sale. I ducked into an internet *cabina* adjacent to the bus terminal. I entered one of the phone booths and took the slip of paper on which I had jotted down Emilio's number from my pocket. As I dialed, the smell of roasting chicken from the small restaurant next door hit me, and I realized I was starving.

"*¡Hola!*" My friend sounded tense.

"Emilio. It's Wilson."

"Yeah. What happened, man? Where you at?"

"Molleturo."

"What are you doing there? What happened? How did my taxi get down in the canyon?"

"So, the cops called you already?"

"Yeah. They said that there was nobody in the car, so they were leaving the scene."

"Did they actually go down there and look?"

Emilio made a sound that was half chuckle and half snort. "I asked them that myself. They said they were able to get a good look with their binoculars, so there was no reason to go down there."

It was my turn to snort. "Afraid they might get their pretty uniforms dirty?"

"Yeah. So, what happened, dude?"

I told him about the shotgun-wielding duo, and he whistled through his teeth. "You okay, man?"

"I will be." I touched my forehead, and it didn't hurt quite as bad as before. "Did you tell them that I was driving?"

"Nah. As soon as I got your text, I reported it stolen. Said I came out this morning and it was gone."

"Smart thinking," I said. "You do have insurance. Right?"

My friend groaned and let out a sigh. "Yeah. I do. Now I got to deal with those bloodsuckers for who knows how long."

"Hey, *amigo*, I'm sorry," I said.

"Ah, don't worry about it. Wasn't your fault. Anyway, I got to go. You can get back home?"

"Yeah," I said. "I'll let you know if I find out anything."

Emilio was silent for a few seconds. "What do you mean, find out anything?" His tone was suspicious, almost accusatory. "What is there to find out?"

"What about this German? What do you know about—"

"He paid, didn't he?" Emilio interrupted. "The German?"

"Yeah, yeah. He paid up front. I'll bring you your cut when I get back to town."

"He paid. So, who cares what happened to him?" The next thing I heard was the dial tone.

I went next door to the restaurant, wolfed down a quarter of a roasted chicken and a pile of white rice and thought about the events that had transpired that morning. When I was finished, I went back into the *cabina* and sat at one of the computer terminals. I pulled up *Google Translate* and entered the phrase that I had heard my passenger scream out before the shotgun butt hit the side of my head.

Es war mein Bruder! It was my brother! That was interesting, but not especially helpful. Like Emilio said, "Who cares?" Well, I did. I made a living as a PI—*Wilson Salinas, Investigador Privado*. It wasn't a great living, but I was doing what I wanted to do. And what I wanted to do was solve mysteries.

I went to the phone booth and called Ana. I told her what I was about to do, and she heaved a sigh but didn't try to stop me. "At least maybe I'll find my phone," I said.

"Be careful, *cariño*," she told me. I promised her that I would and headed back to the bus terminal.

I got off the bus at the intersection with the main highway. A couple of strips of yellow crime scene tape strung across the opening in the guardrail were the only signs that anything had happened there that morning. I looked down at the taxi. In a few years spindly trees would grow up through the broken windows and pampas grass would obscure it from sight, like so many other rusting hulks that littered the hillsides along this route. I know it was only my imagination, but it seemed as if nature had already begun the process. I made my way slowly down the steep slope, managing to stay on my feet by grabbing onto the small bushes that grew out of the hillside.

I tried to think as I descended—no small feat when you're trying to keep from ending up in the *Río Sitcay* that flowed through the canyon, 1,500 meters below. The kidnappers had waited until we had passed the halfway point to Guayaquil before making their move, and then had driven the taxi twenty kilometers back in the direction we had come from, before shoving it down the embankment. They wore clothing that a typical *campesino* might wear, but their red ponchos looked too new, as if they had been purchased just for this occasion. It didn't make sense.

And the German? He had screamed that it was his brother who did... what, exactly? If that was the case, his captors should have realized it by now. But they could have killed him and rigged it to look as if he had died when Emilio's taxi went down the hill, and they hadn't. Why not? They were certainly willing to kill, as evidenced by the way they threw me down the embankment. Only the rock outcropping had saved me. The thought sent an icy chill through me.

The Hyundai didn't look as bad as you might expect, but bad enough. The right front fender was crumpled almost back to the windshield and the hood latch had released. All the tires were flat, and the windshield and one of the rear windows were shattered. If anyone had been in this rig when it went down the mountain, they would be dead for sure.

The shift lever was in Drive and the key was still in the ignition, so one of them had apparently taken a running start and dived out at the last second before the taxi went through the guardrail. My phone lay on the passenger seat, still plugged into the charging port. I powered it up and saw that it was almost fully charged, but I had no service down in this canyon. I didn't have anybody to call anyway, so I stuck the phone in my back pocket and continued to search the cab. An empty soda bottle and a handful of napkins had been dislodged from under the seat, but the rest of the interior was as clean as when the Hyundai rolled out of the factory.

I climbed out of the car and stood for a minute, stretching my back, and contemplating the climb back up to the roadway.

Safely ensconced on the bus back to town, I called Emilio again.

"*Oye*," I said. "Do you know if this German has... had... a brother?"

"I don't know, man," Emilio said, clearly exasperated at the question. "Why do you care?"

"Come on," I said. "Just think for a minute."

He didn't say anything for a while. I didn't hear a dial tone, so I knew he hadn't hung up, but I expected him to at any moment. My friend has never been known for his patience with fools, and it was clear that he thought that I was being one just then.

"Yeah," he said finally. "I think he does. They own that little hostel on *Presidente Córdova*. The kind of place that backpackers stay. You know what I mean?"

"Yeah, you mean cheap."

"Exactly. Got a German name for the place. Posada something. Posada Berliner. That's it!"

"Okay," I said. "I can find it." Something was bothering me, and I quickly figured out what it was. "Wait a minute," I said, "you told me that you take him to the airport every three months or so. That he flies all over South America, sometimes to Europe."

"Yeah. That's right." I could hear the suspicion return to his voice.

"So, why does a dude that owns a little backpacker's hostel in Cuenca need to fly off to parts unknown four times a year?"

"I don't know, man. You're the detective, aren't you?" For the second time that day Emilio hung up on me.

I tried to find some information about my German passenger, using my phone app while I rode the bus back into town. There wasn't much on the Posada Berliner, but I did run across a picture of Gustaf Becker—the guy that I had misplaced halfway to Guayaquil—and his brother, Stefan. They were a jolly pair, both with reddish hair pulled forward to cover their receding hairlines, and flushed faces with chubby freckled cheeks. They appeared to be in their mid-thirties and could have been twins except that Gustaf was a little taller and his face had a few more lines and creases.

Stefan greeted me at the front desk at the Posada Berliner, his smile cranked up to maximum wattage. When I told him why I was there, his smile melted away. It took me a moment to read the new expression that took its place. It wasn't a shock, or even surprise. It was closer to acceptance, as if he had been expecting this very moment for some time. I could see that he was also confused, wondering why a taxi driver was delivering this news instead of the cops.

"What do the police think?" he said finally.

"I haven't told them," I said. It occurred to me then that my aversion to the police, the result of growing up in a poor barrio, was not a sentiment that was necessarily shared by the rest of the world. Stefan surprised me.

"That's good," he said, nodding thoughtfully.

"Is there somewhere that we can talk?"

"Of course." Stefan picked up a small silver bell that was chained to the desk and shook it three times. A young *ecuatoriana* came from a side room and he gave her some quick instructions in flawless Spanish. He led me to a small dining room and ushered me to a table next to a window. He fussed around at a side table and then brought over a carafe of coffee. The carafe was chipped, the mugs and spoons were mismatched, and the sugar and milk containers were repurposed soda bottles, but he carried it all as if it were the queen's own china.

It seemed that Stefan had used the time spent preparing our coffee to gather his thoughts. His Spanish was much better than his brother's, and he got right to the point.

"Your taxi? It was stolen?"

"It's not my taxi. It belongs to a friend of mine. But yes, it was stolen and pushed over a hillside near Molleturo."

"We have no money!" As if to reinforce his point, Stefan looked around the small room, with its battered furniture and walls that could have used a coat of paint.

"I don't want your money."

He paused with his coffee halfway to his lips and frowned. I noticed then that his eyes were green, rather than blue as I originally thought.

"What do you want?"

It took a while to convince him that I just wanted to find out what happened to his brother. As I spoke it occurred to me to wonder if I was trying to convince myself as well.

"We . . . my brother and I . . . run a small export business."

"Just export?"

"What?"

"Don't companies that export usually import also? I always hear the two terms together. You know: *Una empresa de importación y exportación.*"

Stefan mulled that over. "We are not a company," he said finally. "We—" His eyes widened, and his face collapsed. "My brother," he wailed. "He is dead. Don't you think?"

"I don't know," I said. I explained my thinking that if they wanted to kill him, they could have done it up there on the mountain. "They need him alive for some reason," I assured him, and his expression changed just for a moment. I didn't realize it then, but when I think back on it, of course he knew why they wanted Gustaf alive.

Stefan's expression changed again. He buried his face in his hands and started sobbing. His shoulders heaved and big tears found their way through his fingers and dropped onto the table. I heard a sound and looked up. The young Ecuadorian woman that Stefan had left at the desk peeked around the partially opened door. She had to have been listening. The expression on her face as she watched her boss cry was unreadable. When she noticed me watching, she gave me an impish smile and put a finger to her lips before withdrawing and silently closing the door.

Stefan finally recovered. He went to the side table and grabbed a handful of napkins, which he used to wipe the tears from his face. He blew his nose, sniffed one last time, and then was all business. He came back to the table but made no move to sit.

"Thank you so much for coming to let me know what happened, Herr Salinas." He extended his hand, and I shook it.

"Wait a minute," I said, remaining seated. "Your brother screamed something when he saw the two men with shotguns."

"*Ja?*" His reaction was polite, but without any real interest. His little crying jag had apparently served as a grieving experience, and he was ready to face whatever the future looked like without his brother.

"Yes," I told him. "He said, '*Es war mein Bruder.*'"

Other than a slight tightening of the muscles around his eyes, his face remained impassive. He shrugged and began gathering up our cups and placing them on the tray.

"Do you have another brother, Herr Becker?"

"No. Just the two of us." His expression had changed completely, from the jovial innkeeper that had greeted me earlier, to a cold-hearted businessman. He stalked off toward the kitchen with the tray.

"Okay. Well, I just wanted you to know," I said, getting up from the table.

"Yes, yes," he called from the kitchen. "Thank you again. That was very kind, but as you can see, we are quite busy." He rattled some dishes to emphasize his point.

I went out the door that led to the small lobby. The *ecuatoriana* was behind the desk checking in a young couple that I took to be Americans. They wore identical khaki shorts and blue T-shirts. The woman had long brown hair and the man had short frizzy red hair and a wispy beard. As I left the building, the clerk was assuring them that the continental breakfast could be served with gluten-free bread.

It had been a cool day, and it turned colder that afternoon. The townspeople walked a little faster than usual to their destinations. I hurried as well, wearing nothing but a light windbreaker as I set out for the bus stop, a dozen or so blocks away on Calle Presidente Córdova. I had promised Ana that I would make *coq au vin* for dinner. I had put it off as long as I could. Not because there is wine in the recipe and I'm a recovering alcoholic—I could find a substitute for the wine—but because the thought of cooking a gourmet meal made me think of my aborted career as a chef in Seattle. A career cut short by my drinking, drugging, and general fecklessness.

I was cutting across *Parque Calderon* when I heard the click-clack of high heels on the tile walkway behind me, approaching quickly.

"¡*Señor, Señor!*" I heard the young female voice behind me but ignored it at first. Who would be chasing after me, calling me sir? Then I heard her say something in tentative, heavily accented German, and I stopped walking.

It was the young *ecuatoriana* from the Posada Berliner. I couldn't imagine what she wanted from me. She beckoned me to join her on a bench beneath one of the towering Chilean Pines. I sighed quietly and sat down beside her on the cold metal. I had been toying with the idea of finding out what had happened to the missing German. I was over it now, looking forward to a night of domestic bliss, but one look at the fear and anguish on the young woman's face and I was back in. I exhaled again, this time loudly.

"They took the wrong brother," she said, and the tears started. "It was Stefan that—" She stopped talking and really started wailing, drawing curious looks from passersby. I smiled to show that everything was okay and waited for her to compose herself. The sobbing stopped and she wiped at her tears with the sleeve of the black blazer that she wore over a black skirt and a white blouse. The release of emotion seemed to have struck her dumb. Patience has never been my strong suit, but I'm helpless when confronted by a woman's tears.

"Who is 'they'?" I asked, as gently as I could. "What did Stefan do?"

The girl, I never found out her name, sniffed a final time and launched into her story. The brothers were engaged in smuggling relics, artifacts of the indigenous people. Ecuadorian law makes it a misdemeanor for private parties to own such relics, but to take them out of the country is a felony of the highest order. Unfortunately, a lack of funding and a lack of interest on the part of law enforcement means that these crimes are rarely prosecuted. Enter a vigilante group that calls itself "The Guardians of the Patrimony." This loosely organized group has made it their mission to capture and punish those who would pillage their culture for profit.

"Do you think that's who took Gustaf?"

"Of course," she sniffed. "It had to be them. Who else would take him?"

"Why do you think they have the wrong brother?"

She explained that Gustaf was the brains of the organization, but Stefan had the nerve, so he usually made the smuggling runs.

It was hard for me to see the weeping husk of a man that I left at the Posada Berliner as a steely-eyed smuggler with ice in his veins. But I had been wrong before.

"Why do you think I can help you?" I asked. I thought the tears might start again but they didn't. Her face hardened and she seemed to age far beyond her years.

"I doubt that you can, really," she said, "but I had to do something." She started walking away slowly and then her pace quickened. She was practically running by the time she reached *Calle Símon Bolívar* and headed east.

I took out my phone and called my friend Javi Morales.

Javi's moon face and shock of stiff black hair gave him a slightly Asian appearance, and he had put on a few pounds since he was a skinny defender on *Los Tigres*, our youth soccer team. Through an uncle in the force, he became a member of the transit police, but he made his real money using his knowledge of the inner workings of Cuenca's numerous bureaucracies. I used Javi from time to time in my business. The things he did for me were often not technically legal, but they were always for a good cause—in most cases, increasing my bank balance. If anyone could find the missing German, it would be Javi. He might also figure out a way to wring out a few dollars for me in the process. I called Javi and told him everything I knew. It wasn't much, which he was quick to point out.

"*Dios mio*, Weelson. You don't know much, do you?"

"No, *amigo*, I don't. That's why I called you. If anyone can find out what happened to this guy, you're the man."

Javi took a moment to absorb this blatant act of flattery and then got right to the point. It's considered vulgar in Ecuadorian society to talk directly about money. I'd gotten over it by spending fifteen years in the US. Javi, who as far as I know, has never left the country, seemed to come by it naturally.

"What's in it for me?" he wanted to know.

"My undying gratitude."

"You're funny, man."

"I'm doing this one *gratis*, Javi."

It was an idea so alien to my friend's way of thinking that there was a long pause on the line. "For free?"

"I'll tell you what," I said, "if you can figure a way for me to make something out of this, I'll split it with you."

"Yeah, you will." Javi hung up and I headed for the *mercado* to pick up the ingredients for my evening's culinary masterpiece.

Coq au vin sounds like a dish for rich folks, but I knew that French peasants had come up with the idea of using wine to tenderize the tough meat from chickens that had outlived their usefulness as egg-layers. For those of us who avoid alcohol for whatever reason, cherry juice makes a good substitute. The sugar substitutes for the sugar in red wine and the color is nearly identical. I put a pot of water on for the chicken and pitted and squeezed a pound of cherries that I had bought from a lady with a wheelbarrow outside the *mercado Diez de Agosto*. I was sautéing the carrots, onions, garlic, and mushrooms when Javi called.

"I got something for you," he said, and laughed.

"What's funny about some poor dude getting kidnapped?" My friends and I tend to have odd ideas about what's funny, but even I thought that Javi was out of line.

"No, no," he said, "It's not about that. I'm still working on that, don't worry."

"So, what *is* it about. Why are you calling me?"

"*Dios mío*, Weelson. What's got up your butt?" Javi sounded truly hurt. I was stressed about cooking this meal for Ana, and wanted to get back to the stove, but if I didn't humor my old friend, he probably wouldn't pursue my case with all the vigor it deserved.

"Nothing," I sighed. "What've you got?"

"Well," he said. "You know how when you're asking around about somebody and you kind of stumble on something that doesn't have anything to do with what you're looking for, but it makes you say, 'hmm?'" It was a long-winded sentence, even for Javi Morales.

"Yeah, I guess." I lowered the heat and stirred the vegetables, which had already started to scorch.

"You know who the other brother—not the one you're looking for?"

"Stefan."

Javi laughed again. "You know who he's sleeping with?"

"No." I grabbed a fork and checked the chicken breasts that were now parboiling on another burner. "Who?"

"Juan Carrión's wife!"

"What?" I dropped the fork into the boiling water and scalded the tip of my fingers as I tried to grab it.

"Yeah," Javi said gleefully. "He's fucked, isn't he?"

"Yeah," I said. "He sure is." I hung up the phone, opened the tap, and ran the water until it turned cool. I inserted my scalded fingers in the stream.

My friend Javi is usually quite dependable, but he loves to gossip. His need to share with me the tidbit about Stefan Becker and the wife of one of Cuenca's richest and most powerful men completely put him off the scent.

He had, however, solved the mystery even if he didn't realize it. I flashed back to the previous night on the mountain. Two things bothered me about the encounter. If "The Guardians of the Patrimony" had kidnapped Gustaf—thinking he was Stefan—why had they stopped there? The young *ecuatoriana* told me that Gustaf was the brains of the outfit, while Stefan had the nerve, but they were both equally guilty.

The other thing was the clothing worn by the assailants. Their black pants and red ponchos were typical dress for the Indigenous people who worked the land in the area—but the clothes were brand new, as if they had been purchased just for the occasion.

Juan Carrión owned tens of thousands—some said as many as a hundred thousand—hectares of farmland in the hills surrounding Cuenca. Individual families farmed small plots, growing mostly corn, cabbages, and potatoes on the steep hillsides. The land was far too steep to use tractors and other equipment, so everything had to be done by hand. The *campesinos* farmed their little plots, usually no more than a hectare, and the small percentage that they paid to Carrión had added up to the point that he was one of the richest men in Azuay Province. It seemed like a good deal for all parties, but the word on the street was that Carrión was a ruthless landlord. If a family came up short on their share, for whatever reason, they were promptly evicted from the property and another family brought in.

So, the men who had ambushed us were thugs, hired by Carrión to dish out justice for his cuckolding. They had dressed in a manner that would cast suspicion on "The Guardians of the Patrimony." I had to admire the man's shrewdness, but it seemed he had failed to find the best and the brightest to carry out his plan. Someone had to have been watching when Gustaf got into my taxi and relayed the news to the men up in the mountains. The two brothers looked similar, except that Gustaf appeared older and taller. You would think, if you were sentencing a man to, at the least, a severe beating you would try to be more precise in your identification.

I laughed at that thought. One German was the same as another to whomever Carrión had hired. He didn't care.

All of which led to the big question: *Why do I care?* But I did.

I was able to save the vegetables by adding a splash of water to the skillet, and the pain in my fingers subsided when I smeared them with aloe vera. As many times as I had burned or scalded my fingers in my former career, I was surprised I had any feeling left.

Some long-dormant sense memory kicked in and I was able to complete the preparation without a problem. Ana pronounced it delicious, and I have to say I was proud of myself. Still, I was only partially present while we ate. I saw Ana watching me from time to time, a slight smile on her face. She had seen me like this before and knew that it was useless to attempt any conversation while I was in this state. Another woman might have felt neglected or excluded, but not Ana, and I loved her for it.

After dinner we sat on the back patio, a small square of cracked and stained concrete that gave us a great view of the mountains to the west. The house that I grew up in, and that I now owned, was located as far west as one could go and still be within the city limits of Cuenca. Beyond our property was a steep ravine with the opposite bank dotted with little plots of farmland. For all I knew Juan Carrión owned some of that property.

I told Ana what I had learned from Javi and that I felt a responsibility for leading Gustaf Becker into the trap.

"You have a good soul and a good heart, Wilson," Ana said. "I wish that you believed that like I do." She kissed me then and, hugging herself against the cold, went back into the house.

I sat there for a long time, thinking.

I arrived at Posada Berliner a little before nine the next morning and found the massive mahogany doors closed. I pounded on the door with the side of my fist, making only a hollow thumping sound due to the thickness of the wood.

"He won't answer," said a voice to my right. "He's crazy!"

I turned in the direction of the voice and saw a skinny guy with a hawk-like face and a mop of unruly black hair sitting on the stoop of the *tienda* next door. He wore camouflage pants, a stained green T-shirt, and hiking boots. A huge backpack leaned against the wall next to him, the Argentinian flag emblazoned prominently on it.

"He's in there?" I said. "Stefan?"

The backpacker stood up, revealing himself to be about a foot taller than me. *Definitely an Argentino.* "Yeah," he said. "Whatever his name is. He's crazy. Came around at four o'clock this morning and woke us all up. Said we had to leave right away. There was only me and a couple of Americans in Number Seven. We started arguing and he gave us our money back. He wrapped up some bread and cheese for us, and he pushed us out the door."

"Did he say why you had to go?"

The tall backpacker ignored my question, still focusing on the unfairness of the events of that morning. "My bus to Bogota doesn't leave until four this afternoon," he whined. "What am I supposed to do until then?"

I told him I didn't know and walked to the opposite side of the street to get a better look at the two-story building. A rolling metal door had been pulled down over the big street-facing window, and the curtains were drawn in the upstairs windows.

I took out my cell phone and dialed the number on the sign over the door. The phone rang, and rang, and then rang some more. I was about to hang up when the answering machine finally clicked on. I was wished a wonderful day in five languages—English, French, German, Spanish and what I assumed was Mandarin Chinese. Then a voice in English with a heavy German accent encouraged me to leave a message and someone would get back to me as soon as humanly possible.

I waited for the beep and said: "You can't stay in there forever, Stefan. Don't you think they've figured out by now that they've got the wrong brother? I know what you've done, and I know who's after you. I can help you, but you must talk to me." I hung up and waited, wondering how I was going to fulfill the promise I had just made.

After a few minutes I saw a curtain move in one of the second-story windows. The window opened and Stefan poked his head out, looking up and down the street before focusing on me.

The tall skinny backpacker spoke German quite well, and he used it to make his displeasure known. Stefan responded with a rapid-fire outburst full of harsh H and K sounds, his face turning dangerously red as he yelled.

A small crowd gathered quickly, grateful for this bit of excitement in their usually humdrum life. Here and there, arguments broke out as to which of the combatants was in the right. I finally managed to calm the young *Argentino* down, and he shrugged into his backpack and set off down the street to a smattering of applause.

A few minutes later I heard a bolt slide open and the big double doors opened slightly. Stefan Becker leaned out and gestured for me to enter. I had barely cleared the threshold when he pulled the doors shut and slid the bolt closed with a resounding clank.

Stefan ushered me through the lobby and into the same small dining room where we had talked the day before. In the corner of the room, I noticed a bulging suitcase, a smaller carry-on bag, and a laptop case.

"Going somewhere?"

Like the backpacker, Stefan saw no reason to answer my question. "They called me," he said, his voice trembling.

"Who called you? Carrión?"

"No!" He shook his head vigorously side to side. "One of his people, I guess. They've got Gustaf!" I thought he might start crying.

"Well, that's good," I assured him. "At least we know he's alive."

"They wanted to trade him for me," he said, so softly that I barely heard him. He watched my eyes go to the packed bags in the corner of the room and then collapsed onto a wooden chair and buried his face in his hands.

I tried to feel morally superior to the poor slob, but I don't have a brother, and I can't say with any real certainty what I might have done in his situation.

"I assume," I said, "that you were supposed to have met them already."

"Yes."

"Where and when?"

The meeting had been set for four A.M. in the narrow alley behind the *Mercado 9 de Octubre*. A beehive of activity during the day, the mercado would be deserted at that hour, aside from the handful of drunks that gathered there as soon as the market closed.

I said, "Instead of rescuing your brother, you kicked out all of your lodgers and locked yourself in here."

Stefan looked up at me and his eyes filled with tears.

"I'm weak!" he cried; his hands extended in front of him as if begging for my forgiveness. "I'm lost without *mein Bruder*! He's taken care of me ever since our parents died when I was thirteen."

I couldn't think of anything to say to that, so I remained silent.

Stefan's attitude changed then, so quickly that it caught me off guard. Gone was the grieving sibling, replaced by a shrewd businessman. "I have money," he said. "I offered it to them, but they laughed at me."

I could have said, with great indignation, "*Yesterday you said you didn't have any money.*" But old instincts die hard. "How much?" I said.

He grinned and wiped the last few tears from his cheeks. I watched as he made the calculation. Whatever he offered me would be less than he had offered his brother's captors. That went without saying.

"Fifteen thousand," he said. It was more than I expected, and I must have let it show on my face, because he frowned.

I didn't verbally accept the offer—*let him squirm a little, at least*—but there was no way I was going to turn him down. I need money as much as, if not more than, the next guy. I would need help, but the kind of help I needed is surprisingly cheap in my country.

"Have they contacted you since the initial call?" It had been nearly six hours since the first contact, so if they hadn't contacted Stefan again it was a pretty good bet that his big brother was dead.

"They tried," he admitted, showing me his cell phone display. "I was too afraid to answer."

I looked at the screen. Six missed calls, one an hour since four A.M. According to his phone the time now was 9:58.

"Answer, if they call again," I instructed him. Tell them you're sorry. Make up a reason why you didn't show. Beg them to give you another chance."

Stefan nodded his head rapidly in agreement and then gave me a pleading look. "You'll do it then?" he said. Before I could answer, a sly look appeared on his face. "I'm not sure that I can come up with the full amount. Could you consider a little less? Say, ten thousand?"

I despised him then for trying to bargain for the life of his brother, but I was in familiar territory. I had been dealing with people like this my entire adult life.

"Fifteen thousand," I told him with a broad smile, "or I'll take you out there myself and let them kill both of you." I was speaking figuratively. Stefan was bigger than me and probably stronger. It worked, though. Stefan was nodding his agreement when we heard a scratching sound from the front door, followed by a terse whisper.

"Stefan! Stefan! *Öffne die Tür!*"

It had to be Gustaf. The terror in the voice was the same as I had heard when he screamed out, "*Es war mein Bruder!*"

Stefan came out of his funk and his face lit up like a golden retriever who had just noticed the tennis ball in his owner's hand.

He raced toward the door, and I had to grab him by the back of his shirt to stop him.

"It's a trick!" I hissed. "He's not alone."

Stefan struggled to release himself, but I tightened my grip.

"Wait a minute," I said. "I'll go upstairs and look out the window. Just to be sure." I turned away and took the steps two at a time. At the head of the stairs, I entered a narrow hallway with eight closed doors off it. I chose one of the two that were closest to the street. The door was unlocked, and I entered a tiny cell-like room containing a single bed and a wooden chair. I rushed to the window, pulled back the curtains and inched the window open far enough to stick my head out a little.

I was right. Gustaf was not alone. I was pretty sure his companion was one of the kidnappers, minus the red poncho and the shotgun. My satisfaction at being right was tempered by the unmistakable sound of the bolt being thrown open on the front door. I heard the creak of the hinges, followed by a shriek from Stefan and then the muffled sounds of a struggle.

I raced out of the room and started down the steps. Stefan had managed to extricate his brother from the clutches of the goon and was pulling him toward the rear of the building. The thug was right behind them, a nasty-looking pistol in his hand. I launched myself over the guardrail and planted both feet in the middle of his back.

By the time I made it back to my feet, Stefan had retrieved the pistol. Carrión's man lay on the tiled floor, taking in huge gulps of air and thrashing about like a freshly caught trout. I grabbed the gun out of Stefan's trembling hand before he accidentally drilled one of us. I have little use for guns, I've never fired one in anger, and my hand was only marginally steadier than Stefan's, but it was steady enough. Gustaf tied the goon's hand securely behind his back with a length of clothesline. We stood up and let our breathing return to normal. The guy on the floor began to curse and make threats of a disturbingly explicit nature until I flipped him over onto his back. The pain of lying atop his trussed-up arms shut him up quickly, but now I needed him to talk.

"Who else is out there?" I demanded, sticking the pistol in his side.

"I thought you were—"

"Yeah," I said, shoving the pistol in a little further. "You thought I was dead. Now answer the question!"

"Two of them," he hissed out between gritted teeth.

"Go ahead." I must admit I was enjoying the feeling of shoving the pistol into the side of one of the men who had just two nights ago tossed me over the side of a mountain and left me to die.

"One across the street in the alley next to the *panaderia*," he said, "and one at the corner by the park."

"Are they armed?"

"Of course they're armed!" The thug tried a sneer on for size, but it didn't take. "Paco in the alley has a rifle and—" he cut himself off, as if afraid that he had messed up by revealing his partner's name. "The other one at the corner has a little .22-caliber," he said, "but he's keeping it out of sight."

It occurred to me that knowing his partner's name actually might help. I flipped him back over onto his stomach and saw the telltale outline of a cell phone in one of his back pockets. I retrieved it and scrolled through his contacts list. I found a number of text messages between him and Paco, the last one having arrived a few minutes ago, about the time I had launched myself over the stair rail and onto the thug's back.

"What's going on?" the text read.

I quickly responded, "Stand down. Wait to hear from me."

With that taken care of, I turned to find Stefan and Gustaf standing toe to toe. Stefan kept dropping his head, and Gustaf kept pushing it back up. At first, I thought Gustaf was berating his brother for not coming to his rescue, but then I heard him say, "*fünfzehntausend*," which I was pretty sure translated into "fifteen thousand." I shook my head. It appeared that Gustaf was angry at his younger brother for not negotiating a better deal for their rescue. He looked meaningfully in my direction and was about to say something, but I held up my hand palm outward.

"Let's get the hell out of here," I said.

There was no back door to the posada, but on my earlier foray upstairs I had noticed a wooden ladder at the end of the hallway, leading to a roof hatch. The three of us clambered up and emerged onto the flat roof of the building. A pile of roofing tiles lay nearby, and I used some to weigh down the hatch cover. We headed across the roof.

The neighboring building and the one after that had flat roofs that were the same level as the one we were on. The roof of The San Alfonso Catholic Church was steeply pitched, so our journey ended there.

I called Javi. He was at the cop shop, waiting to begin his shift, and agreed to get a van from the impound lot and head our way.

We huddled in the shade of one of the church towers and waited. It was only a matter of time until Carrión realized that his prime goon was taking much longer than expected to return with the correct brother. I tried to think like him. What would he do? I supposed he would dispatch one, and probably more than one, of his thugs to investigate. I had made sure that Gustaf bolted the doors before we left, so that would slow their entry. But for how long?

All in all, though, I felt pretty good about our situation. All Carrión's men would find when they breached the door was the dude we had trussed up and left behind. That would infuriate them, but there was nothing they could do about it. The only way out was through the roof hatch, and I had weighed that down with several kilos of roof tiles. I had ensured that both brothers had their passports, so all we had to do was wait for Javi to come to our rescue.

Ecuador's borders with both Perú and Colombia are notably porous. Perú was closer, but I would let Javi choose which way he took them. Once they were across the border, they were on their own. I was sure that they had more money stashed away than the fifteen grand Stefan had offered me. He was just that kind of dude.

That reminded me that I had yet to collect the money. Did they leave it behind when we escaped the Posada Berliner? I was about to ask when my phone rang. It was Javi.

"Weelson!" *Why was he whispering?*

"What's up?"

"I can't help you, *viejo*."

"What do you mean? You can't help me?"

After a long pause he gave me the bad news. Javi is a man with many contacts, but he's a low-ranking member of the transit police. Juan Carrión was also a man with many contacts, and he was one of the wealthiest and most powerful men in Azuay Province. Javi had said that he would need to bring in someone at a high level in the National Police if we were to put our plan into place. So, someone at an even higher level had been gotten to. That's just how things work in my hometown.

I didn't waste my time pleading with Javi, but I did offer to bring up his percentage of the fifteen grand that I hoped to live long enough to collect from the Becker brothers. When I reached sixty percent with no response I gave up. Javi was patrolling out in the far reaches of town that night, but he did offer to arrange to switch beats with another cop and cruise the downtown area, *just in case.*

"Try to get them to do something big, something that attracts a lot of attention," he said cheerfully. "We'll have no choice but to bust them."

I hung up and saw the brothers staring at me with mournful expressions on their faces.

Darkness falls early on the equator—six P.M., year-round. By eight, the street outside Posada Berlin was deserted. I was shifting position in a vain attempt to get comfortable, when I heard a big *Woomph* and saw a bright orange light reflected in the window glass across the street. I poked my head out far enough to see that someone had sprayed some type of accelerant on the front door and set it afire. *Well, Javi. You got that big attention-getter you wanted.*

"*Das Gasthaus!*" Stefan screamed and ran to the edge of the roof to get a better look at the family business going up in smoke. I thought he might go over, but Gustaf grabbed him by the back of his shirt and pulled him back. They embraced and collapsed back in the shadows. Although Gustaf was speaking in German, I knew that his words were an effort to comfort his stricken brother.

"Carrión's man!" The words flew from my mouth. "He's trapped inside."

Gustaf looked up and smirked. "It will take hours for that door to burn through. It's solid mahogany."

"But the smoke will get in and he'll die long before the door burns through." I was ten meters away, back toward the inn before I looked back. Stefan hid his face, but Gustaf looked me straight in the eye and shrugged his shoulders. I was on my own.

The smoke was just starting to seep in beneath the door by the time I made it back down the ladder and down the stairs to the first floor. Carrión's thug, tied at hands and feet, was squirming along the floor like the inchworm from a kid's story that I vaguely remembered. I removed the gag from his mouth.

"Get me out of here!" His voice sounded raw as if he had been screaming for a while, which he probably had, but the bandanna had muffled the sound.

I showed him the gun and reminded him that his friends had set fire to the door and left him here to die. "I can untie you and get you out, or I can leave you here," I told him. "Your choice." Of course, I wasn't going to leave him behind or I wouldn't have come back in the first place. Still, I felt the need to act tough, figuring that was a language this guy would understand.

He nodded his agreement, and I untied him. I followed him up the stairs, the first tendrils of choking black smoke reaching us. We went up the ladder without incident, but as soon as he set foot on the roof he took off at a sprint. By the time I clambered out through the roof hatch he had made his way onto a neighboring building and was nearly at the top of the steeply pitched roof. I wasn't going to follow him up there and I wasn't going to shoot him, so I just watched as he crested the roof.

By the time I reached the hiding spot by the church towers, the Brothers Becker were, of course, nowhere to be found.

I clambered down a shaky wooden ladder that ended at the top of a guard shack for the neighboring parking lot. The guard inside was watching TV and didn't react when I jumped down to the sidewalk. I thought to ask if he had seen the two brothers and what direction they headed. But Argentina was playing Ecuador in an America's Cup early round and the guard wouldn't have noticed if a bomb went off beneath his feet.

I headed west on Presidente Córdova, the opposite direction from the inn with the burning door. Sirens—police, fire, and ambulance—sounded from different quarters of the city, like wolves howling to each other across the wilderness.

I found Gustaf and Stefan huddled together in a recessed doorway to a clothing shop that was closed for the night. I stood over them like a disapproving parent until Gustaf grabbed me by the arm and pulled me into them.

"He'll see you!" Gustaf's voice cracked with fear and his eyes shone white in the darkness.

"Who?" I disengaged from them but remained in the alcove. "Who will see me?" I hadn't seen anyone on the short walk from the church to our current location.

"Look," Stefan murmured. "At the corner. By that big Jacaranda tree."

I saw the dude then, not much more than a shadow in the dim light. Then I saw another figure hurrying to join him. I recognized him as the thug that I had rescued from the Posada Berliner. He must have clocked which way I went and told his partner, who would have seen the brothers descend from the church and run in this direction.

"Do you think they have guns?" Stefan spoke in a strangled whisper. "If we show our faces, they could pick us off one by one from that distance."

"They're not going to do that," I said. "They want you alive." I pointed at Stefan. "Carrión is going to want to lay hands on you personally."

"This is all your fault!"

I had to clamp my hand over Gustaf's mouth to keep him from revealing our location. He pulled away from me and proceeded to pound his fists against Stefan's chest. "I told you to stop seeing her!" At least he lowered his voice.

"They're coming!" Stefan broke away from his brother's onslaught. "Look what you've done," he hissed in Gustaf's direction. I knew better. Thug Number Two knew where we were from the start. He had just been waiting for his partner to arrive. I could see that they both carried pistols, pointing at the ground but ready for action.

That reminded me that I still had the pistol I had taken from Gustaf's captor back at the Posada Berliner what seemed like days ago now. I took it out and hefted it. I assumed it was loaded because it was heavy. I had never fired a gun in my life, and I had never killed anything larger than a cockroach. Maybe I could use the gun as a diversion. Fire a shot into the air to get them to back off so we could make our escape.

I was fumbling with the pistol in the darkness, trying to find the safety, when I heard the short *whoop, whoop* of a siren. Blue and red lights reflected off the walls of the surrounding buildings. A black *Policía Transito* pickup truck pulled to a stop and my friend Javi Morales exited from it.

"*What the hell are you doing, man?*" Javi was only a few feet away, but he acted as if he hadn't heard me. I thought he was going for his gun, but he pulled a big black ticket book from his pocket. There were three cars parked at the curb and Javi walked around each one as if inspecting them. Placing his right foot on the bumper of an old Chevy sedan, he began writing a ticket. Suddenly he dropped his foot onto the pavement and stuffed the ticket book back in his pocket.

"They're gone," he said, barely audibly. The pickup was a crew cab model, and he opened the rear door. Stefan was the first to pile into the back seat, followed by Gustaf and then me. We made a comical sight I'm sure, trying to stay low while peeking out the rear window to confirm for ourselves that Carrión's goons had fled the scene. Javi calmly got behind the wheel, turned off the lights, and drove us away from there.

"Damn it, Javi," I said when I had finally untangled myself from the two brothers. "You took a hell of a chance coming back here. I mean, I'm grateful but—"

"Don't worry about it." Javi signaled and turned north on Calle Padre Aguirre, heading for the Pan American Highway.

"All they had to do," I said, "was to clock the numbers on your truck and they'll find out it was you that screwed up their plan. I don't think Carrión is the type of guy to just let things go." I was worried about my friend, sure, but I also knew that if they got their hooks into Javi, it wouldn't be long before they connected him to me.

Jav's smile got bigger as he turned west on the highway. "This . . ." He patted the truck's dashboard with affection. "This is what we call a 'Ghost Truck.' The numbers, the license plates . . . All fake. We use it for special operations, like . . ." He trailed off, waving a hand in the air. I got the point. The cops probably had a good reason to have such a vehicle, but I doubt this is what they had in mind.

I had made sure that the Beckers carried their passports with them when we left the hostel. Javi arranged for a couple of mechanics from the National Police motor pool to "requisition" a squad car which they would use to carry the brothers to a small airport in San Joaquin where they would be flown out of the country. It didn't seem likely that even Carrión would try to take down a police vehicle to get at Stefan.

Of course, the fifteen grand reward never materialized. Between what they had on them and what they could get from an ATM, they came up with about five thousand. I gave Javi three gees for his part. He would give the two mechanics, and the pilot, the least amount that he possibly could, but that was his business. He dropped me off near the park and sped off.

The buses had stopped running at ten, so I took a cab. The driver, lo and behold, was my friend Emilio, working the night shift for another cab owner. I paid him the twenty-five I owed him and told him about my adventures that night. He whistled through his teeth.

"I'll get my new rig in about ten days," he told me. "With a big payday like you got tonight, you probably won't want to drive for me anymore."

I thought about the new roof that my house needed, along with new wiring and plumbing.

"Call me," I said, getting out of the taxi. I gave him twenty for the two-dollar fare and went through the gate. A single lamp burned in the living room, where I knew that Ana would be asleep on the sofa waiting for me.

I waved at Emilio's retreating taillights and unlocked the front door, a feeling of warmth radiating through me.

As a writer, everyone I meet is fair game to become a character in one of my stories. The character of Wilson Salinas is based on Emilio M, the first person my wife and I met when we moved to Ecuador in 2014.

Emilio, about thirty-five at the time, drove us from the airport in Guayaquil to our new home in Cuenca. He had recently returned to Cuenca after fifteen years in Minneapolis. Emilio was a great ambassador for Ecuador, friendly and extremely knowledgeable about its history and culture.

I was intrigued, thinking of the culture shock that he must have endured upon relocating to the frigid North at the age of nineteen, and his shock at the changes to his home country when he returned after such a long absence.

While Wilson is loosely based on Emilio, Emilio is a hardworking family man (boring!) so I made Wilson a recovering alcoholic with little in the way of marketable skills, who becomes a PI because he has nothing to lose.

Emilio drove us hundreds of miles over the six years that we lived there, and I have come to consider him a friend. This story is dedicated to him and all the wonderful people of Ecuador.

Billie Livingston *is the author of four novels and a collection of short stories for which she won the Danuta Gleed Literary Award. Her writing has appeared widely in magazines and newspapers, including* Ellery Queen Mystery Magazine, The Saturday Evening Post, Black Cat Weekly, *and* The Daily Beast. *She has been the recipient of The Writer's Trust of Canada Award and has been nominated for a National Magazine Award, the Journey Prize, the Pat Lowther Award for Poetry and the Scotiabank Giller Prize. Her short story "Sitting on the Edge of Marlene" was adapted to a feature film. She is in the process of finishing her first crime thriller novel. Livingston lives in Vancouver, BC, with her husband, actor and writer, Tim Kelleher. You can read more at billielivingston.com*

SAME OLD SONG
Billie Livingston

Jack had been practicing law for about three years when he came home one afternoon and flopped on the couch. Beside him, Maisy pecked at her laptop, hunting for light at the end of the teaching tunnel. In her two years as a substitute in the Los Angeles public school system, she'd been punched, groped, shoved, and locked in a closet. The day the kid threw a chair was the day she decided she'd rather wait tables. Pay couldn't be any worse.

"You're home early." Eyes on her computer screen, she skimmed an article titled: *What Else Can I Do With a Teaching Degree?*

"I, uh . . ." Silence. He picked at a hangnail. "I got disbarred."

"What?!" Maisy slapped her laptop shut. "What did you do?"

"Nothing, baby." When they were first together, they made fun of couples who called each other baby. Now they do it too—reserved for deep cuts and white lies. Sometimes it just feels better when someone you love calls you baby.

She scoffs. "Come on, Jack. They don't just suddenly disbar you."

"Suspended technically. But they're talking two years. *Failure to make reasonable inquiries of clients in the face of overwhelming, objectively suspicious circumstances.*"

"What does that mean?"

Jack considered for a moment. "Apparently, helping clients buy property with suitcases of cash is frowned upon. In particular if said client is found guilty of running an illegal gambling operation. And I may have changed a couple pertinent client details on a contract."

"So, money-laundering and fraud." She closed her eyes and took a breath.

"That's putting it a little harshly."

Harsh but not entirely false. Jack liked to take an edge where he could. He passed the bar exam without spending a day in law school. Perfectly legal in California. But she should have known something was off when he made so much money his first year. Maisy convinced him to park the cash somewhere safe. Put it into a waterfront condo. Santa Monica high rise: two bedrooms, two baths. They'd have the mortgage paid off in no time. Maybe she was just as bad.

"We'll be fine," Jack said and gave her neck a rub. "I'll write the real estate exam. Easy peasy." Probably would be. Jack Adams knew how to hustle. It's how he was raised.

It is about thirteen months later when Maisy stands in the bank arguing with the teller. "What happened to the deposit I made?" These days she works at El Jardin in the Casa del Cielo. The restaurant is in a five-star hotel so most shifts are decent for tips. But now the mortgage payment's due, the dishwasher is broken again, the joint account is gasping, and here's this pinch-faced weasel giving her the runaround.

"You were *overdrawn*," the teller says. Louder this time. "If you transfer funds by end-of-day, you'll avoid an arrears penalty. All this information is on the app."

She wants to tell him to shove the app up his arrears. Instead she takes her readers out to look at the receipt. Maisy's prescription glasses got crushed when she sat on them last week.

Shit. Jack used their joint account to pay the vet. She feels her face getting hot. "Can't you just transfer funds from the other account?" The teller asks what name is on the other account. "My husband's. Jack—I mean John—John Adams Jr."

One station over, a man turns his head suddenly. Tan skin, silver hair, he wears a pale blue overcoat. Probably cashmere. Unusual to see a coat like that in Southern California, but this is one cold January. The man looks back as his teller lays rows of bills in front of him: "Fifty, one hundred, one fifty . . ."

"I can't do that, ma'am." Maisy's teller pulls her attention back.

"Do you guys want your money or not?" Maisy's in a mood. Worked a breakfast shift today. They had guests in for an engineering conference. Wall-to-wall math dorks demanding bacon and Bloody Marys for their hangovers. When the check came, half of them opened their calculators and argued the charges.

The teller gives her a tired stare. "Unless your name is on the account—"

"Fine. Forget it." Wrestling her purse strap to her shoulder, she hustles for the exit. The silver-haired man is just ahead now. She slips through the open door behind him. Standing on the sidewalk, her breath clouds the air. Her reading glasses fog and she snatches them off her face. The man looks east on Wilshire, turns west, and walks smack into Maisy. She drops her glasses.

"Excuse me!" He has a slight accent. Mid-sixties, large bony nose and a square jaw. His eyes are an unusual golden brown. "I am very sorry."

She sees her readers under the sole of his polished oxfords. The man lifts his foot. Crouching, he picks up the mangled frames. Tears well in her eyes. It's not the glasses. It *is* the glasses. And the cat, the dishwasher, Jack, her job, and her lousy education choices.

The man peers at her. "What are they worth?" He reaches inside his exquisite blue coat. "Let me make it right." He takes out his bank envelope.

"No." She shakes her head, thinking of the glasses she sat on. The ones she got with Jack's new health insurance. Another job that he'll probably burn. Looking at the man's soft lapels, she mutters, "Three hundred dollars." The lie sends a bolt of adrenaline through her veins.

"You look familiar." Keeping his eyes on her, the man goes into his envelope, takes out six fifties. "Perhaps I only wish I knew you."

Holding out the cash, he says, "Why don't we have lunch? I am staying at Shutters on the Beach. A magnificent hotel."

"I'm married." Maisy takes the cash. "Thank you," she says and turns on her heel.

The man watches her hurry west on Wilshire. He smiles softly and heads her way.

He cracks open a bottle and fills two glasses. "This comes from the glaciers of—"

"Jack, you can't keep blowing this kind of money on *water*." He once brought home a case of spring water from Slovenia. *Slovenia!* Sixty bucks per liter. Claimed he got a deal on it.

"Stop thinking like a poor person, Maisy-May. Think poor, you'll be poor." As he takes a slice of gourmet pizza from the box and sets it on her plate, Cyril saunters across his lap and settles on the couch between them. He yawns, his white fangs iridescent against black fur.

"That why you spent fifteen hundred bucks to get the cat's teeth cleaned?"

"He had gingivitis," Jack says. "It's the anesthesia. They had to put him out."

"Someone should put you out."

"Relax. I just got paid. Funds transferred. Mortgage secure."

"We got to talk about the mortgage," Maisy says. "We could have a whole house in Silver Lake for way less than what we're paying here."

"Leave Santa Monica? This is our investment. Like you said, there's a finite supply of oceanfront property."

Did she say that? Bigmouth. Slick and swanky is for people making bags of cash. That's not Jack and Maisy anymore. Four months ago, Jack had his real estate license revoked for breaching client confidentiality and failing to disclose something or other. Now he's the activities director in a nursing home. Never say die. She had to give him that.

"At least I'm not into wine. Then you'd have something to bitch about."

True. Jack's not a drinker. His mother cured him of that potential. Died a few years back. Cirrhosis. He raises his glass of pricey water. "To my wife, Scam Artist of the Week."

"It wasn't a scam."

"You pulled off a perfectly executed Melon Drop. Also known as The Broken Glasses scam. You're a natural!" He sighs as if he just fell in love all over again. "Sure paid up easy." Jack picks up a fifty and examines it. "Probably up to something. What'd he look like?"

Maisy shrugs. "Older guy. Trippy amber eyes. And he was wearing this super luxe blue coat. I think he just wanted to dip his noodle."

"As my dad used to say, a con works best when the mark's got some larceny in him."

"For a man with nothing good to say about his father. . . . Anyway, he stepped on my glasses."

He smirks. "Here I'm living like Señor Scrupulous and my wife's out fleecing the sheep."

"I am not." She roots for an excuse and gives up. "You're right. I'm always giving you shit, then I pull a stunt like this." She looks into her glass a moment, then looks at him. "They say if you intentionally perform a bad deed, it leaves a metaphysical residue on you. Bad karma."

Jack laughs. "You become a Hindu when I wasn't looking?" He sees the anxiety in her eyes. She's actually worried. "No, baby, you didn't do anything wrong." He puts his arm around her. "How about we find you something cause-y and altruistic to do with the money?"

She drops her head against his shoulder and nods.

Morning light peeks saffron through the curtains as Maisy sits on the side of the bed and buttons a white work shirt. Jack's in the ensuite toweling off. "I was thinking about your broken glasses cash," he says. "Did I tell you about Miriam? Eighty-six. Sweet, but not all there. When she gets agitated, she takes off her clothes. Could be the middle of bingo—Next thing you know: *starkers*. Anyway, staff keep asking her son to buy her some anti-strip jumpsuits. Give her a little dignity. The guy's been MIA for months. They cost about seventy bucks each. Whaddya think?"

Jack's phone buzzes. Maisy looks at the nightstand. Call-display says *UCLA Medical*. He pads naked into the bedroom, drying his wet hair. Maisy hands him his phone. He wipes his ear, sits next to her. "Hello . . . Speaking . . . When? Is he . . . Yeah, I'll be there." He ends the call and exhales. "My dad had a stroke."

"Your *dad*?" She puts her hand on his arm. "He's here?"

"They called him *Jonathon* Adams. It's John." He fidgets with the phone. "Last time I talked to him, he was heading to a prison in Pensacola."

"Guess he's out. But, why's he here?"

Jack looks at the floor. "I've done some things, not strictly above-board. But he's . . . The Granny Scam is about as low as you go. And all he did was twenty-two months."

She watches him. His tone is bruised. "Is he asking for you?"

Four years ago in Sarasota: a patio just off The Circle. John Adams Sr. waited at a table for two. Spotting his son, Adams rose to his feet, tanned and dapper in beige chinos and a navy blazer. "Started to think you weren't coming!" He clapped hold of Jack's hand and patted his back.

"Sorry. There was a pileup outside Fort Myers."

They sat. Adams gave him an admiring look. "My son, the legal eagle. Let's get some champagne, make a toast!"

Jack grinned. He'd just passed the bar four months ago. "Not for me. You go ahead."

Adams butchered an '80s tune as he sang: "*You don't drink, don't dope, what do you do?*"

Polite smile. Same old joke.

"Just razzing you, pal." Adams sipped his scotch. "Property law. I was bragging to Armen how my lawyer-son flew all the way to Florida just to see his old man."

"Yeah, well, that and Maisy's grandmother broke her hip. Who's Armen?"

"She in Naples? Some money in *that* town. Grandma single?"

A server interrupted. Jack ordered an iced tea. "You sounded anxious to meet. What's up?"

Adams shrugged. "Just want to see my boy. Not every day you graduate law school." He leaned back, breathed the warm air. "So? How's your love life?"

Jack blinked. "Maisy? She's great. Teaching. She's not loving that but . . ."

"Women . . ." Adams gazed up at the blossom-draped pergola. "Some of these old dears don't part company so well. Hell hath no fury." He dropped his eyes to Jack. "Armen figures it'll blow over. We're not talking huge money, but it's a chunk. And I gotta think of my retirement."

"I'm not following you. Who's Armen?"

"It's complicated." His voice dropped. "I got charges against me. They're looking at Armen too. He thinks we should dump it into cryptocurrency. I don't trust that shit. Truthfully, I don't trust Armen. He's a smart prick but he's a prick." He licked his lips. "Listen Jacky-boy, I need some help. Maybe you could tuck it into a property for me. Or maybe you know a different way—some legal tangle that'll keep it safe. Just till things settle."

Jack's mouth hung. "You and this guy, Armen . . . you cheated old ladies out of their—"

"No." Adams scoffed. "You're as bad as the feds. This is about asset management. But if I end up doing time, I can't manage those assets, can I?"

"Just want to see my boy . . . Christ. I almost believed you." He stood up just as his iced tea arrived. He threw ten bucks on the table.

"Would you sit down?" his father said. "You're just like your mother."

The elevator pings as Jack steps onto the sixth floor of UCLA Medical Center. Staff in scrubs crisscross the floor. As he walks to the neurology wing, his pulse quickens. Why is it always like this, seeing his father? Like hope and anger all mixed-up.

As he passes the nurse's station, twenty yards ahead, he sees a silver-haired man in a navy suit come out of a room. The man pulls on a blue cashmere topcoat as he walks. His eyes look gold against his tan skin and Jack's head fritzes with something like déjà vu.

"Can I help you find someone?" A nurse in flowered scrubs.

Jack pulls his thoughts from the man in blue. "I'm looking for John Adams."

"He's in 6044, two doors down, on the right."

Jack thanks her. Didn't the guy with the coat come out of there? Jack continues down the hall until he gets to 6044. Electronic beeps from various machines sound in his ears. He looks at his father in bed, layers of flannel sheets, nasal cannula up his nose, a pulse oximeter attached to his finger. Waveforms and bright bold numbers flash across the monitor next to the bed. Jack clears his throat and walks into the room.

John Adams Sr. rolls his head toward Jack. One eyelid droops slightly, and his smile pulls to one side. Reaching out, he says, "Do you work here? I got to talk to my son."

What is that, sarcasm? "Hey, Dad." Calling his father *Dad* feels like pulling on a wet sock. "How you doin'? Did you just have a visitor?"

John Adams Sr. blinks at his son. "What'd you say your name was?"

Jack's gaze snags on his father's hospital wristband. Adams with an extra D. *Jonathon Addams.* What kind of game is he playing? "Dad, it's me. It's Jack."

"Good morning, Mr. Addams." A woman in green scrubs comes in and walks up to the foot of the bed. Early forties, blond, a medical mask hangs off her chin. Two young men follow her, begin tapping buttons on the monitor and unlocking the bed's wheels. "This is Andrés and Carlos. They're going to take you downstairs for another scan."

John Adams groans. "Why you gotta do so many tests?"

Jack notices a slur now, a slight garble as if his father's tongue isn't keeping up with his brain. He looks at the woman. "I'm Jack Adams. His son."

"I'm Doctor Ellen Mason. We spoke on the phone." They move aside as the aides roll the bed from the wall and push it through the open doors. "We're still trying to figure out if he's had a stroke. His CT scan didn't show anything. But as you may have noticed, he's confused. Speech is a bit slurred. What can you tell me about his baseline? Does he have a history of dementia?"

Dementia? Jack's seen his old man make like he didn't have two brain cells to rub together. Fake drunk, fake brain damage. Used to have a scam he called The Special Olympics.

"I haven't seen him in a few years. He doesn't keep in touch."

"I see. Well, he's got some weakness on the left. Blood work came back clean, so we've ruled out an infection. It's possible he had a seizure. We'd like to do a lumbar puncture as well to give us a more complete picture. At any rate, he's probably going to need some time in rehab."

Jack looks at the space where his father's bed used to be. "How did you find me?"

"He kept asking for you. He had a piece of paper with your name and the facility where you work. Collingwood Home and Health, is that correct? Are you a medical professional?"

How the hell does the old man know where Jack works? Last time they talked, Jack was still a lawyer. "I'm in recreational therapy."

"He's adamant that he wants to be with his son." The doctor smiles.

Hot fury pushes up from Jack's belly. "My wife and I aren't in a financial position to—"

"Collingwood is on Medicare's list of skilled nursing facilities. We've used them before."

Jack rifles through his mind for a way to shut this down. The doctor continues. "You know how Medicare is, they want them out of the hospital ASAP."

"John Wayne! Correct." Jack does his best impression of The Duke to say, "Another point for the Silver Bullets." He gets a laugh from the thirty-three seniors spread around the open concept lounge.

Some in wheelchairs, some in Naugahyde lounge chairs, all listen keenly.

"Final question," Jack says. "Box of truffles riding on this—just in time for your afternoon coffee." Through the windows, he sees a transport vehicle roll into the circular drive and pull up to the front doors. The back of the van opens. Jack's pulse ramps up.

"Read the question!"

He looks back at the creased faces. "Helen, you are feisty today! Final question: Who won the Nobel Prize in Physics in 1945 for his discovery of cosmic radiation?" Jack checks outside again. His adrenaline pumps as the chairlift descends. It's his father all right. The doctors said they found a small brain bleed. Should heal on its own, but it needs to be monitored.

"Percy Williams Bridgman!" The answer pulls Jack back to the lounge.

"Correct! Good old PWB. You people blind me with your brilliance. Okay, Trivia Blast final score: Thirty-five to forty. The Golden Slammers win the truffles!" Outside, two aides wheel John Adams Sr. toward the front doors. Jack feels a roar in his head as if a storm is coming. "Don't forget, tonight's movie is *Some Like it Hot*."

The trivia players ease themselves out of the lounge and head toward the smell of coffee and cake as the two o'clock snack trolleys cruise in.

From the lobby, a young female aide pushes John Adams's wheelchair. The male aide hauls a hard-shell suitcase. Jack's father hugs a black bag in his lap. Looks like one of those secure document cases Jack used to see around his old law firm. As they pass the lounge, John Adams locks eyes with his son. Jack's guts twist. Has the old man really lost his marbles or is he just hiding them? They head toward the south wing and Jack follows.

Once they have John Sr. ensconced in Room 226, the male aide asks if he can take the bag from his lap. "No thanks." The female aide asks if he'd like to lie down.

"Not now, sweetheart." His eyes drift to the door. "Jack? Look, that's my son, Jack. When'd you get here?" That slur again.

"Aww." The aide smiles. "Jack, your dad's so cute."

"Thanks, Lucinda," Jacks says. "I'll take care of him." Once they're gone, Jack closes the door. His father holds tight to the locked bag in his lap. "You going to break up with that bag at some point?" Jack asks. "I can put it on the shelf."

John Sr. sings, *"Waiting for the break of day . . ."* His fingers tap out a beat on the bag. It's a moment before Jack recognizes the words to a 1970s Chicago song: "25 or 6 to 4". Never understood the lyrics, but it was a favorite of John Adams. For as long as Jack can remember, his father would transform everything into some old song. Always singing, humming, drumming on his leg. As a kid, it made Jack nuts when all he wanted was an answer to a question. Now is no different. He opens the door and leaves his father singing.

Tuesday morning at El Jardin, Maisy sets down breakfast at a table for two. Another conference is in town and it's made for a steady turnover all morning—a relief to have her mind on tourists and toast instead of Jack's father and whether he's demented. It's all Jack can talk about.

Heading back to the kitchen, she stops. A silver-haired man with tan skin is at the hostess stand. Is that the bank guy? No blue coat, he's wearing a three-piece suit. Maisy sees him offer cash to the hostess. The hostess looks around and spots her. Dread roils Maisy's belly. She hurries off to the kitchen.

When she returns, the hostess is alone. No silver-haired man. He probably left; the place is jammed. Maisy's got her hands full with three plates. She sets them down at a table. When she turns around, there he is: The silver haired man is in her section. *Shit!* In the corner by the window, he gazes out at the Santa Monica Pier.

Taking a slow breath, she heads over. "Good morning, sir, will anyone be joining you?"

He lifts his chin. "We meet again." Sunlight makes those eyes glow like a wolf's. "Have you purchased your new glasses, Maisy?"

Her skin shivers at the sound of her name. "Can I start you off with a coffee?"

He smiles. "You are the daughter-in-law of my business associate."

"You know Jack's father? Small world. What can I get you this morning?"

"Jack's father and I have an agreement. Now he seems to have disappeared again. You need to tell me where he is. The situation will end more pleasantly if I don't have to hunt."

Blood rushes into her limbs. Her hands tremble as she grips her pen. "He had a stroke."

"You tell him that Armen is coming and it would be wise to keep his promise."

John Adams Sr. lies atop his made bed. Jack walks in and pulls a chair close. His father turns his head toward him. King of the poker face, it's impossible to know what's going on in that skull.

"Your buddy, Armen, showed up at my wife's work. He's looking for you. Making threats."

"You look good, Jacky-boy. What happened to lawyering? Get disbarred or something?"

"Shut it . . . *Jonathon Addams*. Your chart says you were born in June and you're seventy-eight-years old." No response. "You're seventy-three last I checked. We talking Medicare scam? Or did you screw Armen so bad, you had to hide?"

John Adams smiles. His speech is clear and there's a spark in his eyes, like when he used to show young Jack those quicky bar cons: Betcha I can balance a quarter on the edge of a dollar bill. Betcha I can cut this lime with a cigarette. Jack was barely into the double digits when his father took off for good, but those prop bets stuck with him. That's how he met Maisy. Spotted her across the room at a college bar. Bet her a beer that he could get a dime out from under a glass without ever touching the glass. He came up with an excuse to hold her wrists and then stole her watch. At the end of the night, Jack took one of Maisy's hands, looked in her eyes, and laid the watch across her palm. "You make me want to be a better thief," he said. She laughed. He asked for her number. A year later they were married.

"I wasn't feeling too good," Jack's father says. "Needed some TLC."

"Armen was your partner in Florida. Right?"

John Adams Sr.'s face is quizzical. "You look like my son. What's your name again?"

"What're you up to, you old bastard?" Up out of the chair, Jack looks around the room and then shoves open the sliding door of the closet. Not much there. The cleaning staff left a jug of heavy-duty sanitizer in the corner. Next to it sits his father's suitcase. Couple shirts and a pair of trousers hang off the rail. On the top shelf sits the document bag. Jack reaches for it, glances back, and sees his father's face hardening.

John Adams swings his legs over the side of the bed and sits up. "Get your hands off that." His voice rasps like a metal rake on concrete.

Jack smiles. "Off this?" He grips the handles. Christ, it's heavy.

"Get outa there!" His father snaps. "I mean it, y'little prick."

A knock at the door. John Adams shouts, "Help! Somebody, help me!"

Jack lets go of the bag as Lucinda, the care aide, walks in. "Mr. Addams, what's wrong?"

"That man! He's stealing from me."

Jack throws his hands up. "I don't know what's wrong. He just started screaming."

"You're safe." Lucinda keeps a soothing tone and comes toward the bed. "*I'm* here. Your *son* is here. It's time for your physical therapy appointment."

"That's not my son." Adams Sr. sobs. "Get him outa here. I'm not moving till he's gone."

As Jack backs out, Lucinda turns to him, whispers, *Don't take it personally.* Behind her, John Adams Sr. watches Jack and sniffs.

The next day, Jack is in the Collingwood activity hall when Maisy walks in.

"Hey!" He grins. "What're you doing here?" Chair bowling just ended and the players have cleared out. Plastic balls and pins lay scattered on the floor.

Maisy holds a large envelope. "The anti-strip thingies came. Thought I'd bring 'em by."

"Well, aren't you the cat's PJs." He puts his arms around her.

Maisy kisses him. "To tell the truth, I'm still freaked out about that Armen stuff."

"If Armen was going to pull anything, he wouldn't advertise." Jack sets the envelope on a nearby table, picks up bowling pins, and chucks them into a bin. "This stuff with my dad is making me nuts. I don't really buy the dementia crap, but this morning they caught him following a cleaning guy. Tried to swipe stuff off his cart. I know: Dementia patients steal. One minute he's out of his mind and the next, it's like he's playing us all. But if he's *not* playing us, then why is Armen so hot on his heels? And what's with the phony ID?" Jack looks at Maisy. "Pretty sure Armen's the guy he was running with in Florida. I never actually met him but . . ."

Maisy drops the last few neon balls into the bin. "Maybe he and Armen were into some scheme, then your dad had a stroke and the whole thing got derailed."

Jack picks up the bin, puts it in the storage closet. "Another weird thing, he had a locked document bag when he got here. Now it's gone. I asked Lucinda if they'd moved it. Or if it could be in the lost and found. Nope. But that bag was a big deal—he had a conniption when I touched it. Now he pretends he doesn't know what I'm talking about."

"Pretends?" she says. "Jack, come on. You know how it is with dementia. It's just harder when it's your father. I had a roommate who volunteered at a care home. Staff had to sneak dirty clothes out of their rooms or they'd scream their heads off. They'd hide toothpaste in their socks!" She gives him a long look. "You ever going to introduce me to him?"

He bullfrogs his cheeks and lets the air go. "If you promise not to hold it against me."

Inside Room 226, John Adams Sr. stands outside his bathroom. Singing the old Chicago song, he looks at the closed door, and rubs a penny between his fingers.

A rap at the front door. "Dad?" Jack walks into his father's room. Maisy follows.

John Adams doesn't turn, just keeps singing, "25 or 6 to 4." He peers into the crack between the bathroom door and the jamb molding and slides his penny in.

Maisy gives Jack a face full of *See what I mean?*

Jack sighs. "What's going on, Dad?"

Adams Sr. hums another bar, then says, "It's like those cell doors in the joint. Sometimes the inmates'd do a penny-lock. Do it right and the guard can't even turn the key." Looking over his shoulder, he seems startled. "Who's this?" He lets the penny clatter to the floor.

"Dad, this is my wife, Maisy."

"Jeez." Adams Sr. hobbles over, hand extended. "You're gorgeous. Don't go anywhere."

Maisy laughs and shakes his hand. "It's nice to finally meet you, Mr. Adams."

"Call me Johnny. Call me anything you want!" Eyes glued to her, he says, "Jacky-boy, you did good." After a few seconds he lets go of her hand. "I hear you met my friend, Armen. Character, isn't he? Don't let him scare you, it's just his sense of humor. He's Armenian." John Adams winks. "I gave him a call. It's all good."

Armen runs his amber eyes over the spartan décor of Room 226: Laminate wood dresser, hospital bed, nightstand, and a single straight-back visitor's chair. He sniffs the air. With his large bony nose, he has the look of a curious eagle. "Why does it smell like a swimming pool?"

"Bleach," Adams says. "I was trying to unplug the drain. Got a little gum in there."

Armen nods. "Is there not a maintenance department?"

"Don't like them nosing around. Wanna get a coffee? They got a little bistro here."

"I have not come to socialize." He nods at his satchel. "Give me my share and we never need to speak again."

"Jeez, Armen. I thought we—" Adams sits suddenly on the bed. "Christ, these blood thinners make me dizzy. I had a stroke."

"So you said."

"I'm saying it again. Cuz I need a little help." Adams reaches into his nightstand and takes out a screwdriver. "I hid it all in the air duct." He nods toward the bathroom. "Almost killed myself getting it up there."

"In the ceiling?" Armen sighs testily and accepts the screwdriver. He pushes open the bathroom door. His nose scrunches at the acrid smell of bleach standing in the sink. "You should turn on the exhaust fan." He reaches outside the bathroom and flips a switch. The fan whirs into motion. "Do you have a step ladder?"

"Just the chair there."

Armen blinks at the straight-back chair. He snatches the towel from the seat, and flings it on the bed. He drags the chair into the bathroom and sets it under the grill of the air duct. Setting his own satchel on the bathroom counter, he grunts as he brings a foot onto the seat.

John Adams gets off the bed. From the door, he watches Armen turn the screwdriver. Then he looks to the sink. "That bleach ain't doin' much, is it?"

"I cannot hear you over this fan," Armen says. The first screw falls to the floor.

Adams bends down. From under the sink, he retrieves a plastic jar of SuperSkale and unscrews the lid. "Someone's coming," he shouts. "I'll get rid of them."

As Armen fits the driver head into the next screw, Adams dumps lime scale remover into the sink. Green sludge begins to hiss. He steps out and closes the door.

Outside the bathroom, he fishes pennies from his pocket and begins squeezing short stacks into the crack between the door and the jamb molding. He grabs the towel off the bed and packs it under the door. Then he turns off the exhaust fan.

Inside the bathroom, fumes rise from the sink and fog the air. Armen coughs. "John? Open the door." His eyes burn. Each breath razors his lungs. "John!"

John Adams Sr. walks to the dresser, and hauls open the bottom drawer. Fingering the lock's combination, he opens his black bag, looks in at the stacks of cash, and lets his breath go.

It's going on ten P.M. Jack takes a hard right off San Vicente onto 17th. Maisy throws a palm against the glove box, bracing herself. "For chrissake, Jack."

He slows a little. "I should have gone in."

"It was your day off," Maisy says. "Probably why your father invited him today."

Collingwood had called. According to the nurse it was about two hours ago that all hell broke loose. She went into his father's room to give him his evening meds and found a man dead on the bathroom floor. Called 911. Fire department came. Paramedics. Near as they could tell, the man had tried to clear a drain with lime scale remover and industrial bleach. The combination created a deadly chlorine gas. Most of the liquid had drained by the time the nurse came in. Bedroom window open, exhaust fan on, John Adams Sr. was sound asleep.

Jack grips the steering wheel now. "They should've called me right away."

"You father is fine." Maisy looks at him. "It's awful what happened. But what are you going to accomplish at this time of night?"

He's not listening. He's looking for a spot out front of the care home. He circles the block and comes up a side street. Across from the north side of the facility, he pulls into the curb, turns off the ignition. "I think he killed him. My freaking father killed Armen."

"Jack. Stop. Just take a breath."

He looks at her. "No offense, but you don't know anything. I got to get in there."

"You *don't*. Can you listen to me for a second?" Maisy keeps her voice even. "Your dad is sleeping. They moved him to a nice clean room."

Jacks looks toward the traffic on 17th Street. A box truck rattles past. A yellow taxi pulls into the curb at the corner. "I screwed up. I got to talk to him."

She lays her hand on his leg. "He probably doesn't even understand what happened.

Jack looks at the care home. A side door opens. He watches a figure move from the door to the sidewalk, juggling a document bag and a hard-shell suitcase. Hobbling up to 17th, Adams Sr. makes for the yellow taxi.

Jack stares. "You gotta be kidding me." He gets out of the car. "Dad!" When the old man keeps going, Jack sprints after him.

Adams Sr. opens the rear door of the taxi. He glances back and, for a moment, Jack thinks his father might wait. Instead he hefts his bags into the back, climbs in after them, and slams the door just as Jack reaches the corner. John Adams Sr. gives him a two-fingered salute and the taxi rolls out into traffic.

Jack bellows and waves at the disappearing taxi. Eventually his arms drop in defeat. He looks back and sees Maisy in the road. He takes a last look into traffic and then trudges back.

As he reaches Maisy, she says, "God, Jack . . . I'm so sorry."

He shakes his head slowly. "The hell did I do?"

She touches his hair. "You didn't do anything. Your father's a—"

"You don't get it." He reaches into the car, and flips the trunk release. Maisy follows him to the trunk. He lifts the lid and shows her his own document bag. "He hid it in the air duct."

She gawps as Jack fingers the combination and opens the bag.

"I just—It was a game. I swapped the cash for play money, put a real bill on the top of each stack. I was going to tell him. I just wanted to know what the hell was going on. Figured we'd finally have it out. Then Armen showed up."

She stares down at the bundles of cash. "You said his bag was locked. How did you—"

"The song he kept singing, '25 or 6 to 4.' That's the combination. He had some scam going in Florida. I don't know if this is the same money. Obviously Armen was looking for it."

"Can you call your father and—"

"Call him where?" He sits on the trunk. "Nearly five hundred grand. Part of me thinks I should turn it over to the cops. A bigger part thinks: That asshole never paid a dime in child support. Never helped out when my mother died. He—" Jack's mouth shuts because suddenly all he can hear is his old man's old heckle: A guy who's good at excuses isn't good for much else. Jack looks at the pavement. All that hunger and hustle—Maybe John Adams is in his DNA and that's just how it is. Wherever you go, there you are.

"I'm keeping it," he says. "It's mine." Under the pale light of the streetlamp, the words feel dark. He lifts his eyes to Maisy. "Is that bad? Am I bad?"

Maisy meets his gaze. A bolt of adrenaline rushes through her veins the way it did that day outside the bank. She sits next to Jack and takes his hand. "No, baby. You're not bad."

---

*My father, Billy, was a card sharp and a con artist. He wasn't around for much of my childhood, so I wasn't so much raised by him as haunted by him. From what I know, he generally worked with a partner and he liked relatively quick grifts that could instill enough confidence to make his marks hand over hundreds, even thousands of dollars—cons with names like "Old Farmer" and "The Granny Game."

My mother never took part. After they split up, when she talked about him and the things he'd done, her tone was one of disgust but, clearly, she was fascinated. She told me that when she was pregnant, he said, "If it's a boy, I'll teach him how to steal." Alas, I was a girl. They called me Billie, after him, and that's as far as it went. But what would have become of me if I'd been a boy? This story is a "What If?" Who does a boy with the skills of his father and the conscience of his mother grow up to be?

Kai Lovelace *is a writer and musician born and raised in New York City. His stories have appeared in* Ellery Queen Mystery Magazine, *Murderous Ink Press's* Crimeucopia *anthology series, and* The First Line *literary journal. He was nominated for the Robert L. Fish Memorial Award as part of the 2025 Edgars. His past adventures include spending time as a corporate flunky, a bartender, a bowling alley manager, a film producer, a jazz pianist, and a bookseller. Now he writes.*

ONLY A STORY
Kai Lovelace

Striker hitchhiked the last seventy miles to Galveston and had to listen to a born-again Christian in a blue hatchback prattle on about Jesus Christ until he'd had enough and told him to go to hell.

"Out of the car, Mister," the driver's voice quavered as he pulled over. "Nobody talks to me like that."

Striker thought about the .38 wedged into his waistband and the 30,000 in the duffel bag between his legs, calculating the risk of making any moves a hundred yards from the quaint rest stop and gas station shimmering down the road like a toy set.

He pulled out the .38 and set it on the dashboard. The driver started to shake.

"Please, sir. I've got a family."

Striker smiled. "Yeah," he said. "So do I. We're all one big happy family."

He picked up the revolver and aimed it idly toward the driver's seat. The man whimpered. No winks of sunlight signaled approaching cars in the rearview mirror.

"You ought to be happy," Striker said. "This way you'll get to heaven a whole hell of a lot faster."

Henry lowered the paperback when sweeping headlights disturbed the stillness of the lobby. A troupe of shadows rippled across the stucco siding, gray columns drifting between bands of golden light growing larger until they dissipated. An engine groaned like a giant turning over in its sleep. He waited; if it died down the vehicle was heading south on Alston Road and would bypass the motel.

The bands of light merged and brightened. The motor got louder and slowed, underscored by the smooth crunch of tires on gravel.

Henry inserted his tattered bookmark and set the book down. A brilliant flash of orange-yellow bathed the lobby before the vehicle angled away and slowed to a stop. He waited for the engine to cut but it kept on growling, headlights cutting into the scraggly woods past the parking lot. Through the glass doors the back half of a long, boxy, squared-off sedan idled, rocketship wings flaring off the rear corners. Nobody made a move to get out and Henry inclined his head for a better look. The left tail light was cracked and the fender badly dented.

It was going on 1:30 A.M. Before the dark blue Lincoln Continental showed up it was another boring night, seconds oozing by like drops from a leaky faucet.

Henry liked the graveyard shift because it gave him time to get ahead on homework and read his crime stories, but sometimes the boredom was murder.

It wasn't that people never showed up in the middle of the night. They were just too exhausted for chitchat, complaints, or questions. Cash for the room key and a scribble in the logbook. Traveling salesmen dead on their feet, road tripping couples hauling comatose children who'd gotten lost or bit off more than they could chew on a day's run.

Occasionally someone with a different look in their eye would arrive who Henry would have to think about. No luggage or companions. Quiet, self-contained, furtive. Secret agents lying low, hitmen tracking unwitting targets; even G-men and assassins needed sack time.

A couple years ago in junior high comics like *Crime Doesn't Pay* and *The Long Arm of the Law* were his favorites. He'd pick them up at the drugstore on Wilmot Street downtown by the train station. Then he discovered *Tales of Suspense* and *Corruption of the Innocent*—racier, edgier, more convincing.

When he was younger he idolized the heroic lantern-jawed policemen stolidly pursuing their prey. Compared to the upstanding officers, the degenerates who shot a prison guard while escaping a chain gang or kidnapped the mayor's wife and dragged her on a cross-country spree appeared subhuman. Ugly, pinched faces, squat or spindly physiques, each disfigurement a stamp of their fate.

Around his twelfth birthday a creeping suspicion became undeniable, starting as a passing notion quickly dismissed but growing stronger every day like a moldy odor.

Fearless, noble cops versus sleazy scum-of-the-Earth became as stale and thin as the educational Saturday morning cartoons he'd outgrown around the time he spat out his last baby tooth. It wasn't just the repetition or the pat endings where the convicts, feral with self-destructive greed, met justice. It was the *lessons*, like Mrs. Florsheim's sermons against the evils of drugs, alcohol, premarital sex, and race music.

Henry paid attention and remembered things. Officers lurking by the squad car on his way to school, chewing tobacco and hawking viscous brown strands. A wolf whistle at the library assistant, the strained smile stabbing a pang of heat into Henry's chest, reminding him of schoolyard bullies patrolling for lunch-money shakedowns. Bright scarlet flecks under the summer sun tarmac when they'd stomped a vagrant outside the bowling alley, ducking his mother's fingers trying to shield his eyes. They never showed that in *Tales of Daring Crime Fighters*.

He also knew Officer Tim, hero to every child and housewife in the neighborhood. He found that missing girl in the brambles by the golf course over in Stratford that one time, dirt-streaked and frightened but alive, heard the story a hundred times. Why did his mother call him "roguish"? Henry thought the Roman nose and receding hairline made him look gawky, but he accepted the fact that he was a good guy, upstanding. But heroic? Not exactly.

Then last year he'd borrowed a battered paperback of *The Postman Always Rings Twice* from the library and dumped his heap of hero cop comics into the waste bin. *The Secret Agent* and *Red Harvest* lead him to Walter Delaney's *Striker* series, wherein the taciturn antihero escapes prison and embarks on a cross-country odyssey centered around revenge and financial gain.

He had new heroes now. Down-on-their-luck drifters, desperate gamblers, icy killers, weary private eyes, slicing through life like rusty blades because the straight and narrow was a fool's dream.

His mother worried.

He'd said the words many times: "It's only a story, Mom."

Always that skeptical face as she angled her head away and exhaled smoke sideways from a puffed up cheek, plumes dissolving under the hanging kitchen bulb's anemic glow. "These things really happen, Henry."

How could he explain the difference between loving villains and being one? The biggest jerks in his school idolized TV lawmen and treated their classmates like Jack Palance in *Shane*. Henry got straight Bs and had never been in a fight, even when the bigger guys harassed him with questions when he had nothing for the Father's Day presentations. The next year he just skipped it. Going the extra mile for As would have cut into his reading time.

The latest *Striker* book had come out two days before, and the title—*Three Strikes and Out*—made Henry nervous. Surely this couldn't be the end of the road for that raw-boned bastard; he needed peace and quiet so he could find out.

That's why he liked working the graveyard shift at his uncle's motel.

The phone wouldn't answer itself, nor would the ashtrays tap themselves out. Someone had to be in charge of these responsibilities.

The Cozy Road Motor Inn was a long single-story complex with the office at the far end, tucked in a weedy lot far enough off Interstate 684 to be easily missed between the clustered maples and oaks lining the exit to a lonely stretch along the border between New York and Connecticut. The drab beige stucco was lined with a slash of mint green along the base. The roof extended over the pathway to the rooms, dark green paint chipped on the doors, brass numbers reflecting gold winks from the arc sodium lights at the gravel intersection off the highway. Of the eight units about half were typically occupied on a good night.

Between midnight and 6 A.M. the lobby was quieter than the downtown library or the Chester Arthur High cafeteria. Tidy the seating area, sweep and dust. It was seven extra hours for reading and homework.

Sometimes he'd have to switch peoples' rooms if these new Magic Fingers beds stopped working, haul luggage, or dust off the road atlas under the front desk and help with directions. Anything more complex got passed off to the errant handyman Chuck, limping around half-drunk ever since he got back from Korea, or better yet, jotted on the clipboard and shunted to the next day.

His uncle gave him the night shift twice a week. It was an easy job. If he could barely keep his eyes open the next day in school he'd catch up later. Most nights he passed absorbing a lurid paperback, sometimes cover to cover without interruption. His uncle dismissed them with a sneering wave as trash and Henry didn't mention the Tijuana bibles in the back office filing cabinet, wanting to keep the shift.

Usually nothing much happened, which suited Henry fine. But some nights the boredom got to him no matter how good the book was. A barrage of floor lamps lit the maroon carpets, mismatched armchairs, and wooden rack of outdated travel pamphlets. A canopy of maples swayed outside the bay window overlooking the quarry beyond the parking lot.

Was this really it? There had to be more to life than waiting out the clock in the dingy lobby of Uncle Ansel's pride and joy.

A middle-aged couple had checked into Room Six and had not emerged since. Another younger guy had lounged by the coffee table, leafing through an issue of *Life* for about an hour before someone came to pick him up.

Since then the phone hadn't even rung. It was too late in the season for crickets and the stark silence thrummed a phantom tone. Henry turned the portable radio next to him on low to a local station that was normally off the air from midnight to 6 A.M. but had recently started piggybacking off an overnight DJ in New Haven—a godsend. The dials and speaker on the compact turquoise box formed a surprised face and a driving brassy voice crackled from the wide mouth: Billy was begging Stagger Lee not to take his life.

He tugged at a loose thread on the sleeve of his frayed brown corduroy shirt, worn at the elbows and thick with a musk of mothballs and his mother's cigarette smoke, humming tunelessly along to the music. When his uncle was around it was usually a baseball game, maybe some Mantovani or Andy Williams. No chance staying awake all night to that crap.

Striker ditched the Bible thumper's sedan in the bus station parking lot.

Henry was forcing himself to pay attention to the words when the visitor arrived. Just sitting out there on the muddy patch of gravel damp from last night's rain, engine humming, going on five minutes now.

The boy was sliding off his stool—maybe the driver was elderly and needed assistance, he realized belatedly—when the engine cut and the entrance dimmed, lit only by the highway light at the turnoff and the buzzing sign's crimson aura. A door clicked open and a tall, slim shadow shuffled across the tarmac to the trunk of the car. The lid slammed and the figure approached the doors, dusty denim gaining definition as he neared, toting something on his shoulder which threw off his stride.

The doors swung open. A pair of wild eyes darted from a gaunt, haggard, coldly handsome face. His lips were parted and his teeth clenched. He stood surveying the lobby as if expecting a wild animal to jump out any moment. Then a miraculous change came over the visitor, serenity descending from the top of his dirty blonde head down to his soles as his whole body relaxed and his face settled into a pacified smirk, lids lowered over the large hazel eyes.

His scuffed denim jacket was a few shades lighter than his jeans and the top few buttons of a faded Hawaiian shirt were undone, wisps of curly hair matted on his tanned chest. He locked eyes with Henry and crossed the room without breaking contact, not quite limping but favoring his right leg as he approached the front desk and slid the duffel off his shoulder.

"Welcome to the Cozy Road Motor Inn," Henry muttered. They were the first words Henry had spoken in several hours and his voice cracked.

The guy leaned his elbows on the edge of the desk and exhaled deeply like he'd been walking for days.

"Hey, bud." The man's voice was a clear note from a bass guitar. Sweat beaded on his creased forehead as he inspected the boy. "You're a little old to be doing this kinda work, aren't you?"

Henry blinked at him. "I'm fourteen," he said. The guy looked him over for a moment, a skinny kid cutting an absurd figure all alone in the dead of night but carrying defiance in the set of his shoulders. The broad forehead was speckled lightly with acne but his lips were set in a surly twist, curled like a sideways bracket with a slight overbite revealing slivers of two front teeth. The ungainly adolescence ended at the eyes, reserved and cool with the stoicism and suspicion of a young man.

"Oh yeah?" said the visitor. "You look like you're barely out of diapers."

"I'm fourteen," Henry repeated.

"So you're fourteen," the man answered. "I'm forty. Good for us. Who else you got working tonight?"

"It's just me."

"Bullshit," he said, a hint of his former tension coiling tight. "You can't run this place on your own."

Henry opened his mouth to protest, then caught himself and pulled it back, lacing his fingers. "I'm in charge until six A.M.," he said calmly.

The sandy head bobbed backward and the thin lips quirked down, impressed under a layer of offhanded irony. "Head honcho, huh?"

"That's right. You want a room?"

The man winced, rolling his left shoulder and throwing shifty glances around the lobby. "Busy night? I saw a couple more cars out there."

"Not too busy."

"Lotta action since you came on?"

Henry hesitated. "What do you mean?"

"Forget it. Listen, bud. You got a first aid kit?"

"Uh, yeah. In the back."

"Grab it."

"Was there an accident?"

The visitor shook his head. "I had a little scrape a while ago and need to rest."

Henry leaned forward. Something dark stained the bottom of the man's pant leg and his colorless face was slick with sweat.

"You're hurt?" Henry asked. "There's a hospital a few miles over in Kitchawan."

Flash of nicotine-stained teeth. "I don't need a hospital, kid. I asked you for a first aid kit."

"You sure you're okay, mister? I can call you an ambulance—"

A white-knuckled fist slammed against the countertop and rattled the pens in the mug by Henry's elbow.

"Don't need a fucking ambulance either. Get the goddamn kit."

Henry eased off the stool and pushed through the swinging doors into the back office, glancing back to see the man's hand resting in the pocket of his denim jacket.

The room was cluttered with filing cabinets, folding chairs stacked against a mini-fridge, and a standing coat rack draped with unclaimed lost-and-found items. Henry rummaged through a cupboard until he found the dusty green tin box and brought it back to the front desk. The visitor laid his hand on it reverently.

"Thanks," he said. "Sorry about that. I've had a hell of a day."

Henry nodded. "So have I."

That got a raspy chuckle. "I bet you have. You even allowed to do this?"

"I can do anything my uncle can. I calculate the books at the end of the night."

The man tapped the lid of the first aid kit with a fingernail. "Well, look out," he said, "kid's going places," squinted eyes roving across Henry's workspace and lingering on the paperback, chewing on his lower lip as if solving a math problem in his head.

After a minute Henry slid the logbook over, cleared his throat and asked, "Do you need a room?"

The visitor's gaze snapped up. "Yeah. Hey, that one of those Striker books?"

Reaching under the desk alcove for the cash register key, Henry stopped. "You know them?"

"Read every single one. Delaney's a genius."

A grin lit up the boy's face. "He's the best. Striker's my favorite character of all time."

"Which one you like best?"

Henry gestured indecisively. "Oh man, that's tough. *Striker's Score*, probably. No, actually it's *Lucky Strike*."

"With the riverboat casino."

"Yeah!"

"Ever read *Black Mask* or's that before your time?"

An enthusiastic nod. "I got a pile of them cheap from the pharmacy. My mom wants to throw them out but I told her I'd skip school if she did."

"Smart man."

"What about Hammett? And Chandler?"

"Sure. You know a good one? *The Stranger*. Camus wrote it after reading James M. Cain."

Henry's expression clouded and he grabbed a notepad to jot it down. "I'll get it from the library," he said. "But man, Striker is tougher than all of them. He could probably take Philip Marlowe in a fight."

"Tough call. But you want my advice, stay away from Delaney's stand-alones. The covers make 'em look like crime stories but they're domestic melodramas." The shaggy locks dipped and he snored loudly.

Henry laughed. "Sounds boring."

"You said it. Probably as boring as this job."

"Oh no," Henry said, more animated than he'd been all night. "Nothing could *ever* be as boring as this."

"I know how that goes. Waiting for something to happen. What's your name, pal?"

"Henry Haldane."

The man pursed his lips. "Good name. Would look good on a cover. You should write some of these yourself, you're such an expert."

The boy shook his head and his face felt hot, but he couldn't help smiling. He spun the logbook around with a flourish so it was facing the man. "I'll get you number eight down on the end so you can have a queen-size bed, just sign here, Mister, uh—"

The man drew squiggles in the air over the line for a moment before the pen started scratching. "Name's Frank."

Henry looked down. *F. Jones* was scribbled messily in the log line. He dug underneath the desk and came up with a small silver key attached to a plastic oval with an 8 on it.

"Here you go, Mr. Jones."

"Frank, please."

"Okay. Thanks for staying at The Cozy Road, Frank."

"Trust me, you saved my ass." Frank pocketed the room key and stuck the first aid kit under his arm. He hefted the duffel and was turning to go when he cringed sharply and staggered, dropping the bag and sucking air through his teeth.

Henry leapt up from his stool and started around the partition but Frank raised his hand.

"I'm all right." He recovered and took another deep breath. "I'm thinking, Hank. Anyone ever call you Hank?"

After a moment Henry murmured, "Sometimes."

A smirk quivered on Frank's lips. "Henry it is then," he said. "Listen, seeing as how you're the boss tonight, I'm gonna level with you." He toed the duffel. "See this bag? It's gonna change my life."

Henry stretched over to take a look. "What's in it?"

"Don't worry about what's in it. All you gotta know is, it's mine. I got it . . . *won* it fair and square. I laid everything down on the line and it paid off big-time. Understand?"

The boy's brow furrowed and he nodded tentatively.

"Good. You're smart. See, bud, not everyone understands something like that. You know about sore losers, right? On the playground, or the dugout?"

"I don't play a lot of sports."

Frank stared at him for a moment, gray eyes unblinking.

"Yeah," Henry sputtered. "I know about them. Bullies."

The smile returned and lit some life into the craggy face. "Exactly right. Well my point is you got them out there in the grownup world too. And it just so happens some real nasty folks weren't too happy with me the other night. Wanted to take what's rightfully mine. Get me?"

"I think so."

"So I've been laying low til the heat dies down." Frank shifted his weight, crossed his arms, and leaned over on the desk. His voice dropped into a quiet, rumbling purr. "Don't worry, I got away from the pricks. I'm on the home stretch now. But I'm tired as hell. I gotta rest and patch up. Get some shut-eye."

Henry eyed the man up and down and the hairs on the back of his neck tingled. Flecks of brown dotted the right arm of Frank's denim jacket. Besides the stained and frayed cuff of his jeans, streaks of dust and grime mixed with foul sweat dampened the material of his tattered Hawaiian shirt.

"It's not polite to stare, Henry."

The boy started fiddling with the logbook.

"What are you smiling at?" A sharp edge to his words, deliberately paced.

"Nothing, sir. Frank. I was just gonna say there's a couple extra parking spaces out back if you take the dirt path by the trees down at the other end."

"What's wrong with the spaces out there?" Frank jerked a thumb toward the front doors.

Henry shrugged. "You can't see the ones out back from the road."

Frank considered the boy behind the front desk and cocked his head. "Is that right? You know, I might feel more comfortable with a little . . ." He twirled his hand in the air searching for the word.

"Discretion?"

Frank's smirk widened. "Discretion." He chewed his lip, glanced down at the cover of the paperback, an illustration of a scowling, muscular, rough-hewn man tearing across the desert behind the wheel of a black Cadillac with dollar bills blowing in the wind. "I'll do that, Henry. Thank you." He crooked a finger and beckoned the kid closer. "One more thing, bud. Since you're real smart and all, I got a favor to ask."

Henry's face became serious.

"I don't want to make trouble," Frank said, "but on the off chance someone comes by asking for me, or about someone might fit my description? Well, I'd appreciate it you kept—" Frank mimed zipping his mouth shut.

The boy's jaw set and he nodded vigorously.

"Thanks kid. Like I said, I left those friends of mine way back in the dust. But they're wily. You can't trust anybody in this world, you know that? Not your teachers, your parents, or your friends. Not even the police. Especially not them."

Striker knew the flat empty eyes of a cop; he'd seen the same grim look on lifers in the prison yard.

Henry nodded again slower, enrapt.

"Not everybody who pulls a dime-store badge is who they say they are," Frank said. "You got no idea what people are capable of."

"I have some idea," Henry said.

Frank snorted and rapped his knuckles on the desk. "I bet you do. You and me are alike. Not asleep like most of them dinks out there." For a moment the man's face clouded and went nauseously slack. Then it cleared and he gave a tired smile. "Do me a favor, you see anything looks suspicious, you let me know, understand?" A sinewy hand dug in the pocket of his jeans and he slid his palm across the desk.

Henry hid his excitement. "I won't let you down."

"You're my eyes and ears." Frank lifted his hand, revealing a brand new fifty dollar bill. "This is for you, bud. I'll settle up for the room in the morning, all right?"

"Sure thing."

"Thanks, kid." Frank sagged and squeezed his eyes shut, shoulders tensing. He rubbed his face and heaved a deep breath. "I gotta hit it."

"Want me to carry your bag?" Henry asked.

"I'll manage, but thanks," Frank said, rallying. "You're a good kid."

Only after Frank had pulled the sedan around and disappeared behind the main building was Henry aware of the syrupy country ballad seeping from the radio. He clicked the dial off and sat in silence. His heart raced and deep down a pit of fear gnawed his stomach, mingling with the exhilaration that he'd gotten away with something, but he couldn't say exactly what. Gravel crunched and floorboards creaked distantly as Frank ducked into Room Eight, a lanky shadow with a jerky stride passing through the night.

After a few minutes Henry opened the book again but quit after three sentences. The pit in his stomach was crawling up his throat. Something hazy in his mind was coming into focus. In a daze he dropped the folding card onto the counter—*We've Stepped Away From The Desk, Be Right Back!*—and flicked on the light in the back room.

Under the coat rack was a pile of newspapers wrapped in twine. Henry sawed through the string with his house key and unfolded the first paper, dated the day before. He leafed through the front pages, scanning headlines. Unrest in Birmingham after the Bethel Church bombing last summer, marches, riots, scary stuff that seemed to come from another planet. He skipped sports and the cartoons, moving with a graceful indolence as if underwater or taking care not to damage the flimsy paper. When he got through the first one he laid it down and took another, dated two days ago. The itch in his brain was almost unbearable even if he couldn't believe or accept what he was really checking for, keeping an ear out for any activity in the lobby. He didn't usually read newspapers but they helped pass the time and Uncle Ansel had a habit of letting them accumulate creased and coffee-stained in the back room until Henry started tying them up for the garbage. Nothing in the second paper either. Or the third. Doubt crept in—he was just tired and letting his imagination run away. One more paper, crinkled and checked cover to cover. Nothing. Give it up, he thought, you're being stupid. The itch was subsiding, replaced with flooding embarrassment. Dumb kid thinks he's in a movie, sitting in the back room under humming fluorescents next to a pile of old newspapers. Get back to the desk. Show's over.

On the second to last page of the seventh newspaper he found it.

A small item, four or five inches in a single column under a grainy black and white photo of several men in dark suits and hats standing outside a bland brick building. Another man in a police uniform crouched and pointed to something on the ground out of frame.

"Police Track Robber of Hillsborough County Bank by Sheila Kenton."

Feverishly his eyes pored over the story and the words swam together.

"... *FBI, state, and local police are close on the trail of a man who escaped with $28,000 from the Parkville Branch of the Hillsborough County Bank* ..."

"... *shouting, 'I want the money now, up against the wall,' according to Head Teller Martina Harris* ..."

"... *wearing a black ski mask with slits over the eyes but described as a tall, lanky man with a slight limp* ..."

"... *fired three shots, injuring veteran security guard Lloyd Calhoun before making his escape in a stolen 1953 Chevy Impala, later found abandoned several miles to the east* ..."

Henry's hands were shaking as he carefully tore out the article and folded it into his pocket, crouched in the stuffy office. He retied the messy pile of newspapers, swallowed the lump in his throat, and wiped sweaty palms on his jeans, then stood slowly and braced himself against the wall as his vision dimmed into a gray churning void of TV static. Only his shallow breathing kept him tethered to reality. After what seemed a long time it cleared. He shut the lights off and returned to the front desk.

It was impossible. Or was it? Hillsborough County was in New Hampshire. Wouldn't he have made it farther south in over a week? Maybe it wasn't a straight shot, he'd had to make stops, rethink his route. Maybe—

No, there's no way. Nothing so exciting could ever happen out here, least of all to him. He smoothed the fifty dollar bill on the countertop. Crisp, clean, new, like you'd get from a bank. Henry's chest swelled and he giggled, smacked his hand on the desk and shook his head in wonderment. It was a hell of a story either way. He couldn't wait to tell his friends the next day in school. Couldn't wait to tell Mom.

His cheeks flushed with a torrent of guilt. She'd be furious. She'd ask him why he didn't call the police if he was so sure. Because he *wasn't* sure, that's what he'd tell her.

But he was.

The giddy weightless feeling hit him all over again. He spread the article on the desk and reread it. It was like the time he'd seen Lee Marvin in Midtown when his mom had taken him into Manhattan. But more than that, as if Lee had come up to him, singled him out, and asked him to keep a secret, help him out, making them buddies.

A protesting voice deep down spat a fragment of the article back at him: fired three shots, injuring veteran security guard . . .

Did real pros fire their guns? Didn't they keep things under control?

Henry shook his head to clear the confused thoughts. Alan Ladd shot the cop in *This Gun For Hire*. He was the bad guy and Henry loved him. But that was just a movie, this was real life. Veteran meant old. Would the guard live? He couldn't start calling around in the middle of the night to check.

He shivered with another surge of excitement, wishing there was someone who'd understand that he could call and tell right now. Then the roller coaster stomach-drop again: was he protecting a real criminal? A killer? Was the stolen fifty a piece of evidence? He was breathing quickly, fidgeting, staring at the bill, chewing and licking his lip, when a wave of exhaustion pressed down on him. His eyelids were heavy. He looked at the clock on the wall by the rack of travel guides.

2:15 A.M. Almost four hours to go.

Adrenaline was retreating from his muscles and he felt limp as a ragdoll. He blinked and his eyes stayed shut, his head lolled, then snapped back up. Stretching his arms up until his shoulders cracked, he yawned massively. Make some coffee, he thought, it's the only way you'll get through it. All these late nights catching up.

He'd make coffee right after he rested his eyes. Just two minutes. Two minutes until he had to get up for school because he was still in a dream, *wow* what a dream—that he'd been on the night shift at the motel and a real life bank robber came in, spoke to him. The lobby of the hotel swam, contracted, oozed like a lava lamp; cycling in a psychedelic police siren of orange, red, green, and purple.

The stool behind the desk was a leather driver's seat, reclining as the desert landscape sped by him. The Bible-thumper was dead, and that was good.

Wasn't it? Or was he really dead, a real person murdered? Had *he* done it? Terror squeezed him in a vice grip: his mother would never speak to him again. He'd go to prison. What had he done? Think, think, as the little gas station grows on the arid horizon. He could remember if he just concentrated, and yes, here it came. Black and white and grainy, running with words like a newspaper headline, like the old James Cagney movies but no, it was more recent than that, color film like *Rear Window*, here it played out again in front of the judge and the jury, exactly what he'd done.

In an instant, the peace of a Tuesday morning is shattered like a plummeting chandelier. Shouts echo off the marble pillars and glass partition where Martina at counter 3 sees it happening in slow motion before it happens, always the way she thought it would, when the man is just a blooming, quivering silhouette refracted through pebbled glass. Moving too fast, jerky but purposeful. No, it can't be. She's seen too many bad TV shows. It can't be, but it is. They have to base those shows off something. She's nowhere near the alarm button in the vault room when he bursts in and starts yelling.

The man is tall and lanky and moves with a wild grace as he fires a shot into the air, the short hot pop of a firecracker paralyzing the room. Screams, everybody down now, nobody move or you're dead. Pacing and sweeping a short-barreled pistol across the meager, huddled crowd, bright angry eyes burning holes in the black cotton mask as his head darts, cataloging his surroundings like a speed-reader while the barrel holds steady.

"Where's the old man?"

Martina is nowhere near the alarm in the vault room. Her feet are bolted to the carpeting and her knees are shaking, adrenaline thrumming through her slight frame. The two other tellers on duty are frozen stock-still, shooting-gallery ducks lined in a row behind their windows. Where the hell is Lloyd? Usually propped half-asleep by the restrooms from opening to close, rooted to the same spot for twenty-four years it seems but now when they need him vanished into thin air, daydreaming about retirement, close enough for him now to taste. Or maybe not.

"Where is he?" Striker screams as the beige-uniformed wisp of a man, sixty-two come August, elbows his way out of the men's room, adjusting his thick frames and gawping at the intruder while his liver-spotted hand slaps at his side holster. *"I want the money now, up against the wall!"*

No, Martina thinks. This isn't what we're trained to do. Stay in the bathroom, you old fool. Don't go for it.

Lloyd goes for it. The short barrel swings smoothly and discharges. After that it's easier.

Mountains, phone lines, brown smudges of clouds wisp across the moon through the cell's tiny window. Silence and cold like the loneliness of a rotting pine box clogged with earth. Rusty hinges squeal as the lawman marches in, a shadowy face and billowing jacket as he raises the double-barreled shotgun and fires. The explosion of light and sound is a shrill clang that freezes Henry's blood, worse than any gunshot or tearing of flesh and fabric.

Another high searing note like a bell, tolling for him and it won't stop, it rings again and—

Henry mumbled incoherently as he jerked up from the desk. His forearms tingled with pins and needles, damp from the tiny puddle of drool.

"Oh I'm sorry, did I wake you?"

The man at the counter silenced the reverberating service bell with a fingertip. He stood very still, broad-shouldered and stocky with two deep lines running across his small forehead, beady eyes and a wide thin-lipped scowl incongruous on the squared-off face. His curly hair was coiffed up with pomade and he carried the stench of cigar smoke, rough sun-baked copper skin like sausage casing. The slate gray suit jacket was tight-fitting and bulged at the hip, top button undone on the wrinkled white shirt and the thin brown tie with beige stripes tugged loose.

Henry blinked around blearily and checked the clock: 4:42 A.M. His mouth hung open. Asleep for over two hours.

The man with the slick hair frowned. "No child labor laws out here in the sticks, huh? No wonder you were asleep on the job. What's your name, son?"

Henry wiped his mouth and composed himself, looking the new arrival up and down and folding his arms. "Can I help you?"

The man stared at him for a moment. "Uh huh, nice to meet you too. My name's Daryl Geddes, I'm a Deputy US Marshal." He waited a beat but got no reaction. "You know what that is?" His delivery was a quiet, evenly staccato monotone.

A shrug and a nod from the blankfaced kid behind the desk, playing it cool.

Geddes's thick eyebrows twitched. "Okay then." He glanced around the lobby and yawned, fillings in his back molars nestled like burnt kernels of popcorn, then smacked his hand on the desk and shook his head. "This job," he sighed, "the hours are a bitch. You probably know what that's like."

The silence between them grew until Henry cleared his throat and said softly, "Where's your badge?"

Geddes exhaled impatiently, lifting the front of his blazer to reveal tarnished gray metal, a squat shield with an eagle perched on top clipped to his belt. "Satisfied? I'll get to the point," he said dryly, "because I can see you're a busy man. Manager around?"

Henry shook his head.

"Handyman?"

"No, it's just me tonight."

The marshal grunted and appraised the boy with a new grudging sympathy. "That so? Well okay then, tell me. You had any customers come in tonight, tall, rangy, sandy hair? Driving a blue Lincoln?"

Henry's chest flared with heat. "No, nobody like that." Geddes stared flatly and waited for more. "A couple older folks checked into number six earlier," the boy continued, "that's it." His voice wavered slightly and he clenched his teeth.

Geddes watched him. "No one else at all, huh? Nothing unusual?"

"No."

"You seem pretty sure."

"I am sure."

The marshal squinted off toward the window where the dark willow branches swayed. "Damn. Thought I was close this time.

What about yesterday? Anyone stay even just for a few hours, or stop by and decide to move on instead? You hear about anything?"

"I said no," Henry snapped.

Geddes looked back at the boy deadly slow and his brow furrowed. "You know why I'm out here at this hour? A bank up in New Hampshire got robbed last week. The perpetrator killed a guard and stole a woman's car two days ago after another dustup in Massachusetts."

Henry's mouth hung open and a glazed look came to his eyes. "The guard died?"

"You saw it in the paper?"

"No. I mean, yeah I did, but . . ."

The scowl deepened as the square-faced man studied the boy. "We've been trailing him east, state and federals all over the county. Thought I'd spotted his car earlier tonight but I lost him. You better believe I'd rather be home in bed but I can see you're a working man too, you understand. I can't sleep when I'm this close, my nerves are a little frayed and for that I apologize. But I'm eager to bring this matter to a conclusion and any help you might provide would be . . . appreciated."

Henry looked down and tried to do something more natural with his hands than tugging nervously on his fingers, a childhood habit that reappeared in times of stress.

Geddes surveyed the desk, the crime novel, the article. He reached and turned the scrap of paper around with a hairy knuckle. Little spasms played across his frown.

"If it comes out that you saw something," he said slowly, "that you know anything, you're going to be in a lot of trouble, you understand? This whole place," he gestured around with his chin, "we'll shut it down. For letting a damn twelve-year-old work the desk. For a hundred other violations too I'm sure, judging from the look of this dump."

Henry's heart was pounding and his back ached. "I'm fourteen. The guy you're looking for isn't here. He never was. Now get out."

The man straightened and tugged on his lapels, adjusting his jacket before he brushed the tails aside and stuck his hands in his pockets. "Well I'm sure you won't mind if I just take a look around, will you? Being a good citizen, what with nothing going on and nothing to hide." For a moment they stared at each other, Henry simmering and Geddes's beady brown eyes flashing.

"You got a warrant?"

The marshal stopped and regarded the boy like some unknown specimen. "You read too many of those books, junior."

"Is that the law or isn't it?"

Geddes's bemused squint turned meaner.

"Those cars out front the only ones here tonight?"

Henry hesitated only for a heartbeat before saying, "Yes."

"So if I were to follow the tire tracks in the mud out there round back, I'd find what, a fancy outhouse?"

Henry said nothing and forced himself not to look away.

"As I said," Geddes drawled, "I'm going to have a look around. That all right with you, boss man?"

"Go ahead," Henry said.

The marshal was gone barely ten minutes. Henry didn't leave his post. A feeling of unreality washed over him as he shifted objects on the table and thought about what he'd say to Geddes about the car out back. His mind leapt wildly through different possibilities, each one leading to a dead end, so he kept still, unwilling to break this delicate balance. It would work out, he told himself, it would be okay. An idea came to him and before he was consciously aware of it he'd hopped off the stool, ducked into the back office, and returned, turning over what he'd done dispassionately. It was the only way to keep things as they were. Any change carried the ominous disquiet of an approaching cyclone. He folded his hands and shut his eyes. For thirty more seconds there was peace.

Then Geddes shouldered the door open and crossed to the front desk with tense, short steps. His jaw was set and his nostrils flared; a forelock of his greased coif had come undone and lay plastered to his forehead with sweat.

He snapped his fingers at Henry and whispered, "Phone. Now."

"It's not working."

The marshal's face contorted as if inhaling a whiff of open sewage. "Are you fucking with me, boy?"

Henry gestured helplessly to the phone and pushed it forward. Geddes snatched it up and listened, then swore and set it down again. He took a deep breath and spoke quickly and quietly: "Did he threaten you? Is that why you covered for him? Is someone else here in trouble? Nod your head if the answer's yes."

The kid was frozen, not like a frightened deer but with a deeper blankness, a color photograph that blinked. Geddes slid the logbook over and his eyes darted across the page.

"Which room? When—" He stopped at the most recent entry. "Eight, is that it? He's in Room Eight?" When Henry didn't respond the marshal clutched a handful of his shirt. *"Which one?"*

The boy's wide-eyed nod was more like a lurch in the set of his head on his scrawny neck while his Adam's apple bobbed. "Eight," he croaked.

Geddes let go of Henry, unbuttoned his suit jacket, and unstrapped the holster on his right hip, but didn't draw the service revolver. His eyes flashed to the phone and he swore again.

"Stay here."

He was turning to leave when Henry said, "Wait."

"What is it, goddamnit?"

"If you call it in you might scare him off. He's asleep."

"Leave it to the pros, junior."

"Don't you want to get him yourself?"

The marshal glowered at the boy. He left quietly, easing the door shut and stepping gently down toward Room Eight. The vestibule light threw sharp shadows in the gloom, hues of blue just beginning to brighten. When the marshal was out of sight Henry dashed into the back office and plugged the phone extension back into the wall socket.

He felt sick to his stomach; what was he thinking? Back at the desk he scooped up the phone. The hum of the dial tone was a universe of choice.

9-1-1 was just three numbers, couldn't be simpler. Internal calls were only two digits. His finger moved to the dial.

The marshal tread carefully on the walkway, heel-toe silent, palm on the butt of his service pistol.

The front-desk phone swung in a hanging pendulum, dancing a crazy jig at the end of its chord.

Henry cleared the door too quickly and stumbled into the support pillar, shivering in the chill dawn. Geddes was down in front of Room Eight with his revolver drawn and held down by his leg.

Inside the room, the phone rang.

Geddes froze, senses tightening as he whipped his furious gaze from Henry back to the door, teeth gritted, and considered his move with frantic calculations. Rustling and knocking inside the room made the officer step back. He cupped the butt of the service pistol with his free palm and brought his arms up.

"Open up, Hanson," he shouted, "I know it's you."

A series of thunder cracks tore the night. The door frame shook, spitting splinters and popping holes. Geddes jerked backward, arms pinwheeling as his pistol spun in the air. He cleared the edge of the wooden slatted porch and fell hard on his back, sending up a puff of dust and a spray of gravel.

An enormous whip had lashed the world, shattering its fragile composure.

Henry dropped to his knees. Duck and cover.

The fractured door burst open, brass screws and wood shards scattering as the frame rebounded. Frank lowered his booted heel as he sprang out, hair a wild mess, eyes burning over a feral grimace. A short-barreled black pistol dangled from his fist as he took three long strides toward the fallen man. Geddes was trying like a feeble infant to roll himself over. His right hand scrabbled blindly in the dirt for his revolver.

Then the bank robber shot the marshal in the head.

Air drained from Henry's lungs and he collapsed like a punctured balloon, clinging prone and spiderlike to the carpet of the vestibule as he watched Frank standing over the marshal's supine body, gun outstretched, staring down into . . . what?

Into the heart of an impenetrable darkness.

The man snapped out of it and reeled back into the room drunkenly, crashing and tinkling glass resounding. A moment later he reemerged, hefting the duffle bag and skirting along the walkway toward the gravel path like a fox chased out of a hen house, jaw set gravely as he rounded the end of the building.

Henry was alone with the corpse.

The marshal's right foot jittered twice and was still. Henry found himself on his feet, crossing the parking lot with quick, calm steps, heart throbbing painfully, passing a tan Buick he hadn't noticed before parked on an angle. The echo of a motor sputtering to life carried on the crisp cordite and iron-tinged air, the rumble getting louder as the front grill of the Continental rounded the gravel path, rear-end fishtailing as it made for Alston Road.

As the sedan neared the turnoff Frank hissed "*shit*" and slammed on the brakes. The marshal's .45. The cash in his wallet. No time to get sloppy. He leapt from the car leaving the driver's door ajar and stopped short. Fifteen feet away, next to the body, Henry held the heavy .45 caliber straight ahead in both shaking hands. The boy's feet were splayed and tears danced in his eyes.

Frank straightened, a cautious glare easing into the old smirk.

"What are you gonna do with that, kid? I thought you were on my side. Thanks for the call, by the way."

Henry coughed raggedly but kept the gun steady. "You can't do this," he managed. "You can't go around killing people."

Frank's smile soured and he spat onto the gravel. "Shit-for-brains child."

"Stay where you are. Don't move. The police will be here soon." Henry squeezed one eye shut and the heaving chest under the Hawaiian shirt hovered out of focus beyond the sighting notch. His arms burned but the barrel barely quivered.

"Oh yeah, cowboy?" Frank sneered. "You can't even squeeze the trigger."

"I'm warning you," Henry croaked, a shaky note through a broken reed. "If you take another step, I'll shoot."

A ripple of hesitation flashed across Frank's haggard features, then he scoffed and turned toward the Olds.

Henry pulled the trigger.

An explosion ripped the air. Henry's feet left the gravel and the ground slammed into his back. His wrists bent sharply and the heavy weapon was snatched from his hands by the force of the discharge.

"*Jesus Christ!*" Frank cried through the ear-splitting whine of the shot and Henry felt the ground vibrate with heavy footfalls.

The slim figure approached through purple and pink crepuscular pastels, kicking the fallen pistol out of reach and towering in his vision. Cords stood out on his neck and the black bore of the pistol stared into Henry like a phantom eye. The boy lurched to his elbows and crab walked backward until his shoulder blades hit the wooden edge of the walkway.

"You're dead, you little fucker," Frank growled, an amused note swimming in his tone.

Henry closed his eyes and silence stretched. Odd that in this final moment he shouldn't feel fear but only profound sadness, a tired lament at the broken beauty of an undiscovered world.

He waited. Moments or years passed.

His eyelids raised gradually, surreal shades on the figure of the outlaw with the pistol aimed, eyebrows furrowed. The slightest hint of a smile curling the cruel, thin lips and a hard cold glint flickered behind the eyes. Slowly the susurration of the wind returned, the distant wail of a police siren leaking into the tranquil dawn.

The barrel lowered.

"How much you got left on that new Striker book, kid?"

"Fifty pages."

Frank stuffed the pistol into the band of jeans. "Well, then," he said. "Wouldn't be nice of me, would it? You'll like the ending."

The outlaw turned and scooped up the marshal's gun, ducked into the car, revved the engine, and burned rubber in a wide arc across the gravel before bouncing onto Alston Road. Tires shrieked in a hard right and the rocketship fins disappeared past the row of bushes out of sight. The thrumming of the engine died away with the siren still a faint suggestion on the breeze.

Henry's shallow breathing filled the quiet morning as the whine in his ears began to fade.

A black pool was spreading underneath Geddes's ruined face, his arms tangled awkwardly across his chest and legs spread.

The door to Room Six snicked open and a pair of slippers shuffled out followed by the padding of bare feet. The old couple stood gaping, the wife speechless through gasping breaths and the husband murmuring, "It's okay hon it's okay the kid's all right, just hang tight hon it's okay . . ."

The phone in Room Eight was still ringing.

The motel was crawling with cops. Three cruisers were parked at obtuse angles surrounding the marshal's body, now covered with a white tarp, patches of sticky dark red seeping through like stains on a picnic blanket. An officer stood snapping photographs while three more combed the area around the motel, nosing around the back lot and barking into car radios.

A rookie cop with thick glasses interviewed the old couple on the lobby couch, the husband rubbing his wife's shoulders while they talked over each other. In the back office Henry slumped glassy-eyed on the swivel chair with two more officers standing over him. On his left was Officer Tim, stern faced and remorseful. On his right was a shorter, stout man he'd seen on his way to school, auburn hair cropped in a crew cut, beetle-browed, grimly chomping gum and glaring at the boy like he'd just caught a shoplifter. His badge read "G. Woods." Ansel Haldane paced behind them gray-faced, hair ruffled, pajama top buttoned wrong beneath his overcoat.

"He wouldn't have gone in alone," Woods said. "He knew the protocols and who he was dealing with. Something's not right here."

"Go easy on him, Gene."

Woods ignored that and leaned down in Henry's face.

"Tell it again from the beginning. What time did Hanson arrive?"

Henry's gaze wandered, hovering between the officers like he'd been drugged. Finally he shrugged slightly. His lips parted but nothing came out.

Woods snapped his fingers in Henry's face and the boy blinked nervously.

"Wake up, kid. Help us out here."

Officer Tim winced but folded his arms, waiting for a response.

"Problem with the phone," Henry finally murmured.

"That's a goddamn lie," the stout officer snapped. "It's working fine now."

Officer Tim observed the boy pensively. "Son, are you sure you're thinking straight? You want a soda pop or something?"

"He doesn't need a can of soda," Woods said. "We need to haul his ass down to the station for real questioning."

Tim kept his voice level. "You're not helping. He's in shock."

Woods shook his head, scowling. "Doesn't smell right. I think this punk played dumb and got a good man killed."

Smoldering beneath a stray lock of hair, Henry glanced up at Woods and held his eye.

"Why would he do something like that?" Tim asked quietly.

"Cause these damn kids don't respect the law. His story doesn't make sense and you know it. I'm not buying this routine."

Tim smoothed back his lank brown hair. "Geddes may have acted unprofessionally," he said. "We won't know until forensics comes back with the full report."

Woods shot Tim a disgusted look, then noticed Henry eyeing him and bent down further, his face inches from the boy. "What the hell is wrong with you, kid? You know we can try you as an adult for aiding and abetting robbery and murder, don't you?"

Ansel gave a choked cry and stepped forward before Officer Tim grabbed his shoulder and patted the air to soothe him. He turned to Woods. "Step outside, Officer. You're out of line. Let me handle this."

Woods's glare lingered contemptuously on Henry, who had lowered his head and sunken back into a passive daze, then he marched out of the office, slamming the door behind him.

"I'm sorry about him," Tim said. "He's just upset. Geddes was a good man."

Henry raised his head. "How do you know?"

"Excuse me?"

"Did you know him?"

The officer hesitated. "Not personally, no. But I know what this badge represents, the respect it demands and the responsibility it carries. Do you know about that, son? That it's the lifeblood of our community?"

Henry shook his head and hissed a sharp derisive chuckle. "It's only a story."

The officer shifted his weight uneasily. "Listen, I think what you did was right. You kept your head and probably prevented more bloodshed. You knew who it was when he showed up, didn't you?"

Henry pressed his lips into a thin line and kept quiet.

"I believe you were brave, son. I know you and your mother, she's a lovely woman and she's done a fine job raising you. It's my job to keep this town safe, do you understand? We can try tomorrow, you should get some sleep, but it would be very helpful if you could recall as much as possible and walk us through what happened thoroughly. Could you do that for me?"

Henry's gaze was steady and his voice came through deeper and resonant: "I got nothing to say to you."

Muscles twitched beneath the taut skin of the officer's face as the warmth drained from his eyes. "Stay put," he said, "We're not done here yet," and left the lobby.

Henry stared blankly into the middle distance, fished in his pocket absentmindedly, and came out with the folded fifty. The bill showed a bit of wear now and was creased diagonally. "Evidence," he whispered, then crumpled it in his fist and went into the back to flush it down the john.

---

*"*Only A Story" came about as a confluence of stray thoughts: a meta nod to Richard Stark's Parker novels, an image of a lonely motel in the middle of the night, a don't-meet-your-heroes coming of age mood. The fact that they coalesced into something cohesive was, as always, a minor miracle.*

Sean McCluskey *has been a cop of one kind or another since he was twenty-two years old, which means he's never dug a ditch but he never will be rich. More recently, he's turned to writing crime fiction, which probably means the same thing, though he doesn't have to wake up as early. His stories have appeared or are forthcoming in* Ellery Queen Mystery Magazine, *volumes of the* Mickey Finn: 21st Century Noir *anthology series,* The Best Mystery Stories of the Year 2023, *and the* Skinning the Poke *pickpocket anthology. His work has been nominated for the Robert L. Fish Memorial Award and the Shamus Award, both of which he lost to some damn fine writers.*

THE SECRET MENU

Sean McCluskey

*W*hat kind of rich guy meets his mistress in a Waffle House? Len Cox wondered. He wasn't sure, even though he was looking at one.

He'd first seen Hamilton Dunne—"Hammy" to his friends, of which Len certainly wasn't one—in emailed photos from his occasional employer, the Devlin Intelligence Group. Tall, early thirties, wavy-haired and handsome in the athletic-but-not-really style of pro golfers. Aristocratic.

Pictures of Hammy's wife were in there, too, the heiress to her father's commercial real estate empire. Older and plainer than her husband, snaps of the pair attending a campaign fundraiser looked like a high school jock squiring his wallflower cousin to her junior prom.

She was the client, of course. Her suspicions started with friends who'd caught their husbands cheating. A high-end escort service called Sydney Layne Associates was all the rage among their rarified peer group. Sounded like an investment firm, but the only asset management they did was directing beautiful young women to older, wealthier men.

Hammy had a no-show regional director job at Goldstone Realty, LLC, his wife's company. Just a way to pay his allowance from the company till, but lately he'd displayed an unprecedented interest in the operation. He wanted to find new properties for the firm to buy up and lease out, which involved roaming the northeast in the company jet, charging the company card, and spending time away from his wife. This sudden motivation, combined with the rumors flying around her socialite circle, put Hammy's wife on high alert.

The Devlin Investigation Group promised discreet nationwide information-gathering to high net-worth clients. They did that by subcontracting the work to freelancers like Len Cox. Decent short-term gigs, but too infrequent to rely on in northeast Pennsylvania, which wasn't a hotbed of corporate intrigue or dynastic infidelities.

The assignment arrived by email the previous afternoon. Along with the briefing and the photos came background info on Sydney Layne Associates ripped from their website. *Executive-Level Matchmaking, Discreet and Elite.* Arty black and white photos. A gorgeous, sophisticated woman leaned across a lunch table to touch the arm of a distinguished gentleman who'd just said something delightful. Another May-December pair on a sailboat, churning through the spray, him skilled and masterful, her vivacious and windblown. Luxury cars, expansive penthouses, first-class airline seats. Everybody succeeding.

Len, alone in his one-bedroom apartment, browsed the site. Pages of women, catalogued with options: ethnicity, hair and eye color, body type, interests, languages spoken, educational background. Age and weight weren't listed—presumably, lower was preferred for both. No prices, of course. Only comparisons to financial planners, personal trainers, and household staff, all the courtiers men winning at life pay to handle the details. Isn't romance just as important? *If you have to ask . . .*

It reminded him of the time his mother brought home a Sharper Image catalog from one of the offices she cleaned. Young Len was entranced by glossy pages of toys and gizmos. He'd pored over it, filling out the order form. Stuff he wanted, sure, but also things for her to enjoy when she came home late after leaving so early every day. When finished, he brought it to her so she could help mail it off to wherever the goodies came from, some vast factory or warehouse.

It was the first time he'd seen her cry. She told him that those things weren't meant for them. They were for the rich people.

The last thing in the DIG file was a travel itinerary for Hammy's chartered jet from Charlotte, North Carolina, to Wilkes-Barre/Scranton International Airport. It had landed an hour ago at SkyeBlue, the private terminal onsite. Len waited inside, browsing pamphlets about flying lessons. He'd seen nobody who looked like she'd been beamed down from whatever planet Sydney Layne got their girls from. Just harried travelers in off-the-rack suits, and a hired driver holding the same schedule Len had.

Hammy breezed in, casual ensemble broadcasting *You Can't Afford It* on all frequencies. He strode to the driver and dismissed him. "I like to drive myself in a new city," he'd said. "Get the lay of the land." The chauffeur seemed surprised, but Hammy signed off on a full day's pay and pressed enough cash into the guy's hand to elicit a stammering *Thank you*. The driver surrendered the key fob to Hammy, who tossed his bag into the luxury SUV and took off. Len followed, in the anonymous sedan he'd rented at the airport.

Len was optimistic at that point. Ideally, Hammy was enroute to whatever passed for a four-star hotel in Scranton, where he'd meet the demigoddess he'd summoned with the incantation of a credit card his wife didn't know about. Maybe a lingering lunch, oysters for him, salad for her, wine for both. She'd touch his arm across the table.

Then, entwined, to the elevator, an embrace and a kiss as the doors closed. Later, sated, they'd depart, just slightly disheveled. Len would snap photos, upload them to the DIG server, and get money direct-deposited into an account that was skimming perilously close to minimum balance fees. A good day for all.

Instead, Hammy went to Waffle House.

It sat on a prairie of buckled asphalt, along a crumbling retail corridor of strip malls, regional banks, off-brand gas stations, and thickets of *For Sale* or *Space to Lease* signs. If Hammy really was interested in commercial real estate, Moosic, Pennsylvania, was an orchard of low-hanging, rotting fruit.

The tallest structure in town was the black-on-yellow Waffle House sign, three stories high. Hammy gunned the engine when it hove into view. He swung the big SUV into the lot, two wheels bouncing over a curb as he misjudged the driveway. *Should've held on to that chauffeur*, Len thought.

The restaurant's parking lot was shared with a motel called the Montage Motor Lodge, which Len gave half-credit for almost rhyming. Not on the level of *discreet and elite*, of course. Business wasn't booming. There was one car parked over there, a midsize sedan with the same rental company window sticker as Len's car. He swung into the lot, rolling to a stop halfway between motel and restaurant, on the demarcation line of old asphalt versus newer.

Hammy had set the Lincoln crooked across two parking spots, but the lot was empty enough that Len doubted anyone would care. Exhaust still plumed from the big SUV's tailpipe. Maybe Hammy was waiting for the Waffle House valet.

Len unzipped his backpack on the passenger seat. Inside was a folding sunscreen, which he unfurled and shoved into place on the dashboard. He'd already suction-cupped nylon mesh panels to the side and rear windows when he picked up the car. Now he carefully lifted his camera from the bag, a twenty-year-old old digital Olympus he'd gotten secondhand at a yard sale, telephoto lens already attached. He pushed it under one of the sunshade's accordion folds and aimed in.

Hammy was just getting out. He turned in a slow circle, taking in the full panorama, like an astronaut who'd crashed on some barren moon. *Welcome to Planet Poverty*, Len thought. Hammy steeled himself and set off toward Waffle House, pulling up his collar against the wind.

Len tracked him, clicking off a few shots. Then he swung the lens toward the restaurant.

The Moosic, Pennsylvania, Waffle House looked like all its siblings he'd ever seen, a yellow cornice up top and red brickwork down low, broad windows in between. It was mostly empty, in the fallow valley between breakfast and lunch. The busiest booth had five college-age kids crammed into it, whooping it up. Len had seen YouTube videos with people their age filming themselves going into Waffle Houses and demanding items from some secret menu the place supposedly had. Waffle tacos, chocolate pudding sandwiches, and other nonsense. They acted like they were beating the system, "hacking the Matrix," but it was just little pricks harassing working people for laughs.

Len panned away. He saw men in grimy workmen's coats hunched at the counter. A harried couple negotiating with a fussy toddler. A leathery old-timer sipping coffee.

And then, the woman. Len stopped dead when he saw her.

She was . . . Len was no poet. He'd never dazzled a woman with wordplay. But she was exquisite. Glossy dark hair pulled back into a sleek ponytail from an exotic widow's peak. A strong chin and a wide mouth, framed with sharp cheekbones. Tanned, athletic, like a soccer player all dolled up for some ad campaign. Her eyes, dark and catlike, were fixed on Hammy as he walked toward the door.

Len focused in on her. He heard the camera's electronically simulated shutter noise before he realized his finger was tapping the button. The camera's digital display was a more natural frame for her than the viewfinder. A woman like this shouldn't be seen with naked eyes. She belonged on a screen, in some foreign art house film or prestige streaming drama. Actresses who looked like her sent Len to IMDb, to find out who she was. And then to ImageFap or Mister Skin, to see if she'd ever done nude scenes.

Hammy saw her as he stepped in the door. His body language was reserved. He was a man seeing a beautiful woman, but not recognizing her. He stood by the hostess station, ignoring the teenage girl offering him a laminated menu, his eyes fixed on the woman at the table. She nodded, and he approached.

She extended a hand to him. There was nothing demure about her handshake. It was brisk, professional, two quick pumps and done. Hammy sat down across from her. He leaned forward, started to speak, but the woman raised her hand again to stop him as a waitress approached. She waved off a coffee refill, and when the server drifted away, she and Hammy started to talk.

Len framed the pair. The camera had a decent lens. He'd probably overpaid for it, like his ex had screamed at him during one of their last fights. But even it couldn't find any sexual tension between Hammy and his tablemate. The body language all said that this was a first meeting. She did most of the talking, and a lot of it looked like questions. Hammy would pause, furrow his brow or cock his head, then say something short or just nod.

They didn't look like lovers. They looked like two people talking about the weather, or a movie they'd both sort of enjoyed. Or even commercial real estate.

Len sighed. He'd driven two hours from Philly for this?

The woman turned to the window, set down her coffee, and pointed at Len. Hammy swung his head, and now the two of them were looking right at him.

Len froze, as the weightless roller-coaster hit of adrenaline punched through his chest. Maybe the sun had glinted off his camera lens, or she'd noticed the car's exhaust. But they weren't seeing him. They were looking at a rental car with a sunshade. He'd been spotted on surveillance before, especially when just starting out. The first rule was *Don't react*. Most people doubted their own instincts, talked themselves out of things. Len watched. Waited for them to do the same.

Hammy looked back at the woman. He narrowed his eyes and twisted his mouth. *Seriously?* his face asked. She nodded, calm and assured. Hammy turned back toward Len. Took a long look. Maybe long enough to recognize the rental car that had followed him from the airport. Then he raised his eyebrows and shrugged. *Okay.*

They stood. She dropped what looked like a ten on the table and led Hammy toward the door. They set off across the parking lot, side by side.

All right, Len thought. This was still all right. *Don't react.* If they approached the car, he'd stash the camera and pretend to be asleep. If they knocked on the window he'd jolt awake, and invent some shamefaced tale of a tired traveler who'd wanted a cup of Waffle House coffee and a room at the Montage Motor Lodge, but realized he didn't have money for either. They'd buy it. If there was one thing Len could sell, it was embarrassment at being broke. He swung the lens to keep them in frame, and watched.

They didn't approach Len's car. They didn't even look at it. They walked across the cracked asphalt, side by side, at an angle that wouldn't bring them anywhere near it. There was only one place they could be going. The Montage Motor Lodge.

That's more like it, Len thought. Some afternoon delight in a fleabag motel. He fired off more snapshots.

Hammy didn't put his arm around her. She didn't take his hand. They talked, but there were no smiles or fraught glances. Not even the wind in her hair or the blades of sunlight swinging down from the clouds could make it romantic.

Len twisted in his seat and aimed the camera through the car's side windows as they passed, and then through the rear glass. They walked to the door of Room Twelve, where the other rental sedan was parked, and he stood by while she got the key from her coat. Len zoomed in tight. Maybe the threshold would ignite an irresistible passion in Hammy, who'd sweep her into a lingering kiss as they stumbled inside.

It didn't. The front door opened onto a wood-paneled room. A twin bed, a small desk, and a low chest of drawers were wedged around a narrow adjoining door. The woman motioned Hammy through and stepped in behind him. She turned in the doorway and looked back out at the parking lot. The mesh on the rental's back window made her blurry and dark, like an old photo of some aristocratic beauty. She shut the door and was gone.

Len lowered his camera. He settled back around in his seat and thought about what he had. Two people in a Waffle House who hadn't even eaten brunch together, followed by a chaste walk-and-talk. Going into a motel room with a beautiful woman wasn't bad, but it wasn't great. No matter how suspicious Hammy's wife was, it was all too easily explained as a business meeting. The restaurant was too noisy, he could say, with yelling kids and a crying baby. My back hurt from the plane ride, so I didn't want to sit in the car. She'd left her property portfolio in her room, so I looked at it in there. Isn't that all reasonable, darling? No need to derail the gravy train.

Oh, well, Len thought. He'd upload the pictures, bang out a report, get his money, and move on to the next one. For all he knew, it really was a business meeting, just like Hammy said, and the wife was jumping at shadows.

But if the woman sold real estate locally, why was she driving a rental car? And who would come in from out of town to sell property in Moosic, Pennsylvania? Even if the parcels were bank-owned, they would just send someone from a local branch or a law firm.

More importantly, whoever sold real estate in this wasteland didn't look like her.

Len looked in the rearview mirror at the door to Room Twelve and imagined what was going on behind it. Women like that, their eyes didn't even focus on Len. To them he was blurred out, like a crime scene on the news. But for pricks like Hammy she was available at whim. All with an heiress at home. Damn good deal for Hamilton Dunne.

Maybe it could be a good deal for Len Cox, too.

He opened the car door. Hauled his backpack out and stuffed the camera back inside. He walked down to the far end of the Montage Motor Lodge. Room Three was open, and a maid was in there pulling sheets off the bed like his mother used to do. Len hustled past and shoved open the door that said *Office*. Little bells on the frame tinkled.

The guy dozing behind the counter jolted and struggled to his feet. Tall and skinny, scabs on both forearms, his craggy face framed by a crispy blond mullet. "Hey," he mumbled. "Welcome." Behind him, numbered keys hung on tiny hooks. 12 was the only one missing. Unlike Sydney Lane Associates, the Montage Motor lodge had their rates displayed. Monthly, weekly, daily, and hourly.

Len pointed. "Let me have Room Thirteen for an hour."

"Uh, it's not made up yet."

"That's fine," Len hauled out his wallet.

"Room One's good to go," the clerk said. "All fresh."

Len pulled out cash. He barely had enough. "I want Thirteen."

The clerk grinned, bemused, showing teeth like brown coral. "How come?"

"I have triskadekaphilia," Len said. He had come in second at a spelling bee when he was a kid with that word, even using it in a sentence: *People who like the number 13 have triskadekaphilia.*

His mother had frosted the word "Genius" onto a small cake for him, spelled with a J.

"Oh," said the counter guy. "I'm real sorry." He took Len's money and handed over the key. "I been sick, too. Long COVID."

Oughtta wear a mask over those teeth, Len thought. "Feel better soon, man," he said. The door jangled as he left.

Len paused in front of Room Twelve to listen, but the cars and trucks whooshing by on Route 11 were too loud. He unlocked the door to Room Thirteen, stepped in, and eased it shut behind him. Eleven, Twelve, and Thirteen, he thought, all lined up. Felt like synchronicity. The universe telling him he was on the right path.

His room was the reverse of hers. Same bed, same desk, same chest of drawers, all arranged around the same adjoining door. Len crept toward it, his steps muffled by the crusty gray carpet. The walls were thin. As he approached, he heard music. Classical. Maybe Hammy liked to screw in 3/4 time.

Len put his ear to the door. He heard what might have been muffled voices, but the music drowned them out. He set his backpack down and lay flat beside it. The carpet, stiff and scratchy, smelled like a car air freshener stuffed into a sweaty sock. He crabbed forward, pressed his cheek to the raspy floor, and peered under the door.

It had been badly hung, so there was a big gap. The rubber draftstrip was ragged on Len's side and entirely gone on hers. He could see the bureau and the small flat-screen, and a corner of the bed. From down here the voices were clearer, but still indistinct. It sounded like she was doing most of the talking. It also sounded like they were off to the side. Not the bed side. The desk.

Len struggled into a clumsy sit-up and grabbed his backpack. From a zippered pocket he drew out a snarled tangle of plastic-coated cable. One end had an adapter to plug into his phone's USB port. He shoved it in and swiped his thumb over the chipped screen until an app called *SnakEye* fired up. The logo flickered into a wavering image of the ceiling and part of Len's face captured by the tiny camera on the cable's other end.

He rolled over, knelt before the door, and gingerly fed the camera end through the gap. On his phone's screen, the woman's room brightened and unfolded as the lens emerged, shoving through blurry fronds of carpet, an explorer trekking into the grass of a dangerous savannah. Len flexed the cable with his fingertips, making the camera yaw to the side. The view swung, and he saw them.

They stood by the desk, their backs to him, leaning over and looking at something. The camera had a tiny microphone. Through the music Len could hear the hum of her voice, but not the words. What were they reading, the *Kama Sutra*? Did she have a whole Sydney Lane menu for him to choose from? No prices, of course. *If you have to ask...*

Len heard a high-pitched trill. For a second, he thought it was part of the classical music, before he realized it was a cell phone. Hammy took his phone from his pocket and looked at the screen. His face changed, the little smile evaporating. He raised the phone to his ear as he moved away from the woman, toward the bed. Closer to the adjoining door. Len fought the urge to yank the camera back—movement attracted notice.

"Darrington," Hammy said. The wife. In their rarified world, everybody had last names for first names. "Hello, love. Is everything all right?"

The woman leaned on the desk, watching him. At the wife's name, she closed her eyes and pursed her lips.

"No, I didn't mean that," Hammy said. "I'm sure everything is fine. I'm just surprised you called." He listened. "Because I'm working, that's all. Of course I want to—what? That's music. The radio. I'm in the car, listening to music."

Hammy stepped out of view. The woman watched him. She had a look on her face like someone listening to a friend's young child tell a long story. Benevolence, mild interest, a wisp of impatience. She folded her arms and glanced at her watch.

The radio shut off. "Yes, love," Hammy said from somewhere out of view. "You have my full attention." Without the music, his voice was clear, and Len realized how thin the walls were. He focused on holding still, despite the pain flaring in his knees.

"An emergency?" Hammy asked. "In Westchester? What do you—?" He paced back into view, phone pressed to his ear. Len heard the chirps and squawks of Darrington's voice. It went on for what felt like a long while. Finally Hammy said, "All right.

See you soon." He ended the call. Looked down at his phone, shaking his head ruefully.

"Is everything all right?" the woman asked. Her voice, husky, was gorgeous as the rest of her.

"There's a crisis in White Plains," Hammy drawled. "A real estate crisis."

"Oh, my."

"And only I can resolve it," he continued. "With her by my side, naturally."

"Naturally."

Hammy stepped closer to the woman. "My wife suspects that I'm having an affair."

The woman put a hand to her chest. "You, sir, are a cad."

"Rumor has it I'm patronizing an escort service, which pairs me off with nubile vixens."

"An efficient cad, at least."

"You know how I've always supported entrepreneurship. Speaking of which . . ." He reached into the pocket of his field coat, which had probably never crossed a field more rugged than a country club lawn, and drew out an envelope. Len recognized the Wells Fargo logo on it as Hammy handed it to her. "I won't be offended if you count it."

She put it on the desk beside her. "Relationships are built on trust."

"I wouldn't know," he said, chuckling. He turned and strode from view. "She's already put the jet on standby, so I'd best be off."

The woman followed. "Mustn't arouse more suspicion."

"But I very much look forward to our next meeting, when time won't be an issue. Maybe then we—" Len heard the front door of their room open, and Hammy's voice was drowned out by a truck roaring past on Route 11. The woman said something in response, but he couldn't make out the words. Then the door shut, the traffic noise gone.

The woman crossed back to the desk. She picked up the envelope, drew out a fat wad of bills, and flicked through it, counting. Brisk, efficient.

Len struggled to his feet, knees popping like bubble wrap. He tottered to his window and tugged aside the gritty curtain.

Hammy was halfway across the lot, hustling toward his SUV. Not the languid swagger he'd displayed with the woman. When Darrington cracked the whip, she got results.

Except this time, she'd screwed herself. Called her man away just before the *delicto* could get nice and *in flagrante*. Now she'd be paying for pictures of nothing. Two people walking across a parking lot. Len would get his pittance, but Hammy's gravy train would keep on rolling.

Maybe there was room on it for one more. Maybe Len could invent his own entrée, and order it off the secret menu.

Len walked back to the adjoining door. Turned the lock and opened it. On the other side was hers, the mirror of his. He stood there, staring at it. He felt a flutter in his chest. Maybe the heart murmur that had kept him off the police force; probably adrenaline. He took a deep breath, blew it out. Raised his fist, held it for a long few seconds, and knocked.

"Hey," he called. "Listen. I know what you're doing."

Silence.

"I don't want to mess it up," Len continued. "I just want a piece. Not even a big piece. Just a taste."

Silence.

Then, footsteps.

The lock clunked, the knob squeaked, and the door swung open. She stood there, scarf and shoulder bag in place, ready to put this dump behind her. Up close she was flawless, except for a tiny scar across one eyebrow.

I'm right, Len thought. *She wouldn't open the door for a strange man if I were wrong.*

The woman looked past Len, into the room. Down at the camera cable and the phone he'd forgotten to retrieve, lying on the floor. Then back at him.

"So," she said. "What do you know?"

I know I'm right.

"I know about Sydney Lane," Len said. "I know that guy was Hamilton Dunne, his wife's Darrington Dunne, and he's cheating on her. With you."

She looked to the side and pursed her lips. Taking it in.

"But it's okay," Len continued. "She's suspicious, so she hired me. But I'll say he was a good boy. Drove around looking at real estate, just like he said. Won't mention you at all."

She looked up at him. Didn't say anything.

"You keep coming here, I'll keep covering for you. So you two can just keep . . . you know." Len shrugged. "Doing whatever."

"And what do you get out of it?" she asked. "Money?"

"Yeah." Len grinned, hopeful and ingratiating. "Only a seat on the gravy train."

Len watched her think about it. Her eyes moved, like she was sliding beads on an invisible abacus. Finally, she nodded. "That's fine."

"Really?"

"Money's not a problem for him," she said. She reached into her shoulder bag and pulled out the Wells Fargo envelope. "Here. Count it."

The flap was ajar, and Len saw a thick wad of bills. Was that Ben Franklin? As he reached for it, the packet slipped from her fingers. He caught it, attention focused, so her other hand was a blur in the corner of his eye as it hooked around and slammed into the side of his head.

Len staggered. Raised his fists, but she was faster. She jabbed him in the belly, and when his hands dropped, she punched him in the head again, right in the same spot where jawline met ear. His vision stuttered and blurred, a filmstrip breaking loose from the sprockets. He collapsed onto the corner of the bed and bounced face-first to the floor. The woman dropped onto his back, her knees crushing the air from his lungs. Len thrashed, struggling to push up, but one arm was trapped under him and the other was wedged between his flank and the bed.

"Relax," she said. Her bag whacked him in the head. She was rooting around in it. "Hold still."

She twisted on top of him. He got one arm free and flailed back at her, just as he felt the jab in his thigh. *Jesus Christ!* he thought. *She stabbed me!*

The woman stood up off him in one smooth motion. Len flipped over and scrambled away from her, heels skidding on the thin carpet. She didn't pursue. Just stood there looking down at him. There was a needle in her hand.

"What the hell did you—" A chill fluttered across his skin, and the world lurched around him. For an instant he stood beside her, looking at Len Cox worming around on the floor. Then he was back, but his body was seizing up. The chill washed over him again—this time, it stayed. He was drowning in it, except he could breathe. His heart slammed around in his rib cage. He lay flat, straining to rise, but he was turning to lead.

"It's just ketamine," she said. She picked up the money. "It won't hurt."

She was right. His body was numb. The world looked like a cutscene in those videogames he sometimes played. Like he was viewing her on a screen.

She picked up his phone. Knelt beside him, held it to his face to unlock it, and tapped at the display. Len, fading in and out, heard muffled voices, her and Hammy. *"Relationships are built on trust."*

She shook her head. Exhaled sharply through her nose. "Okay."

She stood and walked around the bed. "One of the side effects of ketamine is amnesia," she said over her shoulder. "But it's unreliable." She picked up a pillow. Len blinked, and she was beside him again.

Len tried to speak. *I'll forget the whole thing.* But all he managed was a groaning sigh.

"I respect the hustle," she said. "I really do. But there aren't any more seats on this gravy train."

She lifted the pillow to his face, then stopped and pulled it back. Leaned close to his ear. "And for the record," she whispered, "he isn't paying me to fuck him. He's paying me to kill his wife." The pillow came down, and the world went black.

---

*Like all good Americans, I've always been fascinated by wealth. My day job has granted me limited exposure to the world of people to whom being rich is just the natural state of things, as routine to them as breathing. Observing them feels to me like some Bronze Age wanderer keeping a wary eye on a distant storm, inconceivable power expended toward unknowable ends, and

*wondering if the gods are headed my way to alter my life. The only thing I've seen that's more dangerous than blundering into their path is the people who actually try and place themselves in it, to curry favor by climbing the slopes of Olympus. For a lot of them, the only thing that trickles down is an avalanche. When Stacy Woodson and Michael Bracken solicited stories for the brilliantly conceived—and named—*Scattered, Smothered, Covered & Chunked: Crime Fiction Inspired by Waffle House *anthology, in which this story first appeared, it gave me the chance to focus on one of those hapless climbers.*

Richard A. McMahan *is a retired federal agent who served as a criminal investigator for over a quarter of a century. Currently, he's a detective at the Kentucky Attorney General's Office. In 2020, McMahan's story "Baddest Outlaws" was in the* Best American Mystery Stories of the Year *edited by C. J. Box. His writing has appeared in various publications over the years, including having stories selected twice for Mystery Writers of America anthologies.*

MISTER GEORGE

Richard A. McMahan

I was reading about the Wildcats' chances at the Final Four while I was finishing my breakfast when my mother called.

"Bo, I need you to do something for me. Work like," Mama said when I answered the phone.

"Yes, ma'am." Putting the paper down, I glanced at the envelope unopened on the table. Still unopened for over a week. During my dozen plus years with the Kentucky State Police I've had plenty of people ask favors of me, but never my mother. The way I was raised, you don't tell your mama no, regardless of how old you get to be.

"It's Miss Rose," Mama said. "Someone went and killed Mister George, and I want you to find out who." She told me Miss Rose was waiting at home over in Shelby County, and that Mister George was in the kitchen, very dead. I promised her I would go see Miss Rose.

After putting on my coat, I slid my badge on my belt right next to my Smith 10mm, but I paused before I reached the front door. My eyes were drawn back to the unopened envelope propped against the salt and pepper shakers on my kitchen table. I had left my breakfast plate sitting at the table, a benefit of not answering to anyone. I grabbed the envelope and shoved it into the inside pocket of my sport coat. *Today. I'll read it today.*

Once in my car, I radioed Post and told them I was 10-8, in service and en route to Shelby County. The ride was uneventful, except for some cross talk from Shelby County sheriff's deputies.

I pulled into the gravel drive of a house on State Road 53 midway between La Grange and Shelbyville. Miss Rose's place was built back when Ike was running the country, with both yards and houses made big and rambling. A Buick long as a yacht was moored under the carport. Before I could ring the bell, Miss Rose swung open the door and greeted me with a smile of tightly pursed lips. "Bo, thank you for coming over," she said, ushering me into the living room. Her eyes were red, but her makeup was in place, not a bit smudged. She had on a dress, her best earrings, and a pearl necklace—June Cleaver at seventy.

Her living room was quiet except for the ticking of the grandfather clock in the corner. On the coffee table in front of the couch was a dulled silver serving set. I sat in a stiff wing chair that smelled of mothballs, and Miss Rose took her place on the couch. She poured me a cup of coffee from the serving set, handing me a bone-china cup with a chipped saucer before she broached the subject of why I was there. "Your mother said you've done quite well with the State Police, a sergeant no less. I hate to bother you on your day off." When she said this, her eyes strayed to a black and white photo on the mantle of a young man in his Air Force dress blues.

"Don't worry, Miss Rose; I'm on duty." I took a sip of the coffee. "I'm a detective."

"Oh, you're a plainclothes man," Miss Rose said, sagely nodding her head. "Just like the lawmen on *Law & Order*."

"Yes, ma'am, just like them."

"I'm sure you'll want to see"—Her lower lip trembled slightly less than her voice—"his body."

"In a moment," I replied. "Why don't you tell me what happened." As she spoke, I worried with the wedding band on my ring finger. It's a habit I do to make myself stay calm and keep my tongue quiet while I let someone tell me their story. I learned a long time ago if I just listened to folks instead of firing questions at them that I learned a lot more. I've done the twist-my-ring trick so many times I'm sure I've worn a permanent groove into my finger.

"I heard him go out the back door like always for his daily walk," she said. "He usually leaves around six, and he's back by six thirty, even if he makes a few stops. This morning, he didn't come back until seven. He just came into the kitchen and fell over." At this point her voice failed, and the tears started.

I put my cup on the table, and I reached over and patted her shoulder as I mumbled that I would be back. I left her to her grief and went into the kitchen. Though the décor was straight out of *Ozzie and Harriet,* the kitchen was spotless, except for the pool of blood leaking across the floor from Mister George, and the droplets trailing back to the small pet door set inside the backdoor.

Retrieving a pair of latex gloves from my jacket pocket, I snapped them on and knelt beside Mister George. I lifted each paw and put it back down. All of them were dirty, just as you would expect. Then I ran my hands over the body, pushing through the matted fur. Mister George was about the size of a Cocker spaniel, and he had the wiry hair of one of those annoying lap dogs. I found the gunshot at the top of his spine where his left front leg joined his shoulder. Lifting his legs, I saw a small hole at the bottom of his chest behind his right leg. Downward angle, I thought. I've seen plenty of gunshot wounds in my time, and administered some myself, so I figured the bullet was from something small, a .22, .25, or .32. Something small but fatal. The little guy had heart to come back home with a hole in him.

The floor creaked, and I looked over my shoulder. Miss Rose was in the doorway, her arms crossed, hugging herself. "Someone killed Mister George?"

"Yes, ma'am, it looks like he was shot," I said.

"Maybe a hunter shot Mister George by mistake."

"No, ma'am. I think someone shot him on purpose." I thought about what she had said. "You mentioned he makes stops when he's out in the morning."

"He stops by Buddy's or John's or Estelle's," Miss Rose replied. As she talked, she was pointing toward the back of her house. "They all think I don't know that they feed him table scraps."

I peeled off my rubber gloves and tossed them into the garbage can under the sink. As I stood, my knees popped. I told Miss Rose I was going to see where Mister George had gone, and I pushed open the backdoor, intending to follow Mister George's blood trail. I've done this many a time over the years, both when I'd winged a buck and had to track him through the woods, or when I'd found homicide victims who'd tried to escape their attacker as their life bled out. The ink-black drops on the dewy grass were easy to spot every foot or two as the blood trail led back to a barbed-wire fence. On the other side, a dozen Jerseys stood chewing their cud.

By the spacing of the droplets of blood, I could tell that Mister George had struggled to bring himself home to Miss Rose. I felt foolish—a sergeant in the Kentucky State Police running a dog shooting—but I keep my word. So, foolish or not, I slipped between the barbed-wire strands and followed the blood trail across the cow pasture. The Jerseys eyed me as I made my way to the crest of the hill and the next fence, which formed the boundary of the backyards of other houses sitting on the road that ran into State Road 53. As I looked down from the hill, I knew which house I was going to—the one with the ambulance, two Shelby County Sheriff's patrol cars, and an unmarked Crown Vic out front. A pair of EMTs were loading a stretcher into the back of their ambulance. The body had a white sheet over it, so they weren't rushing.

As I made my way around the side of the house, I noticed a large sign near the road proclaiming Buddy's Fine Country Antiques. Two sheriff's deputies stood on the front porch; their thumbs hooked into their gun belts. I recognized the older one, though I couldn't recall his name.

The older deputy said, "You State boys got here awful quick. Detective's inside." He held out a clipboard with a Crime Scene Entry log attached.

Pulling a pen from my pocket, I signed the entry log, then I nodded and went inside without correcting him. The house was muted and still. The interior was similar to Miss Rose's, with the front door opening onto a formal living room, though it looked as if it had been turned into a showroom, cluttered and jammed with mismatched furniture and knickknacks. At the back of the room was a large wooden desk about a mile wide, just like the ones teachers had when I went to school.

"Irv," a voice called from the kitchen area.

Irv Calhoun—he must be the older deputy. "Irv's outside," I said, moving over and looking at the desktop. There was a gray metal money box open with the plastic tray discarded on the floor in a glinting sea of silver and copper coins. Next to the desk was an open display case, with its shelves overturned. I could see empty ring boxes and empty places where gold chains had lain over a velvet display arm.

"Well, if it ain't Beauregard Stokes," Laura Murphy said lightly. She wore a sensible pantsuit and stood with her hands on her hips, looking more like a teacher than a cop. She held out a pair of latex gloves, and I put them on, wondering—not for the first time—if I should invest in the company that makes them. "I haven't heard anything from you since Los Amigos. What was it, two or three months?"

"Three, I think. I've been trying to run silent and run deep." I glanced away. "Thanks for smoothing that over for me."

She waved a hand in a forget-about-it gesture. "The Sheriff said he'd call the Post to get me help, but I never expected help to be so quick coming." Laura gave me her best schoolmarm smile. I wasn't fooled. The thugs who thought she was a pushover because she was a small woman found out she packed a mean left hook, especially when she swung her Maglite. And I knew her sweet smile had helped send many a wandering heathen to Eddyville, where they busted big rocks into little rocks. Well, not really. We're an *enlightened* society, so instead most of them pumped iron in the prison yard or watched daytime soaps in the rec room.

"Post didn't send me." She gave me a puzzled look, so I explained. "I'm here because of Miss Rose."

"Rose Thompson?" Laura asked, looking down at some notes on a legal pad.

"I think so. I've known her my whole life as Miss Rose. She and my mama grew up together, and both had husbands who got drafted to fight in Vietnam. My dad just gave a few toes to jungle rot during the siege of Khe Sanh, while Miss Rose's husband's F-4 was shot down in North Vietnam. All things equal, my dad got the better deal. He came back. This morning, my mother asked me to come see Miss Rose."

"About Buddy being killed?" Laura asked.

"No, she called about Mister George." The confused look again. "Mister George is, or rather was, Miss Rose's dog, and she called to report to my mother that someone killed him, and my mama asked me to find out what happened."

"You're investigating a dead dog?"

I could see she thought I was pulling her leg, until I went on to explain about Mister George's morning walks, the bullet hole in him, and how I followed the blood.

"The trail led here?"

"Sure did," I replied. "What happened here?"

"This is Buddy McGovern's place," she said, though I could tell she still wasn't convinced I was serious about Mister George. "Buddy lives, or rather lived, and ran his store out of here, mainly coins, jewelry, and antiques. Around seven this morning, a neighbor, John Charles"—*that would be the John Miss Rose had told me about*—"heard a car peel out of Buddy's driveway. Charles said the car was an old Ford Tempo. He's retired from the Ford plant, so he's sure of his Ford cars, or so he said to me." Laura allowed herself a smile. "I've put a Be-On-The-Lookout to the surrounding counties."

Smart move. A BOLO report meant that now, hopefully, a bunch of cops would be eyeballing every Ford Tempo, looking for an excuse to stop it.

"Anyway," Laura continued, "Mister Charles thought a car this time of the morning was odd since Buddy hadn't opened yet, so he came over to see if anything was wrong."

She led me back through the living room to a hallway where I could see that the doorway leading from the carport had been forced open. I commented that the marks on the doorjamb looked like a crowbar or tire iron.

"Exactly what I was thinking," she said. "Our killer forced the door in, and Buddy confronted them right here." She led me back toward the living room and the teacher's desk. Behind the desk was a lot of blood splattered on the floor, the wall, and an overturned chair.

"They beat him to death," I said. "And took the murder weapon?"

"Right." Laura pointed her pen at the metal cash box. "It looks like a robbery. Another neighbor, Estelle Williams"—Again, she flipped to a new page on her legal page—"Mrs. Williams works part-time for Buddy, and she gave us a list of what's missing. Jewelry, coins, cash, a couple of guns, and a solid silver tea serving set."

As Laura talked, something caught my eye. Kneeling, I looked up at Laura, and she nodded it was okay to move things. Careful to avoid the congealing blood soaking into the hardwood floor, I reached under the desk and pulled out a large hardback book. *War and Peace.*

"That must be the book Williams was talking about," Laura said. "According to her, Buddy kept one of his pistols in a hollowed-out book."

I flipped open the book. All the pages were cut out in a square. "Paranoid, huh?"

She glanced toward the blood splashed across the walls and the desk. "Maybe not paranoid enough."

I didn't have a response, so I just grunted.

"Buddy was a real snake oil salesman," Laura explained. "He was always trying to put one over on customers. He'd do the bait and switch trick, supposedly selling an antique, and when the customer came to pick it up, the antique was nothing more than a knockoff. He acted sorry, saying it was his old age making him forgetful, but you could tell he was always plotting ways to put one over on you."

The cell phone on Laura's hip rang out music from the William Tell Overture, which, when I was a kid, I'd only known as Lone Ranger's theme. I left her to her call. Moving toward the side of the living room, I looked through the doorway into the kitchen. Sitting on the table were a coffee cup and a newspaper folded open to the same article I'd been reading that morning about Kentucky's Final Four chances. Here in the Bluegrass State basketball is a religion. On the stove sat a saucepan and a box of Quaker Oats. On the floor was a small bowl. It looked like Buddy had oatmeal for breakfast and had fed Mister George the leftovers.

There was a backdoor in the kitchen but no pet door. *So how did Mister George get out?* I went outside and through the backyard to the fence, until I spotted the dog's blood trail. I followed it back to Buddy's house. It didn't lead to the kitchen door; instead, it led to the caved-in door between the carport and the house.

Now that I had the pattern of Mister George's blood, and I was focused on it, I backtracked through the house and was able to discern the dog's bloody trail. I pulled a SureFire light from my pocket and used the flashlight to help me find the black drops on the dark hardwood floors. Now that I knew what I was looking for, I was able to make out a few gory paw prints going down the hall past the living room toward the rear of the house where I found a bedroom to my left and a bathroom straight ahead. Slowing down, I saw the fine mist of a blood spray on the doorjamb of the bedroom.

"I think Mister George was shot here," I called out. I heard Laura cut off her conversation and snap shut her cell phone before moving to where I was shining my flashlight on the floor. Just inside the bedroom door was a chipped piece of wood where a bullet had burrowed in. "I bet we can dig the slug out of this oak floor."

Laura's attention was drawn to something in the bathroom, and she knelt inside the doorway and pushed aside a small garbage pail. Using her ballpoint pen, she picked up a shiny brass spent cartridge. "Thirty-two caliber, UMC manufacture."

"No one heard gunshots?" I asked.

"No, but the pop of a thirty-two wouldn't make much noise."

"But Buddy wasn't shot?"

"Bo, I'm not sure," she said. "He was a mess, so if he had a bullet hole, I might have missed it, but I don't think so."

I fished an evidence bag out of my pocket and held it open while she dropped the casing inside it. We returned to the living room where Laura had paper and plastic bags marked with evidence numbers sitting on an old divan. She picked up a clipboard with a diagram of the house and started annotating the new finds on the chart. Then she flipped to another page where she added the casing to her evidence log.

Looking out the window, I saw a woman standing at the railing of a front porch. Down below on the grass stood a man. The woman had a hand over her mouth, and the man was talking, his hand pointing in the general direction of the house. "Are those the neighbors?"

Laura glanced and said, "Yeah, our only two witnesses for what they're worth."

I thought of something. "Mind if I talk to them?"

"Be my guest," she said, waving her hand as her phone started playing the Lone Ranger's theme again.

I made my way out the front door, past the deputies, and to the couple on the front porch across the street. They were about the same height—right in the middle of five foot five. He was a stick man wearing a pair of faded jeans and a belt hitched to the smallest point, which was still too big on his waist. On top, he wore a flannel shirt over a ribbed T-shirt. He was clean-shaven with wispy white hair.

The woman was as thick as he was thin. In her youth, she was probably shapely and soft with curves in all the right places. The years had layered her body with extra flesh. She wore a bright print dress that hurt my eyes. Her hair was still blond, and just like Miss Rose, this woman's makeup was in place.

"Miss Williams," I began, after I introduced myself to them and showed them my badge.

"Estelle," she said with a smile.

"Right, ma'am. Estelle, did you tell the deputies what all was taken from Buddy's place?"

"Oh, yes. They had him covered up when those deputies had me to look around his place, but I could see it was bad. Real bad."

"How do you know what was taken?" I asked.

"Oh, I've got a good memory. My body isn't what it used to be," she smiled, "but my mind is still sharp. I have always been good with remembering things. It's just my knack. I worked for Buddy, kind of a clerk and a housekeeper. The man couldn't keep a plate clean. So, I knew everything that was in his house."

"And what did they take?"

"Oh, the cash for sure, and some ring sets and silver dollar collector sets out of the jewelry case, a couple of solitaires. Engagement rings and such. Oh, they also took a mint condition silver tea serving set—teapot, tray, spoons, and even silver cups. It's a shame, too, that they took it since John was going to trade Buddy for it, weren't you, John?"

John nodded.

"How much cash was there?" I asked.

"I kept telling Buddy about keeping so much money at home, but he didn't like making trips to the bank. He always kept a couple thousand on hand, he said to buy anything he wanted from a customer before they changed their mind."

"Did Buddy keep any guns around?"

"Two pistols," Estelle answered. "Like I told the officers, he kept one in a hollowed-out book by his desk. He talked about another, but I never saw it."

"One was a Colt Python," John said. "He kept it in the hollowed book on his desk where he did business. And the other was a Colt pocket .32 I remember because the gunman in the *Maltese Falcon* film carried one."

"Where was that one?"

John smiled. "Buddy kept the .32 in his medicine chest in the bathroom. He figured he could get to a piece at either end of the house if something happened."

"Trooper, would you like some coffee? I don't know where my manners have been." Both had porcelain mugs, and the coffee smelled strong and fresh. I told her I would love a cup. Actually, between breakfast and Miss Rose, I'd had enough coffee, but I couldn't disappoint Estelle, the perfect hostess who hurried across the yard toward her own house, leaving John and me alone in the yard. We stood there not talking to each other, both of us watching the scene unfolding across the road at Buddy's house.

"I saw who did it," John Charles finally said in a steady voice. His hands were shaking as they held a coffee cup, but I wasn't sure if it was fear at how close he had come to death or just an old age ailment. "I didn't get a good look at them, but I saw them just the same. I was sitting right there," he indicated his living room on the other side of the big picture window, "watching my morning shows when I heard them pull out, kicking up dust and gravel." I hadn't asked for the retelling of his tale, but he probably wanted to try it out, so he could tune it up before he told it to a larger audience. "I looked out my window and saw a Tempo, all rusted out. I worked thirty-two years for Ford. I know my Ford products," he said proudly. "So, I'm telling you it was a Ford Tempo. I think only one person was in the car."

Dutifully, I flipped open my notebook, clicked open my pen, and scratched notes on the paper while I made encouraging noises.

"I saw Buddy's side door open," John continued. "From my window here, you can see right into his carport and it ain't right for his door to be open. I got a bad feeling."

"You went to check on him?" I asked, prodding. "You and Buddy close friends?"

"We're the only ones left." He nodded his head, but I could swear he seemed a little perturbed—as if I had gotten him out of his story-telling rhythm. "The others who built here have died or sold out, so we are the last original ones, and we have to watch out for each other. The four of us are all that's left."

"You were saying you were worried about Buddy?"

"The side door," John said. "Right. I went over, and I knew right away something was wrong. I saw all the blood and Buddy wasn't moving, so I called nine-one-one."

The screen door behind us banged, causing John and me to start. Estelle was crossing the yard with a metal serving tray held in front of her. "I didn't know if you took yours with or without cream, so I brought it all with me." I took my coffee black, like all cop stereotypes do.

I asked John, "While you were at Buddy's, did you see Mister George?"

"Mister George?" This came from Estelle and not John.

"Yes, ma'am," I explained. "Do you all know Miss Rose and her dog?"

"Of course," John said. I noted the irritation in his tone. "I just told you we're the last of the original folks living along here. We're all four widowers, though Rose was a widow long before any of the rest of us. Like I said, we all watch out for each other; if we didn't, we'd end up in some home. As soon as you get old, people want to shove you in a home."

"What about Mister George?" Estelle asked, setting the tray on the rail of the porch. She retrieved a coffee cup ringed with lipstick smears.

"Someone shot him," I said. "I think the same person who killed Buddy."

"Oh, no," Estelle said. "Rose is going to just be a mess."

"She's got to be all tore up," John said.

I told them that Miss Rose was indeed upset about Mister George's death.

"You sure the same person killed Buddy and Mister George?" John asked.

"I think so," I replied. Before I could elaborate or ask them any more questions, I heard Laura call my name and saw her waving to me as she jogged toward her cruiser.

"That lady detective is trying to get your attention," John said.

"Looks like she is at that," I said. I handed Estelle the mug and thanked her for coffee as I headed toward the road. Laura was already backing out of the drive.

"I think they have our guy," Laura said as I slid into the passenger seat. She nodded at the radio. "Right now, Jefferson County is chasing a Ford Tempo. What do you want to bet it's our killer?"

I told her I wouldn't take that bet. In mystery books and on television, murder is a whodunit, but in reality, most murders are rash crimes committed on impulse and are not well-planned—that's one of the reasons the clearance rate of homicides is pretty high. Criminals are stupid and make mistakes. He or she is caught because he and the victim had argued in the past, or the killer can't keep his mouth shut and brags to someone. Or, as is often the case, the lawbreaker is caught by his bad driving. I can't even begin to count how many of my cases have been solved by an alert patrol officer and the stupid actions of a criminal. Ted Bundy was caught because of his bad driving.

As we made our way to the interstate and Laura pointed the car west toward Louisville, we listened to the Louisville Metro police officer calling out the progress of his chase over the radio. I could hear the adrenaline edge creeping into his voice. A few moments later, the officer came back on the radio. This time, he asked for an ambulance and rescue squads to start rolling to Wolf Pen Branch Road.

"The Tempo just T-boned a Jeep Cherokee. Everyone in both vehicles is going to need EMS," the officer on the radio said.

By the time Laura and I arrived at Wolf Pen Branch, the road was blocked by cruisers with flashing lights, two ambulances, and a fire truck. The curve was a nasty switchback, and the Tempo and the Jeep were mangled together against a large oak at the side of the road. We pulled into a driveway and went over to a group of cops clustered around the fire truck.

As we drew close, a voice called out, "Well if it ain't Bo Stokes hisself." The voice was deep and gravelly, which was incongruous with Frank Bernard's short, skinny frame. Except for being Black and being a competent cop, Frank reminded me of Barney Fife, a skinny man swaggering and perpetually hitching his belt up on his hips. Frank broke away from the group and came over to greet Laura and me. "Hell of a thing," he said. "I was hoping for a nice quiet shift today, and now we have this." He jerked a thumb toward a young, uniformed officer at the center of the gaggle of cops. "Rookie's lucky the bad guy was a bad shot."

"What happened?" Laura asked.

"Well," Frank said, warming to telling the story. "The kid was running radar on the highway, and he needed to take a leak, so he decided to swing off on Blankenbaker Road and hit a Dairy Mart for a john and free cup of coffee. He's not even off the ramp when he sees this Tempo blow by. At least he remembered hearing the BOLO that you guys had put out, but he must have forgotten the part about the guy being an armed murder suspect. Instead of doing a felony car stop, the kid just initiates a regular traffic stop."

"Oh, no," Laura whispered.

"Oh, yes," Frank said. "The rookie's not even out of his car when the driver of the Tempo unloads at him through the rear window of the car. Luckily the guy couldn't shoot straight with his big hand cannon. The rookie took cover, and the bad guy took off. At least the kid had the wits about him to chase after him, and then this happened." Frank looked over at the mangled cars, shaking his head. I noticed two EMTs loading a black body bag on a stretcher. My second, and hopefully last one for the day.

"Is that our perp?" Laura pointed at the stretcher.

"We should be so lucky," Frank replied. "It seems the good Lord looks over kids, drunks, and murderers. The suspect was bounced around the inside of the Tempo like a pinball, but he's alive. This poor schmuck driving the Jeep was wearing his seat belt and probably driving the speed limit and gets sideswiped and killed."

"Where's the perp?" Laura asked.

"Already in the first ambulance, heading to the emergency room."

"Do we have an ID on him?"

"Ronnie Vittow," Frank replied.

"Damn!" Laura exclaimed, more in an exasperated voice rather than a shout.

"You know him?" I asked.

"One of our local cranksters," she answered. "He's been out of the pen less than a year, and I've locked him up three times on felony charges that should have sent him back to prison but haven't. Our judge keeps letting him out."

"I don't think the judge will let him out this time," I said.

"No, not this time," Laura agreed. "Not a robbery-murder."

Frank nodded, and then jerked his head for us to follow. He led us to the rear of his patrol car where there was a cardboard box advertising Chiquita bananas. Inside the box were plastic cases with Liberty Dollars and Kennedy half dollars, as well as boxes complete with marked tags of earrings and rings and necklaces. Lying on top of the box was a nickel-plated Colt Python and a box of shells. "This stuff spilled out of the car when it rolled. My guys are still looking around to see if anything else was tossed out." As he said this, we all glanced toward the side of the road where several uniformed officers were scouring the roadway and underbrush near the accident. "He probably was heading to a fence to pawn the stuff here in Louisville."

Laura and I both grunted in agreement.

"And the *coup de grâce*." Frank pulled a brown Kroger grocery bag from inside his car. Opening the bag with a flourish he showed us the contents—a blood-coated tire iron. "Possibly the murder weapon."

"Most probably."

Laura and Frank began talking about the crime spree.

Something bothered me, something I hadn't seen in the box. Leaning into the car, I looked at the entire contents of the Chiquita box and made sure neither one was there. Then I wandered across the road to inspect the wreck.

Firemen in their heavy coats and suspendered pants were packing away a large saw, the Jaws-of-Life, which it looked like they used to try to save the Jeep's driver. The Tempo had T-boned the Jeep square in the driver side, pushing the door almost to the Jeep's center console. The Tempo was folded like an accordion, the window spiderwebbed and caked with a blood spray similar to the one I'd seen at Buddy's house. The driver's side door was ajar, so I leaned in and looked around, but all I saw were some Whopper boxes. I got out of the car and walked around to the rear. The trunk had popped open on impact and spit out the rear tire, which was lying in someone's driveway on the opposite side of the road. I still didn't see either item I was looking for in the trunk or in the roadway, so I walked back to the wreck. This time I walked around, looking underneath and around the cars. I noticed a stethoscope hanging from the rearview mirror of the Jeep, along with a laminated ID badge. I reached inside the Jeep and examined the smiling face on Dr. Steven Burnett's badge. Then I heard a sound from the back seat of the Jeep. Something was whimpering.

Leaning into the car, I saw a plastic box with a door. A pet carrier. I opened the metal door and all I saw was a small ball of red-brown and a pair of floppy ears.

"Come here, fella," I called softly. I lifted out a dachshund puppy that couldn't have weighed more than four pounds. I quickly realized the fella was female, and she had a small cut on her nose and a tag on her collar that read Peanut. She wagged her tail and wanted to be pet, which I did as I walked across and rejoined Laura and Frank at his cruiser.

Frank said, "Don't tell me this guy stole a dog."

"No, but he might have killed one," Laura said.

I didn't jump in and agree with her, which made Laura give me an odd look, but she didn't ask me anything else.

"She was in the Jeep," I said. "Maybe the family will want her back."

"This is all I need," Frank said. "As far as I know, this victim doesn't have a family. He lives in a condo down the road. The first thing I did was send one of our detectives there, so a loved one wouldn't wander down the road and see this guy splattered across the pavement. No one was home, and a neighbor told the detective the guy was divorced with no other family." Frank sighed. "I guess I'll have to call animal control."

"Frank, don't you have a heart?" Laura asked.

"Yeah, it's on my desk at the station."

"I'll take care of it." I'd spoken without thinking. "I'll take care of the dog, it's the least I can do for your solving our case here." But he hadn't solved all the cases. At least not mine.

After the tow trucks hauled away the wrecks, all the public servants packed up and dispersed, so there wasn't much for us to do. Climbing into Laura's cruiser, I put the dog carrier in the backseat and asked Laura if she wanted to talk to Ronnie Vittow.

"No," she said. "While you were playing PETA man, I called the hospital. Ronnie's out with a concussion and sedated. I'll swing by this evening and talk to him if he comes around, but I think with everything we've got, he's my man."

I didn't take her bait right then. Instead, I asked her why she thought Ronnie Vittow murdered Buddy. But I knew the answer. Like I said most murders are straightforward, about money or vengeance. Laura pegged Ronnie Vittow's as money.

"He's a crankster," Laura said. "And once you get hooked on meth, you know what happens, Bo."

And I did. Paranoia and meanness.

"Ronnie probably thought Buddy was an easy score," Laura continued. "Maybe he'd been in the shop before and saw all the cash in the money drawer, so he decides to push in the door this morning. Buddy went for his pistol or had it in hand when he confronted Ronnie. But Ronnie was probably so hyped up that he just started swinging the tire iron and didn't stop."

I had to agree, that was a probable scenario. And if not exactly the way it happened, it was pretty damn close.

We rode for another fifteen minutes with only the sound of the police radio to entertain us, until Laura finally asked me about Mister George. I told her what I thought and what I planned to do. She listened and said nothing. No comment for or against, so when she let me off at Miss Rose's place, I leaned down into the open window of her car. All she said before driving away was, "Do what you got to do, Bo."

"I'm just doing what I think's right," I said.

"Like at Los Amigos?" she said with a smile.

"No," I said simply. "That was wrong." Unconsciously, my hand strayed up to my chest, patting where the envelope sat inside my jacket.

I toted the pet carrier up the steps like a traveling salesman carrying his briefcase of wares. Miss Rose opened the door before I was halfway up the steps. We both took our places where we each had sat earlier in the morning. Miss Williams had already told Miss Rose about Buddy, and she was in a daze. I told her how I followed Mister George's trail to Buddy's house, and how Laura Murphy and I went to Louisville where the police captured Ronnie Vittow. I didn't mention anything about ballistics or details of that nature. I just told the story as I had planned. When I was finished, Miss Rose asked no questions, but her lip trembled some, probably wondering why her companion was dead and why a neighbor was dead as well.

Peanut had been quiet throughout the story I told—most of it the truth, mixed with a few lies—but now she let out a bark. I opened the door, and the little wiener dog ran out and scurried around wagging her tail with the puppy enthusiasm that sees everything as new and exciting. She tried to climb my leg, whining, wanting to be pet, and when I ignored her, she went over to Miss Rose and barked to be picked up.

"Beauregard," Miss Rose said, looking down at the pup, "you didn't bring that dog for me? I don't think I can take another heartbreak."

"Yes, ma'am, I did," I said. I told her how the pup belonged to a dead man. "If you don't take her; I have to take her to the pound, because I don't know anyone else that would have Peanut. Both of you lost someone today, and I thought maybe you'd want to take her in."

Miss Rose picked up the puppy and tried to hold on to the squirming little animal that was licking and wagging her tail all at once. "Beauregard, I don't know if I feel right about this, what with Mister George dead."

"If it's not right in a few days, you call me, and I'll come pick her up from you," I lied. "I need to get going."

Miss Rose eyed me as I walked toward the door. Her wrinkled hands were stroking the dachshund as she spoke to me. "Beauregard, thank you for humoring an old woman's silly need to find out what happened to her friend, even if her friend was just a little dog."

"You're welcome, ma'am." I left Miss Rose, but I really wasn't done.

I started my car and drove less than a mile before I parked in front of one more house I had been to today. This time the door was opened before I climbed out of my car.

"Trooper, you came back." John Charles came out on the porch to meet me.

"Yes, I did, and you knew I'd be back."

His head nodded.

"Why don't you tell me how you killed Mister George?"

He looked at me for half a second and then looked down at a spot on the floor. He didn't even try to deny it. He slumped against the rail of the porch. He didn't say anything; he just looked off into the distance.

I decided to help him out. "How's this for what happened? You saw the Tempo peel out of there, and you did rush over to check on Buddy. He was already dead. But you didn't call nine-one-one right away."

John Charles shook his head. "I was in the service, and I fought in Nam just like Rose's husband did, but I was on the ground. I saw plenty of dead folks over there. You don't forget that. I knew I couldn't do anything for Buddy."

"Since you couldn't help him," I said, "you decided to get what you wanted before you called nine-one-one. The silver serving set."

He nodded. "I had helped Buddy at the flea markets for two months, and all I wanted was the silver set. He promised it to me."

"But he didn't keep his word."

"No, he didn't," John said. "And he hadn't paid me for my work."

"But you had really wanted that serving set," I prompted.

"Yes," he said looking me in the eyes. "But not for me. For Rose. I figured he had kept the set just to spite me. He knew I wanted to give it to her, and he just kept it to be mean. Buddy was that way sometimes. So, I figured he'd keep the set in his bedroom."

"The one next to the bathroom at the end of the hall?"

He nodded. "It was there on his nightstand."

"And then what happened?"

"I heard a noise," John said. "I thought maybe the robbers had come back. It wasn't rational, but you saw Buddy and what had happened to him. I knew Buddy kept the Colt .32 in the medicine cabinet, so I ducked into the bathroom and grabbed the gun. I had the gun along my leg, and was looking down the hall, when something bumped into me."

"Mister George?"

He nodded.

"The gun went off."

He slowly nodded. "I didn't mean to shoot Miss Rose's dog," John said. "He just spooked me."

"You panicked and grabbed the silver serving set and the gun and hurried home to call nine-one-one," I said, finishing his tale.

Again, he slowly nodded. "I'll get it." His shoulders were hunched over as he disappeared into the house, only to return a moment later with a pillowcase that clanged as he walked. He handed me the heavy sack. Inside was the silver tray and a small Colt pistol. "I suppose you got to take me in," John said in an even voice. "Can I at least call Miss Rose and tell her what happened?"

"No," I answered. John Charles gave me a curious look. "I'm not taking you in, and I don't think you should tell Miss Rose anything. As far as she knows, the same man who murdered Buddy killed Mister George, and that's the way it'll stay."

"I think I should tell her."

I shook my head. "No, John, you shouldn't. It would break that lady's heart, and she's already had her heart broken once today. What she needs right now is a good friend more than she needs the truth. I think there's a shovel somewhere in Miss Rose's garage. You might want to go over and offer to help her put Mister George to rest."

He nodded slowly, looking me in the eye. "I reckon I should be heading over to see Miss Rose."

"I think that's a good idea," I said as I picked up the heavy pillowcase and headed off the porch.

I climbed into my cruiser. The unopened envelope in my pocket was heavy. I pulled it out and ran my fingertips along the seams, worrying with it. Then, I tore one end off, just like pulling off a Band-Aid. Do it quick, and the pain is less. The letter was on watermarked paper. I read it through slowly. Twice.

As I said earlier, the sun was setting behind John Charles, the killer of Mister George. I know he'd meant no ill will when he killed the dog. I know some would argue I had no right to lie to Miss Rose, but I felt it was the right thing to do. It would kill Miss Rose to find out who had killed her companion.

And I understand how love can drive a man to do foolish things. Love had made a fool of me. I was playing fate and giving John Charles a second chance, even if I hadn't gotten one.

Reading the decree in my hand gave the divorce a tangible finality. Like so many people, my ex-wife—a woman I had loved, married, and had two beautiful girls with—had become someone I took for granted. One day, we woke up and realized we were strangers sharing a bed. She asked me to move out, and she moved on.

I tried to reconcile with her several times because I couldn't let go. I thought we could fix what was broken. Los Amigos was the final straw. She had agreed to have lunch with me at her favorite Mexican restaurant. I thought we were going to talk, maybe work things out, but she brought her attorney along to hand me the papers. I grew rowdy and created a scene. I talked, I pleaded, and I shouted, but as my voice rose, I saw the light in her eyes sailing away. The special thing we once had was gone. If it weren't for the good Detective Laura smoothing things over, I might have gotten locked up that day.

And the short letter in my hand was the bitter end of a life together. Finality. I reread the letter, letting the official words wash over me. Tugging at my left hand, I worked the wedding band free. I folded the letter and slid the single sheet of paper back into the envelope. I dropped the ring in on top of the letter. Tucking the envelope back in my breast pocket, I wondered if ever there'd be someone who would bring me a second chance like I had done for John Charles.

I sure hoped so.

"Mr. George" is probably the story I've written that has taken the most circuitous route to publication. I originally sold the story to a yearly anthology edited by Michael Bracken. The sale happened before my first child was born. The anthology closed before my story could be published. "Mr. George" went back out to make the rounds to various publication slush piles. I thought it had found a home when it was picked to be part of an International Association of Crime Writers anthology. Yet again, the collection died on the vine, and the story went unpublished until I reconnected with Michael Bracken and asked if he would take a look at the story again, and he published it in Black Cat Weekly. *The publication path of "Mr. George" was a long one. How long? Well, the son who wasn't born yet when I wrote the story is now in college.*

Lou Manfredo *is the author of three highly acclaimed NYPD Detective Joe Rizzo novels:* Rizzo's War, Rizzo's Fire, *and* Rizzo's Daughter. *Kirkus declared Rizzo, "The most authentic cop in contemporary crime fiction," and the novels have been compared favorably to the late Ed McBain's legendary 87th Precinct novels. In addition, he has authored two short story collections:* A Dozen Ways to Die *and* Footsteps in the Shadows. *Manfredo's work has appeared in various publications including* Brooklyn Noir, New Jersey Noir, *and* Ellery Queen Mystery Magazine *as well as editions of* The Best American Mystery Stories; The Best of Best American Mystery Stories, The First Ten Years; EQMM*'s* The Crooked Road, Volume Two; Israel's The Short Story Project, *and* The Mysterious Bookshop Presents the Best Mystery Stories of the Year 2023.

A Brooklyn native and twenty-five-year veteran of its Criminal Justice System, he currently resides in New Jersey with his wife, Joanne, his first copy and language editor as well as creative associate.

DREAM STUFF
Lou Manfredo

When it took two days for me to notice my wife had left me, I decided it may be time for some lifestyle changes.

Once my mind was made up, it was amazing how easy it was to stand up and walk away. Advertising had been good to me: it made me rich, encouraged me to drink a lot, and forced me to realize just what a grand, ignoble beast that man truly was. But, most importantly, it hadn't *killed* me, and thanks to some eccentric and legendary campaign ideas, had even provided me with shining moments of genius. In the past, the good old days, the simpler, happier, happy days, my ad campaigns were famous for outrageous excesses and even offensive tones.

When a Midwestern electronics manufacturer turned to my New York Madison Avenue agency for help against the latest wave of Japanese products, I put together a proposal that blew the crew-cutted Iowan president of sales away. One thirty second TV spot featured actual color footage of US Marines in combat on Iwo Jima. It was interspersed with grainy black and white vintage film of a Japanese factory floor, with row upon row of identically attired, hunched, and somber young women working at primitive assembly tables. We used a voice-over actor who turned in a damn near perfect rendition of Mike Wallace's narrative from the old Victory at Sea documentary.

The FCC killed the spot after receiving a few thousand complaints, but not before the publicity had nearly doubled our client's sales. That year my wife was turning thirty-seven. To celebrate, we bought an eight-room beach "cottage" in the Hamptons.

Arguably though, my crowning achievement was the Bonz.

I had been a superficially hip, totally today kind of advertising man with a Starbucks in one hand and a cigarette in the other. But—and here lies the irony—my most successful campaigns had their roots in Bonzo Burger. For those of you who may have missed the dot-com yuppie heyday 1990s, Bonzo Burger had done to the Big Mac what penicillin had done to syphilis. And it was *my* ad campaign that sold it—lock, stock, and artery-clogging trans-fat globules—despite Oprah's periodic diet rants against it. One of the print ads was modeled after a 1950s-style magazine cigarette spot, depicting a distinguished-looking doctor type with one of those headband eye things affixed to his brow. He's pictured leaning in over his cluttered desk, eyes locked on the camera lens.

"Life is short," the copy caption has him saying boldly. "You might as well enjoy it. Bonzo Burger—take my advice: It's the right way to go."

That one eventually fell to an American Heart Association counter-campaign, but the raucous kick-up gave a serious boost to my client's ability to steal fully packed, sweat-pant-wearing burger chompers away from McDonald's and Burger King.

That year, I bought a Jaguar.

But, truthfully, my heart was never in it. Somewhere in the back of my money-hungry, twenty-first century brain someone else was lurking. A Humphrey Bogart, Robert Mitchum kind of guy. A guy who would forsake frozen yogurt for chocolate Breyers, granola bars for Hershey's, trail mix for Lucky Strikes. A tough guy. A *real* man.

So, after nearly twenty-five years in the make-believe, surreal Madison Avenue world, I simply relocated myself to a nicer somewhere else. And my wife deciding to leave me made it that much easier.

It seemed so reasonable. Since I was earning my living in a fantasy world anyway, I might as well do it in one of my choosing.

And on the day I finally walked away, 401K bursting at the seams, pockets stuffed with sold-out partnership cash and eight million dollars in assets whacked up fifty-fifty between me and the bride, it all felt so *right*.

I visited a retro clothing shop in the East Village and spent a small fortune on estate sale mid-1940s Rogers Peet handmade suits. Another bundle went for two dark felt Fedoras, a charcoal gray Stetson, and a spiffy deep blue Dobbs, all in their original boxes.

Next I signed a lease on a three-room walk-up office on Manhattan's Broadway near Murray Street. I hired my sweet young secretary away from Broward, Gulliver, and Hutton by paying her twice what she was worth. With a shiny new investigator license in hand, I set up shop.

Philip Marlowe. Richard Diamond. Sam Spade. And now me, Billy Hutton.

I had been known as the oddest duck in the Madison Avenue flock, so no one was truly surprised when I morphed from advertising whiz kid to dapper, 1940-ish shamus. Looking back, that probably should have offended me. My closest friends seemed to just shrug and say, "It figures." Go figure.

Ah, but how quickly and ironically reality reared its ugly head.

I spent the next two years de-bugging former business associates' offices and occasionally tailing one of their cheating spouses. I digitally recorded blue collar workers as they painted their houses or worked off-the-books jobs while simultaneously collecting disability checks for phony job-related injuries. I spent long, boring hours doing title searches and finding witnesses to auto accidents for negligence lawyers and insurance companies.

On that summer morning, as things turned classically beautiful, you can imagine my joy. At last, my insane fantasy world took a step toward true existence. Mary Lou, my previously noted overpaid secretary, poked her cute little head into my office, shielding me from any view of the reception area, not to mention her delightfully lush body. "There's some classy dame here to see you," she said softly. I should mention, Mary Lou is a clever young thing. She's not above a bit of role-play dialogue in order to keep me signing her exorbitant paychecks. She's a greedy little gal and quite the pragmatist. Sometimes I think I'm in love with her. "A dame?" I asked, looking up from the racing form which I could barely make sense of, my feet propped on the corner of my desk. "Did I have an appointment we forgot to remember?" She shook her head and cracked her chewing gum. Merely one of her imaginative props. The movement of her shoulder told me she was scratching at a thigh. Mary Lou had long ago made a point of letting me know that, in the spirit of my bygone era lust, she sported garters beneath her tight skirts. Apparently, they sometimes caused an itch. For me as much as her, I suspected.

"Nope," she answered. "A walk-in. Says it's *real* important and looks like she's got the dough to make it so. Wanna find out?"

I swung my feet off the desktop and tugged my vintage Sanforized Arrow shirt. I tossed the scratch sheet into the open top drawer and slammed it shut, rattling the Jim Beam bottle in a lower drawer.

"Send her in," I said.

The woman was tall and beautiful, of course, a living doll wearing a skimpy white dress and tanned to the color of a shiny penny in your pocket. She seemed to be about thirty, but the big-time money aura oozing from her pores like honey told me she could be older—well maintained and expensive to keep. She had jet-black hair cut short and in the style of a bygone time, and the only God-honest violet eyes I've seen in my life. When I first looked into those eyes, I found out what I'd been missing. I rose to greet her. "I'm Billy Hutton. Who might you be?" She reached out a slim hand to take mine, her nails shiny red, and we shook as though it meant something.

"I'm Angelina Winslow. *Mrs.* Angelina Winslow."

I nodded. If Mary Astor had an edge on this dame, I didn't see it. "Please," I said, releasing her hand and pointing my chin at one of the two leather chairs in front of my desk. "Have a seat."

She sat slowly, like honey moving in a jar. I found myself wondering what the dictionary meaning of "lascivious" was. I made a mental note to look it up. This broad, I suspected, was "lascivious."

She crossed her bare left leg, a flashing golden thigh making a tantalizing promise, and began to open her handbag. Despite the distracting glimpse of flesh, I noticed the bag was a Fendi.

She had caught me checking her out, and her violet eyes were smiling when I managed to meet them again.

"Do you mind if I smoke?" she asked, her tone telling me she intended to.

"Not at all," I said, taking a near empty ashtray from a drawer and placing it before her. She produced a Marlboro red from the Fendi. No Virginia Slims or ultra lights for this dame. And before I could fish my antique 14 carat Ronson Adonis from my pocket, she had fired the Marlboro with a matchbook match, blowing out the yellow-blue flame with a long, round, scarlet-lipped breath. I watched her as I lit my own Lucky Strike. She pulled deeply on her smoke, collapsing her cheeks a bit. If she had intended to start my mind wandering, she had succeeded extraordinarily well.

"What can I do for you, Mrs. Winslow?" I asked after all the rituals seemed to have played themselves out.

She leaned deeply forward and dropped the spent match, now perfectly folded in half, into my ashtray. Her eyes never left mine, so despite my instincts, I allowed only my peripheral vision to partake of her cleavage.

"Someone poses a threat to my marriage. I'd like you to visit him, then use any method of persuasion at your disposal to dissipate the threat." *Well*, I thought, *I may only have one more line before the first commercial break*. I wanted it to be a good one.

"That's too bad," I said, poking in the ashtray at her folded match with the hot tip of my Lucky Strike. "Any idea who might be posing this threat?"

She smiled—lasciviously, I think—and I swear, I felt a vibration in my groin.

"Why, of course. It's my lover, he's been behaving quite bizarrely of late. Even more so than usual." I kept a neutral expression, like a real pro. Like a tough gumshoe who heard this sort of thing all the time. Like a jaded guy who'd seen it all.

I knew I needed something punchy for my close-up, so I reached across the desk and pressed the intercom button on the phone.

"Yeah, Boss?" Mary Lou said through the speaker. Her choice of words and inflection told me what I already knew: She was starring in her own little drama.

"Hold my calls. No disturbances. Got it?" I said.

What calls? I heard her thinking, her pretty little mouth all screwed up in an ironic smile. "Got it," was the line she delivered. I leaned back in my chair and opened a drawer, producing the Jim Beam and two almost clean rock glasses.

"We need to talk some more," I said.

Mrs. Winslow's smiled again. "Yes, we most certainly do." Her eyes fell on the bottle of booze. "Bourbon," she said, pink tongue tip poking out between ruby lips at word's end. "But of course."

I didn't waste any time after she left. Her check for twenty-five hundred dollars sat where she had placed it on my desk. It was drawn on her and her husband's joint account, and that struck me as being a bit odd. Why hire private heat to scare away her boyfriend, then pay with her husband's check? A paper trail should be the last thing she'd want, and I figured two-and-a-half Gs was nothing more than pocket change for her. Why not pay in cash? But then, why use paper matches? You'd figure a dame like Angelina would be lighting her way to lung cancer with Tiffany's finest Colibri jeweled lighter, not book matches from Ahmed's newspaper kiosk.

She was an all-around enigma, and with the good looks to make a guy want to solve the puzzle.

Mary Lou poked her head in. "I'm going out for a late lunch, Billy. See you later."

I nodded. "Okay," I said and reached for the phone.

He answered on the fifteenth ring, better than average for a state court employee.

"Joey?" I said. "Billy Hutton here."

"Hey, Billy," he said, a happy anticipation in his voice. "I'll call ya right back."

I smiled and hung up. What with all the recent courthouse scandals in and around the Big Apple, old Joey was not taking any chances. Or at least, not taking as many. About five minutes later, he called back from his personal cell.

"What can I do for you, Billy?" he asked, thinking about which Tribeca hot spot he'd be blowing my dough in soon.

Joey Zinna was a court clerk in the Manhattan New York State Supreme Court's County Clerk Division. For three C-notes and an unsigned Christmas card every December, Joey and I had entered into a sort of professional retainer arrangement. And I wasn't his only benefactor, and pretty small potatoes to boot. What with all the PIs, process servers, title companies, and law firms in the borough of Manhattan, I figured Joey was good for about twenty, twenty-five untaxed Gs a year to supplement his state paycheck. So every business day was Christmas to him. Ho-Ho-Ho.

"Well, it's like this, Joey. I want to know if there's a prenup on file for a Mr. and Mrs. Alexander Winslow. Wife's name is Angelina. And a copy of any will at Surrogates Court. Can you do it?"

Joey chuckled. "It's done, Billy. But it'll cost me a toll with the Surrogates clerk. You want this stuff faxed to you?"

"Sure."

"Well, that's another expense. I gotta go out to Fed Ex, can't risk it on the house fax."

"How much?"

He sighed. He was gonna do me a favor. "Being as it's you, just two bills. No, better make it two-fifty. It can get done for two-fifty."

I nodded, realizing once again that America's brand of entrepreneurial capitalism is, and will always remain, far and away the most efficient of all economic systems, period. The thought caused me to swell with warm, patriotic pride.

"Done," I said. "You're the man, Joey. Fax it a-sap and drop by when you can. See Mary Lou for the dough."

"Have a nice day, Mr. Hutton. Pleasure doin' business with ya." His tone dripped with sarcastic subservience.

The politicians who ran the courthouse would just have to appoint him Chief Clerk someday. He was born for the job.

By six thirty that evening, I believed I had it figured out. The Winslow prenuptial agreement was clear. If Mr. and Mrs. Winslow ever divorced, she and her delectable thighs would be screwed. She'd get a living out of it, sure, but she would lose her shot at millions. And Angelina hadn't impressed me as the type of dame who'd be inclined to let something like that happen.

So, she comes to see me—the delusional ex-advertising genius cum retro PI who she read about in last year's *New York Times* Metro Section. I stand six two, one ninety-one, lean and mean. I've got a 1951 Colt Commander revolver slung in an Olsen-Huckleberry shoulder holster and a set of authentic speakeasy brass knuckles tucked inside my belt. When I first got my PI license, I took a self-defense course and aced it. I was an authentic tough guy, and I had a paper certificate with a little gold sticker to prove it.

Of course, the last actual *fight* I had was back in the seventh grade, and then I got my clock cleaned by the chess team president. But hell, Angelina Winslow didn't need to know that.

Yeah, I had it all figured out. Her lover boy was getting greedy as well as a little *too* lovey-dovey. It would be very easy for a guy to fall for this dame, fall hard, and she'd find herself in some serious economic distress if love conquered all. So she needed me to go see the guy, scare him a little, make him think I was maybe going to land on his spine with both feet, and with her money and juice backing me up. She was planning on not going steady anymore and dodging a divorce, and the poor sap boyfriend was maybe planning on taking her to the prom. I figured I could do it for her, charge her another grand or so, then bitterly sip some Jim Beam in memory of yet another love story gone tragically awry.

The next call I made was to an old college buddy of mine, an attorney my ex and I had often doubled with on dinner dates and Broadway plays. I reached him at his office.

After the catch-up chitchat of two guys who have recently discovered they have nothing much to talk about anymore, I got to the point. After I read him the one clause of the prenup I told him she had left me and I wasn't sure I had fully understood. He laughed.

"Sounds like the lady had herself a damn competent attorney. That clause completely releases Mrs. Winslow from the prenup if, during her marriage, her husband becomes socially impeded to the point where he can't continue to provide her with what would legally be considered a normal marital relationship. You know—comfort, companionship, slipping her some wood once in a while—like that."

"What would happen, exactly, if that clause *did* kick in?" I asked.

I could almost see him shrugging at the other end of the line. "All bets would be off. If for some reason hubby *did* become unable to function in a normal marital manner, any divorce proceedings initiated for any reason would be legally unbound by the prenup. The case would go through divorce court like any other."

"And she'd come out flush?"

He laughed. "Billy, I know Alexander Winslow by reputation. If she managed a non prenup divorce from him, under NY state law, she'd come out flusher than a bus full of ex-Trump wives."

I nodded. "Thanks, buddy. Let's get together soon."

As arranged, Mrs. Winslow called the office the following morning. My intercom buzzed and Mary Lou's voice carried through the line like silk.

"It's her, boss man," she purred. "And right on time."

I figured, what the hell. Ever since Angelina Winslow graced our gray little world with some good old pulp pizzazz, Mary Lou had been sashaying around the joint, shaking her butt and being all breathless and sexy, really getting into her role. She deserved a little feedback, some encouragement, so instead of shooting back with a quick, "Okay" over the box, I said, "Thanks, doll. Want to listen in?"

She gave me a throaty laugh, fully up to my challenge. "Not in my job description, boss. Three-ways will cost you extra."

I picked up the phone.

"Hutton," I said.

"He's at home right now," Angelina told me. "I just spoke to him. He'll be in all morning, but he has an audition at one."

Seems her little playmate was an aspiring musician of sorts. Tenor sax, she had told me.

"Okay, I'm on my way. Do you want to meet me somewhere near his place?"

She gave a cold laugh. "Mr. Hutton," she said. "I have never been near his place throughout our affair, why on earth would I go *now*?"

I frowned. "You've never been to his apartment? How come? Does he have roommates?"

"No, he lives alone. But—for God's sake—he lives in *Brooklyn*. *I do not go to Brooklyn*. Regardless of how many journalists continue to sing its praises."

I smiled into the phone. "I see. Well, I do go. Quite often. I'll call you later and let you know how I made out. But just so we're clear: You still want him scared off, correct? No last minute change of heart looming?"

"Correct. Out of my life."

"Okay, then, I'll get going. I'll call you later."

"On my cell, of course."

"Yes, Mrs. Winslow. On your cell."

We hung up. I stood and slipped into my coal gray, double-breasted Rogers Peet suit jacket. I placed the dark blue Dobbs on my head and rubbed first one, then the other wingtip shoe against the back of the opposite pants leg. Somewhere, Archie Goodwin was smiling.

I went down to Broadway and grabbed a cab. "Second Place and Clinton Street. Over in Brooklyn, just across the Brooklyn Bridge," I said to the cabbie.

He turned in his seat so quickly, the turban nearly fell off his head. The pink and green hole in the center of his gray beard barked at me. Suddenly, I was back to the future.

"Brook-line? Brook-line? I don't drive to Brook-line."

I glanced at his name on the hack license displayed on the dash.

"Well, Omkar," I said, leaning toward him, my eyes hardening, "that's where you're going this morning, or my next stop will be the Taxi and Limousine Commission's field office at the Immigration building. So step on it." I swear, I felt my lip curling, just like Bogie's. He glared at me but turned and slammed the cab into gear.

"Sum-uff-a-bit," I heard him mumble. New York City had naturalized yet another soul. We had a nice quiet ride to Brooklyn.

The brownstone was just off the corner on the south side of Second Place. It stood four stories, and lover boy lived in the small walk-in-basement apartment. I passed through the wrought iron gate and stepped around five garbage pails. Three very steep and crumbling stone steps led down to the apartment door.

I ran the script through my mind one last time, gathered myself up and, trying to ignore the knot that was beginning to form in my stomach, descended the steep steps. Time to deliver the message: Stop any threats aimed at the Winslow marriage. *Mrs.* Winslow has left the building. From now on she was just a fond memory in the long, lonely nights ahead.

The steel gate that usually guarded the plain wooden door stood wide open. The door itself was ajar. I leaned on the doorbell and waited. No one responded. I tried again.

That's when I heard it. The shrill, high-pitched whine of an off-the-hook landline telephone receiver. I pushed my head in closer and listened at the entryway. Yeah, no mistaking that sound. I stepped back and poked at the door. It swung open, eager to show me. So I looked in. The doorway opened into a small foyer; a closet door faced me. To the left, a small, sparsely furnished living room stood in midmorning semidarkness. The screaming phone lay just within my sight, knocked from its cradle, abandoned on the worn carpet that covered the floor.

I stepped in a bit more. A small table stood next to an empty umbrella stand in the foyer.

And there on the living room floor was lover boy, not looking all that attractive.

He was flat on his back, clad only in a pair of those weird-looking boxer briefs that seem designed to crush whatever you've got and usually making it look like you could maybe use a little more.

A raw red wound appeared near his heart. His body lay in an ocean of dark blood.

All of a sudden the movie that had been playing in my head switched off, the screen going all grainy, then blank. I turned and bolted from the place. The last dead body I had seen was my ex-wife's ninety-two-year-old uncle, and he had been laid out as pretty as a newborn in an expensive East Side funeral home.

That's it, I knew. Show's over, time to get real. When I got across the street, I pulled out my cell phone and dialed 911. Then I fished out my Lucky Strikes.

The cops confiscated my sixty-year-old Colt Commander without compliment or comment. A homicide detective scribbled out a receipt and handed it to me in exactly the same manner that my internist writes and hands out prescriptions for Aciphex. He listened to my story and jotted some notes.

"Go sit in the kitchen," he told me. "And don't touch nothing."

They had lover boy all covered up with a morgue sheet, but I could still smell his blood as I walked by. It smelled like Smith & Wollensky prime.

The cops let me sit there alone for a very long time. Then the homicide dick came in and sat across from me at the small table. He grimaced before speaking. I couldn't help thinking, seventy years ago the guy would have been played by Broderick Crawford.

"We found your cabbie pushing his hack over in Manhattan," he told me. "And by the way, the guy don't like you very much. But he did confirm your story—his trip log registers when he picked you up in the city and when he dropped you out front a few minutes before your 911 call came in. The victim was dead at least an hour or so before that. I called your office and your secretary says you were there all morning 'til you left for Brooklyn." He sighed, obviously unhappily resigned. "It looks like you may be clear on this."

I gave him a tight smile. "Sorry to disappoint you, Detective," I said. "Can I have my Colt back? It's kind of valuable."

He frowned at me and stuck a pointer finger into his right ear, scratching frantically as he answered.

"No gun yet. If it turns out this guy took a thirty-eight round to the chest, we'll have to clear your piece through ballistics. That'll take a few days. If it's a different caliber killed him, you can get the Colt back sooner. I'll let you know. You can claim the gun at the Property Clerk's office over at the Plaza. Just show them the receipt and your carry permit and hope nobody stole it yet."

I stood up. "So can I go now?" I asked.

He looked up at me absently, his large brown eyes watery. His bulbous nose looked like a road map, scattered burst capillaries running purple and red across it.

"Woulda been so easy if it turned out it was you," he said, almost to himself. "Now we gotta check out this broad—what's her name?—Winslow? *And* her husband. And twenty others, most likely. Then, after all that, it'll wind up some strung out junkie burglar killed him and we'll never find the guy anyway."

"Detective?" I prompted.

He focused on me a bit. "Yeah, yeah, okay, I'll walk you out past the uniforms. I'll be in touch if I need more from you."

We left the small kitchen and walked through the living room again. Now the body was uncovered and some stout woman with stringy hair and a gold detective shield draped on a chain around her neck was snapping photos with a digital camera. I saw no resemblance to any female television show sex bomb female cop. She belched loudly and long just as we passed.

"'Scuuuuze me," she said musically to no one in particular.

I kept my eyes away from the body and glued on the open front door and the bright afternoon sunshine streaming through it. There were few things I had ever wanted more than to get out of that apartment and into that sunlight, right then, right away, right now.

But, alas, it wasn't to be.

When we reached the small entry foyer, my eyes fell once again on that small table standing next to the empty umbrella stand.

But this time, I noticed something. Something I had missed earlier, something no one else would have reason to notice or care about if they had.

There, on the table, in a small glass ashtray, there it lay. Neat as could be. One simple burned up paper matchstick. Folded.

Folded perfectly in half.

And she said she had never been to lover boy's apartment.

Not even one time.

I turned and looked at the homicide dick. "Detective," I said. "This may turn out to be a lot easier than you think."

A few days later I sat at my desk, the office blinds shut tight against the morning sun, a small desk lamp the only light in the room. A glass of Beam sat next to the Lucky burning in my ashtray.

It was the first thing I had done. Right after finding the body and calling 911, I had reached for my smokes, lighting one with trembling fingers.

It was what any smoker under stress would do.

It was what *she* had done. Right after she shot him and watched enough blood leak out to assure her he would die. Just before she left. She would naturally light her smoke inside the apartment, take that first stabilizing drag, then step out to leave. Couldn't afford the time to pause out front to light up. No, she'd want to move steadily away, probably in a blond wig, wearing big sunglasses and cheap, baggy clothing that she could later discard.

But old habits die hard.

So, unconsciously, her mind awash with other concerns, she shook out her match, folded it neatly in half as she had done thousands of times before, and dropped it into the ashtray. She was, after all, a classy lady, and classy ladies do not toss spent matches into the street.

Not even a God-forsaken street such as one found in, of all places, *Brooklyn*.

I sipped the bourbon and reflected. Whereas I had thought it odd for her to be leaving a paper trail when she paid me by check, it had all been cold logic to her.

"But, really," she could say to cop or lawyer or Indian chief. "Why would I retain a private investigator to confront poor, dear Richard if it was my intention to *kill* him? Really, that would be quite illogical."

And with hubby off to jail for twenty-five to life on a murder-two, he could not possibly be any more "socially impeded." Goodbye prenup, hello divorce court. Divvy up that dough, toss the lawyers their cuts, and off she goes into the wild blue yonder, free as a bird and rich as Paris Hilton.

It was all so neat. And me—the perfect sap. She knew enough about me to figure I'd self-delude myself right into her hands. Flash me a thigh, bat an eye, and whamo—a wanna-be Sam Spade turned into Pee Wee Herman in one blinding flash.

And her plan certainly required a patsy. By sending me to the guy's apartment an hour or so after she shot him, all the pieces would fall perfectly into place.

She knew I'd have to explain my presence at the murder scene. She knew I'd tip the cops to her affair and tell them she believed, and maybe her husband had reason to believe, that lover boy had posed a threat to not only her marriage, but maybe her husband as well.

That would point the cops to both of them. Then she stacks the deck a little, and hubby takes the fall all by himself.

And she's rid of the three of us. Lover boy is dead, hubby is bye-bye, and me: I'm paid in full. Just an errand boy she sent off to Brooklyn to smell the blood and point the cops in the right direction.

I fingered the fax copy of the prenup on the desk in front of me, then reached for the phone.

Before I could get to it, the intercom buzzed.

"Yes?" I asked.

"It's Detective Basso, Billy," Mary Lou said. She had been rather subdued the last couple of days, considerably less theatrical.

Interviews with homicide dicks can have that effect on sweet young things.

Detective James Basso was sort of a buddy of mine. He worked Manhattan's silk stocking nineteenth precinct and did me favors routinely. In return, I paid some of his mortgage, in an indirect, public spirited sort of way, of course.

I had asked him to use his connections to keep me up to speed on the murder investigation in Brooklyn.

"Hello, Jim," I said. "What's new?"

I heard him laugh. "You got a few minutes, Billy? I got the whole rundown, plus the latest breaking news. All I need is film at eleven and I'm the friggin' network."

"Shoot," I said.

"Well, if it's a frame, it's a good one that's probably gonna stick. They arraigned the old man an hour ago. Murder-two. After they had gone in with a search warrant and found the murder weapon hidden behind his fireplace, it was a no-brainer. The gun was wiped clean, no prints. They got partials off the cartridges. It was him that loaded the piece. Claimed he had no idea why it was stashed behind the fireplace. He usually kept it under his side of the mattress."

I frowned. "Why shoot a guy with your own registered handgun, then wipe it clean and stash it inside your home?"

He laughed. "'Cause he's the stupidest son of a bitch on the planet, or because she framed him. Stupidity is relatively easy to prove, frames ain't. Especially this frame. If it is one, that is."

"You have doubts?"

"Sure. There's always doubts. That's what the jury of high school dropouts and English language–challenged immigrants is for—to figure out what nobody else can."

I sighed. "So they formally charged him? They're going to ignore the folded match?"

I heard him laugh again. I began thinking maybe I hadn't given the advertising game a fair chance.

"How shall I tell thee? Let me count the ways. On the one hand, there's this here folded match of yours. The vic was a nonsmoker, so why is there a match in his ashtray? We don't know. And why is it folded in half, just the way you claim Morticia Addams Winslow has been known to do? We don't know. Want to hear her lawyer's explanation?"

"Probably not, but tell me anyway."

"The husband *planted* the match to make it look like *she* did it. And that's why the gun got wiped down: to make it look like she used it. After all, he legally owned the gun; his prints *should* be on it. See, her lawyer figures old man Winslow was framing *her*. Beautiful ain't it? This is the same lawyer who gave her that escape clause in the prenup. This guy's a friggin' genius, I gotta get one of his cards."

"So there's the folded match on one side of the ledger," I said. "What's the total on the other side?"

"You got a pen and pad ready? Jot this down. It's his gun, he says he's home all morning, no alibi, he's alone. She's got a receipt from some fancy-ass dress shop on Fifth Avenue. American Express receipt, timed at midmorning. Doesn't prove she couldn't have done it, time of death is flexible enough, but it sure doesn't hurt her any to have it. About a month ago, the husband started to suspect she was passing around a little tail and hired a PI. Probably where she got the idea to hire you. The PI gave the old man the victim's name and address, complete with color photos. Covers the motive and means angle pretty good, don't you think? As for opportunity, remember, Winslow claims he was home all morning. The cops found a message on his answering machine with date and time received. Guess what? The message is from his wife on the morning of the murder. She's on the machine, quite surprised he's not picking up. Wherever could he be? she wonders."

I could just hear her voice, purring with perplexity. I suddenly caught a chill.

"Those machine dating programs can be doctored," I said.

"Sure, and maybe OJ is innocent." He sighed. "It's just another nail in Winslow's coffin, Billy. Your theory is this dame gets caught cheating. She sees the marriage going down and the prenup kicking her in the ass. So she decides to whack the boyfriend and pin it on the husband. Okay, I get it. But where's your evidence? The folded match? Gimme a break. Look, my advice to you: Cash her check and forget about it. She's gonna walk and he's going away for a long time. Hell, maybe he did do it. Who knows? Cash the check and walk, pal. That's my advice."

It was almost lunchtime when Mary Lou knocked on my door. She came in silently and took a seat in one of the leather chairs. She glanced at the bottle of bourbon and saw that much of it was gone.

"You okay?" she asked. Tentatively.

I looked across the desk at her. She was a good kid, really. It hadn't been fair of me to hire her for my little dress-up farce, isolated from people her own age, answering phones for the King of the Lost Boys.

"Yeah," I said. "Peachy."

Her eyes fell to the sheaf of papers I held in my hands. "What have you got there?" she asked.

I glanced at the papers: the prenup.

I smiled. "Oh, this?" I said. "This is nothing, sweetheart, nothing at all. This is just the stuff dreams are made of."

I let the smile fade from my face.

"Just nothing at all."

Humphrey Bogart was born on Christmas Day, 1899, almost exactly thirty years before, Dashiell Hammett published The Maltese Falcon. *Some ninety-five years later, that combination of extraordinary talent helped birth a most unworthy ancestor: "Dream Stuff."*

I had just finished watching, for perhaps the twentieth time, the film version of Hammett's classical novel, starring Bogart as Sam Spade. It sparked my memory and brought to mind the description of Spade from the first page or two of the novel, so remarkably similar to Bogie himself. It improbably seemed Mr. Hammett had somehow met personally with the movie icon and thought, "Yeah, that guy is my Spade." I have no idea if the two ever actually met, but it seems unlikely any such meeting could have predated the 1929 appearance of the novel. Uncanny.

But rewatching the film had certainly pushed my memory button. For some reason it brought to mind my maternal grandmother, an Italian immigrant and seamstress, who had, well into her sixties, labored with needle and thread on the handmade suits of the Rogers Peet Company, suits contemporary to both

Hammett and Sam Spade, and unaffordable to the men of my grandmother's Brooklyn neighborhood. For much of the twentieth century, those suits were legendary.

And thus was born the formula: Hammett, Sam Spade, Bogie, my nonna (grandmother), and all things Rogers Peet–like. I went directly to my Smith-Corona electric portable (yeah, I'm a dinosaur) and got to work, pecking away. The result now stands honored on these lofty pages.

If you haven't read The Maltese Falcon, *do so. And of course, see the film. Movie star Paul Newman once reportedly said, in response to a question regarding his long successful marriage to Joanne Woodward, "Why go out for hamburger when you have steak at home?"*

So—you've had your "Dream Stuff" hamburger. I suggest you now indulge in a fine porterhouse, one prepared by Hammett himself. I can assure you, it's quite a feast.

Karen Odden *earned her PhD from New York University, writing her dissertation on the ways the medical, legal, and popular literature around Victorian railway disasters created a linguistic and theoretical precedent for PTSD. Subsequently, she taught at UW-Milwaukee, contributed introductions for Victorian titles in the Barnes & Noble Classics series, and wrote and edited for academic journals including* Victorian Life and Culture *(Cambridge University Press) before turning to fiction. Her decades-long fascination with the Victorians has led her to set all her published novels in 1870s London. Her first,* A Lady in the Smoke *(2016), about a railway disaster, was a USA* Today *bestseller and won the New Mexico–Arizona Book Award. The most recent,* Under a Veiled Moon *(2022), was nominated for the Anthony, Agatha, and Lefty awards for best historical mystery and features Scotland Yard Inspector Michael Corravan, who also appears in this short story.*

Originally from upstate New York, Odden now lives in sunny Arizona, teaches writing workshops nationwide, and has served on the national board of Sisters in Crime for three years. Connect with Odden at karenodden.com.

HER DANGEROUSLY CLEVER HANDS

Karen Odden

London, 1879

The Metropolitan Police Divisions had known of the Wrens for years, but like their winged namesake, the all-women thieving gang from Whitechapel was quick to flit away, hard to catch, and prepared to move their nest as needed. They also prudently stuck to thieving—nothing violent, nothing vicious, mostly pilfering items worth less than ten pounds, even if it was hundreds of them each month around London, which meant it was the local divisions, not the Yard, who responded to their cases.

But one day, I entered the division to find three inspectors blocking the hallway with a newspaper opened too wide for me to pass. White and Bristow read avidly over Montrose's shoulder.

"What is it?" I asked.

"Oh, Corravan," White said. "You might know her. She's from the Chapel."

"Ugly murder," Montrose said.

I peered between them to see the headline: "Whitechapel Woman Fatally Stabbed!"

"Name's Margaret McHugh," Bristow said, peering up at me. "Heard of her?"

"No," I lied, shouldering my way around them. "Chapel's a big place, and I left near fifteen years ago."

"Poor thing," Bristow said. "Stabbed four times."

I stepped inside my office and shut the door.

I'd known Margaret McHugh as "Maggie"—now head of the Wrens—since I was a boy, for she'd come into Ma Doyle's shop, like most Irish in that part of Whitechapel did for their sundries. Ma once admitted to me that Maggie amused her, but she trusted Maggie only so far as she could reach into her pocket, which might not make sense to outsiders, but I understood. All the Wrens had special cavernous pockets sewn into their skirts, reinforced against their crinolines to support the weight of merchandise. One of Ma's friends' daughters had once stood in our kitchen and laughingly shown me how the pocket's wide opening could allow her to slip four pairs of gloves, two yards of ribbon, a pair of lady's slippers, and half a dozen handkerchiefs inside without a West End shop clerk suspecting a thing.

A knock interrupted my thoughts, and the door swung open. My usual superintendent Mr. Vincent was away, and his superior, a gimlet-eyed man named York, stood with his hand on the knob. "You heard about the murder? This woman McHugh?"

I nodded.

"You're Whitechapel Irish, a'n't you?" he said with distaste. "Why don't you take it?"

I bit my tongue and watched his mouth twitch. I knew what he thought of my race, and he was just waiting for me to rise to the bait and balk. "Yes, sir," I replied evenly.

"Victim lived in Coburn Street, number six." He turned on his heel, leaving the door wide open.

I took a cab to Leman Street and climbed out, about a quarter of a mile from her house. I liked putting my boots on the ground here because I could sense changes like a new odor in my nose. I wondered where the Wren nest was these days; as a precaution, it was never close to where the leader lived, so she could keep her work separate from her home. I also wondered if Maggie's murder was an internal matter or something else. If this was a feud among the Wrens, they'd close ranks, and I'd have a devil of a time convincing anyone to talk to me.

Maggie's house, on one of the better streets, was white-painted brick, with a wood door. I put my hand behind the black mourning wreath to find the knocker and struck it once; the door was opened by a maid, slender and young. Her face was pale, her brown curls pulled back, her eyes red-rimmed. "Good morning," she said, her voice quavering.

"Good morning. I'm Michael Corravan," I said, softening my voice. "An inspector from Scotland Yard. I'd like to speak with you, please. What's your name?"

Her brown eyes widened. "Katie Wells." It came out little more than a whisper. She closed the door behind me with a subdued click. She led me into the parlor. "Do you want to see the housekeeper, Mrs. James?"

"Both of you," I replied. "Is there anyone else in the house?"

"Nay, just us two. A charwoman comes in to help every other day."

Mrs. James, a sedately dressed woman of about thirty-five, entered the room, a silver chatelaine snug around her waist. She did not ask me to sit, so we all stood in the parlor. At first, Katie fidgeted with the ties of her apron, until Mrs. James gave an admonishing look, and Katie meekly dropped her hands to her sides. I asked the usual questions about how long they'd worked for Mrs. McHugh and what their routines were. Both women lived in the house, and Mrs. James had worked here twelve years, Katie seven.

When I asked if anything out of the ordinary had happened in the days before her death, any unusual visitors, or if Mrs. McHugh had seemed out of sorts, Mrs. James shot Katie a look that might have silenced her. But Katie's eyes were on me, and she didn't see it.

With some surprise, Katie said, "Why, yes, Mrs. McHugh did have a visitor."

"Two days ago," Mrs. James added, pursing her lips. "A woman named Mrs. O'Connell."

"She was very pretty, with long dark hair and green eyes," Katie said, a touch wistfully. "I don't think they were friends, though. It sounded as if they were having a row."

"About what?" I asked.

Mrs. James gave a warning cough, and Katie amended, "Well, it probably warn't a row exactly. We didn't listen in—"

"She means we could hear their raised voices," Mrs. James interrupted.

"Had you ever seen her before?" I asked.

Both shook their heads, and Mrs. James said, "When she left, Mrs. McHugh told me not to admit her again."

I looked to Katie for corroboration. "Aye, her face was red, and she was fidgety the rest of the day."

"Anything else you noticed about Mrs. O'Connell?" It was a common enough name in this part of Whitechapel.

"Well, 'twas odd," Mrs. James said. "Her dress was right fashionable, though her bonnet and shoes were old."

"There's one other thing," Katie said, her cheeks flushing, and she gave a quick look at Mrs. James before turning back to me. "I heard her say 'Damn Honora,' later that night."

I was writing in my pocketbook when I heard that, and I froze, then continued to push my pen across the paper, scrawling nonsense for a line or two and hoping I gave nothing away. But I knew that name.

If it was the same Honora O'Connell I'd known years ago in Whitechapel, I'd been a little in love with her, when she was twenty to my fifteen. It had been she who showed me the special pockets Wrens had in their skirts, one time when we'd played cards together in Ma Doyle's kitchen, and she'd taught me how to spot someone's tell and how to bury an ace up my sleeve for later. She had the prettiest dimples and a sly, approving wink for me when I mastered the sleight of hand. When I lay in bed at night, thinking of girls I might fancy, they all had her green eyes and dark glossy hair. But after I left the Chapel, I'd never seen her again. Had she left, to get married? And why would she fight with Maggie? They were Wrens together.

Feeling a poke of gratitude that Katie and Mrs. James had been so forthcoming—as I'd anticipated, they weren't Wrens—I asked a few more questions, took down their names, and left, pointing my boots toward Ma Doyle's shop.

Ma Doyle had adopted me, taking me in when I was thirteen, after I'd kept her son Pat from being beaten to death in an alley. A cheerful, clever, competent woman, she had a way of offering a cuppa and sympathy without causing offense, so she knew a good deal about people who lived nearby. More than once, when I needed to know what was happening in the Chapel for my work, I'd gone to her first. As I reached the shop, I looked in the window and saw Elsie behind the counter. The shop held about half a dozen customers, some of whom I knew, others I didn't. I observed Elsie for a moment. She was just twenty—and prettier every year, with the braids that used to hang long down her back now coiled around her head in a way that made me think of a flower. There was no sign of Ma, so I started for the back stairs that led up to the living quarters above. I inserted my key in the lock and turned it, calling out, "Ma, it's me," as I stepped inside.

"Mickey," she said and presented her cheek for a kiss.

We sat down with our tea and thick slabs of bread and butter.

"Are y'here about your work or to visit with me?" she asked with a knowing smile that dented a dimple in her cheek.

I looked at her apologetically, and she patted my hand. "I'm only having a spot of fun. I'm glad for whatever brings you."

"I'll see you Sunday for tea, but this is work," I admitted. "Maggie McHugh was killed last night near her house."

"Aye, so I heard," she said indifferently and slipped her knife into the butter.

Surprised, I asked, "Am I not remembering properly? I know you didn't trust her much, but I thought you were friendly."

"With Maggie?" She looked up from buttering her bread. "Why would you say so?"

"Well, I've seen you talking and laughing with her in the shop."

She gave me a look. "I visit with everyone in the shop."

"True," I said. "Why don't you like her?"

She merely shrugged. "'Tis no matter. Haven't seen her in years, since she moved out of the Mews and started putting on airs of bein' respectable."

Ma was a fair judge of people and tended to get on with most, so I took note of her dislike.

"Ma." I sipped at my tea. "What ever happened to Honora O'Connell?"

While the mention of Maggie's murder barely raised Ma's eyebrow, this question made her skitter her teacup into her saucer with a clink and stare at me. "What on earth made you ask about Honora?"

When I hesitated, she shook her head. "You can't like *her* for Maggie's murder! She's in Swan River, in Australia!"

"What?" It was my turn to stare. "The penal colony? When? How did I not know?"

"'Twas after you left. And you didn't come back for a good while, if you recall."

I winced, knowing what my abrupt departure from Whitechapel had led to, the hurt it had caused the Doyle family.

"So why would you pull her name out o' thin air?" Ma asked.

"It isn't out of thin air. She might have been in Australia, but she's back now. She was seen by witnesses. Here in London."

She frowned. "She's warn't due back until October. That's the month she was shipped off."

"Sometimes they'll let them go a mite early, depending on if there's space in steerage."

She shook her head, slowly at first and then more firmly. "Honora wouldn't kill Maggie. I know her, Mickey. She wouldn't."

People change, I thought. *Especially in a penal colony*. But I kept that to myself. "Why was she transported? Was she picked up for thieving?"

She made a *tsk*ing sound, her tongue against her teeth, a sign I knew. She thought Honora had been dealt an unfair hand. "It was the worst of luck. Honora went out with . . ." She paused, thinking. "Eliza Bell, that was her name. A fool of a girl."

"A fool how?"

She sighed. "Ah, she was empty-headed. As many times as she was told not to smirk at the shopkeepers or sashay when she left a store with summat in her pocket, she couldn't help herself. So most times, she was the decoy." A shrug. "She was pretty."

I knew the importance of a decoy. Sometimes it took the shape of a young boy who pretended to steal a Wren's purse in the shop—and while she was screeching over it, a second Wren was quietly filling her pockets. Other times one Wren did a bit of flirting with the shopkeeper, to occupy him.

"Why would the Wrens keep a girl like that?" I asked. "Seems like they'd drop her faster than a hot coal."

She gave me a look. "She's O'Hagan's niece."

"Ah." Seamus O'Hagan kept the bare-knuckles boxing club where I'd worked until he ran me out of the Chapel for not throwing a match. O'Hagan had a straight line to James McCabe, who oversaw most of the crime here.

"So Honora was caught because of Eliza's foolishness," I said, and she nodded. "And this was seven years ago?" Seven was the usual sentence for thieving.

"Nae." Ma shook her head. "Fourteen. At her trial, the judge told Honora she had dangerously clever hands, and a dangerously corrupting heart, teaching a young innocent girl like Eliza the dark business of thieving. So he doubled the sentence and gave Eliza none at all."

I did a quick calculation: I was eighteen when I left Whitechapel, and I was thirty-two now. "Why, this happened *very* soon after I left," I said in surprise.

"Aye. Only a few weeks, if I remember rightly."

So Honora had served her sentence and returned. I wondered what kind of vengeance she had in mind for a sentence she probably felt she didn't deserve. And why Maggie might have been on the receiving end of her anger. And if Eliza might, too.

"Were you at the trial?" I asked.

"Nae. The trial happened almost straightaway, like they did back then, and it was the autumn Elsie had pleurisy. So I didn't know of it till later, from her mum." She winced with regret. "By then Honora was already on one of the ships. They had to fill 'em, you see, and they needed one hundred women for each."

"Women only?" I asked.

"Aye." She looked askance. "Couldn't put men and women together on a ship for six months, Mickey. 'Twas bad enough the crew were men."

"Ah."

"Once a ship was full, it left. She was gone 'afore I could say goodbye."

"Do you have any idea where I'd find her, where she'd stay in London now?" I asked. "I just want to talk to her." Ma bit her lip anxiously. "Ma, you know if she didn't do it, I'll make sure she isn't accused. I want the person who did it, not just the person easiest to blame."

"I know that!" She looked indignant. "I was just tryin' to think who she might have gone to. I'd have thought she'd come to me. Her mother was my dearest friend."

"I'm sorry she didn't."

"So am I," she said unhappily. "Let me ask 'round. Come back tomorrow, will ye? I'll find out what I can."

I thanked her, finished my tea, and kissed her goodbye.

The next morning, I stopped into the Yard only long enough to report that I was attending Maggie's funeral. It had been announced in the paper for eleven o'clock, at Sacred Heart. I knew the church well, for many a night I'd hidden in the priest hole, eating stale bread and moldy cheese with other boys, before the Doyles took me in.

Funerals were one of the best places for discovering truths about people's lives. Mourners thought no one was watching, with everyone too racked with their own feelings. But some people sobbed because they relished a chance to go into hysterics, some were stoic, some sincerely grieved, and some secretly gloated that the person was dead.

Rain drummed at the windows as I entered the church and sat near the back to watch. There weren't more than thirty people, but I saw two women who must've been Maggie's relations; they had the McHugh red hair and round chin. Nothing out of the ordinary happened during the mass, but at the end, a burly, slightly balding man approached one of the McHughs to say he was sorry, how Maggie had always been a fine woman.

She gave him a baleful look, and my instincts drew me closer, so I could listen.

"If you thought she was so fine, why didn't you marry her?" she demanded. "If you had, she'd still 'a been alive. That witch wouldn't 'a killed her."

He stood with his hat in his hands, blinking in bewilderment.

She turned and swept around the pew, as his mouth opened and shut like a trout.

I had a split second to make the choice between the two. She knew something, while he seemed not to know his arse from his elbow. So I hurried after Maggie's relation and approached her sideways, withdrawing a card from my pocket, with my name and Scotland Yard's insignia, almost like a gentleman's calling card.

"I'm Inspector Michael Corravan," I said as I passed it to her. "I'm looking into Maggie's death."

"Murder, you mean," she snapped. "Or you wouldn't be here, would you?"

"Are you a relation?"

"Her cousin." Her gaze went over my shoulder. "My sister Mary is too."

"I have questions for you," I said. "But if you'd like to answer them later, I can come by your house."

She weighed that for no more than a second. "I'll speak to you now. Not sure when I'll be home after this."

"Who was that man with the thinning hair?"

Her mouth pursed. "Sean Tooley."

"A friend of Maggie's?"

She grimaced. "Ach, you needn't bother with 'im. He wouldn't have nothing to do with 'er murder, the big, spineless, sad-faced oaf, more's the pity." Her voice faded toward the end, and I wouldn't have heard, if I hadn't been intent on every word.

"Why not?" And when she didn't reply. "Did he misuse her?"

"Nae. But . . . he . . ." She shook her head. "He lured her along, like, played with 'ffections." Her eyes drifted over my shoulder again, and I turned to follow her gaze. Her sister was beckoning urgently. "I must go. We have the graveside yet, in all this rain."

I watched her leave, put up my umbrella, and headed back to Ma's shop. It was late afternoon, when Ma usually sorted the day's shipments and parcels. With a wave to Elsie behind the counter, I pushed the door that led to the storeroom and entered. The tang of tea, coffee, brown sugar, and the cloying odor of tallow candles brought back my time as a boy, when I'd help Ma with the counting, tallying the sums on a square of slate. "Ma?"

She put her head around the corner, and her face brightened then fell in regret. "I haven't found Honora yet. But I put out word."

"It's all right," I said, dropping onto one of the wooden barrels. "Something else I want to ask. Who's Sean Tooley?"

"Ach, Sean." She winced, as if she felt sorry for him.

"He was at the funeral today," I said. "Maggie's relations didn't seem happy to see him."

She frowned. "Dunno why that would be. Maggie and Sean were friendly, so far as I know."

"What can you tell me about him?"

She plumped down on a barrel opposite. "Well, Sean grew up here, same as you. He's a foreman at the St. Katherine Docks." She paused. "He was sweet on Honora for years—and she was fond o' him."

That put a cold feeling down my spine. "And when Honora left?"

"Ach, it nigh broke 'im. Oh, he took up with this woman and that, but he never married. I suspect he couldn't stop comparing everyone to her." Her mouth twitched. "I'd say there was a time when you felt the same."

I grinned. Naturally Ma had noticed. "Well, she was beautiful and clever. And a great one to laugh. She taught me card tricks."

She chuckled. "Aye, she did." Then her smile faded. "Clever hands, she had."

"Did Sean ever take up with Maggie?"

Her expression changed to shock. "Good lord, Mickey. Is that what you're thinking? That Honora might'a killed her out of revenge over that?"

I spread my hands. "She went to Maggie's house, Ma."

She pursed her mouth and looked thoughtful. And in the silence, the door swung open, and we both turned.

Honora O'Connell stood before us, and I caught my breath. She was still beautiful, with green eyes and rich coils of dark hair, though her face was thinner. "Beggin' your pardon," she said, appraising and dismissing me with a glance. She stepped toward Ma with her hands out. "But I heard you wanted to see me, Mary."

"I did." Ma put out her arms, clutching Honora to her. Then she stood back and looked Honora straight on, their eyes speaking words I couldn't decipher. "Dear girl, I'm very glad you're home, safe and sound. I didn't think you were due yet."

"They credited my time on the ship down and let me go a mite early." She kissed Ma affectionately on the cheek.

"We'll have a proper visit later," Ma said. "But Mickey needs to talk to you. He's a Yard man now."

"Honora," I said. "I'm glad to see you looking well."

She turned and blinked rapidly. "Mickey? Corravan? Good lord." She came closer and peered at me. "Well, I see it now. You've changed a mite."

"I know."

A smile tugged at Ma's mouth. "I'll just step into the shop."

As the door swung to and fro behind Ma, Honora sat on one of the barrels and folded her gloved hands in her lap. *Mrs. James had been right*, I thought. I didn't know much about fashions, but it seemed to me her dress looked new, though her bonnet looked worn.

Her gaze ran over me. "So you're an inspector now? Last I heard you were running away from O'Hagan."

"I began in Lambeth, as a constable. Worked my way up."

"Ah." A flush that might have been from embarrassment came to her cheeks, but her chin came up. "Your ma told you where I've been?"

"Australia," I said. "Sentenced for fourteen years."

A slow nod.

"When did you return to London?" I asked, my voice casual, but she understood.

"Eight days ago." She cocked her head. "And you're here because you think I murdered Maggie."

I put up a hand. "Honora, I was assigned the case. I didn't choose it, and I had no idea you'd be involved. But frankly, I'm glad it's not someone else. We're friends, and I want to help. But I need to know what happened."

She looked indignant. "*Nothing* happened!"

I turned both palms out. "You were at her house, arguing two days before!" I wasn't going to let her lie to me. "The maid heard Maggie cursing you by name after you left."

Her eyes darkened. "I didn't kill her, Mickey."

"I didn't say you did. But what were you arguing about?"

Her expression flattened, and she crossed her arms over her chest. She gave a mirthless laugh. "Well, you and I might'a been friends once, but you're police now, that's sartin."

"For God's sake, Honora!" I burst out. Her face was hard, her eyes full of distrust. I stood and came close, reached to touch her elbow, but she shied away, and I let my hand fall. "If you didn't kill Maggie, you could only be convicted for it over my dead body. I swear it. I've no desire to pin it on you. In fact, if my superintendent knew just how far I'd lean to your side, he'd take me off this case."

She gave a snort and a skeptical shake of her head. "Begging pardon if I don't believe you, but every police I ever knew lied to me." Her eyes were full of pain, and her voice dropped. "And worse."

Her tone carved out a dark place in my chest, and I sat back down on the barrel, curling my palms over the rim. "I'm bloody sorry about that, Honora." We sat in silence a moment before I continued. "But I'm looking at what's in front of us. And at the moment, you are the first and only suspect."

Her mouth tightened. "I had a right to confront her after what she done. Not that you'd understand."

"Honora," I protested, and then I stopped. I couldn't prove myself to her other than by playing a fair game, with honest questions. "Do you blame Maggie for your getting caught?"

"Course not." She gave a scornful look. "She warn't even there. If I was going to blame anyone, it would've been Eliza Bell."

"So why did you argue?"

"Maggie was my friend, and she didn't even come to my trial! She knew the police had caught me, and she could'a testified how Eliza warn't no innocent young girl that I'd corrupted. Eliza'd been thieving as long as I had, and . . . other things besides." Her eyebrows rose.

"Like what?"

She shrugged. "Baitin', for one."

Setting up as a prostitute in a brothel and then drugging men and taking everything out of their pockets and off their fingers. Illegal, of course, but Eliza's crimes didn't matter to me.

"So Maggie could have helped you get seven years, instead of fourteen," I said. "What did she say?"

Her mouth curled in contempt. "She told me it would 'a been a risk to come. Except no other Wren would 'a said a word—and who else could've recognized her as one?" She shook her head. "I'd 'a done it for her, even if I had to disguise myself, or wear a veil, or dress like a boy."

"She was cowardly," I said.

"And disloyal." Her voice was thick with feeling. "I'd lie awake some nights in Swan River, achin' over her not caring enough to come." There was a world of hurt and anger in her eyes. "So, we argued the other day. But I didn't kill her. You think I'm going to do something stupid that will have me hung? I'm no fool."

To my relief, my instincts told me she was being truthful. "I know. Sometimes you'd save the ace for the next hand, even if it was burning up your sleeve. Being prudent, you called it."

She gave a grim smile. "Swan River was fourteen years spent learning to be prudent, putting my anger into stitches and hems. I'm not ruinin' what's left of my life over her wrongdoing."

"What are you going to do now? Will you stay in London?"

"Oh, aye." Her expression eased. "I've found a position. I worked for a dressmaker in Swan River, and the superintendent recommended me to one in Oxford Street. Wedding dresses, veils, fancy costumes. I start tomorrow."

"You made the dress you're wearing?"

"Aye." A wry smile tugged at her mouth as she plucked the skirt. "Stepped off the ship, looked about me, realized how I must look, and spent two days sewing. Knew I'd never get a job at a good shop if'n I was dressed like I was."

"Where are you staying?" I asked.

She hesitated, her expression wary again. "You can reach me through your ma." At my frown, she added, "I won't leave London, a'right?"

Likely she was staying with one of her old Wrens and didn't want to betray her, so I had to be satisfied with that. I gestured toward the back door. "Then you leave ahead of me, so it won't look like we've been talking."

"All right, Mickey. Tell your ma I'll come back later to visit."

As she stood, I asked, "Do you know where I'd find Eliza Bell now?"

She rolled her eyes to the ceiling. "No."

"One other thing. Who do you think will take over the Wrens now that Maggie's gone?"

Wren leadership was passed down from mother to daughter, and in the absence of daughters, to the second in command. Leadership carried more risks, but it was lucrative, as ten percent of the value of every pawned item was given to the head.

Honora shrugged. "Couldn't even guess."

But I remembered her tell. She didn't take her eyes off me, but there was the slightest head tip to the left. She was lying.

"Can you think of anyone who might want Maggie dead?"

"P'rhaps some other friend she betrayed."

I pulled the door open and watched her go.

Then I followed her. Left, right, left—then, around a corner that she took quickly, I lost her.

I paused and felt a rueful smile curve my mouth. Honora had known I was following.

I walked back toward Whitehall Place along the Victoria Embankment, up the broad stone steps, and through the rough cobbled yard behind the division, mulling my next step. It wasn't likely Eliza Bell would still be at the same address as fourteen years ago, but someone who knew her might. I wanted to know what she remembered.

The records room held books with the names of people we'd arrested. They were organized by year, so I began with the year 1861, the year of Honora's trial, pulling each book down off the dark wooden shelf and reading through the alphabetized listing. It might not seem difficult, except that sometimes names were added in later, in an addendum, or scribbled in the margins.

I looked through every book until the present year and found no mention of E or Eliza or Elizabeth Bell. I swore under my breath just as Barton stuck his head in.

"What's the matter, Corravan?"

"Trying to find a woman," I said dryly.

"The everlasting problem." He chortled and raised a finger. "The problem ain't finding a woman. It's finding the right one."

"Well, she isn't in here," I said, slapping the last book closed.

"Who're you looking for?"

"Thief and baiter named Bell."

"When was she arrested?"

"I guess she wasn't," I said. "But she should have been. She was an accomplice."

"Was she let off to turn witness?" he asked.

I blinked. The way Ma and Honora had told me, it seemed Eliza had been tried alongside Honora and "given nothing." But Ma hadn't been in the room, and Honora hadn't specified one way or the other. If there was no physical evidence of Eliza having committed a crime, she could've been turned.

"A good thought," I said to Barton and grabbed my coat. My first stop was the Home Office, which kept the Criminal Registers and the trial calendars. It took the clerk nearly an hour to find the notation and the indictment number for Honora's case. Armed with that, I went to the Old Bailey to look at the trial transcript. If Eliza had been a witness, her address would be on it.

There she was: Elizabeth C. Bell, of Russet Street, number eight.

The only defendant named was Honora O'Connell, with a shopkeeper Mr. Dross and Eliza as the sole witnesses. Mr. Dross identified the pair, and Eliza protested that she'd had nothing in her pockets and had only been in the shop to buy some ribbon.

But something odd caught my eye. In his testimony, Mr. Dross had called her "Eliza," though the judge had called her Elizabeth, as had been listed on the first page.

Instinct made me check Mr. Dross's address. Meryton Mews, number six.

I shuffled the papers back into their proper order and replaced them in the folder.

At that time, Maggie McHugh and her father had also lived in Meryton Mews.

Coincidence? I rather thought not.

As luck would have it, an envelope had been slid partway under Eliza Bell's door when I arrived, and I gave it a gentle tug. It appeared to be a receipt of some kind, addressed to Mrs. E. Bell. Satisfied that I had found her, I replaced the bill and gave the door a sharp rap with the knocker. No one answered, and I rapped again.

"Comin', comin'!" I heard and the door opened.

A very pretty woman of about my age, with heaps of auburn hair, an upturned nose, and bright blue eyes looked up at me. "Yes?"

I glanced down at the floor. The envelope had vanished into her pocket.

"Mrs. Bell?" I asked, and at her nod, I said, "I'm Michael Corravan, an inspector at the Yard. I was wondering if I might ask a few questions."

A young boy was peering over the fence, and he hooted.

She hissed at me. "Not so loud. D'you want the world to hear?" She gestured for me to come in, and I stood in the foyer. Her home was decent, but the bench in the entry was threadbare, telling me that despite the respectable address, she strained to make ends meet.

"Do you remember a woman named Honora O'Connell?" I asked.

"Nae."

"You were in the Wrens together," I said. "Fourteen years ago."

She blinked, and her jaw jutted forward as she crossed her arms, but as I held her gaze, she pouted. "P'rhaps. Don't recall."

I put my hands into my coat pockets. "I read the trial transcript. If you don't want me to come around here every day, making it look like you're in trouble with the law, you'll tell me everything, including why you weren't tried with Honora."

She was silent, and I waited. Finally, her chest heaved with a sigh. "It was Maggie. She made the roll for the day and told me not to take anything from the shop."

"Maggie McHugh?" I asked, that cold feeling running down my spine again. "But she wasn't running the Wrens back then, was she?"

"When Jacinta were feeling poorly, sometimes she did."

I kept my voice even. "You were sent with Honora and told not take anything."

"Aye."

So Maggie had set Honora up to be caught. "Why would Maggie do that?"

She shrugged. "I dunno."

But I was beginning to assemble the pieces into order in my mind.

"Who will take over the Wrens now that Maggie's gone?" I asked.

"I dunno that neither. I'm not in it anymore. I'm respectable now."

Probably due to money O'Hagan gave her, I thought. Whatever I thought of the man, he was loyal, like most Chapel Irish. He'd take care of his niece.

"Thank you," I said and put my hand on the knob. "One more thing. Do you know Sean Tooley?"

Her face paled. "Get out! Just get out! And if you come round here again, I'll—I'll tell my uncle. He let you run off back then, but he still frets over you when he's in 'is cups."

"All right, all right." I left, letting her think she'd succeeded in scaring me off.

What the devil was that about? Why so snappish about Sean Tooley? I wondered. *Was Eliza one of the women he took up with "on and off," as Ma said?*

But I had the growing certainty that Maggie had wronged Honora beyond not appearing at her trial. My question was whether Honora understood the extent of it.

It was time to go see the man whom I suspected knew even less than I did.

Sean Tooley wasn't difficult to find. I began at one of the Irish pubs frequented by dockworkers and found him at the third. "Over thar," the barman said and sent a thumb over his shoulder without even looking.

I went to the corner, and there he was, sitting with a newspaper and a pint. The light coming in at the window showed the lines on his face more harshly than the light at the church. I'd put him at five or eight years older than I, around forty.

"Mr. Tooley," I said.

He looked up. "Aye. 'at's me." He took in my coat, my hands, quiet at my sides. "You police?"

I pulled out a chair. "I wanted to ask about some friends of yours."

You can tell a lot about a man, his general level of guilt, by the way he responds to that sort of opening.

Tooley folded the paper and set it aside, clasped his hands, and landed them on the table, meeting my gaze. "A'right."

This man didn't have much to hide. Or he was very good at feigning.

"How did you know Maggie McHugh?"

"Ach." His face fell. "A turrible thing. We both grew up here. Knew each other since we were . . ." His hand gestured to somewhere around the table's height.

"Did you ever take up with her?"

He drew back. "Nae!" And then he shrugged. "Not saying we didn't have a pint together once or twice. But I didna care for her, not that way."

"And Eliza Bell?"

He stiffened and ran a hand over his chin. "Aye. We were friendly for a bit."

"And Honora O'Connell?" I asked.

His whole body stilled. "Why're you asking about her?"

"She's back from Australia."

His back thunked against the wooden panels behind him. "Wot?" It came out in a hoarse whisper.

Satisfied that he hadn't known, I said, "Only just back, a week ago."

"You seen her?" He tensed as if he'd jump up and run to her that very moment.

"Settle down," I cautioned him, and he swallowed and put his spine back against the panels. "And yes, I've seen her. Did you ever speak to her after she was arrested fourteen years ago? Get a letter from her, from Australia?"

"Nae. I couldna read then, so I doubt she'd 'a written."

"Did you care for her?"

His mouth twisted, and he looked down at his hands. When he looked up, his gray eyes were suspiciously damp. "Is she a'right? Healthy, I mean? Safe?"

My heart went out to him. If he didn't truly care for her, he would have asked different questions.

"She's fine," I said.

He drew a ragged breath. "And she's here in the Chapel?"

"I don't know where she's staying," I said. "But I'll get her word that you're asking after her, if you'd like."

"Thank'ee." His broad chest was rising and falling out of rhythm.

I guessed this was a man who had no idea at all that Maggie McHugh loved him—mostly because he loved Honora too much to notice anyone else more than in passing.

My second guess was Honora had known he loved her. And if she still loved him in return, this was another reason she wouldn't risk committing murder. She had a position and someone to love. What more reasons to live? What more reasons not to ruin it by killing an old rival—especially if she didn't even know that Maggie had sent her out with Eliza to be caught, to be sent away for years, maybe so Maggie might have a chance with Sean Tooley?

"Back when Honora was caught," I said, "who was running the Wrens?"

He frowned, wary of revealing that he knew. "Why can that matter? She's dead."

"Honora's suspected of killing Maggie, and I think the reason has to do with whoever was in line for the head." I saw him hesitate. "I'm police, but I was born and raised here by Mary Doyle."

A flicker of recognition sparked in his eyes.

"Honora taught me how to play cards and slide an ace up my sleeve at Ma's table."

His eyes narrowed, and the left side of his mouth twitched. "Jacinta Wells."

I rose. "Thank you."

He put out a hand to halt me. "Is she staying?"

My mind had already leapt elsewhere, and it took me a second to realize what he meant. "Aye. She's taken a position with a dressmaker."

He released a sigh of relief. "She was always clever with 'er sewin'."

I left him smiling into space, his newspaper and pint forgotten.

Jacinta *Wells*. Katie *Wells*. It couldn't be a coincidence.

Maggie may have put on airs of respectability, but remarkably, she had Wrens living in her own house. I shook my head in surprise and headed back there.

Katie answered the door, looking calmer and more poised today. That wasn't suspicious, in and of itself. It had been another two days, after all, and as I had reason to know, the shock of sudden death does wear off.

Clearly she expected someone else, for she started, and her former air of timidity reappeared a shade too suddenly. "Do you want to see Mrs. James?" she asked, her eyes wide.

Good lord, I thought. *She should have been an actress, the way she could mold her expression.* "No," I said. "I want to talk to you."

She blinked but held her air of innocence. "All right."

I didn't let her direct me to the parlor. The light was better here, and I wanted to see her face. "Who is Jacinta Wells to you?" I asked.

She stiffened. "My late aunt."

"You know she ran the Wrens, back in the '60s, before Maggie did."

A long beat as she took that in, and then her eyebrows rose. "You can't possibly suspect her of Mrs. McHugh's death. My aunt died years ago."

"Did your aunt have any children?"

"No."

"And do you have any sisters? Any other cousins?"

This line of questioning shook her, but the only tell was a slight flare of her nostrils. "I didn't kill Mrs. HcHugh so I could run the Wrens, if that's what you're saying."

"Answer my question."

"I've an older sister, Alice," she said with a shrug. "But she's respectable, same as I am."

"Where can I find her?"

"Putnam Street, number twelve."

As I noted it in my pocketbook, Mrs. James appeared on the stairs, her pale hand sliding down the banister, her eyes on me. "What's the matter?"

I turned to Katie Wells.

She looked up at the housekeeper and replied in a tone of mock seriousness. "He thinks my sister Alice killed Mrs. McHugh. So she'd be able to run the Wrens."

Mrs. James simply stared.

For the second time in as many days I watched two women speak to each other with their eyes. I needed to hear what lie had been concocted for this situation, and if both of them told it.

"Look here," I said, rising and standing between them. "You can avoid any unpleasantness if you tell me what Honora and Maggie fought about. This house isn't large enough for you not to have heard *something* they were saying."

From the second-to-last step, Mrs. James looked down at me and began with a seeming reluctance. "They were friends, from a long time ago, only Honora was jealous of Mrs. McHugh on account of Sean Tooley."

Katie explained further: "Mr. Tooley was in love with Mrs. McHugh. He'd come round and ask her to go for a pint or they'd sit in the parlor together, and anybody could see it, the way he looked at her, though she didn't think of 'im that way."

"Ah," I said and put an expression of belief on my face. "But why was this a problem for Honora?"

"Because," Mrs. James said slowly, as if explaining it to a fool, "Sean wouldn't look at Honora twice, and she thought Mrs. McHugh was the reason. Honora blamed her for being transported and for her broken heart."

If I hadn't seen Sean's face when I told him Honora was back in London, I would've believed her. She was that good a liar. But the way the two women elaborated and bolstered each other's stories told me a good deal.

"So Honora killed her," I said, with a look of sudden enlightenment, as if I were that fool, "because she was bitter over being caught and jealous over Sean Tooley."

Mrs. James and Katie both nodded.

They were in it together.

"Thank you," I said gratefully, though I let them see some exasperation. "Why you didn't tell me this right off, I'll never know."

"Do you know where to find Honora?" Mrs. James asked.

"No," I said. And then, as an afterthought, I added, "Do you?"

They both shook their heads.

"No ideas where I might find her? You're sure?" I asked again. They'd have been suspicious if I didn't push.

Katie spread her hands.

I left and walked down the street until I found a constable and showed him the house to watch. "If anyone tries to leave, take them to the Yard."

His eyes wide, he nodded and took up a post at the corner, where he could see the door.

Leadership of the Wrens went by inheritance, I knew. But even if Alice was a few years older than Katie, she'd still have been too young to take over from their aunt Jacinta years ago. So Maggie, second in command, had been made leader. Given that Maggie had no children, Alice could certainly make a legitimate claim.

Putnam Street was only three streets away, and I found number twelve with no trouble.

The woman who answered the door looked a good deal like Katie, to be sure, but older and a bit careworn. A small boy clung to her skirts. "Aye, what is it?" she asked. "Who are you? Police?"

I wondered when I'd taken on the air of police so clearly that I couldn't pass for Whitechapel Irish anymore.

"I need to talk to you about the Wrens."

She laughed as if I was ridiculous and showed me her left hand. It was badly burned, with skin that was puckered and scarred. Her fingers moved stiffly. There was no possibility she could thieve with it. "I was never a Wren and know naught about it."

I winced. "When did that burn happen?"

"I was eleven," she replied.

It was unfortunate, but it was a sure guarantee that she was telling the truth.

She bent to pick up the boy and settled him on her hip. "I don't need to be thieving, or any of the rest of it. My husband earns a fair living."

"What does he do?" I asked.

She looked sorry she'd mentioned him. "He's a tackle porter, weighin' goods at London docks."

I raised a reassuring hand. "I'm not going to cause him any trouble. I'm just asking. I worked the docks myself for a while. Lighterman."

It's funny how sharing that could make a difference. She stepped away from the door and gestured for me to come in. I took a seat at the tiny wooden table and sat catty-corner from her.

"How long has Katie been a Wren?" I asked.

She went still and used her son tugging her curls as an excuse to avert her gaze.

I set my forearm on the table and leaned in, my voice frank. "I grew up here, and I know how it is. One of my friends was a Wren. For some, it's either that or being a prostitute. I don't blame her. I'm just asking. When did it start?"

Her eyes met mine. "'Twas after our parents died. Katie was fifteen." She sighed. "She's always felt cheated. She's younger 'n me and don't remember what it's like not to have a decent house and new dresses. But after our parents died, we had to sell most everything. Katie hated it. So she went to Maggie and asked to join. Maggie let her, 'specially when she saw . . ."

"Saw what?"

"Katie was talented," she said simply.

"Maggie had to know Katie might want to lead the Wrens eventually, as Jacinta was her aunt."

"Well, o' course," she said. "Katie's been loyal to Maggie for years, and she was sure Maggie would reward her. With Maggie havin' no daughters, Katie would 'a been the natural choice. But a few months back, Maggie told her she was thinking of giving it to someone else."

"Thinking of?" I asked. A few months was a long time to keep someone on tenterhooks. Plenty of time to make someone feel fidgety and impatient.

She nodded. "Maggie said she was worried Katie had too much of a temper. Clever hands, but too impulsive." She sighed. "She's right, so far as that goes."

"Who was this other person?" I asked, an uneasy feeling settling in my chest.

"I don't know." Alice's son reached toward the loaf of bread on the table, and she leaned over to hand him a slice of bread, which he took happily. "Just she wouldn't be able to make her choice until later in the year."

Perhaps October, I thought.

"What's the matter?" she asked. "You look peculiar."

"Nothing," I lied.

For now, I could guess who Maggie had intended to name her successor. Perhaps Maggie thought she could make up for some of what she'd done by offering Honora leadership of the Wrens. The extra seven years Maggie had cost Honora might be compensated by a good income for life. Had Maggie made the offer and Honora refused it?

I thought of what Honora had said when I'd asked who else might have a reason to kill Maggie. She'd told me to look at any other friends Maggie had betrayed.

I could imagine Katie feeling betrayed. I knew what that did to a person. Hurriedly, I left Alice's house, turned my feet once more toward Maggie's house, and began to run.

I found the constable up front. "Anyone leave?" I asked breathlessly.

He shook his head. "Been watching the whole time."

I banged on the door. No answer. Banged again. "Mrs. James! Katie! Open the door!"

No answer. By this time the constable had come up next to me. "No one came out, I promise!"

"Stay here," I told him and ran around the back, peering in a window. No lights, no movement. I took out my lock picks and opened the door. The house was silent. I raced upstairs and found no signs of them.

Where the devil had they gone? Where did Wrens fly when they were about to be caught?

And would they try to silence Honora before they left? She wouldn't be on her guard. Was there any chance Katie knew where to find Honora?

Damn Honora's distrust, I thought. *I wish I knew.*

Swearing under my breath, I ran straight for Ma Doyle's house. I prayed Honora was staying close by, and I took the outdoor stairs two at a time and hammered on the door. "Ma! It's me!"

The door jerked open, and Ma stood staring up at me. "Mickey! For goodness's sake!" My eyes went beyond her to the empty room.

"I need to talk to Honora, to warn her. Where can I find her?" I demanded. "Do you know?"

"I'm here," Honora said, emerging from the hallway, with what looked like a wedding veil in one hand and a needle in the other. "What's the matter?"

My heart jumped in relief before beating again, all out of normal rhythm. "Honora, when you confronted Maggie about not coming to your trial, did she offer you leadership of the Wrens? As a way to make it up to you?"

Honora tucked the needle into the hem and set the sewing on a shelf. "You ask that like you already know the answer."

"What did you tell her?"

She hesitated. "I said I'd consider it. Not because I really would, mind you, but I . . ."

"What?"

"She was . . . " Honora shook her head. "She wasn't like I remembered. It was like . . . she resented me, which felt absurd because she was the one who injured *me*. At first, I refused outright, but she came at me, her face full of scorn and anger and asked how could I of all people turn it down? I was already a convict." She shrugged. "She frightened me, the way she looked, beyond reason. So I said I'd think about it and left."

That equivocation was why Katie thought she might say yes, I thought. *Why she thought Honora was a threat.*

A groan escaped me. But at least everything was coming clear.

"Mickey, what's happened?" Honora asked.

I rested my hands on the top rung of one of the wooden chairs tucked around the table. "The day you were arrested, Maggie sent you out with Eliza on purpose because she knew you'd be caught. She told Eliza not to put anything in her pockets, and one of the men who worked in the shop was Maggie's neighbor. He knew to look for you."

Her face paled. "But why?"

"Nearest I can figure, she was in love with Sean Tooley. She thought with you out of the way, she'd have a chance."

"Sean!" Her eyes were wide with shock.

"When I went to see Maggie's maid and housekeeper, they said that Sean loved Maggie, you loved Sean, and that's the reason you killed Maggie. Because you felt that she stood in your way with him all those years ago."

Her green eyes flashed. "That's not true!"

"I know," I said. "I saw Sean's face when I told him you were here."

Now her hands reached for the top rung of a chair, in imitation of mine. But hers trembled.

"I told him you'd returned, and he asked how you were, if you were healthy and safe," I said. "He wouldn't have asked those questions if he didn't love you sincerely and still. I doubt he ever gave Maggie a second's thought."

She scraped the chair away from the table, sat down, and rested two hands, palm down, on the wood surface.

My heart clutched, for I knew where she'd learned to do that, and why.

"I told you he'd find the truth," Ma murmured and settled a gentle hand on Honora's shoulder.

She looked up at me. "You believe me now, that I didn't kill Maggie."

"I think Katie Wells heard you arguing and thought she could—pardon the expression—kill two birds with one stone."

"She could take leadership of the Wrens *and* pin the murder on me," Honora said hollowly. "What a little . . ." her voice faded then became bitter. "It makes me think I should've stayed in Swan River."

"Why?" Ma asked.

"At least there you knew to expect people lying and cheating! This maid don't even know me, and she's aimin' to have me hang for what she's done!" Tears rose to her eyes. "I just want to live and work and . . . try to find a decent life for myself here. Why can't I just do that?"

"You can and you will, Honora," I insisted, leaning over the table to face her. "But right now, Katie and Mrs. James have disappeared. At first, I was afraid they might try to kill you before they left—that's why I ran in here the way I did—but now I think they just want to get away. I'm going to the Yard to ask constables to go to the railway stations and keep their eyes out for two women, traveling together, looking as if they're leaving town. I can give descriptions, but do you have any idea which direction they'd go? What would they consider a safe place?"

Honora thought for a moment, her expression intent. "Look for trains going north. Jacinta Wells had family in Liverpool, along the Mersey," she replied. "And tell them to look for two women *without* bags or trunks or even satchels, Mickey. They have pockets. That's all they'll use, if they're running."

I nodded and left.

Katie Wells and Mrs. James were caught at Liverpool Station, on a northbound train. Just as Honora said, they carried no bags, just reticules, with their valuables stowed in their pockets. Katie drew a knife on the constable who approached, but I'd warned everyone about their dangerous hands, and he escaped with only a scratch.

Honora began her stint as a dressmaker and married Sean Tooley in a quiet ceremony two months later. I stood up with them, and as I handed her the silver ring she had chosen for Sean, she laid her hand on my arm and smiled up at me, her green eyes bright with something like mischief. "Thank you," she murmured. "You're a good man . . . for an inspector."

That evening, in my room, as I removed my coat, an ace slid out of my sleeve onto the floor. Grinning, I picked it up and tucked it into the frame of my mirror.

As often happens, the idea for this story evolved from a surprise tossed into my path. In 2021, my daughter was spending a semester in England and I went to visit. (Claims that I was coming to assist her with the language barrier were met with skepticism.) One rainy night, we stopped in at the Great Scotland Yard Hotel for a drink and found a bar called "The Forty Elephants" as well as a lobby lined with glass cases containing some fabulous Yard memorabilia—the boots of criminals, rap sheets, mug shots, truncheons, and such. The QR code on the table explained where the name "Forty Elephants" came from—it had nothing to do with British imperialism in Africa or India, which I'd assumed—and I began my research into the all-women thieving gang centered on Elephant and Castle Inn in Southwark, using that as a foundation for the Wrens of Whitechapel. I am grateful to Brian McDonald for his invaluable book Alice Diamond and the Forty Elephants *and to John Connor and* Crimeucopia *for the initial publication.*

Unable to let go of this ingenious group of talented women, I've made them the topic of my new, full-length mystery novel, coming from Soho Press later this year, about a ring of women thieves—think Oceans 8 *meets 1870s London.*

After serving twenty years in middle school classrooms, **Anna Scotti** *retired a hero and now teaches adults online. She specializes in presentations on grammar and business writing for corporate clients. This is Scotti's third inclusion in* Best Mystery Stories, *following "A Heaven or a Hell" (2022), and "It's Not Even Past (2024)," both first published in* Ellery Queen Mystery Magazine. *Earlier this year, Down & Out Books published the first nine "librarian on the run" stories from* EQMM—*along with two new stories—as a collection entitled* It's Not Even Past. *In addition to mysteries, Scotti writes poetry and young adult fiction. Like everyone else in LA, she spends afternoons at the beach, sipping mocktails and dreaming of writing a screenplay. Learn more at annakscotti.com.*

A NEW WEARINESS

Anna Scotti

In the few years I'd spent in LA, I'd never met a movie star, or even seen one up close. I'd attended a few galas as the assistant to a woman who ran a nonprofit when she wasn't hunting down drunk drivers, but I'd been a hired hand, lucky if I caught a glimpse of Reese Witherspoon nibbling tossed salad at thirty yards, or Dwayne Johnson coming out of the restroom through a protective phalanx of publicists and handlers. I'd met celebrities' kids as an aide at a high-end private school on Mulholland Drive, but my contact with the senior Spellings and Wests and Arquettes had been minimal. So it was a bit ironic that now, on a narrow road in a third-rate beach town in South Carolina, I was about to get my first taste of Hollywood glam, up close.

A very large lady in lavender shorts and a matching flowered blouse touched my arm. She was a tenant in my complex, but I couldn't think of her name. "Move over, Sonia, and I'll give you a soda," she offered. I eschewed the Mountain Dew, but scooted over on the curb to let her sit. She eased herself down, huffing, and took a long swig of her own chartreuse drink. "It's a male star, we know that much," she confided. "They're filming a rescue on the beach. It's a male star and a whole buncha college-kid extras."

Right on cue, a herd of bikini-clad girls poured out of the honeywagon, giggling and shrieking for no discernible reason. Just five or six percent of American women are blond, but you wouldn't know it from this sample, whose tresses ran the gamut from brass to platinum. From another trailer, a complement of boys emerged, each one more toned and cut than the last. Most of them were showing off well-oiled chests, but a few wore tees or sweatshirts—University of South Carolina, Clemson, Webster, and one golden boy sported a sun-streaked man bun and a teal Coastal Carolina tee. There was precisely one person of color in each group, a light-skinned Ken in orange-and-purple Clemson shorts, and a matching mocha Barbie.

Technically, I'm supposed to avoid crowds; it's part of my agreement with the Federal Witness Protection Program. I lie low and keep my nose clean, and in return they do their best to keep me alive, at least until the murderous, drug-dealing cartel-mates of my ex-inamorato, Mateo Andres, are brought to trial. But nobody in Solana Beach was paying attention to a thirty-something gal in ragged yoga pants and a messy bun, not with all this youthful pulchritude abounding. Nearly everyone in the mixed group of locals and tourists was snapping photos on their phones, so I slipped on my Ray-Bans and shook my hair loose just to play it safe. Some of those pics were sure to end up online, or in the paper.

I'm not much of a movie buff, but I was kind of hoping it might be Robert Downey Jr., or maybe Idris Elba, or pretty much any of the legion of Hemsworths. But this whole setup looked a little downtown to be housing any really big-name star. The trailers were not pristine, and the tall canvas folding chairs set up in the shade looked a bit battered. Instead of being emblazoned with specific names, they just read "Director" and "Male Lead," and some of the letters were worn away.

As aides with walkie-talkies and headsets herded the extras toward the beach, the door to the smallest trailer opened and a pretty young woman came down the steps, simultaneously checking her phone and making notes on a clipboard. The onlookers gasped and those who were sitting surged to their feet. "He's comin'," my overly extroverted companion said excitedly. "He's comin' out now! I b'lieve it's, I b'lieve it's—Austin Butlah!"

I blinked. The man coming down the trailer steps was young and blond and extraordinarily good-looking, but he was not the Elvis star, though of a similar type. Instead, it was a guy I'd never thought to see again. The last time I'd spoken with Dylan Albright, he'd been living in a squalid dump in North Hollywood, a couple thousand miles from Solana Beach, working toward a mechanic's license. Dylan had been shockingly handsome even then, with thick tawny hair and coffee-brown eyes fringed with lashes any girl would envy. He'd also had a missing front tooth, a hick way of speaking, and two years under his belt for manslaughter.

I scrambled to my feet, thinking I'd melt back into the crowd and retreat to my apartment, but as I got up, Lavender Lady called out to the actor. "Yoo-hoo, honey, look over here!" Dylan turned and his eyes landed on me. Surprise registered on his face and I forced myself to remain expressionless as I took a step backward into the crowd.

I cursed under my breath. I was Sonia Sutton, the down-on-her-luck manager of the down-on-its-luck Serenity Shores Beachside Apartments. Since I'd shed my Cam Baker identity, I'd bleached my hair back to sandy blond, ditched my brown contact lenses in favor of my natural gray, and packed on a good five or six pounds of muscle. But there had been an undeniable shock of recognition in Dylan Albright's startled face.

When I first went on the run, I was angry, more than anything. It hadn't seemed real. I didn't accept, for a long time, that my life as a hardworking librarian at the world-famous Harold Washington Library in the Chicago Loop was over. As the peril became real, I spent so much time being scared that I forgot to be mad. But now, knowing I might have to pack up and move on yet again, I mostly felt sad, and maybe a little bored. It was as if my life was on auto-repeat; as soon as I started to settle in anywhere, my cover would be blown and I'd be starting over again.

"Whereof what's past is prologue," I whispered, crossing the street back toward my apartment. "What to come, in yours and my discharge." Sometimes even Shakespearean scholars think Antonio is telling Sebastian that history repeats itself, but that's not at all what he meant, as he urged Sebastian—and himself—to murder. He meant that everything in your life up until this very moment—whatever that moment may be—provides the basis, the context, for you to act, to seize your own destiny. I knew that my being recognized could be a blip, a moment in Dylan's day soon forgotten in the glamour and bustle of his apparent new life as a film actor. Or being recognized could mean my cover was blown, my life was once again in danger, and I'd be packing up and moving to a new destination before I'd even had a chance to perfect my backstroke and burnish my tan. "What to come, in yours and my discharge, Dylan," I said again.

My first instinct was to call Owen James. He'd been my WITSEC handler for years, since I'd first gone under as redheaded Juliet Gregory in Billings, Montana, after witnessing Mateo's brutal murder of my best friend. I'd crushed on Owen, off and on, but just when things had finally started to feel serious, he'd abandoned me, claiming he'd been reassigned. Now I was in the hands of Colleen Kendricks, a severe pinstripe-suited Black woman a few years older than I who made straitlaced Owen look like Willy Wonka. Colleen had to be a former marine—a lot of federal marshals are, because their years in service count toward seniority when they apply to the Feds. But whatever Colleen's background, it had been apparent the first time we met that we weren't going to cozy up and be girlfriends. I got a stern lecture about the number of times I'd had my cover blown, and a warning that one more fiasco could lead to my being held in jail until Mateo's trial.

I grabbed a Corona from the fridge and took it out to the balcony. Put my feet up on the rail and tried to focus on the bestseller I'd downloaded to my tablet. I knew that I should call Colleen, but I also knew that odds were the production company would move on in a day or two and I could settle back into what passed for my life without her ever being the wiser.

That seemed like a pretty good plan until about ten thirty, when the peace of our little complex was broken by the calls of a voice I remembered all too well.

"Cam? Cam Baker? Where you at?"

I put my beer down, deliberately calm, although my heart was pounding in my chest and ears. That name could very well get me killed. I hurried down the steps. Dylan was wearing a loud Hawaiian shirt and board shorts that sagged from behind, showing a strip of brightly colored underwear. "Shut up," I whispered, and then, more loudly, "I'm the manager here. Sonia Sutton. Maybe I can help."

He turned around slowly, a big stupid grin showing off his gleaming incisors. When I'd met Dylan, he'd had a habit of covering his mouth with his hand, to hide a missing front tooth. Not anymore.

"What you talkin' 'bout, girl—" Dylan began. I grabbed his skinny upper arm and stared hard into his brown puppy eyes. Something must have penetrated Dylan's happy cloud of alcohol, self-centeredness, and sheer stupidity. He nodded and followed me up the stairs to my place.

I got him inside and locked the door behind us. Dylan tried to give me a big Hollywood hug, but I stepped back and he stumbled, then caught himself on the kitchen counter.

"How did you find me?" I demanded.

Dylan shrugged. "Din' know you was hidin', Cam. One a your neighbors tol' me you live over here, but she din' know which unit."

I winced. Lavender Lady.

"She kep' callin' you something else, Susie Smith, or somethin' like that, but I knowed it was you soon as I seen you—"

"Sonia Sutton," I said absently. "That's my name, Dylan. Forget the other name."

He grinned. "I'm s'glad to see you," he said, helping himself to a seat at the table. "I got a new name too! I mean, I'm still Dylan, but now I use my middle name for my last name: Dean! I guess you can see I'm a actor, now, Cam. I mean, uh, *Sonia*. I'm the star of a movie! A *movie star*! I'd love to have you visit the set and meet ev'body!"

I closed my eyes. Dylan Albright had done two years in prison for removing warning signs from a swimming hole near his folks' place on the Kern River, resulting in the death of a young man and his dog. I'd felt sorry for Dylan—beautiful, naive, and dumb as a box of rocks—until a video had surfaced of him angrily, drunkenly refusing responsibility or remorse.

"Dylan," I said. "I have a new name because I need to lie low. Did you tell a lot of people about me? That you know me from back in California?"

Dylan bit his lip. "Naw," he said. "My manager, she says the less I talk about—*you know*—the better. The tabs—that means tabloids, Cam, those little newspapers that print gossip—the tabs'll find out about it, but it's better if my movie gets released first, so people can know me and love me before they learn about my time of incarceration."

Infinite-monkey theorem be damned; in ten thousand years, Dylan could not have strung that many words into a coherent sentence on his own. His manager had to be a hell of a coach.

He continued. "Diane says, when I run into anybody who knew me—you know, *then*—I should just preten' like I don't see them if possible, and keep the discourse short and to the point if not." He giggled, exhaling a cloud of spirits that made me put down my own bottle with a sigh. "*Discourse*," he said. Then, horribly, he winked. "But I din' wanna preten' like I don' know *you*," he went on. "I allus thought you was hot, and it's nice to see a face from home. So, what? You got boyfriend troubles? Who you hidin' from?"

I took a deep breath and looked around my place. John Ruskin said, *Every increased possession loads us with a new weariness.* I didn't own a lot: my tablet, some clothes, and my mother's engagement ring. The rest of my most cherished things—a silver locket from my dad, my laptop, a well-worn copy of *Boston Adventure*—had been ditched in the mad scramble to get out of town when I'd blown my Cam Baker cover. My sole friendship, my mother's safety, and my dog had been casualties of my recklessness as well. I couldn't afford any more mistakes, but now I was looking a big one right in the gorgeous, chiseled-cheekbone face.

I felt myself going under the spell of Dylan's beauty, despite his terrible speech, his cluelessness, and his blemished past. Maybe that's what they mean by star power. I could never be attracted to him; I prefer a more rugged, decidedly masculine type. But I did want to—what? Hug him like a child? Feed him scraps from my plate like a puppy?

I shook my head impatiently. "You've got to get out of here, Dylan," I said urgently. "You can't tell anyone you saw me, and if you already did, tell them you were mistaken."

"Listen," Dylan said. "I got a lot of people around me, anytime I want them. Manager, PAs—that's production assistants—bit players . . . you could hang with me in my trailer and be safe, you know?"

I sighed. "Until you move on," I said wearily. "In what, two, three days?"

Dylan shrugged. "Well, yeah. But we could have us a helluva time till then!" He put a tanned hand on my knee and grinned, letting his blond bangs fall down into his eyes. His professionally lightened hair really did flatter him. No doubt that investment paid dividends on a fairly regular basis.

"Dylan," I said, removing his paw. "Run back to your trailer and see if one of the extras wants to keep you company. I've got things to do. Just, please, don't tell anyone you saw me."

He got up off the couch and moved reluctantly to the door. "Well, I'm not gonna force myself on you," he said. "Hashtag me too!" He grinned and rolled his eyes like it was a joke. "But you know where to find me if you want to hang out, *Sonia!*"

When he'd gone I sat for a while, trying to think. After the LA debacle, I had begged Owen to put my mother into protective custody with me. It wasn't as though she could go back to business as usual, now that Mateo's men knew that she'd seen me. They had no way to know that we weren't in contact, and Mateo had shown that it wouldn't trouble him in the least to use violence to find out. But Owen had refused, saying being together would make both my mother and me easier to find. He would tell me only that Mom was with my cousin Marsha, and that both were under the watchful eye of the US Marshals Service.

I had to call Colleen. Refusing to play by the rules had cost me a lot already. It was possible that she'd let me stay put, but I'd find out in the morning. I wanted at least one more night in my comfortable bed with the ocean breeze stirring the curtains, a can of bear spray, and my MK3 folding knife—a gift from Owen—under the pillow.

I showered and put on cut-off sweats and a tank top to sleep in. In my long-ago first life, I'd enjoyed the sensuality of sleeping in the nude. Getting rousted out of bed by a team of US marshals waving badges and guns had sucked all the naughty fun right out of that. I slept in comfy clothes with track shoes, phone, and keys in arm's reach.

I set an alarm so I could grab a swim at dawn before the film crew got moving. I'd been reading for an hour or so when there was a tapping, light but deliberate, at the door. I sprung out of bed and snapped the knife open. Stuck my phone in my pocket and crept to the peephole.

Dylan Dean, né Albright, was back.

I snapped the blade closed and opened the door, cursing. "What the hell, Dylan? What do you want?"

He pushed by me and I smelled perspiration, alcohol, and fear. "You gotta help me, Cam," he said urgently.

"*Sonia*. And no, I don't *gotta* do anything," I snapped. "What's the matter?"

Dylan sank down into a squat and put his head in his arms. Even stinking as he did, his feline grace was remarkable. I closed the door and put my hand on his shaking shoulder. "Come on, get up. Come sit in the living room and tell me what's wrong."

He looked up at me, black lashes sparkling with tears. "I went to drink a beer with the crew over in the honeywagon, and then when I got back to my trailer . . . Cam—*Sonia*—there's a *dead guy* lying on the floor! I din' do it! I din' do *nothing*! But you know they're gonna blame me, because of—you know!"

He wasn't wrong. I've heard that the guards at Lompoc send their parolees off with a warm "See you back here soon," betraying an unbecoming lack of confidence in the penal system that employs them. I slipped the knife into my pocket and took out my phone. "We've got to call the cops, Dylan. I'm sorry. I know you're scared, but we have to. I know a guy—I can ask for this detective I know, and tell him you're—"

I stopped. What exactly would I tell Detective Bill Randall, the grizzled old pro I'd met a few months earlier when a dead girl had turned up in the street outside my complex? I didn't know anything about Dylan other than he'd done his time. The only thing I could say about his character—based on that long-ago videoed rant—was not exactly flattering. For all I knew, he *was* responsible for the body on his trailer floor, tears notwithstanding. He was an actor, after all.

Dylan stood up. "Just come back with me," he pleaded. "Maybe you can tell if—like, if it looks like it was just a accident, like if he tripped or somethin', then okay. You can go, and I'll call the cops." He stood up and brushed a lock of gold from his eyes. "The thing is, Ca—*Sonia*, if Diane finds out—I haven't been a movie star very long. This is my first pitcher, I mean *film*! They've hardly started the principal shooting, an' they could drop me. . . . Diane says we're gonna go straight to *People* magazine, right to the top, the day the movie opens, and tell them I done time, but until then—she wouldn't even let the local newspaper interview us, me an—"

"Whose body is it, anyway, Dylan? And what makes you so sure he's dead?"

Dylan winced. "He's dead. There's a puddle of blood by his head. I'll show you." I slipped on the Rainbows I kept by the front door and followed him out.

The little trailer colony was quiet and dark. Movie people go to bed early and get up early. My Malibu boss, Beth Keller, once told me that even when actors and directors aren't on a project, they won't go out late because then people will know they're not working. It had seemed silly at the time, but I'd been living a life of subterfuge for so long that I no longer judged anyone for their pretenses. We've all got our reasons to lie.

This close to the water, the sound of waves slapping shore was alluring. It was hours till dawn, but I couldn't wait to slip into the cool water and float beneath the brightening sky. Dylan led me up the steps of his small trailer and pushed the door open. It was dark inside, but the bare bulb over the minibar was enough to show that there was no body on the floor, nor in the bed or at the little corner banquette. I tiptoed to the head with my knife in hand as Dylan cowered by the door. Nothing.

I felt a surge of relief and realized I'd been holding my breath. "There's no one here, Dylan," I said. "Your boy must've been breathing, because he definitely got up and walked out of here." I squatted and touched a dark spot on the floor. Sniffed my fingers. Lysol. "Even cleaned up after himself. I'll bet it was a local—maybe one of the extras—snooping around in here and banged his head."

I smiled up at him. "It's easy enough to mistake an unconscious person for a dead one." Dylan looked uncertain but I got up and patted his arm. "You're okay, buddy," I told him. "Remember what I told you, all right? Don't come by my place again, and if we run into each other, you don't know me, except as a new fan named Sonia Sutton." He nodded, still looking a little green around the gills.

"I got it," he said dully. "But I was pretty sure that guy was *dead*."

"Go to bed so you're fresh on set tomorrow," I advised him. I looked around the trailer, at the empties stacked by the sink, the cramped single bunk built into one corner. It hardly seemed like a better life than the one he'd abandoned. "Congratulations on your new career, Dylan. Have a nice life. And start locking your trailer door."

The night was so cool and fresh that I couldn't resist heading down to the beach for a quick run on the packed sand. Although it was nearly midnight, a full moon cast a mellow glow on the dark water. The beach wasn't entirely deserted; I could hear the soft murmur of women's voices from the dunes, and a man relaxed by the water's edge, feet tickled by the gentle surf.

I pulled my hair back and knotted it into a ponytail. Stretched for a minute. A woman rose from behind a clump of beach grass. She was tall, wearing cuffed shorts and a light cardigan. "Let's walk on the beach a little," she called to someone unseen. The woman's figure was youthful, but when she called out, I thought she must be in her fifties or so. Another figure rose from the dunes. Despite the moonlight, it was dark, and I could see only that she was also slim, dressed in dark pants and a tank. I thought she might be the assistant who'd come down the steps in front of Dylan earlier that day.

I waved casually as I took off running, but they didn't seem to notice. I was about two hundred feet down the beach when a shrill scream roiled the placid air.

I'm a bit chagrined to admit that my first thought was for my spoiled run. As soon as I called Colleen in the morning, she'd most likely be hustling me out of town to parts unknown. I had never expected to love the slow lifestyle and solitude of Solana, South Carolina, but I did. I was lonely, yes, but that had been a constant in my life for so long that I barely noticed anymore. I turned around, kicking at the sand, and saw the two women by the figure of the man I'd noticed earlier. The older woman crouched over him, seeming to be giving inexpert chest compressions, as the younger one fumbled with her phone.

I jogged closer. It was kind, and rather resourceful, of the woman to be attempting CPR, but I've seen enough of death to know this fellow was well past appreciating her courtesy. His eyes were slitted open, unblinking, and there was a stillness to him that a living body never achieves. It was the golden boy I'd noticed earlier sporting a sun-bleached man bun and a gorgeous tan. I estimated he'd been about six feet tall, probably 190 pounds, and every one of those pounds had known right where it belonged. I wondered how many hours Man Bun had spent in the gym to achieve the perfect physical form he'd never enjoy again. He wore only a pair of beige board shorts; his teal CCU T-shirt must have been abandoned to the heat of the day.

The woman looked up at me, her hands still on the boy's chest. Her eyes glistened. "He's one of our background performers!" she said frantically. "Mark, I think. Or Matt? What *happened*?"

I shrugged. "Drowned, maybe?" I knew that wasn't so. The odds that this was anyone other than Dylan's mysterious disappearing corpse ranged from slim to none. I knelt across from her, over his body. Felt his neck for a pulse, just for show, and then turned his head slightly. "He bled here," I told her. "Banged his head on something." The side of his head was matted with dried blood and sand.

"Oh, dear God!" the woman cried. She stood up fast, regaining control. "Elsa, did you manage to get nine one one?"

The girl nodded. "There's an ambulance on the way, Diane."

I blinked. Diane. Of course. This was Dylan's admired and feared manager. It would be ironic if he'd carried or dragged the body all the way down here just to have her be the one to discover it. Could he have, drunk as he'd been? Man Bun had outweighed Dylan by at least twenty pounds, but Dylan's lean muscles weren't for show. He had the hard, wiry physique of a guy who's grown up working hard and playing harder. He could conceivably have carried Man Bun to the water. But if he had, why the charade about expecting to find the body in the trailer? And Dylan didn't seem intelligent enough to have fooled me. But then, he was an actor. Surely, in addition to his blinding beauty, he had to have some talent as well.

A siren pierced the stillness of the night, growing closer. "I can stay," the girl told Diane, "If you want to take the car and head back to the motel."

There was no motel large enough here in Solana to house those of the cast and crew that didn't rate—or didn't want—a trailer near the set. I figured they'd most likely be at the Budget Inn in Myrtle Beach.

"Yes," Diane said decisively. "Good, Elsa. And see if the Uber knows a place to pick up an herbal tea on your way back. I'm going to have trouble sleeping tonight."

I snorted rudely, then covered the sound with a cough. The closest place to pick up an herbal tea this late on a weeknight was probably Norfolk, three hundred miles north. Elsa would be lucky even to get an Uber this late. This lady had forgotten she wasn't in LA anymore.

I knew that the police would want to talk with both of them. But I wasn't judging; I planned to do a fade myself. It seemed trite to bid the ladies good evening, and callous to wish them a better day tomorrow, so I simply turned to continue my jog along the water's edge. I'd brought enough attention to myself for one day.

Two or three miles north, some college kids were drinking Buds around a campfire. I accepted their invitation to stop for a beer, but declined an offer to light up a bowl and/or share a fold-out couch with a sleepy-eyed jock who'd somehow ended up without a partner for the night. He was cute, and I was lonely, but I do have standards.

Sort of.

The truth was, swiping right had lost its appeal since buttoned-up Federal Marshal Owen James had given me a chaste kiss on the forehead and moved on to a new assignment. I'd never seen much of Owen, but I missed his popping in and out of my life. He'd been about the only constant in eight years on the run. Owen had choked a bad guy to death with his bare hands to rescue a terrified Juliet Gregory in Billings, Montana. He'd sat beside Cam Baker in the sand and broken the news of her father's death, then swept her out of town, nearly hysterical with remorse and fear, steps ahead of a hired killer. Owen had watched—only slightly disapprovingly—as Cam had made a fool of herself first over a married detective, and then, worse, when she'd nearly given her heart to a man who'd murdered one child in cold blood and had tried to kill another. He'd let Juliet and Audrey and Serena and Cam mock his dorky bow ties and dadlike khakis, unflinching, and flirt with him nearly to the point of actionable harassment. He'd bought me a knife when I confessed I was afraid to own a gun, despite my aptitude on the range, courtesy of the dashing detective aforementioned. And through all my incarnations, Owen had been . . . well, a perfect gentleman: intelligent, brave, chivalrous, and exceptionally good-looking, which never hurts.

"Night, kids," I told the lustful jock and his friends. I headed back down the beach, walking now. Something was bugging me. My eyes burned with fatigue, and I dreaded morning, but it was more than that. Mark, or maybe Matt, had been in Dylan's trailer at some point, and had presumably been killed there. I had Dylan's admittedly dubious word for that, but I also had the wet patch on the carpet where Mark had bled. Either he'd been moved after death—and that would have been quite a feat for Dylan to accomplish, let alone surreptitiously, and while drunk—or Mark had somehow gotten himself down to the beach post-injury, and died there. To my eye, the severity of the head wound made that seem unlikely, but head wounds do bleed rather dramatically.

But even if he had stumbled down to the beach on his own, I doubted he'd have had the courtesy, *in extremis*, to scrub his own blood out of the carpet.

There were lights on around the makeshift village, but Dylan's trailer was dark. I waited until I was sure I was unseen, and then crept up the steps and tried the door.

"Jesus, Dylan," I whispered, letting myself in. "Do you ever learn?"

I heard a sigh and the creak of springs as he sat up. "Cam? I mean, Sonia?"

I flipped on the overhead light and sat down at the little banquette. It was perfectly sized—for an eight-year-old. "They found your runaway corpse," I told him. "Down by the water, just lying there like he was enjoying the sun. Except it was nearly midnight, and the side of his head had been bashed in with . . . I dunno. A golf club?"

Dylan flinched.

"In fact, your manager found him."

Dylan gasped audibly. "*Diane?*"

"And her sidekick. Elsa?"

Dylan groaned. "I heard the siren, but I thought, well, I'ma jus' stay out of it, y'know?"

I laughed, but fingered the knife in my pocket. "Dylan, honey, pretty sure you're already in it up to your belly button. You blew it leaving the door unlocked. If you were afraid there was a killer on the loose, you'd have locked the door. So how about you come clean?"

"That door don' keep nobody out," Dylan said sullenly. "An' I ain't ascared. Bring it on!"

"Okay," I said. "So why was Mark—or Matt—here in the first place? Did you catch him snooping around looking for souvenirs? Did you invite him in?"

"Mac," Dylan corrected sullenly.

I nodded. "*Mac*. So you did know him. He was a good-looking guy, Dylan. Were you—"

He swung off the bed and scratched his package as if for reassurance. "Jesus H. Christ, Cam! I mean Sonia! I ain't no, uh—" He put his hands out, palms up, as if at a loss for words.

"Yeah, horrors, Dylan. I'm asking if you're gay. Or I guess, more specifically, I'm asking if you and Mac were doing the wild thing. Is that why you killed him? Afraid he'd tell?"

Generation Z, along with Carl Nassib and Matt Bomer and Duncan James, had pretty much turned stereotypes about sexuality and masculinity upside down. It was hard to imagine anyone in 2022 fearing being outed. But I knew it was possible. Homophobia was still very much around, and it would be hard to promote Dylan as a heartthrob to young women if he was actively throbbing elsewhere for young men.

"Come on, Sonia. I've hit on *you*. You know I ain't no homo!"

I ignored the slur, along with his assumption that hitting on women precludes a man from homosexuality.

"Dylan, sit down. Tell me why Mac was here. Were you drinking together?" He shook his head almost violently. "I mean, as *straight* buddies?"

He went to the refrigerator and got a Coke. Rinsed and spit into the sink. "No, no, and no," he said firmly. "I tol' you. I came in and foun' him lyin' there. Then I went and got you."

I couldn't identify anything in the tiny trailer that could have caused the injury to Mac's head, if he'd somehow tripped. The side of the banquette, perhaps, but it was so low as to make the would-be accident implausible. And the blood spot on the carpet was in the wrong spot for that scenario.

"Mind if I use the john?" I asked, and Dylan nodded absently.

I'm not a big person—average height, I guess, and slim—but the bathroom was so tiny that I could barely get the door shut without straddling the toilet. There was just one shelf that held a worn toothbrush in a plastic cup, a single roll of toilet tissue wrapped in paper, and an optimistically large, but factory-sealed, box of Trojan Pleasure Pack condoms. The shower was cramped and bare. I flushed to mask the sound of opening the cabinet beneath the sink: a bottle of Lysol and a toilet plunger, nothing else. The minuscule plastic trash can held nothing but a few bits of tissue.

Coming out of the john, I wiped my hands on my shorts as if I'd just washed them. "Mind if I get a soda?"

Dylan waved toward the hip-high fridge magnanimously. "Help yourself, Sonia. Stay as long as you like. It's good to have a friend right now, lemme tell ya."

I ignored him. There was nothing in the refrigerator but a cardboard twelve-pack of Coke, a few bottles of Heineken, a styrofoam takeout box, and a half-eaten mocha doughnut, sitting unappetizingly on the bare wire shelf. In the classic Roald Dahl story, a woman bludgeons her husband with a frozen leg of lamb. But Dylan's meals would be provided by craft services, or by a PA running into town for carryout; there was no freezer here, no oven, no cabinets for food, no cans to use to bash someone's head in.

The time for pretense was over. I went to the bed, ripped back the covers. Nothing. Slid my arm beneath the mattress. Zilch. "Hey!" Dylan exclaimed. "What the eff, Sonia?"

"What did you kill him with, Dylan? There's nothing here—no golf club, no baseball bat." I laughed. "No Oscar on the mantel. Not even a mantel!"

Despite my accusation, it was hard to imagine Dylan a killer; he was foolish and ignorant, impulsive, and immature beyond every expectation for a man who'd spent two years in the state pen. Dylan inspired pity more than fear. But Dorian Gray, too, had started as an innocent, guilty only of reveling too much in his own beauty and in the rewards it brought.

Dylan sighed and sat on the edge of the bed. "You know, Sonia, a long time ago I made a mistake. I took that warnin' sign down, and a guy drownded. I assepted the blame and did my time."

That was not exactly true, the part about accepting blame, but I let it slide.

"I put my faith in the system," he said righteously, "and now it's time for the system to put some faith in me!"

"Dylan," I said as patiently as I could. "What are you ranting about?"

He looked indignant. "*You*. You *assume* I killed somebody, just because I have a record. It coulda been anybody!"

"It could have been," I agreed, sitting beside him on the narrow bed. "Except Mac died in *your* trailer, Dylan, and someone has taken pains to conceal that fact. Where's the murder weapon? Whatever you—or someone else—hit him with, where is it? What did they use to clean up the blood?"

Dylan's pupils dilated, black circles in the warm chocolate of his eyes. Something I said had surprised him, or perhaps a new thought had somehow taken root in the wasteland of his consciousness.

"I got to take a shower," he said abruptly. "Call time is seven." Indeed, I saw out the window that the sun was struggling to rise, casting a wan, watery light over the beach and the trailer village. Dylan crossed to the john, shrugging out of his shirt along the way. He stepped out of his shorts but had the grace to keep his boxers on until he'd shut the door. They were something a child might wear: navy blue, spangled with red and yellow airplanes.

"Stay as long as you want, Sonia," Dylan called through the door. "But I'ma be comin' out in my birthday suit!"

It was dawn, and I had to tell the police what I knew about Mac's death. But I couldn't figure out how to do so without admitting I'd known Dylan in a former life. How else to explain why he'd come to me when he found a body in his trailer? Detective Randall and I weren't buddies in any sense of the word. I could imagine that big bulldog mug staring me down if I tried to give him half the story.

The set was just waking up, extras arriving with bathrobes and hoodies over their swimsuits, production people checking and inspecting and importantly making notes on their ubiquitous clipboards. A man stood by the water, incongruously dressed in a lightweight brown suit with an out-of-date yellow tie. Bill Randall, SBPD. A petite Asian officer stood nearby, arms crossed over her chest, already sweating in full uniform and cap. They'd driven stakes into the sand and strung caution tape around the area where Mac's body had lain, but the body itself was gone. Wind and water had erased whatever tracks might have remained from the evening prior.

"Detective," I greeted him.

Randall nodded. Looked me up and down, taking in the cut-off sweats, the skimpy top, the face no doubt haggard with alcohol and lack of sleep. "What dreadful noise of waters in my ears," he said, over the rush of surf.

I hesitated, not sure I'd heard correctly. "What sights of ugly death within mine eyes," I replied at last.

"Clarence to the keeper." Randall laughed aloud. "You're surprised, Ms. Sutton." I was pretty sure the folds lifting in his bloodhound face signaled delight. "You were thinking we don't cover Shakespeare in high school here in the South?"

I shrugged. "*Romeo and Juliet*, or *Midsummer Night's Dream*, are more standard fare, I think. Nobody does *King Richard* because there aren't enough roles for girls."

Randall smiled. "Claudia Hamilton was an excellent Buckingham," he said. "Although I might be partial; I married her a couple years later." The young officer shifted from one foot to the other. "Officer Tang," he informed me, with a cursory jerk of his head.

"So," he said, turning his attention back toward me. "No homicides in Solana Beach for eleven years, and now we've got two in less than six months. You may be a bad-luck charm, Ms. Sutton."

I shrugged. "I've been called worse. Listen, Detective. I'm heading back to my apartment. Want to walk with me?"

He gave me a hard, appraising look. Nodded and followed me across the sand toward the parking lot.

"Poor kid," I said tentatively. "Any idea why—"

"MacDonald Mason," he said brusquely. "Twenty-one, journalism and pre-law major, no frat, head of the school paper, good grades, still lived with his parents in Charleston, had a nice girlfriend. Spent his time working out and studying." He looked over at me. "And, oh yeah. The kid probably didn't die where we found the body. That's what I got, so cut the crap. Your turn."

I swallowed hard. "You're going to want to question Dylan Dean," I said. "The star? He claims he found Mac's body in his trailer last night, but when I went back with him to check it out, Mac was gone."

"Jesus Christ in a handbasket, girl!" Randall stopped. "Are you out of your mind? You knew this last night, and didn't report it?"

"It's not a crime to fail to report a crime," I said archly.

He smiled. It wasn't pretty. "Let's see about that. Aiding and abetting, accessory after the fact, hindering a police investigation—those sound like crimes to you?"

"Well, I'm reporting it now," I said firmly. "In fact, I was there when the ladies found the body on the beach."

"You," Randall said grimly. "You stay put while I make a call."

He turned and hunched over his cell. All around us, the set was bustling now. A lean gray-haired man I took to be the director was inspecting the extras, Elsa now dogging his footsteps instead of Diane's. Dylan perched in a folding chair beneath a stubby palmetto tree, chatting with an actress wearing nothing but a flesh-colored swimsuit. I stepped back, then back again, then dropped into a crouch behind a parked car. Randall would know where to find me, and I'd have to face his wrath, but first there was something I needed to check.

It wouldn't have been a problem to pick the simple doorknob lock on Dylan's trailer, but he'd left it unlocked again. I went straight to the refrigerator. The bottles of Heineken I'd noticed the day before were still there. I wrapped a paper towel around my hand and took one out. It seemed clean. So did the second. I knew that Randall, or the backup he'd called, would be swarming the trailer any moment, but I forced myself to remain calm and methodical. The fourth and last bottle wasn't quite like the others. Its label was wrinkled and had clearly been wet—perhaps held under running water in an attempt to wash it clean. At the bottom of the label was a telltale reddish-brown stain. I'd found my frozen leg of lamb. I set the bottle carefully back in the refrigerator alongside its innocent companions.

The frosted doughnut was gone, but the takeout container was still on the shelf. Without removing it, I pushed it open delicately with the edge of a plastic fork, just enough to peek inside. Teal and rust. Mac's shirt was wadded inside, stiff with crusted blood.

A light tread on the trailer steps gave enough warning for me to stick the fork and paper towel in my pocket and slam the fridge door shut. I expected a police officer, but it was Elsa who slipped in and closed the door behind her.

"Forget something?" I asked.

She shrieked, stifled herself, and looked around wildly. "You shouldn't be here!" She seemed unable to keep her eyes from roaming to the refrigerator behind me.

"Nor you," I agreed.

"Dylan is thirsty! He asked me to grab him a beer," Elsa said huffily.

I peeked out the window over the sink. The director and the flesh-clad woman were in angry debate with a uniformed officer, a Black man I'd nicknamed Specs during our last encounter. Dylan slumped in his tall chair, doing a palm plant so like the ubiquitous icon it was nearly comical. Nearly. Detective Randall stood over him, hands shoved in the pockets of his brown suit, saying something that Dylan clearly found objectionable.

"Now, you know that's not true, Elsa," I said bluntly. "Looks to me like they're closing the set down. Dylan doesn't want a beer; he wants his mommy. And I know exactly what you came here to get."

I was entirely prepared to get tough, but to my surprise, Elsa pushed at her eyes with her fist and cleared her throat in an unsuccessful attempt not to cry.

"You don't understand," she said desperately. "This is the first film production in Solana Beach *ever*! They're orderin' takeout and pizzas and beer and sodas like nobody's business, and hirin' extras and people to work crew an' all, and Diane says she could use me back in Hollywood, 'cause I'm really good at followin' orders, an'—"

"Elsa," I said gently. "A temporary job and a pleasant boost to the local economy are no excuse for murder."

She looked up, shocked. "I didn't murder anybody! *Nobody* murdered anybody! There was an accident, that's all. Diane and I came in here looking for Dylan to go over some paperwork, and we found Mac there on the floor, so we just, just—*moved* him down to the water for exactly this reason! So's they wouldn't get the wrong idea and shut the set down. Please, can you just—"

"Elsa," I said firmly. "It was murder. Haven't you figured out why Diane hid Mac's shirt and rinsed off the beer bottle? Or did she have you handle that?"

"We couldn't take that stuff with us," she said weakly. "We could barely lift him, the two of us together, with his arms over our shoulders, an'—"

There was another tread on the step and Office Tang came in, hand resting lightly on the holster at her hip. Ignoring Elsa and me, she checked the john and eyed the rumpled bed warily. "This trailer is inside a closed perimeter," she told us blandly. "You'll have to leave."

"Elsa has something to tell you," I told the cop. "And then you'll want to be very careful with the stuff in the refrigerator."

Tears were streaming down Elsa's face. Officer Tang looked interested now. "Everything I did, Diane made me," Elsa sobbed. "And she's gone, she got away! I already dropped her at the airport!"

At times, I'll admit, LA and South Carolina seem like different countries, but I was pretty sure there was an extradition agreement between them. "You just tell Officer Tang the whole story, Elsa," I told her. "How you and Diane decided to cover up a crime. If you're lucky, you can make a deal to testify against her."

I left them to chat and went out.

Dylan was still with Randall, who looked over as I approached, looking frustrated.

"So you mentioned that Mac was a reporter for the school newspaper," I said to the detective, ignoring Dylan. "I think you're going to find that Mac came to see Mr. Dean, hoping to discuss a news story he must have stumbled across when he was Googling the production. It's a really sad story about a boy and dog, and a girl who loved both of them."

Dylan looked at me desperately, his eyes begging for mercy.

"The boy died, and the dog too," I said. "But the good news is, the person responsible went to prison for it."

Randall nodded, catching on. "That kind of backstory could sink a rising star," he offered.

Dylan sat up straight. "To hell with the damn dog," he said. "It was a mistake! An' I paid for it. It was just a accident!"

"Mmmm," I agreed. "*That* death was an accident. But Mac figured out that Dylan Dean and Dylan Albright were one and the same, and he was excited to run a story about it in the school paper. How'm I doing, Dylan? Have I got it about right? Maybe Mac thought he could go wider—take it to the local paper! So you bashed his head in with a bottle of Heineken, and *that* death was no accident."

Dylan stared at me, his brown eyes slitted with fury. I recognized the man I'd seen in a video long ago, a man whose hatred and rage were no longer masked by beauty. "That damn kid had no right! He had no *right* to just come in and trash somebody's career! He wanted to *interview* me about it, like I'm gonna help him *destroy* my own effin' career afore it even starts!"

"I'm going to read you your rights, Mr. Dean," Randall interrupted.

But Dylan couldn't stop. "After we gave him a *job*! We put 'im in a *movie*!"

"Dylan," I told him. "You're entitled to a lawyer. Stop talking now."

Randall motioned to Officer Tang, who was coming down the trailer steps with Elsa in handcuffs. Dylan must have realized what was happening. "You stupid bitch," he shouted. "What the hell did you do?"

"Elsa and Diane were trying to help you, Dylan," I told him. "If you hadn't dragged me into it, nobody would have known where Mac died. You can really blame yourself."

Dylan had regained control, but he was so angry that his jaw trembled. "You think you're so smart, *Sonia Sutton*," he said softly. "But I ain't the only one with secrets."

Tang handed Elsa off to another officer and accepted the cuffs he offered. As she hoisted Dylan to his feet and read him his Miranda rights, Randall took my elbow and steered me away from the activity.

I was awfully tired. My eyes burned and everything had a gritty quality, as if I were watching an old newsreel. It was well past eight and I'd never gone to bed the night before.

"I ran you, Ms. Sutton," Randall said gently. "I'm sorry. Had to. I'd have backed off, soon as I figured out why you seem to have sprung into existence the day you arrived in Solana. But I guess it triggered something." For once, his bloodhound face looked kind. "There's a lady waiting for you."

I froze. Strangers looking for me never brought good tidings, and had upon occasion delivered chaos, danger, and death.

"It's okay," Randall said, and again I thought that his eyes were curiously soft. "She showed me some pretty interesting ID"

"Is she a tall Black lady with extremely rigid posture?" I asked, and he nodded. We walked through the parking lot to my complex.

"I guess you'll need my statement later," I suggested.

But he shook his head. "We may have to build our case without it."

And with that I knew that Colleen had filled him in, and that my time in Solana Beach was over. My hand was nearly lost in Randall's big paw as we shook. "You're welcome back to the Palmetto State anytime you like, Ms. Sutton," he told me soberly. "When whatever this is you're going through is over."

His kindness surprised me. Both Elsa's guilt and her innocence had surprised me. Dylan's treachery had surprised me. I didn't think there would be any more surprises that morning.

But I was wrong. There were several to come.

Colleen met me at the door and hurried me in, her big Staccato 2011 in hand. "I can give you half an hour to pack," she said briskly. "And I can offer you a choice—Las Vegas or suburban Maryland." That was new; Owen had never let me pick a location, or even told me where I was going until we arrived.

"Marshal James told me that this would be over by now," I protested. "I know my cover's blown, but Dylan Dean will be in custody pretty much forever. Even with a good lawyer, he won't make bail right away, and—"

Colleen shook her head. She wore discreet, no-nonsense pearl studs in her ears, and a matching string around her neck. They glowed against her dark skin. "Ms. Yarborough," she began, and the shock of hearing my real name delayed the shock of what came next. "Mateo Andres is dead."

I felt a warm wave start in my gut and move outward to every extremity, like ripples on water. "Oh, thank God, thank God," I murmured, sinking onto the battered sofa. Colleen was still talking, but my mind was spinning. I would see my mother again, and the cousin who'd looked after her for so long. I would start my life again—maybe finish my degree. "And Owen!"

I slapped my hand over my mouth, realizing I'd spoken aloud.

". . . necessary to keep you under just until we can assess—" Colleen was saying, but she broke off when I spoke.

"Ms. Yarborough, I understand that you grew . . . *close* to Federal Marshal James while he was assigned to your case."

"No," I exclaimed. "Not at all! Not like *that*—I just—" Her expression stopped me. Overfamiliarity with a witness in protective custody could end a marshal's career. "Is that why he was reassigned?"

"Please, Lori, listen." Colleen sat down beside me, but I noticed she kept her piece in hand, letting her arm rest loosely at her side. "Owen James wasn't reassigned. He left the US Marshals Service voluntarily. He went out on his own, and he shot Mateo Andres to death during a botched attempt to take him into custody."

I gasped. Mateo's comings and goings had never been clandestine; he'd been under surveillance since he'd murdered my best friend and triggered my desperate flight. Mateo could have been arrested and charged a dozen times, but federal agencies had delayed, vying to take down the cartel kingpins while letting lesser crimes and criminals go unpunished and unchecked. Owen could only have been trying to end the eternal back and forth by forcing their hand. He could only have done it for me, to free me.

"Is Owen in trouble," I asked Colleen. "Is he under arrest?"

And there it was, the very last surprise of the day.

"No," Colleen said gently. "I'm sorry, Lori. Owen is dead."

Lori lost her father in 2020, an event that triggered her rebellion from witness protection and a string of disasters that continue in "A New Weariness." I lost my own father in 2014, and in him my most enthusiastic fan and cheerleader. He never got to see my first story published in Ellery Queen Mystery Magazine, *my first poem in* The New Yorker, *or my first inclusion in this prestigious series. But he's there in every story—reflected in Lori's intelligence, her resourcefulness, her courage, and her unwillingness to, as Saint Paul and my father both advised, "suffer fools gladly." Lori represents my best self—or, rather, a self better than I could ever be, the one parents envision their children becoming—and we're both grateful to our editors, our readers, and our fathers for our continuing survival and success.*

Shelagh Smith *is the PEN New England Award winner and Derringer Award nominated author of several short stories. Her previous publications include stories in* Best New England Crime Stories *2024, 2018, and 2017, and her work has also appeared in* Tales of Sley House, Hearth & Coffin, *and* Dark Reads *by Thin Veil Press where she explores the darker side of life and death. Her debut novel* Fall River, *a retelling of the Lizzie Borden story, is forthcoming in 2026.*

She teaches writing for Bridgewater State University and Massachusetts Maritime Academy, and lives in a tiny village on Cape Cod with her long-suffering husband and two pathologically ungovernable dogs.

SNAPSHOT
Shelagh Smith

Burying my dad wasn't the hardest part; it was cleaning out his cottage.

The place was a wreck, not in a filthy hoarder kind of way, but in an old man who's lived by himself too long kind of way.

I sat amid a pile of old magazines—*National Geographic, Smithsonian, Guns & Ammo*—and paused for breath. Salty, my blissfully dimwitted mutt, lifted his head, and let out a soft whine. "I know," I told him, and then to my best friend Carla, "Would someone want these?"

She looked up from going through his old roll-top desk, dust motes swirling around her face, and wiped her brow with the back of her hand. The air was thick with the humidity of the late June day creeping in around us, and Salty's moist doggy breath didn't help.

"Maybe the library?" she suggested, and then held up a box of paper clips. She set it atop the other twelve boxes. "Did your dad steal these or what?"

"No idea."

"I'm done here," said Carla, standing and stretching. "I'm going to the bedroom, but before I do, let me ask. If I find something that's a little . . . um, sensitive? Would you want to know? Or just toss it?"

"What do you mean?"

Carla arched an eyebrow. "He was a guy."

"You mean like porn or something?"

"Or something."

I considered it and finally said, "Use your best judgment."

Carla disappeared upstairs. I heard the floor creak overhead as she moved about the bedroom where he'd passed. A sudden swell of emotion rose in me, so I hauled myself to my feet, called Salty, and together we went outside. I leaned on the deck railing as Salty leapt down to survey the yard. I watched him crisscross the lawn until he found something interesting and started to dig.

"Hey!" I yelled. "You're trashing the property value!"

Unimpressed, he continued to dig, then lost interest, and began another circuit. There wasn't much space for him to roam, but childhood memories painted the space much more grandly.

The yard had seemed immense then, when it was just me, my older sister, and a rusty swing set that had eaten up hours of my childhood. I swore I could still hear the creaking swings echo against the woods around us. The memories, so sweet at first, began to sting as I realized our lives—all I knew and loved—were ebbing away. First Mom, then Dad, and now it was just me and Colleen, but even she had been drifting in and out of my life since we were young.

Gone nearly five months now, Dad had died alone here, going to sleep one night at eighty-three and simply never waking. There were a lot worse ways to go, I supposed, and he'd died the way he'd spent most of his life: alone.

He'd divorced Mom when I was eighteen, had had a series of relationships that never lasted, and ultimately married his job. Being a beat cop in a small town wasn't particularly challenging, but he had loved it, and I'd always loved him for it. He'd been there to break up fights, pull over drunk drivers, bring lost dogs home. He'd been the model of a good small-town cop, something many people nowadays forgot ever existed, and I treasured our times together, here in this very cottage, after my sister departed on bad terms for the West Coast and the life she wanted.

"Hey, Moll?"

The unsettled note in Carla's voice twisted my guts. Oh god, I thought, please don't let it be . . . Well, I didn't know what it *could* be, but whatever it was sounded upsetting. "Well, shit," I muttered, and then called Salty.

Salty gave up the spot he'd been digging in a flower bed and ran to me.

I found Carla in my dad's room, perched on the bed, a pile of scrapbooks splayed open around her. She held a photo—an old-fashioned snapshot where you drove to a tiny parking lot kiosk, handed over a roll of film, and prayed for seven to ten days that the pictures had actually come out. This time it had. The white border around the photo and date on the back placed it almost exactly fifty years ago.

It was a young blonde woman, hair ringed by daisies woven into a chain. She smiled at the camera, blue eyes alight. It was impossible to miss that she'd been in love when this was taken, and it made my heart hurt. I had never felt that, not even once, but here she was, eyes shining as though she'd finally figured it all out. It took a few seconds for me to realize who she was, and when I did, my stomach clenched.

"Oh my god," I whispered.

"Who is that?" asked Carla.

"Delilah Festis," I said softly, recalling the case that had rocked our small town and ended my carefree childhood days playing alone outside, even in our own backyard. "A missing girl from a long time ago. They never found her."

Carla gestured to the scrapbooks and photo albums. "Looks like your dad had a thing for her."

For some reason, her words sent a chill down my spine. I shook it off as I looked at page after page about the case, about Delilah.

"This was so long ago." I breathed, pausing to examine a black and white school photo from the newspaper, staged, formal, and worlds apart from the one in my hand.

"He was obsessed," she said.

"It was a pretty big case," I said. I flipped through clippings and newspaper photos of Delilah, forever eighteen. The editors seemed to like the black and white graduation photo, which to me seemed unfair. The photo I held showed her alive and in love. Why not use the one that told more of her story?

In the snapshot, she stood against a woodsy backdrop, hair teased by an unseen wind. Sun dappled the leaves, throwing shadows against her cheeks, and shrouding eyes that seemed lit from within. Flowers bloomed at her feet, buttercups, and just out of frame, the hint of a strangely angled pole, white and red like a candy cane, nearly matching the woven red band and dangling half charm around her wrist. That band, more than anything else, made me sad. Who held the other half of that friendship bracelet? Were they missing her still today?

"Oh my god," said Carla in a suddenly hushed whisper. "Moll, do you think he killed her?"

I stared at my best friend. "Are you insane? Have you actually gone insane?" I asked in something close to amazement. "You're talking about my *father*."

Carla looked chagrined, but only for an instant. "No, I'm just saying, it happens. Didn't you see that documentary where the woman found her serial killer dad's souvenirs from—"

I cut her off. "You watch too much murder TV. It's rotting your brain."

"I'm sorry, I just . . ." Her voice trailed off, and I found a smile for her. I supposed if my very best friend couldn't bring up such outlandish ideas, who could?

"It's fine." I continued to turn pages.

"Do you think the town PD would want this?"

I considered the new detectives—an entirely new evolution from the cop my dad had been, in the same way wolves had evolved into domesticated dogs—poring through his collection. No, I thought. They wouldn't appreciate an old man's obsession.

Plus, the killer was undoubtedly dead.

I made a show of looking at my watch. "You've got to pick up your kids."

"Don't remind me," she said, but she stood and brushed dust from her shorts. "Pick it up again Saturday?"

"You bet."

We shared a brief hug, she gave Salty a scratch, and we watched together as she backed down the narrow drive.

Across the way, afternoon light shimmered on the pond where I'd learned to swim. How many times had I woven my way through thick brush to the water, causing my mom to yell after me, "Dear God, Molly Gallagher! You better not drown!"

Parents back then were a different breed too.

"C'mon, dog," I said, heading inside to stare at the photo albums. But still Carla's words rang in my ears. *Moll, do you think . . .*

I resisted the urge to light up a smoke. I'd quit when Mom passed of lung cancer, not from smoking, but some genetic fuckery that left her in misery for the last year of her life, not long before Dad's passing. I wondered if her dying had hastened his. Even though they'd stopped being married they'd always remained close, despite the unique challenges of managing a fractured family.

There had never been any noticeable acrimony between them during or after the split; all that venom had been spilled when my sister, older by twelve years, left home for her new life. Perhaps that ugliness was enough for one lifetime.

Occasionally, though, a word or two would bubble up about each other. "So he's seeing *her*," Mom would say with a sniff. Or my dad might say, "Well, she got what she wanted" whenever Mom married the new man in her life.

I wondered idly if Mom had blamed Dad for my sister, Colleen's, leaving, but she had never mentioned it to me. Who can say what might have passed between Colleen and Mom when the prodigal daughter returned with wife in tow to nurse Mom through cancer treatments?

I pushed the thought aside, turned to the albums, flipping to a newspaper article dated nearly a quarter century ago.

Missing Girl Case Enters
25th Year—Waiting for Answers

Delilah Festis—"Daisy" to friends and family—was only 18 years old when she vanished from Rocky Point on a scorching July day in 1974. Today, she would be 43.

And today, there are still no answers. With no new clues, it's up to Daisy's family to keep her memory alive.

"Everyone loved her. She marched to her own drum, you know?" said her sister Patty. "She was a free spirit. She trusted everyone. I guess she trusted the wrong person."

I studied the accompanying photo of Patty and my cigarette fingers itched again. She looked sad, old, worn. A cigarette burned in the ashtray beside her, and I wondered how that had slipped by the editors, even back then. Smoking was verboten now, the same way hitchhiking became forbidden in the late seventies and eighties when horror stories of missing girls started to come out. Was Delilah—Daisy —one of those girls?

I turned the page to avoid the pull of nicotine and stumbled into a series of Dad's handwritten notes, all dated the same July day in consecutive years, like some grim anniversary.

July 12, 1975—spoke to Det. Carver—no leads.
July 12, 1976—called Det. Carver—no leads. Still working.
July 12, 1977—called Det. Mercantonio—no call back.

They went on for years—decades—until eventually the notes stopped because the detectives stopped returning calls. I felt a pang of regret for Dad that he was ignored when he so clearly cared about the case that happened on his watch, in his town. They ended with one last note, just three years ago.

July 12, 2021—Done.

I turned next to printouts from online missing persons' forums where the bored and lonely lived—and died—vicariously through others' misery. Most posts were links to anniversary articles. Some offered suggestions. One writer, SleuthSlayer, had an abundance of theories, all printed and annotated with Dad's increasingly wobbly hand.

> Did anyone check her sister? Younger than her but kids do crazy things. Look at the Kennedy family murdering that Moxley girl.

And my dad's note: *Crackpot.*
And later:

> What are cops not telling? Small town cops must have known this girl. Looking like that, she probably had a lot of male attention.

And the response:

> We're assuming male attention.

Dad's note in the margins: *Revisit.*

I leaned back in my chair, idly stroking Salty's head in my lap. I wondered if Dad had softened enough in his later years to consider that very idea, that it might not have been a man who took her. It seemed his acceptance of other people's lives had grown as he aged, although as far as I knew, he'd never reached out to Colleen to make amends.

Revisit.

Did he mean the case? Or did he mean his broken relationship with my sister? I supposed either could have been true.

I didn't sleep well that night, a victim of my often unchecked anxiety, thinking over all the things I had to do. The thoughts came relentlessly, clawing at my peace, and the one that cut deepest: *Moll, do you think . . . ?*

I finally dozed off in the last hour before my alarm chirped, and that pissed me off. I fed Salty, drank a rank cup of coffee that had been in the pot since yesterday, and planted myself in front of the computer to tackle the detritus of living. Paying bills. Checking emails. Reading social media. When I'd exhausted those distractions, I dived into the thing that had kept me spinning in my sheets overnight.

Why Delilah? Why *that* case? And Carla's words: *Moll, do you think . . . ?*

I researched the sleuth forums. As I skimmed, I dug into foggy memories from that time in my life. I wondered how many people actually remembered with any clarity what they did in the summer of their eighth year.

I recalled vague conversations among grownups, back when things like missing and murdered women weren't celebrated with such macabre glee. Aside from a cursory "Don't hitchhike," there were no stranger-danger talks. I used to think I was lucky to have grown up during a time when the only instructions were to get home before the streetlights came on. Parents didn't care where you were; they were just happy you came home at all.

Well, most parents anyway.

I thought of Delilah's parents. They'd gone to their reward without ever knowing what happened to her, and soon, no one would remember her at all. After fifty years, how many follow-up stories could a newspaper print?

With nothing new online, and my own memories sketchy at best, I did the only other thing I could think of. I drove to my sister's house.

Her wife answered the door. I hadn't seen her since the funeral.

"Hey, Laura," I offered. "Colleen here?"

She ushered me in and summoned my sister. She came out of her office wearing a tight smile and I knew she wasn't entirely happy to see me. That was okay. The last time I'd been here had been to tell her I'd found Dad dead in his bed. Her reaction then had been reserved, but at his memorial service, she'd wept openly and spoke about the loss of the father she'd loved, then hated, then . . . what? What had evolved between them in his later years I would probably never know.

"What?" she demanded.

"I wanted to check in about the house," I said. It was a weak excuse. She hadn't cared about the house before and she didn't care now. But it would get the conversation rolling.

"Do what you want."

Laura threw her hands up and said, "You two. I'm going to put on some coffee. You want?"

"Sure," I said. To Colleen, I added, "It's going on the market next week. I'm cleaning it out."

"I don't want anything."

"Okay."

Silence hung between us until she let out an exasperated sigh and said, "Stop worrying I'm going to hate you for something later. Do what you want. Keep it if you like."

"I don't want it," I said, and the vehemence in my own voice surprised me. Where had that come from?

"Then sell it."

"Yeah, but—"

"But nothing." And then, raising her brows over the frames of her glasses, said, "What's *really* on your mind?"

There it was. She'd always been able to see through me, but maybe that was part of being so much older. She'd left home shortly after I'd started eighth grade—she needed to be free, Mom said. Dad had said much worse.

"I found some stuff."

"Porn?" she said with a sly grin.

"Oh, my god."

"Please tell me it was gay porn." A genuine smile lit her face, her eyes gleaming. I couldn't help but smile too.

"I'm sure you'd like that."

She cackled wickedly, and suddenly the ice was broken between us. She gestured to the living room as Laura brought our coffee. She backed out, saying "Family business," even though we encouraged her to stay.

Colleen sipped and grimaced. "How does she fuck up a perfectly good cup of coffee?" she whispered conspiratorially, and I had to agree. The coffee was shit. "It's a Keurig for fuck's sake."

"Do you remember the Delilah Festis case?"

Colleen blinked slowly, and I thought she might be trying to place the name, but the way she set her cup down made the hair on my arms stand up. "Daisy?" she asked. "Why do you ask?"

"He had a ton of stuff about her."

Colleen hesitated again and said, "Not surprised. He was a cop."

"Yeah, but I mean *a lot* of stuff."

He was obsessed. Moll, do you think . . . ?

"Like what?"

"Newspaper articles, internet posts, photos."

She pressed her lips tight together and said with a hint of bitterness in her voice, "He always wanted to be a detective, just couldn't pass the tests. He wanted to be something he wasn't—wanted *us* to be the family we weren't, right?"

Suddenly, I regretted excavating bad memories. "I didn't mean to upset you."

She forced a smile and said, "It was a long time ago."

I struggled for something to say, then returned to the reason I came. "What was Delilah like?"

Colleen shifted in her seat, crossed and uncrossed her legs. I could sense her unease from across the room. "She was nice. Pretty. She was . . . missed." Colleen stopped talking suddenly, and I wondered if she was struggling with her emotions. Spots of color rose in her cheeks. "Her absence was felt by the whole town."

"Was she a good friend of yours?"

"We knew each other," she said, blowing out a sigh and slapping her hands on her thighs. "Long time ago. I barely remember 1974. Too many drugs," she joked.

"One thing I didn't find," I said, "were any photos of us. Isn't that strange? Dad didn't have a single photo of *us*. Just *her*."

"Mom had those. Wait here."

She hurried to another room and emerged with a photo album, not unlike my dad's. In fact, they were identical. Synthetic fabric backing gone dingy with age. She plopped down beside me, leaning into me, and it brought a tear to my eye. How long had it been since we'd sat like this? I wiped it away before she could notice.

She opened the book, and under see-through pages lay the story of her—of *our*—youth.

"Oh my god, is that Patches?" I asked, studying a picture of our old dog in the backyard of the cottage. "And this was Mom?"

The photo was my mom in an evening gown, a metallic pink party hat atop her head. The banner in the background read *Happy New Year!* I couldn't remember her ever looking so young.

"And Dad," said Colleen, pointing to my father, tuxedoed, arm around another woman. "That's Mrs. Sullivan. She lived next door."

"Oh, wow," I said, and heard my sister mutter under her breath, "Swingers no doubt."

"Oh!" I cried, and nearly slammed the book shut. "That's disgusting."

"That was the seventies. Free love, baby."

"I don't believe you."

"You don't have to, but I was there," she said, and together we turned pages until she found a picture of us together.

We were in the backyard, my feet climbing the sky as she stood behind me, pushing me on the swing set. I could almost hear the creaking metal as the set tried to break free of its mooring, feel the burning chains in my hands, and whooshing of air as I leapt off, midswing, landing amid a field of sunny yellow blooms.

"Do you remember this?" I asked.

"How could I forget? You loved that stupid swing set. You thought you were a bird. I thought it looked like demented candy cane."

I stifled a grin. Colleen was right. It did look like a demented candy cane, its red stripes over rusting white metal. It was an eyesore, but it had been my eyesore, until suddenly it vanished one day, another victim of the hysteria that followed Delilah's disappearance.

Carla's words came to me again, causing my stomach to drop to my feet. I knew if I didn't ask it now, I never would, and I'd regret it forever.

"Colleen, do you think Dad had anything to do with her disappearance?"

She stared at me, her face a blank slate, and not for the first time I wished I could read her the way she could read me. "Why would you ask that?"

"You know why."

"Because he was obsessed?"

I nodded, unable to speak.

"No," she said with certainty. "He was a lot of things, but he'd never hurt a woman."

With that, she slapped the book shut, handed it over with a tight smile, and said, "I've got to get back to work. Do what you need to do. I'll be happy when it's gone, and I think you will too."

I wanted to be hurt by what she said, but she was right. The cottage had been important to me then. Now it seemed like something else, something I didn't want to consider too deeply. "Thanks, Sis," I said, and she hugged me tight before I left.

I couldn't sleep again that night. I lay awake in the dark, listening to Salty's snoring. It was strangely comforting, and I wondered if everyone felt this way about their dog. They *had* to. There were few things in life better than the unconditional love of a pup. I thought back to Patches, back to the album that sat untouched on the coffee table. I couldn't bring myself to look at it, to revisit old memories—the good, the bad, and the ugly—of our childhood.

I knew that raising teenagers was hell, and it couldn't have been easy raising me, but raising my sister must have been much more challenging, especially back then. Colleen was different, a lot like Delilah, I thought. She, too, walked to the beat of her own drum. Sometimes I admired her eagerness to go out on her own and find herself, her life, and her truth. Honestly, I was still a little jealous.

It was sometime before dawn when I nudged Salty out of my way, crawled out of bed, and slipped into the past.

The photos were dated, of course, documenting a time when things were easier or, maybe not *easier*, but hidden. I studied pictures of my sister, a freckled Irish girl like me, with dark hair, splotchy skin, and stance that said she was uncomfortable in her skin. Her shag 'do fell over her eyes as she slouched in jeans and T-shirts in the backyard. If teen resentment was a person, it was Colleen. Some photos were of us together, Colleen the tomboy, me in frills and lace that did little to hide my plump figure and unfortunate hair. We Gallagher girls would never be Delilah.

I turned pages, fingers fondly stroking Patches, then Thumbs, an old cat who long ago crossed the Rainbow Bridge, and then I settled on the photo of me and Colleen, at the swing set I loved and she hated. This one I would frame for a gift, I thought.

I laughed out loud at how miserable she looked, not at me, but past the lens to the photographer. I imagined if it were a selfie today, she'd throw up a middle finger, but certainly not back then, and certainly not if Dad was taking the picture. I looked with some chagrin at my own goofy smile, just happy to be around my older sister, and then to her hands, one resting on my shoulder, the other on the candy-striped swing set pole.

Then I saw it.

Around her wrist was a flash of red, a woven band, and hanging from it, the other half of a silver charm.

I stood on the back deck of the cottage watching Salty make his circuit. I didn't hear the car door shut, but Salty did. He ran to greet Colleen.

"Where's Laura?" I asked but words were hard to get out. It felt like I had gravel in my throat.

Colleen shrugged off the question, took a bracing breath, and leaned back against the railing, staring at her reflection in the sliding glass door. "Why am I here?" she asked.

I took the photo of us on the swing set from my pocket, handing it to her. She looked at it once, then handed it back. "What about it?"

"I was going to have it blown up for a gift, but thought better of it." My words caught, but then I managed. "I thought we shouldn't memorialize evidence that Dad killed Delilah."

A soft gasp, not quite a laugh of disbelief, escaped Colleen. "What are you talking about?"

"Look at it." I shoved it at her. Color rose in her face, redder than I'd ever seen, and maybe, for the first time ever, I *could* read my sister. "You know it too, don't you? That's why he was obsessed."

"Moll," she said slowly. "You need to let this go."

"Oh, come on, Colleen," I said, and felt tears start to build. "She was *here*. She was in this yard. With us. With *you*. Look!"

I pulled out the photo of Delilah, held it beside the one of us, and pointed out the swing set's matching legs. I pointed to the friendship bracelet, a forever promise, on both their wrists. "She was here, Colleen. He killed her. Why else would he track the case so carefully? Why?"

Colleen shook her head. I could see her swallowing hard again and again, and was afraid she'd be sick.

"Tell me I'm wrong," I said, clutching her arm.

Then, with a dead certainty in her voice that stopped me cold, she said, "You're wrong." She wiped angrily at her eyes, so full of sudden tears that they spilled down her cheeks, and when she met my gaze, I felt my knees go weak.

"I'm not wrong," I said, but deep inside, I knew I was. I knew what she would say next, and I wanted to scream no, no, no to drown out the words that would come. I clamped my mouth shut, bracing myself for it, for the truth.

"It was me."

I felt the world spin. I steadied myself on the railing. I wanted to scream that she was lying, just fucking around, but the desolate expression in her eyes told me otherwise.

"What are you saying?" I whispered.

"Daisy and I weren't just friends. We were . . . seeing each other," she said, her voice barely audible. "We were over there." She gestured feebly to the spot where the swing set once stood. "We were messing around, you know, and Dad saw us. He flipped out."

I took a breath, imagining the scene, imagining his rage when he came upon them. He had mellowed in later years, but still I recalled the ugly words he'd spoken to my sister when she told him her truth. I could see it. I could hear it.

"He grabbed her. I tried to stop him. There was a struggle." Colleen fought for the words. "I tried to push her out of the way and she fell. She . . . fell." Colleen covered her mouth with her hands, and I watched as the horror of what had happened came alive in her mind. "She hit her head on the swing set. She started shaking. Convulsing."

"No," I said, but I *could* see it in my mind, like a movie playing endlessly before me.

"She died so quickly. I still can't believe it," she said, and short, ragged sobs tore out of her.

"Why didn't you call the cops?" I demanded, suddenly angry.

"Because Dad *was* a cop," she said as though I was an idiot. "Do you know what that would have been like? He was a town cop, Moll. His lesbian daughter gets caught with the homecoming queen and she dies *here*, in our yard. What do you think would have happened to him? To us?" She fought back more tears, and said brokenly, "You once asked if I knew Dad loved me. Moll, I know he did. He covered it up for us. For *me*."

The next question was obvious, but still it stuck in my throat. I couldn't ask it because I already knew the answer in my heart and soul. My hands shook as I gazed at the photo of Delilah here in our yard, beside the swing set, among the field of buttercups at her feet.

I looked at the yard today, at the spot where the set had once stood, and saw Salty digging, digging, digging in a patch of flowers that bloomed in the shape of a young woman's body.

Hidden secrets, twisted motives, shocking revelations, and warped family dynamics are my jam. That's where I find the best material to work with, and growing up with a too-big family in a too-small house gave me lots to work with. This story, however, came from a very different place, though no less twisted.

When a friend's ex-cop father died, I was tasked with helping clean out his home and the things we found . . . well . . . that will have to come in a much longer work. Rest assured, though, there is a lot *more to share in future stories!*

I hope you enjoy "Snapshot" and, when you're done, ask yourself this: What would you *do to protect the ones you love?*

Born and raised in Southern California, **Casey Stegman** *started reading mysteries and thrillers at a young age. After snagging his mom's John Grisham and Stephen King paperbacks, he'd spend many nights turning pages until the wee hours of the morning. Those books and those authors later inspired him to become a writer. His fiction has been published by* Tough, Shotgun Honey, Dark Yonder, Bristol Noir, *and* Punk Noir Magazine. *He also writes the article series "Murder in the First" over at* Mystery Tribune. *He is honored and privileged for his story to have been selected by Otto Penzler and John Grisham for this year's publication and for it to appear alongside so many talented writers. For more about Casey, please visit: caseystegman.com.*

EFFIE'S OASIS
Casey Stegman

Effie's at the counter in the Oasis's front office, separating out her pills for the coming week in the plastic container with individual boxes for each day.

Doc Sommes suggested she buy it to keep track of her multitude of multicolored medications, seeing as Effie's previous method of relying on her memory had failed her on more than a few occasions. Effie said it was the fault of those goddamned orange pills. "They cloud my thinking, make me so damn sleepy and forgetful," she'd said at her last appointment. "They keep the pain away, Effie," he'd told her. "And Lord knows you need that. Especially as this thing progresses." He went on to prescribe her a new blue pill and a red pill. That was on top of the chalky white one, the green one, the clear one, and—of course—the damned orange one.

She finishes up Monday's box and is moving to Tuesday, when she glances up at the wall calendar the Ralston County Rotary Club sent her last December. It's still on June. The picture's an aerial shot of the minor league ballpark in Davee. She shuffles over and flips to July, which has a picture of a rodeo rider holding on to a bucking bull. She checks tomorrow's date—July 11.

"Well, goddamnit." *How the hell does someone forget their own birthday?* "Those orange bastards."

That's when she hears the car pull into the lot.

It's an older model, *whatever-it-is*. The engine—a V8, if she had to put money on it—has a rattle and rasp to it.

Adjusting her bifocals, Effie squints beyond the dirt-speckled glass door to see the car pull to a stop in what is technically the handicap spot. Looks like a Mustang. A '77 or maybe a '78. Yellow in color. The car idles as the front passenger door opens and out steps a young woman in tight black pants and a denim jacket, wearing her hair cut short.

A second later, the front door swings inward. The bell above makes a hollow *clang*. And a blast of hot desert air precedes the woman.

First thing Effie notices are the woman's V-shaped facial features, from her chin to her mouth to her nose—all sharp. She's wearing Wayfarer sunglasses, which she takes off to survey the wood-paneled and green shag-carpeted office. "You're open!"

"Never close," Effie says. "Except for a week back in Ninety-Seven, when I rewired the electricity myself."

The woman smirks. "That so?"

Effie nods.

The woman steps up to the counter and sweeps her gaze across the pill bottles. "Well, don't this look like a good time," she says with a smile. She's got straight white teeth, which make Effie think of a shark she saw on some show she's forgotten the name of on the Nature channel last week.

"From the road, this place looked abandoned. Almost everything else we passed was. What little there was. My husband's the one who spotted the 'vacancy' sign."

Effie reaches under the counter and pulls up the guest ledger and mechanical credit card imprinter. "How many nights?"

"Not quite sure. Could ya put us down for one with the possibility of an extension?"

Effie nods, sliding the woman the ledger and a pen. "I'll need a credit card and an ID."

After she finishes scribbling in the ledger, the woman reaches into her inner coat pocket and pulls out a fat roll of bills. They're all hundreds. Must be fifty of them. Or more.

"Would you be willing to accept cash instead?" She peels off ten bills and lays them on the counter.

This ain't the first time Effie's been given this option. But it's probably the first time it's been another woman on the other side of it. Every other time it'd been men. Men who roamed these highways and byways and who, from one glance, Effie knew to be up to no good. But that weren't none of her business. And she'd said as much back in '99 to Tom Folton, *God rest his soul*, when he asked about the Oasis Motor Lodge's less-than-respectable clientele while the two of them were sipping that fine Tequila he'd gotten in Chihuahua. "As long as their money ain't funny," she'd said, "I don't give a rat's behind." They'd toasted to that.

Effie grabs the key to Room Six off the rack behind her. "Second to last one over by where you come in."

"Appreciate it, Miss . . ."

"Effie."

"Effie," the woman says, winks, and turns to go.

Which is when Effie remembers. "Wait."

The woman turns on her heel a few inches from the door.

"I forgot that room ain't been cleaned."

"Oh . . . we don't mind."

"No," Effie says, "Trust me."

What Effie doesn't say is that Matilda and one of Matilda's regular clients, Jesse Spears—a Davee councilman last Effie checked—had "stayed" in that room for a few hours two nights ago. While Effie usually cleans up right away (despite having less than two customers per week), she'd forgotten all about it this time. *Goddamned orange pills.*

Effie takes the key for Room Seven off the hook and exchanges it with the woman. "Last room at the end of the complex."

"Thank ya, Effie," the woman says, and is outside and back in the car inside of a minute.

Effie returns to her pills, filling Tuesday's box with two chalky whites when the muffled sound of a trunk lid slamming home distracts her. She looks out through the large bay window.

The husband's about the woman's height, maybe an inch or two taller. He's dressed in black jeans, cowboy boots, and a half-buttoned dress shirt. Clean-shaven, with slicked back hair, his head is doing a full scan both ways as he steps up toward the room door. In his hand, he has a black backpack nearly bursting at the seams.

Next to him walks the woman, pulling along a child by the right hand. Looks like a little girl, no more than six or seven, dressed in brown jeans and a blue shirt, with red curly hair. Before the three disappear into the room, Effie can swear the little girl is crying.

But through all that dirt caked onto the glass, it's hard to be sure.

Turning the ledger around, Effie looks at the chicken scratch on row eleven. It reads: *Mrs. and Mr. Fields*.

It's a little before three P.M. when Effie loads up the cart with the requisite cleaning supplies. She's just had her afternoon snack of cottage cheese and saltines—not a favorite, but one of the few that doesn't cause terrible gas and sharp pains. After that, she'd taken her round of pills. Despite the pull of the beaten BarcaLounger in her little apartment behind the main office, she decides to buck up and do her basic duties. Lest she forget again.

She rolls the wobbly cart with the one bad front wheel down to Room Six. Before unlocking the door, she glances over at the Mustang, specifically at the hood with the faded King Cobra painted onto it.

Definitely a '78. Gus Rogers had one kinda like it. *Didn't he?*

Gus had been one of Tom's friends. Owned a two-pump station along Route 18. Probably still does, for all she knows. Effie and Tom had stopped there on their way up to Gentry just over the state line back in the summer of '98. Tom said Gus served good hot dogs at his station. "Best wieners in five counties," he'd told her. She'd recognized a setup when she heard one. Replied there weren't much competition. This had made Tom howl. When they got there, Gus treated Effie like an old acquaintance from the get, despite that being their initial meeting. Prepared two dogs apiece for her and Tom. Weren't too shabby neither. Had this homemade sauce on 'em he called *"special slather."* Afterward, he'd shown them round back where his car was. "A midlife crisis purchase," he'd claimed.

And, yes, now that she recalls it, it had definitely been a King Cobra. A '78 matter-of-fact. Because he'd said it was the first year they made them.

Same yellow color, too.

As she enters Room Six with the cart, she wonders how many of them are still in circulation. Probably quite a few.

But how many of 'em are that same yellow?

The sheets on the king bed are all askew. Effie rolls the cart over and puts on a pair of rubber dishwashing gloves. She's stuffing the bed linen into the cart's laundry bin, when she feels something solid bunched up inside the fitted sheet. As she unballs it, there's a metal clanking sound. She has a good idea what it is a second before she sees it.

Bingo.

A pair of handcuffs with this frilly pink fabric on the ends. They're unlatched and without a key. And despite their goofy—or, maybe to some, *erotic*—appearance, they're basically your standard set of cuffs. Heavy too.

It's while she's in the bathroom, emptying the trash of its bunch of wadded tissues and two condom wrappers that she hears a muffled voice from next door yell: "Shit!"

Mr. Fields.

Next, what sounds like the woman. "What'd Mike say?"

Or . . . Mark maybe?

Effie leans in a bit closer. Hovers her ear a few inches from the wall. Mr. Fields says something to the effect of, "He can't get us across until tomorrow. Says it won't be safe till then."

Effie misses a few words and fills them in with what makes the most sense. *Maybe my medicated brain is making up stuff.*

Mrs. Fields says, "Shit!" louder and angrier than her husband's exclamation.

After that, there's silence. Or, at least what at first seems to be silence. In the background, despite the wall and Effie's less than perfect hearing, she can hear what sounds like crying.

A child crying.

A second later, Effie hears Mrs. Fields yell, "Shut the fuck up, you little bitch."

And then, it's silence for real.

Effie takes the padlock off and unspools the long chain wrapped around the back shed's door handle and pulls the heavy wooden sonofabitch open. She shuffles in and flips the switch to her right.

The single bare bulb in the center of the fifteen-by-twenty space flickers to life.

The light it casts is dim. But it's enough to see the narrow pathway between the plastic bins filled with Christmas decorations and the janky tower of over forty paint cans, which she'd ordered special from Burt's Hardware in Davee twelve years ago. Burt himself had gone to a lot of trouble to get the oil-based paint to match the Oasis's original bright, aqua-blue tint. And every time she came in here, it pained Effie that she'd yet to start the massive repainting project. According to Burt, the oil-based paint would go bad in another couple of years. He'd also said they were combustible if left out in the heat. So far, they ain't exploded despite the temperature in the shed getting well past a buck twenty in summer. So, maybe they'd still be good beyond their expiration date. Or maybe beyond hers. Whichever came first.

At the back of the shed, she opens the large bin containing fifty-one years of left behind and forgotten items. Everything from suitcases and toiletry bags to more unsavory things, like a rusted hacksaw with curious red stains on its teeth and several varieties of knives. No one ever came back to retrieve these things. Not a one. Still, Effie kept the *Lost and Found* bin going. Maybe Matilda would want these frilly cuffs next time she came back. That's if Effie remembered they were even in there.

She's respooling the chain around the shed's door handle when she hears: "Effie."

Startled, she drops the lock, which rolls down the tiny ramp to the dirt. "Shit," she says.

Mrs. Fields picks it up and dusts it off and hands it back to her. "Didn't mean to give ya a start."

Effie doesn't say anything.

"My husband and I are gonna end up staying another night." She pulls the roll of money back out of her jacket, and peels off two hundreds. "I don't imagine that'll be a problem, will it?" She smiles again. All those white teeth.

"No."

"Perfect." Mrs. Fields holds out the bills.

But Effie doesn't reach out for them. Not yet. "Meant to come by earlier. Ask if you needed a rollaway for your daughter."

Mrs. Field's smile goes away.

"Seeing as Seven has only the single king," Effie says.

Mrs. Fields takes a beat before responding.

"No. We're fine. She . . . *my daughter* . . . doesn't like to sleep alone when traveling. Likes to sleep between me and my husband." Another beat. "Has nightmares."

Effie gives a slow nod. All she's thinking about is this woman yelling *Shut the fuck up, you little bitch*, and that crying coming to an immediate halt in response.

Mrs. Fields steps forward and fully extends the two hundreds.

Effie eyes them for a long moment before taking them.

The next morning, Effie wakes before the sun's up to sharp pains in her gut. It's like a bunch of tiny men in there with ice picks are stabbing her repeatedly. She grabs for the bedside lamp's chain, yanks it on, and rolls out of bed clutching her stomach tight and hobbles over to the sideboard where she has the extra bottle of orange pills. She struggles to get the childproof cap off.

"Sonofabitch," she says through gritted teeth as the tiny stabbing men increase their speed and efficiency. When she finally gets the cap off, she palms three and dry swallows.

After collapsing back in bed, she holds her stomach and rocks back-and-forth on top of the sheets until the orange pills work their magic and she falls into their warm abyss.

When Effie wakes again, the digital clock next to the lamp reads 10:19 A.M. The pain has subsided. It ain't gone away completely, but it's in the background. At least as much as it can be.

As Effie's hoisting herself up, she remembers.

"Well, goddamnit."

As she's taking her morning piss, she hums "Happy Birthday" to herself.

Eighty fuckin' years old.

After that morning's helping of pills and a serving of dry toast and unleaded instant coffee, Effie dresses and drives her Ford Courier the twenty-five minutes to the Qwick Stoppe over on Old 237 North.

As she enters through the double automatic doors, she gives a wave to Hector behind the cash register and grabs a basket.

"Buenos dias, Señora Effie," Hector says.

"Buenos días, Hector."

Near the slushie machines in the back, she scans the boxed dessert items on the middle shelf. There's several types of off-brand Jell-O, puddings, and three cake types: vanilla, chocolate, and double chocolate. Her finger oscillates between chocolate and double chocolate for a long time until finally, she thinks, *You only turn eighty once*, and mumbles, "I hope."

At the register, Sheriff Ramirez is standing arms akimbo as Hector rings up four to-go coffees in Styrofoam cups and eight energy drinks adorned with lightning bolts made to look like exclamation points.

". . . And that's just the start," Sheriff Ramirez says, before his head turns when he hears Effie's rubber soles hit a squeaky patch on the linoleum. "Lookee here. We got Effie May in the house." His eyes go to the single box of double chocolate in her basket. "What's the occasion?"

"Another trip around that bastard sun," she says.

Ramirez smirks, still eyeing the double chocolate. He pats his sizable gut hanging several inches over his belt before his eyes return to Effie's. "Well, happy birthday."

"Feliz cumpleaños," Hector says.

"Yeah, yeah." Effie juts her chin at the coffees and energy drinks. "You fixin' to stay up the whole week?"

"Probably. Me and the whole damn department gonna be time and halfin'. Figured I'd be a good boss and get them some fuel to see 'em through."

As if for effect, Sheriff Ramirez takes one of the coffees and downs a considerable amount. "Whatcha get for having little more than a handful of deputies to patrol damn near two thousand square miles. Not like those assholes in Davee give a shit."

"You politickin' for re-election?" Effie asks. "Goin' door-to-door to scrounge up the vote?"

Sheriff Ramirez guffaws. "Whoever wants this job next, they can have it."

Hector loads the coffees in a to-go carrier and bags the energy drinks. "If you do run again, you got my vote."

"Missus Ramirez will have my head if I don't join her in glorious retirement two Januarys from now."

"So, what's got you all up in a twist?" Effie asks.

"You hear about that bank robbery up at the state line two days ago?"

Effie thinks about it for a moment. She recalls something about it on the TV. But she usually watches the idiot box after taking her nightly dose of an orange. "Mighta."

"These three fuckin' monsters—pardon my language—killed a guard, a bank teller, and two customers. Made off with one point five million. Shot their way out, like they's some cowboys or something, with a woman and her kid as human hostages."

"Jesus," Effie says.

"Yeah, real goddamn bloodbath," Sheriff Ramirez says, taking another swig from one of the coffees. Effie ain't sure it's the one he drank out of previously. "Cops on scene say they *think* they got one of those assholes pretty good. But with all the bullets flying every which way, they can't be too sure. FBI seems pretty certain they're on their way to the border, if they ain't crossed already, which could bring them around these parts. So, we're doin' the rounds and keeping our eyes peeled. Speaking of which . . ."

He digs into his rear pocket and pulls out a folded piece of paper, which he hands to Effie.

Effie sets her basket on the counter and unfolds the paper. There are three grainy pictures in square boxes. Overhead shots, like from a security camera. Two are of men with beards and eye masks, like the Lone Ranger. The third is of a woman with long hair and the same eye mask. The words, *Wanted: Armed and Dangerous*, are above in bold type.

"You see anything suspicious, you give me a holler," Ramirez says.

Effie stares at the picture of the woman, whose facial features are sharp. Almost V-like.

"Will do," Effie says, not looking up.

"Y'all take care," Sheriff Ramirez says, grabbing his caffeinated beverages and heading out.

When Hector says, "This it for ya, Effie?", she looks up at him.

"Yeah. This is it."

Effie's in her living room on the BarcaLounger, remote in hand, clicking between Channel 2 and Channel 3. Both show the four o'clock news. So far, it's been stories about those assholes in Congress and a war in a place she couldn't find on a map if her life depended on it.

It's at 4:16 P.M. when the anchor on Channel 3—the guy with the dimpled chin and the smug smile—starts talking about a "robbery gone wrong" at a gas station along Route 18.

As opposed to a robbery gone right?

Within a few seconds of seeing footage of the gas station, Effie understands what he means.

The reporter on scene, a young woman with kind eyes, says deputies responded to a report of a vehicle fire. A shot of the charred remains of a sedan behind the gas station supplies the imagery. Inside the vehicle, the reporter says, firefighters found the bodies of two individuals: a man and a woman. The former was determined to be the owner of the gas station. The latter is still waiting on a positive identification, but "sources close to the investigation" say that authorities believe the woman to be

Rosaland Jeffries. The image cuts to a photo of Miss Jeffries at what looks like a Christmas parade, with her arm around her young daughter, who's no more than six or seven. Both are smiling. And both have curly red hair.

The image cuts back to the reporter on scene as she recaps how the woman and her daughter were taken hostage during the "brazen bank robbery" at SunLand Savings up on the state line. As the reporter details how authorities are on the lookout for the three perpetrators and their remaining hostage—should the body found in the burned wreckage be confirmed as Miss Rosaland Jeffries—Effie's imperfect eyesight focuses on the sign behind the reporter. She can just barely make out the words "Hot Dogs" and "Special Slather."

It's when the footage cuts back to the studio that Effie hears the bell above the door in the Oasis's front office *clang*. Effie hits the off button as the dimpled anchor continues discussing the robbery.

"Hello," she hears Mrs. Fields call.

As Effie stands, her left knee makes a *pop*. She shuffles toward the door to the office and stops when she sees it's open a crack. *How loud had the TV volume been? How much mighta seeped out?*

"Miss Effie?" Mrs. Fields calls.

"Yeah, coming." Effie takes a deep breath before heading through the door.

Mrs. Fields is leaned up against the front counter, a smirk on her face. "Good news, old gal, we're pullin' up stakes tomorrow." She pulls out her wad of bills and slaps another hundred on the counter. "Wanted to settle the bill."

"You don't owe me nothin'."

"Consider it a tip. Put it toward . . . I dunno . . . sprucing up the place a bit." She slides the bill halfway across the countertop. "It ain't a bad establishment. Damn shame you don't get more customers."

Effie keeps her hands at her side. "We do okay."

"We?" Mrs. Fields makes a show of looking behind Effie. "You got someone else back there I ain't seen?"

Effie shakes her head. "Just me, by myself. Been that way for . . . a while."

"Well, we're heading out early in the morning. You want us to just drop the key off here?"

"Sure."

"That your little apartment back there?"

"Yeah," Effie says. "That's where I live."

Mrs. Fields smiles her perfect white teeth. "Wonderful."

The sun's going down and Effie can feel the stabbing sensation starting to rise in her gut. The tiny men in there with their ice picks are waking up, and soon they're gonna be going full steam.

She's in her tiny kitchenette. The plastic pill box is on the counter with Tuesday's lid open. The remaining day's pills are still inside. And despite the pain, Effie's decided that's where those pills will remain.

She's staring at the egg timer on top of the stove. Two minutes left and she's using this time to run through her options.

As soon as Mrs. Fields walked out of the front office, Effie thought about calling Sheriff Ramirez.

A bloodbath. That's how he'd described the shootout at the bank.

She knows enough about dangerous people to know that when they're backed into a corner, they'll do anything and everything to get out of it.

That young man who'd sought to relieve Tom Folton of his wallet in Mexico City back in the fall of '02 had been surprised when Effie stepped out of the hotel. And in that moment of panic, his finger, which was already on the trigger, squeezed a little too tight. Later, at the American Embassy when Effie was making arrangements to ship Tom's body back to the States, the woman finalizing the forms had attributed Tom's death to an "unstable situation."

Effie thinks about that little girl. She imagines a scenario in which a blaze of bullets between cops and robbers creates another unstable situation.

No.

Effie runs through the remaining options. Which ain't many. And by the time she arrives at a decision, that egg timer buzzes. She silences it and grabs her oven mitts.

"What?" Mr. Fields says.

He's got the door cracked open only a few inches and is staring at Effie with a mixture of anger and annoyance.

Effie smiles and holds up the plate with three large pieces of cake covered in Saran Wrap.

"I can't eat all this myself," Effie says, "At least my doctor wouldn't want me to. So figured y'all might like some."

His eyes go to the cake, then he looks behind him, nods, and disappears inside as Mrs. Fields takes his place. She keeps the door cracked the same small amount.

"What's this?" Mrs. Fields says. Those white teeth putting in an appearance.

"I'm celebrating . . . well, a *significant* birthday today. But I baked me a larger cake than I can handle. Wanted to see if y'all cared for some."

"Well, happy birthday," Mrs. Fields says.

"Cut off an extra-large slice for your daughter," Effie says. "I know how kids like sweets."

At this, Mrs. Fields's faker-than-hell smile drops for a split second. "Yes. Yes, they do."

"All right," Effie says, and starts to shuffle off. "I'm gonna sleep off this sugar coma I feel comin' on."

"Wait."

Effie turns back.

"What kind of cake?"

"Double chocolate," Effie says. "And orange."

It's 11:37 P.M. when Effie knocks on their door again.

She's got the Colt pistol with the four bullets in it that a guest had left on the bathroom sink in Room Four back in December 2006. She ain't sure it fires, and she's had limited experience with guns. She's had it on her since this afternoon, and for a half-minute she reckons she's gonna have to use it. But after the second round of knocking and more than a minute of no one answering, she starts to believe otherwise.

Effie slides the skeleton key into the lock. She takes a deep breath before turning it.

Inside, the two bedside lamps are on. Both Mr. and Mrs. Fields are on the bed. He's lying across the foot of it, one arm over his chest, the other at his side, breathing slow and snoring some. She's lying perpendicular to him. Her knees are pulled up midway to her chest. She's also breathing slow.

On the bedside table next to her is an automatic pistol. Big, black, and bulky. Effie ain't sure on the type, but one look at it tells her it can do a lot of damage.

Effie next looks at the radiator on the far wall. And there, she sees what she was guessing she'd see. The little girl with one hand tied to the radiator with thick rope. Her eyes are open, staring up at Effie. They're a deep red. Darker than her hair. On the floor in front of her is the plate that had the slices of cake on it. Only crumbs are left now. But Effie knows the kid got the smallest piece. Because she's awake. And the other two ain't. Which is what she figured would happen.

You can always count on assholes to be selfish.

Effie puts her finger to her mouth. At the bedside table, she lifts the heavy, black handgun and puts it in the right pocket of her housecoat, which causes it to sag considerably. She holds up the Colt pistol, business-end toward the ceiling and leans over Mrs. Fields.

She snaps her fingers two inches above Mrs. Fields's face, steps back, and aims the gun.

But Mrs. Fields doesn't so much as twitch.

Neither does Mr. Fields.

Good job, ya orange bastards.

Over the next ten minutes, Effie executes the plan she'd initially anticipated would only take her five. The primary reason for the delay being the tiny stabbing men in her gut, which feel like they're damn near close to breaking out of her intestines. The other reason is that her arms are sore, on the verge of burning, from heavy lifting.

Despite the pain and the soreness, she keeps going. And through it all, the little girl watches with a look of growing curiosity slowly overtaking the one of total despair.

Effie goes to the cart outside the door and returns with the long chain. She secures one end around the foot of the radiator with a lock and extends it taut to the bed. Pulling out the set of frilly handcuffs from the other pocket of her housecoat, she snaps one cuff around Mr. Fields's right wrist and the other around Mrs. Fields's left. Then she secures the cuffs to the end of the heavy chain with another lock.

Finally, Effie pulls a switchblade from her back pants' pocket, and cuts free the rope around the little girl's wrist.

Outside, the little girl watches as Effie puts the key into Room Seven's door and turns it hard, breaking off half of it inside the lock, then tossing the broken end over her shoulder. It makes a *ping* somewhere in the night as it hits the ground.

Atop the cleaning cart is a square glass bottle filled a third of the way. A wadded red rag stuffed into it sticks out the end. The little girl's gaze follows Effie as she pulls a lighter from her right pants' pocket, strikes the flint, and puts the flame to the end of the wadded rag which catches.

Effie chucks it like a football into Room Six next door where it hits the ten open paint cans stacked on top of each other. Below them are a bunch of soaked rags. The glass bottle explodes on impact and the paint cans immediately come alive with flames. A pungent smell of paint and gasoline mixes with acrid smoke.

Effie grabs the little girl's hand and leads her to the Ford Courier, idling perpendicular behind the Mustang. She helps the little girl into the passenger seat and secures the seatbelt, before shutting the door.

The little girl watches through the window as the glow of orange and red fire inside Room Six grows more and more intense through the open door. Black smoke flows out and up into the night's sky. As Effie gets behind the wheel and buckles her own seatbelt, a faint glow becomes visible through the closed curtains inside Room Seven.

"Hey," Effie says.

The little girl turns. Her eyes are no longer as deeply red.

"What happened to the other guy? The one was with those two?"

The little girl points at the Mustang. "They put him in there. He got hurt and died. So, they put him in the trunk."

Effie nods as she shifts into drive.

"Where are we going?" The little girl asks.

"Figured we'd go up the road a piece. There's a Qwick Stoppe." Effie turns out of the parking lot and onto the main road. "They have ice cream there, I think. You like ice cream?"

The little girl is staring at the dark road in front of them, illuminated only a little by the Courier's headlamps, as she nods.

"Me too," Effie says. "It's my birthday, you know."

"Happy birthday," the little girl says, the same way a person might say "Bless you" to someone who sneezes.

Effie shifts into a higher gear and drives on.

Not once does she look in the rearview.

Motels are such interesting settings. Primarily because their main purpose is to be temporary. A place to bed down for a few nights or, even, a few hours. They're also designed to not be memorable in any way. From the nondescript furniture choices to the uninteresting paint (both inside and out), they are meant to be forgotten. They exist—for most of us—solely as a bland midpoint in a much larger journey.

Except for the people who run them.

When I saw editor Barbara Byar's call for Motel: An Anthology, *I knew I wanted to tell a story about someone whose motel experience was far different from most everyone else's. For this character, I wanted the setting to be permanent—the one constant running through a lifetime of memories, both good and bad. I also knew that, for this angle to have the most impact, the character would need to be at the end of that lifetime and facing her own looming checkout.*

That's how Effie May and the Oasis Motor Lodge came into being.

Effie has since become my favorite character. Her voice, her grit, and her strength stand alone among the many other characters I've created before or since. I reckon that will likely continue to be the case going forward. Which is fine by me; and—I'd like to think—would be fine by her too.

Lamont A. Turner, *the grandson of a police sergeant and the nephew of a captain of detectives who was also a popular magician in his spare time, was exposed to wild tales of crime and adventure from a young age. Being named after the fictional crime fighter The Shadow by his maternal grandmother, a fan of the radio program chronicling his exploits, probably sealed his fate. He is the author of the novel* Never the Night, *featuring PI Robert Doverman, as well as six collections of short stories. He currently resides in Louisiana with his wife, four children, two cats, a dog, and his best pal, an alligator named Fido.*

THE LOST AND THE LONELY
Lamont A. Turner

I sat there watching three hundred pounds of louse chew on a cheap cigar between sips off a bottle of local beer that sat sweating on a desk only a few inches wider than the slob behind it. Despite two fans, one in the open window behind him and a smaller one blowing directly on him, you could have filled Lake Pontchartrain with the water you wrang from his expensive button-down. Maybe if he'd been a water moccasin he would have been better suited for the Louisiana summertime, but he was something lower than a snake. The big man was a loan shark, drug peddler, and pimp—not the kind of person who usually had me over to watch the big game. If the promise of an unusually large sum of money hadn't stirred my curiosity, I would have declined his invitation. The pile of green propping him up was the only thing I could trust about him. He had enough cash in his pockets to buy cops and judges in any market, not just the ones in New Orleans who came cheap.

"What's this about, Larry?" I asked, already bored with watching him perspire and longing for the company of the fifth of whiskey in the cabinet at my office. "You know I don't work for the mob."

"This is straight up legit," Larry replied, his voice a little softer than the way I remembered it. "I need you to find my little girl." He stopped dabbing at his forehead with a handkerchief that cost more than my suit long enough to fish a photograph out of his desk drawer. The picture wasn't very good, but I could tell Larry's girl was a lot prettier than he was, and not all that little. Even in black and white, she looked like a girl a lot of guys would have been happy to find.

"I can understand why a guy in your line of work wouldn't want to talk to the police, Larry, but you've got plenty of connections." I couldn't move my gaze from the girl. "You couldn't turn anything up your own self?"

"Nothing," he said glumly. "We can't find a trace of her anywhere, and it's been two weeks. I'll pay twice your usual rate if you can find her. And there'll be a bonus at the end, too."

"You'll pay three times my usual rate, half up front, half when I come through for you. And, I'll also take that bonus." I expected him to throw me out on my ear. Instead he just nodded and made a pile of moola appear on his desk. It was a neat trick.

"Okay," I said, pocketing the picture along with the cash. It was a tight fit. When a guy like Larry Gerguson is that willing to part with his money, I pay attention. Snow on the bayou would have been less rare. "Let's go down the checklist. I assume no ransom notes have turned up in your mailbox?"

"You think anybody would be dumb enough to kidnap my daughter?" he asked, slightly offended.

"Sorry. I forgot you were so big and scary. What about a boyfriend? Anybody you didn't approve of who she might have run off with?"

"Maggie only had eyes for one man, and I was all for it. He comes from a good family, a old family here in Nawlins, and plans on becoming a doctor. He's a good boy."

"And how does this future doctor's good family feel about their son running around with a pimp's daughter?"

Larry shook his head and took a long drag off his cigar. "I've kept Maggie away from all that. She doesn't know how I make my money. As far as she and her friends know, I just rent out jukeboxes."

I didn't quite buy that Larry had managed to keep his little girl in the dark, but I let it slide. "Tell me about the last time anybody saw Maggie."

"She was shopping with Valerie, my wife, on Canal Street. They had a spat, and Valerie took a cab home, leaving Maggie to get home however."

"You let your girls run around loose? I'd think a guy like you would want to keep close tabs on them. What? Your boys all busy busting heads and stealing the pencils from blind men that day?"

"Valerie doesn't like any witnesses around when she spends my money," Larry replied with a sigh, ignoring my jab. "She got pretty good at slipping her bodyguards. I can't come down on her too hard. It's not like I can keep up with her."

"I'm interested in this fight between your wife and daughter. Any idea what it was about?"

Larry fidgeted with the knob on his desk fan, looking for a higher setting that wasn't there. I wondered if he would have time to answer my question before he turned into a puddle.

"Maggie and Valerie never hit it off," he said almost pensively. "Maggie never trusted her."

"And you do?"

"I never trust anybody!" he shot back. "I like my head without holes in it."

"All right, I guess I'll start with Valerie if you have no objections. Where do I find her?"

Larry jotted down an address on back of an invoice and slid it across the desk. He looked at his wristwatch. "I'd recommend heading right over there."

"Why? She have an expiration date?"

"You might say that. She usually starts tossing 'em back around noon. It's a quarter past one right now."

After a handshake with the fat man that felt less than sincere, I headed out to talk to Valerie. Spending the afternoon with a lush with bad taste in men wasn't my idea of a picnic, but the wad of cash in my coat pocket made me feel a little better about it. I looked at the invoice with the words "Track Amusements" printed in bold black letters across the top. It wasn't a lie. Gerguson got a cut of the profits from every jukebox, slot machine, and pinball game in New Orleans. That was just the semi-legitimate tip of the iceberg, though. There was nothing amusing about the pile of ruined lives, broken dreams, and dead bodies it rested on. Every time I was tempted to feel sorry for Larry, I thought of all the kids who ended up on slabs in the morgue after shooting up the junk he peddled, and of all the girls, girls just like his daughter, who ended it all rather than be forced to spend another night getting slobbered on by some geezer old enough to have voted for Lincoln. As happy as I was to be able to finally pay off my bar tab at Mocasso's, even the money Larry was offering wouldn't have been enough to make me join his team if that was all there was to it. It had been the photo of Maggie that had sold me. Maybe I was wrong, and it wouldn't be the first time, but I had the quaint notion that the fruit might not be as rotten as the tree it fell from, and that his girl deserved the same chance as anyone whose father *wasn't* a professional murderer.

The address on the back of the invoice was for one of those big but not too ostentatious houses on the lakefront. Sandwiched between all the other big houses, Gerguson's fit right in. It was just posh enough to demonstrate the success of its owner without attracting the attention of anyone who might question how a guy who rents out jukeboxes was able to afford it. It was a nice, respectable house in a nice, respectable neighborhood. As I swung my jalopy up the circular drive, I wondered how many of Gerguson's neighbors suspected what he was, and how many of them cared. For all I knew, the whole block was a viper's nest.

I've never been what you would call a car guy, but I knew enough to figure out the sports car I parked next to wasn't supposed to have scratches down the side, or be half parked on the meticulously manicured lawn. It was just a guess, but I took it as a sign that Mrs. Gerguson had started drinking early. On my way up the stairs to the porch, I found half of a pair of red pumps somebody had left there after breaking off its heel. I decided I was wrong about Mrs. Gerguson. She hadn't started early. She had ended late.

There was a buzzer with a speaker box, but I didn't need to bother with it since the door had been left half open. Peering in, I could see a blonde in a red evening gown sprawled out on the carpet next to the sofa. She looked dead.

Under the circumstances, I didn't think anybody would mind if I let myself in, but the little man who appeared out of nowhere to shove a gun in my back informed me that I was mistaken.

"You got some nerve waltzing in here like that, pal," he growled as he ground the barrel into my left kidney.

"I just came to return the lady's shoe," I said, nodding in the direction of the blonde on the floor, "but it doesn't look like she'll be needing it. You have something to do with putting her there?"

"Don't be stupid." The gentleman's thick neck turned red and threatened to pop the buttons on his collar. He was short, but what little of him there was seemed to be all muscle. "She's just sleeping it off; not that it's any of your business."

"So, you must be the cleanup crew," I replied, trying to ignore the pain in my leg the *first* War to End all Wars had left me. It hurt, but it meant I got to sit the Second World War out.

"How do you know Larry?"

"I'm working for him. I'm a PI trying to find his daughter, Maggie. If you'll screw that gun out of my back I can show you my credentials."

"You can show me what you got, but the gun stays screwed in where it is," he replied, giving me an extra poke to illustrate his point.

"Fine. It's in my wallet in my back pocket. You going to let me get it, or are you looking forward to frisking me?"

That wisecrack earned me a crack on the back of the skull with the butt of his revolver. When I came to, I found I had taken Mrs. Gerguson's place on the floor. The lady had relocated to the sofa where she was trying to drink herself back to a state resembling consciousness. My friend with the gun stood over me, studying my driver's license. He'd had to put his glasses on to do it. Oddly, they didn't make him look any smarter.

"You should have called first," he said as he dropped my license on my chest.

I felt for the wad of bills in my coat pocket, and, finding it still there, decided to lie there a little longer while my head did a few more laps around the room. My new pal was having none of it.

"Come on, get up." He nudged me in the ribs with a shiny black wingtip. "You got questions to ask, get up and ask 'em."

"You talked to Larry?" I asked as I pulled myself up onto the sofa. I hoped Valerie wouldn't think I was getting too familiar, but standing wasn't a trick I was up to performing just yet.

"You're still breathin', ain't ya."

Taking that for a "Yes sir, I did speak with Mr. Gerguson," I turned my attention to the blonde sitting next to me. Even in her current condition she was a knockout, and one I was sure I had seen somewhere before. I couldn't quite place her, especially since I was still seeing two of her, but I knew this wasn't the first time we had met. Not coming up with anything, I decided the trip down Memory Lane could wait, and waded right in.

"Mrs. Gerguson, what can you tell me about your daughter Maggie's disappearance?"

"She's not my daughter! Do I look like I'm old enough to have a twenty-year-old kid? I bet *you* make the ladies swoon!"

I decided it was best to leave that one alone. I was just starting to see straight again, and didn't need another knock on the noggin.

I tried again. "I take it you and your *step*daughter don't get along." My emphasis on *step* seemed to do the trick.

"We have our difficulties," she said while failing to light a cigarette with a hand that had more shake to it than a hula dancer. I lit it for her before she managed to burn her nose off.

"So, what made you decide to take her shopping on the day she disappeared?"

"It was supposed to be a new start for us; a mending of the ways, you might say. Larry wanted so badly for me and her to get along."

"But it didn't work out that way?"

"No. She started in on me, calling me a golddigger and making nasty insinuations about my past. I called a cab and left her high and dry on Canal Street."

"Buy anything while you were out?"

"What possible difference does that make?" she asked while blowing a cloud of smoke in my face, letting me know that I was about to wake up a sleeping dragon.

"If you wrote a check, it helps me confirm your story," I explained as delicately as possible.

"I didn't," she retorted. "I always use cash. I don't care to have anybody know how I spend my money."

I understood she meant she would rather her husband not know how she spent *his* money, and, knowing her husband, I didn't much blame her. As far as I was concerned, the more she spent the better. At any rate, I figured she had the difficult life coming to her for being willing to cozy up to a slug like Larry. It couldn't have been pleasant.

I was about to launch into the next round of questions when I noticed my date was looking a little green. Mr. Clean Up, who had been standing around glowering at me the whole time, noticed it too, and dropped a brass trash can in front of her. It was the sort of thing some people keep around to hold big pastel ostrich feathers or stalks of sea oats, but she barfed in it anyway.

"Mind showing me Maggie's room?" I asked, directing my question at the only person in the room still able to answer.

"Larry said to give you whatever you want," replied Clean Up. "It's right up those stairs, if you think you can make it."

"Don't flatter yourself. That love tap you gave me barely made an impression."

"You made enough of an impression on the floor after you hit it, funny guy," he shot back.

I had to give him credit. I didn't have my back to him this time and, being a few inches shy of my nose, he had to crane his neck back to insult me to my face. Of course, the gun in his pocket gave him a few extra inches.

"Lead the way," I said, gesturing toward the stairs. "I mean, as long as you're sure your boss's wife doesn't need another trash can." "She'll be just fine," he replied with the certainty of a man who had done it all before.

Mr. Clean Up stood in the doorway of Maggie's room, watching to make sure I didn't pocket any of the jewelry that sat on the dresser. There were piles of it scattered around with the usual hairbrush, makeup, and assorted trinkets. What caught my attention, though, was the empty picture frame. It suggested Maggie had planned on disappearing, and had taken with her the one thing she valued the most. I assumed the frame had held a picture of the boyfriend.

"Know anything about the kid Maggie was seeing?" I asked Clean Up, figuring I might as well make the most of his delightful conversation since I was stuck with him.

"His name's Joey Richards, and he seems like a nice kid," he replied grudgingly.

"That all you got?"

"I mind my own business. He seemed like a good kid, but I never said much to him."

He didn't say much else to me either as he just stood there glaring at me until I looked under the pillows and slid my hands under the mattress.

"Think you'll find her under the bed?" He chuckled at his own joke.

"What happened to minding your own business?"

"*I'll* decide what my business is!" Clean Up snapped, his grin replaced by the scowl I had come to know so well—which actually suited him better than any number of expressions I could think of.

"I'm looking for a diary or address book. Maybe even a bus schedule with some numbers circled on it. You know, detective stuff. You wouldn't understand."

"You mean like that book there on the nightstand?" he replied. That hurt more than the slug he had given me earlier. I'd missed it, a big pink rose on the cover and all. Clean Up's scowl must have been contagious because I caught it. I picked up the address book and paged through it until I found *Joey* written next to a drawing of a heart.

"I'm taking this with me. Any objections?"

"None from me, shamus. The sooner you're gone, the better."

I was going to say goodbye to Mrs. Gerguson on the way out, but she had already reclaimed her spot on the carpet where she snored away, her arms wrapped around the brass can. I couldn't say I liked him much, but I had to admit that Clean Up earned every penny they paid him.

After a thousand good ol' college tries, I finally got ahold of Joey, who told me he was too busy to talk about his missing girlfriend. I figured maybe he wasn't as nice as everybody said he was, or he knew things he didn't want to share. Betting on the latter, I dropped a hint that I might already have a few clues, and let that eat at him for a while. I only had to wait for a half hour before he called me back, looking to set up a meeting. I was told to go to Brewster's, a dive bar over in Bucktown far away from the eyes of that good family of his I had heard so much about. It wasn't the kind of joint where a clean-cut college kid would blend in, and something stank about the whole setup. I would be there, but I would make sure the .38 in my glove box was loaded.

Before I headed over to Brewster's, I did some checking and found out the place was owned by Sal Masetti, one of my client's chief rivals. Masetti was new to the area, but had managed to chip away a big chunk of Ferguson's turf. While Ferguson still had a pretty tight grip on New Orleans proper, Masetti had set up shop on the outskirts, buying up the clubs in Kenner and Metairie, before spreading out to the Westbank. So far, Ferguson had tolerated the intrusion, provided it was *his* slot machines in the back rooms, but sooner or later he was bound to resent the competition in the junkie market, or the negative attention Masetti was drawing by paying the right people to let him set up shop too close to schools and churches. It was only a matter of time before the lid blew off the pot.

Alarms went off in my head when I pulled into the empty lot at Brewster's. Somebody had gone to the trouble of running off all the drunks and junkies before the guest of honor arrived. Deciding I had more pressing engagements elsewhere, I put my jalopy in reverse. As I shifted into drive, a kid in a pink shirt appeared in the doorway to flag me down. He was all smiles, but the goons milling about in the background behind him seemed less friendly, so I had to decline his invitation. My car sputtered before launching off as I tried to murder the gas pedal, but I doubted I would be followed. Whoever wanted me out of the picture knew they had already blown it. At some point I would have to deal with them again, but I was confident they would want me to keep breathing until they could find out what I knew. I didn't have to sweat the sharpshooters or mailbox bombs this time.

At least my trip out to Bucktown hadn't been a total waste. I now knew squeaky-clean Joey had some dirt under his nails. He was in with somebody, probably Masetti, but what was his angle? While it would mean having to part with some of the spoils, I knew that I would have to call in some help. Somebody would have to tail Joey while Masetti was tailing me. Managing to make it back to my office with all the blood still in my body, I took a swig from the fifth on my desk and dialed Billy Ray's number.

Since retiring from the New Orleans PD, Billy had spent most of his time fishing, but I found he could still be lured back to the cause if the money was right, or his curiosity was sufficiently aroused. This case met both criteria, and Billy was in. I gave him all I had on Richards, then headed home with my bottle for some well- deserved sleep.

Tired of soaking my sheets with sweat, I got up extra early the next morning and headed down to the nice air-conditioned offices at City Hall. I didn't expect to find much in the public records, but Donna, who kept all the files nice and tidy, pretty much knew everything about everybody. If you wanted to know what your neighbor had for lunch on June third, 1949, you could ask Donna.

"Good morning beautiful!" I dropped the bag of pecan pralines I had picked up on the way over.

"I love you, but my waistline hates you." Donna plunged her hand into the bag. "Is this a bribe?"

"You object?"

"Not at all," she replied, examining her prize approvingly. "But I guess I should wait to find out if what you want is legal before I eat one."

"I just need some info on a missing girl by the name of Maggie Gerguson. Margaret, I guess. Or maybe Margarete."

"Lawrence Gerguson's daughter?"

"That's the one. Know anything about her?"

"I know they've kept her on a short leash since the day they brought her home from St. Elizabeth's. As far as I know, she hasn't been in trouble a day in her life."

"St. Elizabeth's? The orphanage over on Napoleon?"

"Yep. Mr. Gerguson's first wife wanted a kid, but for some reason they couldn't have one."

"Well, that explains how an ape like Gerguson can have such a human-looking child. I should have figured that from the start. What about the current Mrs. Gerguson? Know anything about her?"

"I know she drinks. Gerguson has had to pay out quite a lot to cover for her antics."

"I figured that part out for myself. How long have the happy couple been together?"

"Her predecessor passed away about a year after they adopted Maggie. I think he married his second wife a few months after that. I'd have to check the files to be sure, but I remember she moved in pretty quick."

"Any idea where he picked her up?"

"None." She seemed embarrassed by the gap in her knowledge. "She wasn't born in New Orleans. I could see about hunting down a record of her in the area prior to her marriage to Mr. Gerguson, but it's going to cost you another bag of goodies. How about some bacon pecan brittle next time?"

"I keep a year's supply on hand just for you," I said, flashing my prettiest grin. "Mind doing me another favor by letting me use your phone?"

Donna pushed the phone at me, and I dialed my office. After a few rings I heard the melodic voice of Vicky, my secretary, telling me I had called the offices of Jack Craig, Private Investigator.

"Vicky. It's me. *Jack*. Did Billy Ray check in yet?"

"He did, but you aren't going to like what he had to say," she informed me in her usual languid manner. It was hard to read Vicky. Even after five years, I still wasn't able to tell what was coming by her tone of voice.

"He lost Joey Richards?"

"Not in the way you might expect. He'll explain it to you himself over at Deacon's Sea Food. He's waiting there for you now."

I hung up, promised Donna she'd get her candy, and headed back to Bucktown. If I remembered correctly, Deacon's was just a few blocks from Brewster's. I was heading back into enemy territory.

Nobody would ever have pegged Billy Ray for a cop even when he still was one, making him the perfect tail. I found him sitting on the bench out in front of Deacon's. Dressed in a T-shirt that might have been white once, and faded overalls, he sat sprawled back with a newspaper over his face, hiding the gray stubble that always parked there.

"Have trouble with the kid?" I asked, giving his boot a kick to rouse him.

"Easiest tail you ever put me on," he replied from under the paper. "Go have a look around back."

As I made my way to the back of the restaurant, I wasn't feeling very optimistic. I felt even less so when my way was blocked by a man in blue who made me show him my identification before he let me pass. There were a bunch more of the blue boys hovering around the dumpster, watching a man with a camera compete with the flies for a glimpse of something inside. My PI license got me close enough to take a look for myself, though I had already guessed what the show was about. Resting on top of a pile of empty containers and dinner scraps was a dead man in a pink shirt. The bulging eyes and purple tint of his face and neck told me he had been strangled. It had probably happened before I had even made it back to my office the night before.

"Working a case?" asked a familiar voice.

"Yeah," I said as I climbed back down. "One that just got a whole lot more complicated."

Phil Landry, lead detective of the NOLA PD Homicide Division, handed me the rag he'd used to wipe his own hands earlier, and waited patiently while I swiped away at the slime I'd picked up from the dumpster. I had known Phil since our days together tracking down bootleggers for Uncle Sam, and he was a big reason for me hanging my hat in New Orleans, but I hadn't seen much of him since his boy took a bullet to the head at Iwo Jima. He had pretty much kept to himself since then, doing his drinking alone. Phil wasn't the type to let other people see his tears.

"One of your friends?" he asked me, nodding toward the dumpster.

"I wouldn't say that. He used to be a medical student named Joseph Richards."

"Have any idea how he ended up in the trash?"

"Nope. He looked pretty healthy last night when I left him at Brewster's. He was having a sing-along with some of Masetti's boys."

Phil let out a whistle. I remembered the last time I had heard him do that we had just found one of our star witnesses in a murder case hanging from the rafters.

"What the hell was Adam Richards's son doing with a sleaze bag like Masetti?"

I filled him in on what I knew, which wasn't much, got a lecture on working for dope peddlers, and promised to stop by the station to give a full statement first thing in the morning. The meat wagon was just pulling up to collect what was left of Joey as I headed back to play catch up with Billy Ray. As far as I was concerned, they should have left the kid in the garbage.

As the sun sank into the Mississippi, Billy and I were still at Mocasso's, sitting under the ceiling fan on the balcony, drinking up Gerguson's money. It was beginning to look like I wouldn't be getting any more from Billy. He'd hit his happy spot and was more interested in doing card tricks for the waitress than in dead medical students. I had no idea where to go from here, and Billy wasn't offering any suggestions. Suddenly remembering my date with the boys down at the station house in the morning, I was about to call it a night when we heard a commotion from inside. I really didn't want to know what it was all about, but Billy was a little more curious, and insisted we check it out. It was the cop in him, coming out at the first sign of a disturbance.

By the time we got to the doorway, it had already gone silent in the barroom. Everyone was staring at the tall blonde and the taller man who stood in front of her. The empty glass in her hand and the big wet stain on his shirt told the whole story. I recognized the woman as none other than the faultless Mrs. Gerguson.

"Touch me again and I'll give you *another* bath!" she snarled with a backwoods twang I hadn't noticed before.

Recovering from the shock of being put in his place by a woman, the tall man grabbed her wrist and raised his hand to administer a slap that never landed. I was already halfway across the room when I saw him start to make his move, and cleared the rest of the distance just in time to interrupt him with a punch to the side of his head. He was big enough, and drunk enough, to shake it off, and came at me with two fists of his own. And then, just that quick, he was gone. Before I could decide whether to jab or dodge, Billy had him kissing the floor with his knee in the guy's back. He gave the guy's arm, which was bent in a direction nature never intended, a tug, and asked him politely to calm down. The guy only replied in grunts, but Billy apparently understood him, letting him scamper off like a roach trying to keep from getting stepped on. Considering who he was about to slap, we had probably saved his life.

By the time it was all over, Valerie Gerguson had already lost interest. I found her slumped in a chair at one of the tables, gazing mournfully at her empty glass.

"I didn't ask for your help," she hissed as I pulled up a chair and sat down across from her.

"You needed it just the same. Your hubby know you're running around loose tonight?"

"To hell with my husband!" she shouted, displaying that country accent again. "If you *really* want to help me, you'll get me another drink."

"Oh no," I replied. "That part of your evening is over. Now we've come to the part where I drive you home so you can keep your appointment with that brass trash can."

"Oh. *Now* I remember you," she said, squinting at me like I had suddenly become transparent. "You're that detective friend of Larry's."

"I'm no friend of your husband!" I snapped, wounded by the insinuation. "I doubt if he has any."

She got a kick out of that, laughing all the way up to the point where her head hit the table. Mrs. Gerguson had checked out.

Billy Ray didn't object when I suggested he help me get Sleeping Beauty to the car, but was a little less gracious when he found out I meant *his* car. I felt a little guilty about sticking him with my heap of machinery, but Masetti's guys knew it, and I couldn't risk them tailing me back to Gerguson's place. Before heading off, I took the time to go through Sunshine's pocketbook. I found the usual driver's license, keys, feminine doodads, more cash than most people could have spent in a month, and an old photograph of a woman holding a baby. The photo was tattered around the edges, and badly faded. She had apparently been carrying it around for a good while. I compared the woman in the picture to my passenger. Subtract a few pounds and the crow's feet around the eyes, and it looked like a match. I left the money, but pocketed the picture.

Billy was still fighting with the door latch of my jalopy and cursing me as I drove off. I tried to remember if there was enough gas in the tank for him to make it back to Houma, but couldn't recall filling up that morning. I made a mental note to bring some extra cash for Billy when I went to pick my car up, and hoped I wouldn't get knocked out trying to give it to him.

Mr. Clean Up didn't seem at all pleased to have his beauty sleep interrupted, especially by me, but he softened up when he saw the present I had brought him. Together we hauled her up the steps and deposited her on the sofa. He tossed a quilt over her, and then just stood there looking down at her, shaking his head.

"You'll find her car parked at Mocasso's over on Decatur," I said, handing him her purse. "You might want to talk to her about playing nice with the other kids. There was a guy wearing her drink tonight who wasn't too happy about it."

"Thanks," he said, surprising me with his new set of manners.

"It's no big deal. I was passing by here anyway," I lied.

"No. I meant for *that*." He nodded at the split knuckles on my right hand.

It was funny I hadn't noticed. As I descended the steps past the marble columns that lined the porch, all I could think about was how mad Billy Ray was going to be if I got blood all over his car.

The next morning as I was splashing cold water on my face in an attempt to drown the elephants dancing on my skull, I heard a pounding that wasn't coming from inside my head. Irritated, I stomped over to the front door and flung it open, ready to chew somebody's head off.

"Jack Craig?"

"Who's asking?"

"I want to know what happened to my son," demanded a man in a suit that belonged on a mannequin in the window at Rubensteins. There wasn't a hair out of place, or a drop of sweat to be seen, despite the humidity and the three-story climb to my floor.

"I have an office," I snarled, ready to slam the door in his perfect face.

"I phoned your office," he replied with an air of disapproval. "You hadn't bothered to show up yet."

"Let me guess. You told my secretary a sob story, and she gave up my address."

"Actually, I looked you up in the phone book." He brushed past me to plant himself on my sofa, his suit clashing horribly with the threadbare cushions.

"Coffee?" I asked sarcastically. "Or maybe a foot rub?"

"I want to know who killed my son." He was obviously in no mood to deal with objections from the peasants. "They threw him away like a piece of trash, and somehow you were involved."

Call me slow, but it just then dawned on me that I was speaking with Adam Richards, father of the late and unlamented Joey. I'm not one to kick a guy when he's down, but I decided to go ahead and take him down a peg or two. "Your kid had gone sour, friend. He was running with a bad crowd, and doing bad things, including trying to set me up to be murdered. You want answers, then go wade into the sewer and ask a slimeball called Masetti."

Richards Sr. sat there glaring at me like I was something he wanted to step on, but was afraid to get his shoe dirty. He pulled a notebook out of his coat pocket and waved it in front of my face. "I found this in my son's room. It mentions getting a payment from somebody named Masetti." He stood back up—all thirty feet of him.

I was beginning to regret being so rude. Mr. Richards had brought me a lead. I took the notebook from him and settled down on the sofa, reading while Richards paced around like he hated my carpet and wanted to kill it. Twenty minutes and half a pack of cigarettes later, I put the notebook down and took a deep breath.

Masetti had sent Joey Richards in to get the dirt on Gerguson, and the kid had come through for him. It was all there: dates and locations of pickups, the amount of money being exchanged, and the names of the people making the transactions. Somebody on Gerguson's team kept good records. With this book, Masetti could hijack Gerguson's shipments, or cause him a lot of heartache if he showed it to the right people. But Joey never handed it off to Masetti. Somebody, probably Joey himself, had scribbled "Maggie" on the pasteboard cover, and under that he wrote Masetti's name surrounded by dollar signs. Joey had been playing Masetti, probably leaking tidbits in exchange for payoffs. He was going to milk it for all it was worth. Masetti likely didn't even know about the notebook. If he had, Joey's father wouldn't have been in my apartment waving it around. In any case, Joey would probably still be dead. Playing games with a snake like Masetti is like playing Russian roulette with six bullets.

"You're leaving this book with me," I said. "Go home and polish your gold. I'll handle things from here."

"How much is it going to cost me to see this man dead?"

"I'm not a hitman, but I will see your son's killer gets what's coming to him. If it works out, it won't cost you a dime. I've already been paid."

Richards didn't seem entirely satisfied with my proposal, but he wasn't in a position to raise a fuss about it. I showed him the door and finished getting dressed for my appointment with Phil at the police station.

I was just stepping out the door when the ringer of my phone pulled me back in. I hoped it might be Phil, calling to tell me the station had burned down and I was off the hook, but it was Billy Ray.

"I got a guy in my bushes," he bellowed, nearing blowing the ear piece off my phone. "He's been camped out there all morning. Something tells me he might be looking for you."

"One of Masetti's guys must have spotted my car and thought I was in there with you," I replied. "Good. We'll let them go on thinking that."

"You expect me to stay cooped up in here all day?" Billy objected. "I was planning on taking my new pole out to the Rigolets today."

"I'll make it up to you. Just stay put and try not to beat anybody up until I get there."

"I'll be saving the beatings for you if there are any scratches or blood on my car," he growled before slamming the phone down.

After giving my statement to Phil, and learning Masetti had become invisible since the morning they fished Joey Richards out of the dumpster, I headed out to Billy's place. I figured anybody watching the house would be focused on the front where they could keep an eye on the gravel drive that was the only way in or out. By hoofing it through the woods, it would be a cinch to sneak up on them if I didn't step on any water moccasins along the way.

I parked the car on the shoulder behind the burgundy coupe my date had probably arrived in, and got out. Walking up a few yards, I could look down the drive far enough to see my car parked in front of Billy's house. Masetti's boy was there too, just where I had expected him to be. A big stupid looking mug, he was leaning against a tree out front, swatting at mosquitoes with his hat. It was no wonder Billy had spotted him. The guy was wider than the tree he was hiding behind. I could probably sneak up on him with bells tied around my neck.

He didn't look like he had the ambition it would take to put up a fight, but I decided to make sure by introducing myself with a punch to his head. He stumbled forward, more shocked than hurt, then wheeled around, reaching for the gun in his belt. I stopped him with another punch, grabbing his gun as he fell back. It was almost too easy.

"Thanks," I said, smirking. "I left my gun in my glove compartment last night, and my friend has the keys."

By this time Billy was already heading across the yard eager to get at the man who had kept him from trying out his new rod. I just hoped he didn't think that was me.

"Where's my damn car?"

"It's on the road just past that swamp you call a backyard, safe and sound and scratch free."

"Did you know your junker's outta gas?" Billy asked me, pointing at my jalopy. "I had to walk a damn mile to get a Coke bottle full 'cause it was all I had. I should've left the shit-eatin' thing by the side of the road. Or in a ditch more like it."

My captive snickered. "Looks like you got bigger problems than me."

That was a dumb thing to say to a man with a gun pointed at his chest. I grabbed a handful of his shirt and shoved the muzzle into his gut. "I want to talk to your boss," I snarled, making sure to spray his face with spittle. "Either you can tell him that, or I can pin a note on your corpse."

"He wants to talk to you too," he replied more coolly than I would have expected. Either he had more backbone than I had given him credit for, or he was just too stupid to be afraid.

"Good. It's nice when we all agree," I said.

The stink coming off of him was starting to make my eyes water, so I gave him a little push to put some distance between us. He stumbled back, stepping on the hat I had knocked off his head.

"Tell Masetti I'll be at my office at nine tonight. He can come and see me when he swings by to pick up your car."

"My car?"

"Yeah, your car," I said, holding out my hand for his key. "I just found out mine's out of fuel."

He muttered something nasty under his breath and tossed me his key.

"Good boy!" I proclaimed with mock enthusiasm. "If you walk fast, you might just get to a phone in time to give Masetti my message. I'm sure he'd like to spruce up before our meeting."

The goon stood there for a minute fondling what was left of his hat and trying to melt me with his stare, and then headed off toward the road. As I watched him lumber off, I noticed Billy was giving me that look again. It was the kind of look you give a guy you see trying to pet a lion.

"I know what I'm doing," I said defensively.

"I guess there's a first time for everything," replied Billy.

A little after eight, I was sitting in my office staring out the window at the Bentley that had been parked out front for at least an hour, when the phone rang. I was pretty sure I knew who was calling.

"Jack Craig?" inquired the voice on the other end of the line.

"Yeah, Masetti. This is Craig. You going to make it over tonight?"

"Why? So you can have your cop buddies pick me up? Do you think I'm stupid or something?"

"I don't know what the hell you are, but I have something you want, and you have something I want. Inviting the cops would spoil our trade."

"And what is it I want, smart guy?"

"If you hadn't been so eager to bump off the Richards boy, you might have learned he'd managed to get his mitts on Gerguson's record book. Guess who has it now?"

I waited while Masetti digested the feast I had just fed him.

"What's the trade?" he asked, just as I was beginning to nod off. "Richards's reports on Gerguson's daughter, Maggie," I said. "I know he was bleeding her for info, and I want every word of every conversation they shared."

"Okay, okay. I'll be there. But there better not be any surprises."

He hung up before I could say anything cute, and I turned my attention back to the Bentley. I had assumed one of Masetti's men was behind the wheel, but suddenly I wasn't so sure. I was still looking out the window when a sedan rolled up and spit out Masetti and two of his gunsels. Masetti looked like somebody who would have been at home in a mausoleum. Dressed all in black, and with a cadaverous complexion, he could have passed for Dracula's cousin. I recognized one of his companions as my playmate from that afternoon. Glowering under the mangled brim of his hat, he looked like a man eager to settle a score. The other thug was just as big, and looked just as stupid as the original model. Maggie Gerguson was nowhere to be seen. That was okay. I didn't have the notebook with me either. This meeting was just to work out the details.

Masetti had just stepped up on the curb in front of my building when I heard a shot, and saw a gun sticking out of the window of the Bentley. Masetti's boys saw it too, and sent some lead of their own back in its direction. I assumed at least one of them scored a hit because the Bentley, which was already in gear, and had started to pull off, drifted a few feet out into the street and then sputtered to a stop. Seeing the driver had checked out, Tweedle Dee and Tweedle Dum threw down their guns and raced each other back to the sedan, leaving their boss lying in the gutter. I couldn't blame them much. He wouldn't have made very good company with that hole in his skull.

By the time I raced down the stairs of my building and crossed the street to reach the Bentley, I was breathing hard, but that was a good thing, because the driver wasn't breathing at all. He sat slumped over the wheel, bleeding all over the cream interior. I leaned him back, and saw the face of Adam Richards. Like Masetti, he had a hole in his head, and, like Masetti, he was definitely dead. He had rubbed out his son's killer, and rubbed out the trail leading to Maggie Gerguson with him. That was it. I was all out of ideas. Masetti's crew would all be heading out of town to lay low after this, taking all the clues with them. I lit up a smoke and sat on the curb next to Masetti to wait for Phil to show. It was the kind of thing he took a professional interest in.

After explaining to Phil how one of New Orleans's most prominent blue bloods had come to get in a shootout with an up-and-coming crime lord, I retreated back to my office to spend some time with the bottle in my desk drawer. As I worked on drowning the few brain cells I had left, I went through the stack of mail Vicki had left in a neat little pile on the corner of my desk. Mixed in with the usual overdue bills and sales fliers, I found a note from Donna saying she couldn't find anything on the mysterious Mrs. Gerguson. There were no records of her being in the area until she suddenly popped out of a hat to marry Larry twenty years before. I took out the photo I had pinched from her pocketbook and studied it some more. Again, I got that feeling that I had seen her somewhere before. Then suddenly it hit me. I remembered that a PI pal of mine from up North had sent me a clipping about the disappearance of a girl who looked a lot like the one in my photo. I ransacked my files until I came up with it, and read the letter he had sent me. He was working an inheritance case, searching for the long-lost daughter of some whiskey tycoon who had died and left a load of money for her. Before she ran away, she had been Marjorie Patton. By the time he had traced her to Newport, Kentucky, she was stripping under the name Vesper Wilde, at which point she got herself involved in something ugly and ran again. That was twenty-two years before. She had been declared dead a long time ago, but old man Patton had stipulated in his will that one last effort be made to find her before all that green went to charity. Somebody had told him they thought she had moved to Louisiana, so I ended up with her picture in my mailbox. At the time I hadn't given it much thought. My gumshoe buddy didn't really expect to find her, and I didn't think he would either. He was just checking off the boxes to earn his fee.

I set the two pictures on the desk next to each other. There was no doubt it was a match. I had found the missing woman. Too bad it wasn't the woman I had been searching for. Or was it? I recalled Joey had scribbled Masetti's and Maggie's names next to the dollar signs on that notebook. I was starting to see that the pieces I had been working with had been from the wrong puzzle. Masetti had always been just a bit player in the story. I decided to pay a visit to the star of the show.

Clean Up welcomed me with the kind of enthusiasm usually reserved for bill collectors and salesmen peddling things you don't want. He told me nobody was home, and I told him that was fine; I just wanted to take a look around. I had to remind him that I had a pass from Larry before he raised the gate to the castle, but once I was in, he mostly stayed out of my way. It was late anyway, and undoubtedly past his bedtime. I had him show me to Valerie's room, where I started with the closet. It didn't remind me of any rich woman's wardrobe I'd seen before, and I'd played around in plenty of them over the years. You'd be surprised how many rich guys don't trust their wives, and hire guys like me to keep tabs on them. Usually the latest Paris fashions would be hanging toward the front, and there would be a pair of shoes for each day of the year. While I wouldn't exactly call Mrs. Gerguson's ensemble threadbare, there was a lot of empty space, and what was there smelled like last year. I checked for price tags and didn't find any.

On my way out, I noticed a picture frame on the dresser that looked a lot like the empty one I had seen in Maggie's room. This one contained a picture of a smiling young girl. I was beginning to think the acrimony between Gerguson's wife and daughter had been overstated.

"Has Mrs. Gerguson always been a lush?" I asked Clean Up, who had been waiting for me in the hall.

"That's a fairly recent development," he replied, looking a little pained.

"Well, if she can still understand English when she gets home, tell her she left something in my car that I'd like to give back. I'll be at my office all day tomorrow."

"I'll be sure to tell her." He shooed me out the door like I was a fly he had been too slow to swat.

"One more thing," I said before he had a chance to slam the door closed. "Why do you stick around? You don't seem like the type to play nursemaid."

"I got my reasons," he answered a little too defensively.

"I'll bet they're all blonde with blue eyes. A lot of guys have ended up dead for having reasons like that."

That was his cue to finish slamming that door in my face. I didn't mind, though. Everything was starting to make sense for the first time since I'd taken the case. From here on out it would be all puppy dogs and sunshine.

The next day Mrs. Gerguson stormed into my office. It was noon, which was early for her, but she was wide-awake.

"I want my property!" she demanded.

"Good afternoon," I replied as I waved her into the chair in front of my desk. "Have a seat."

"Hand over the picture!" she demanded as she kicked the chair out of the way so she could slam her palms down on my desk.

"I'll do better than that. How about *two* pictures?"

I handed her the newspaper clipping and watched as she stared at the headline above the picture of her younger self.

"Murder Witness Missing," I recited, just in case she was a slow reader.

"I know what it says!" she snapped as she tossed the article back at me. "What's this all about?"

I kicked back in my chair. "It's about a girl who ran away from home, and saw some things she shouldn't have seen. She had a new baby, and liked living just enough to do the smart thing and put some distance between herself and the bad guys. Sound familiar?"

"Go on," she said as she grabbed the chair and sat down.

"She ran all the way to New Orleans where she decided the baby would be safer with somebody else, so she dropped the kid off at the orphanage, but she couldn't bring herself to let go, and kept tabs on the child, even after she was adopted by a local businessman and his wife. Not long after that, the businessman's wife died. Wanting to be with her daughter again, now that she felt the heat was off, she made a play for the guy and scored a diamond ring."

She rose to leave. "I've heard enough."

"I can tell *you* the story, or I can tell *Larry* the story. What's it going to be?"

She slid back down, glaring at me like I was the guy who just let all the air out of her favorite balloon.

"It wasn't long before she discovered the business her new husband was running wasn't the type approved of by decent society," I continued. "It was worse than the mess she had left behind in

Newport, but she didn't care. She was with her daughter, and she had enough dough to give her anything she wanted. Life had its ups and downs, but generally it was tolerable until a punk named Joey Richards came along."

I saw her tense up at the mention of Richards, and knew I was on the right track. I offered her a smoke, which she accepted with a shaking hand.

"Joey came on like Prince Charming, but he was rotten. You realized the kid was a trojan horse sent by one of your husband's rivals, but by then it was too late. Maggie had already let him in. Probably without realizing what she was doing, she passed on something to Richards she shouldn't have. Afraid of how Larry would take it when he found out his adopted daughter had sold him out, you tried to get it back, giving Richards the idea that the notebook might be more valuable to you than it was to Masetti. That's when the blackmail started. Joey was feeding Masetti just enough to keep him happy, while keeping the book to hold over your head.

"It was then that you got the idea that Maggie should do what you had done twenty years before. With your daughter safe from her father's wrath, you would be able to deal with Richards on your own terms. You started stockpiling the money your husband thought you were blowing on shoes and jewelry, only withdrawing a few hundred at a time so he wouldn't get wise. Finally, when you thought you had enough to send with her, you handed her an envelope with the cash, and the picture of you from her dresser, and put her on a bus. You had her leave all of her clothes and other possessions behind so Larry wouldn't get the idea she had run off on her own."

"That doesn't make sense," Valerie interjected. "Larry would have to figure it out at some point. You're just spitting in the wind."

"Maybe," I said as I offered her another cigarette. "But would he figure it out before Masetti took him down? With Maggie out of the picture, Joey's blackmail scheme would go up in smoke, and he'd sell everything he had to Masetti. Larry would have his hands full. But you sold Larry short. He cared a lot more for the girl than you imagined, and he brought me in to screw it all up."

"Are you finished? I think I've heard enough of my life story." She rose again to go.

"Not quite. There was that murder your houseboy committed."

She sank back down, stunned. She tried to put on her best poker face, but I could see through the cracks.

"What murder?" she asked, her Kentucky accent coming out again.

"Well, Valerie, or Vesper, or whatever it is you're calling yourself today, Adam Richards got the wrong guy. Instead of gunning for Masetti for killing his son, he should have had a talk with your Mr. Clean Up."

"Mitchell? What does *he* have to do with all this?"

She seemed genuinely surprised, and I was inclined to believe she might be. She was too rattled to put on that good of an act.

"I wondered why the body had been left in a place where it was likely to be found instead of going into the lake, which is just on the other side of the levee across the street. I didn't put it together then, but after thinking about it, I surmised it might have been because whoever dumped it there wanted it to be found. He knew I would blame Masetti, and spend a lot of time chasing my tail, which I did."

"And why would Mitchell do all of that?"

"Maybe because he's in love with you, but that's not news to you."

She got that shocked look again, but it wasn't as convincing this time. I shook my head to let her know I wasn't buying it, and continued. "Come on! He's a bright guy. You couldn't have pulled off your stunt with Maggie under his nose without him noticing things. No, he was in on it from the start. That's why when I questioned him about Joey Richards he started to worry. He was so worried he decided to shut Joey up before I could pry anything out of him. Framing Masetti was just a bonus."

"I swear I didn't know anything about that," Valerie stammered. "I had no idea he had done that."

"I believe you."

"So what now? You tell all of this to Larry?"

"If I had planned to do that, you wouldn't be here," I reassured her. "You've got a lot of money waiting for you in Kentucky. That business you got mixed up in is ancient history now. Go back. Get settled, and then send for Maggie. Start over. Maybe this time you can manage to stay away from guys who carry trouble around with them as easily as they breathe."

"What about Larry?"

"Don't worry about Larry. Some friends of mine on the police force will be more than happy to read a certain notebook currently in my possession. I plan to see that they get it."

"And Mitchell?"

"Clean Up? I'll have to spill the beans on him. Of course, it might take me a while to write down my story for the cops. If somebody tipped him off that he should get out of town before then, I wouldn't have much to say about it. Joey Richards was a heel, and probably belonged where he ended up."

The woman who left my office that afternoon didn't seem like the same one who had come in. She walked a lot straighter, like a huge weight had been lifted off her shoulders. Pausing at the door, she turned and showed me a smile that had probably been hidden since she had posed for that picture of her holding her infant daughter.

I'd never collect the rest of that money from Larry. After all, I wasn't going to deliver what I had promised. After he was in jail, where he couldn't cause too much trouble, I would stop by and let him know the girl he had raised was doing all right. His concern for her was probably the only tiny bit of decency he had in him, and I owed him that much. When he asked where she was, I would tell him I didn't know, which happened to be the truth.

I sat there in my office for a while, thinking about the whiskey tycoon who never stopped searching for his daughter, and the runaway who had traveled across the country and spent twenty years married to a monster to protect her own daughter. I thought about the cop who had shut himself off from the world when he lost his son, and the rich man who had killed for his, even though his son had been no good. I thought about the criminal who'd kill a man over a dollar, but was willing to spend whatever it took to find his little girl, and how he had brought me into the whole mess. Finally, deciding I would never figure it out, I called a tow truck to haul off the pile of junk I had left at Billy's, and set off for Mocasso's in the burgundy coupe.

---

*My late father-in-law loved to tell stories of his youth in the New Orleans of the 1940s and '50s and of his interactions with the colorful and sometimes dangerous characters who lived there. It was with him in mind that I decided to have my PI, Jack Craig, a Treasury Agent in some earlier tales set in the 1920s, migrate to New Orleans and set up shop as a detective in his later years. I didn't have to stretch too much to set my tale in this particular era. Jack Craig would be long gone by now but New Orleans hasn't changed all that much since the 1950s. There are fewer fedoras, and a lot less cigarette smoke, but the characters are just as colorful, and some are probably just as dangerous.

Joseph S. Walker *lives in Indiana. He is the president of the Short Mystery Fiction Society, and the author of more than one hundred published stories. He has been a finalist for the Edgar, Derringer, and Shamus Awards, and is a two-time winner of the Al Blanchard Award. "Run and Gun" is the fourth of his stories to be included in* The Best Mystery Stories of the Year. *Visit him at jswalkerauthor.com.*

RUN AND GUN
Joseph S. Walker

The man in the armchair in the corner of Tania Shaw's bedroom was impeccably dressed. Although it was past ten at night, his tan linen suit, the color complementing the slightly bronze cast of his skin, was crisp and unwrinkled, the red tie perfectly knotted, tight against his throat. His black hair was neatly trimmed, his wire-rimmed glasses elegantly understated, his legs casually crossed. The hand resting on the small handgun on the chair's arm was freshly manicured.

Tania turned on the light and came several paces into the room before noticing him. She took half a step back and looked at the door.

"Mrs. Shaw," the man said. He nodded at the bed. "Please, have a seat."

"I've seen you before." Tania Shaw was a tall woman. She wore a simple black dress that ended just below her knees, and she carried a pair of matching high heels in her right hand. Her face had the slightly startled look of recent cosmetic surgery. "Your name is Watson or something."

"Watt."

"Nemo sent you."

"I don't work for your ex-husband. I work for a group of men whose interests typically accord closely with his." Watt pointed one finger at the bed without lifting the rest of his hand from the gun. "Sit down."

Tania dropped the shoes. Moving slowly, she sat at the head of the mattress. She rested her hand on top of the nightstand.

"It might save us some time if I tell you I disassembled the gun in that drawer," Watt said.

Tania moved her hand from the nightstand to the nearest bedpost and gripped it tightly. "You're very free with other people's property."

"Nemo Shaw received a blackmail demand today," Watt said. "Texted to his personal cell phone. Only a handful of people have that number."

He waited a beat. Tania Shaw looked away from him and stared at the floor.

"The message included an image from a video," Watt continued. "Mr. Shaw was under the very strong impression that he had the sole copy of that video, stored on a thumb drive hidden in his home office. Only a few people have access to that office. Speaking of, as we were, being free with other people's property."

Tania Shaw curled her toes into the carpet. She did not look up.

"Mrs. Shaw."

"I don't have it," she said.

"But you did."

"I sent it to someone I thought would hurt him." She looked up. "He deserves to be hurt."

"I need a name, Mrs. Shaw."

Tania Shaw put her shoulders back. "You're not going to shoot me," she said. "It would draw too much attention."

"Mrs. Shaw." Watt's face was perfectly serene. "The posts on that bed are very strong, as are the sashes on your many bathrobes. Let's think together about the places on your body that don't show when you're dressed. Let's think together about the things I could find in your bathroom. Emery boards. Nail trimmers. Curling irons. Razors."

"Jesus," she said.

Watt waited.

"Luisa Abbott," she said.

"The activist?"

Tania Shaw sighed. "I read a profile of her in the paper. Everything in the world Nemo is for, she's against. I mailed it to her. Anonymously."

Watt nodded. "And you kept a copy?"

"No." She shook her head sharply. "I didn't want the vile thing here. Tempting me."

Watt considered her. "If you're lying, I'll be back. If I come back, there won't be any talk."

"I'm not lying," she said. "I'm sorry I did it. Don't you ever do things you know you're going to regret?"

"No," Watt said. He took a cell phone from his breast pocket, hit a button, and held it to his ear. "Luisa Abbott," he said after a moment. "Address, vehicle, finances. Family. Email everything when you have it." He put the phone away and stood up. "Sleep well, Mrs. Shaw."

She was still shaking twenty minutes after he was gone.

Sitting behind his desk, in the office of the auto repair shop that bore his name, Huey was impeccably dressed. His black suit was custom tailored, his white shirt so clean it seemed to glow. Put him in a tie, swap his cowboy boots for fashionable loafers, and he could have been seated at any high-end restaurant in the world with nobody blinking an eye. Of course, he would never wear a tie, and never surrender the boots. Huey was irreducibly Huey.

The office he worked in fit the man perfectly. Although dozens of cars a day went through the shop—some legitimately, some less so—there wasn't an oil stain to be found in the room. No calendar hung on the wall with a scantily clad model holding a power tool. In fact, nothing hung on the walls. The only things in the room were a desk, a locked filing cabinet, and three chairs. The only things on the desk were a laptop computer and a neat row of five cell phones. The employees charged with cleaning the office were told it should be sanitary enough to serve as an operating room.

Today Huey's workday had started after the sun was gone from the blistering Dallas sky. Phone calls to Japan, Dubai, Johannesburg. Containers on a ship halfway across the Atlantic, dodging a hurricane. Inquiries from Colombia. Lately, new billionaires were cropping up all over the place. They all wanted cars. Very specific cars. Cars not always for sale.

There was a tap on the door and Rashad, one of his managers, came in. The scar on his left cheek was shiny against his Black skin. Light gleamed off his freshly shaved skull, and his work clothes were faded, but clean. "Lyle Mulaney is here," he said. "Asking to see you."

Huey raised an eyebrow. Rashad shrugged. "He brought in half a dozen catalytic converters cut out of Toyotas. Seems to think that buys him a word."

Huey closed his eyes for a moment. Rashad waited.

"Make sure he is not wired or armed," Huey said. "And take his phone."

"Happy to," Rashad said. "Always wanted to see how cops like getting frisked."

Five minutes later Mulaney came into the room. He was not impeccably dressed.

He was a big man in his mid-forties, his muscle beginning a slow transformation to fat. He wore khaki shorts, a stained T-shirt, and a Rangers cap pulled low on his head. It had been a few days since he shaved. Huey didn't stand or raise his folded hands from the desk. A flick of his eyes directed Mulaney to a chair. A minute nod told Rashad, hovering in the doorway, that he could withdraw.

"Huey," Mulaney said. "Thanks for taking the time. Really. Lots of people seem to have no use for me these days."

Until six months ago, Lyle Mulaney had been a sergeant on the Dallas police force and one of the most cheerfully corrupt cops in Texas. Some people called him the mailman, because all he did, most days, was drive around town collecting envelopes. One of those envelopes came from Huey, a grand a month in exchange for a warning of any raid or investigation coming near his operation. None ever did.

Then *The Dallas Morning News* broke a story about a ring of cops selling drugs right out of a downtown evidence room. The story grew when it turned out another longtime member of the department, a captain, also had a lucrative side business getting brutality charges quashed, and still another, a shift commander, used police cruisers to take hookers to "dates" arranged online. Within days there were protests across the whole city, demanding reform from the top down. Instead, the outraged public had to settle for sacrificial lambs: twenty cops with the worst records in the city, very publicly handed their walking papers. Lyle Mulaney was one, leaving a lot of the worst people in Dallas in need of a new bagman. Luckily, they weren't hard to find.

By all rights, Huey never should have had to see Mulaney again. But here the man was, slouched back into his chair, his big legs splayed open.

Huey didn't say it was good to see him. "You wanted to talk."

"I need a job."

"Here? I was not aware you were a mechanic."

"Not that kind of job." Mulaney patted his flat hands against his bare knees. "I been pounding the pavement for months, Huey. Gone to every PI agency and security firm in town. None of them will touch me."

"You find that odd?"

"Well, yeah." Mulaney deepened his voice and smirked. "I have a certain set of skills."

Huey gave no sign of recognizing, let alone appreciating, what Mulaney regarded as a world-class Liam Neeson impression.

"What is it you think you can do for me? I have all the security I need."

Mulaney shrugged. "You pay people to bring in cars, yeah?"

Huey looked at him levelly.

"I could do that."

"I think not."

"Where's the harm?"

"In dispatching an amateur to steal cars? An amateur whose name and face have been in the news? The harm is manifest. I cannot say what the gain would be for me."

"Anybody ever mention the way you talk drives them nuts?"

Huey made a gesture encompassing the building. "Think of this as a baseball team. I am the manager. I have a few all-stars, a Bryce Harper, a Mariano Rivera. The ones I call when I need a

Lamborghini taken from a gated community and put in a shipping container to Saudi Arabia in twelve hours. Highly skilled, highly paid. Then I have the bench players, who fill out the roster. The ones who bring in street cars to be chopped for parts or taken across the border. Contract players making a living."

"There you go. Sign me up, coach."

"Then," Huey went on smoothly, "there are the flabby, middle-aged men who come to fantasy camp so a third-string catcher can tell them they have a little pop on their fastball. We applaud them for getting the ball out of the infield. Then we forget them. The dreamers trying to relive the days of blow jobs under the bleachers."

"Hey, come on. I'm not some clown off the street." Mulaney poked his finger against the top of Huey's desk. "I did two years in Auto Theft, man. You know what they teach cops in Auto Theft? How people steal cars. I have a set of the tools and everything."

"The tools."

"Hell, I practiced on my own ride on the way over. Started her without the key. And I brought you them converters."

"Six catalytic converters. Half an hour of work for a teenager in a parking lot."

"Give me a chance," Mulaney said. "I'm not looking for one of the glamour spots, man. I just need to get paid."

Huey was quiet.

"One shot," Mulaney said. "Listen, what do you need more of than anything else? You name it, I'll bring you one inside a day."

Huey let out a deep breath. "Two things I can always use," he said. "Ford pickups and Honda Civics. There are so many of them on the road that people constantly need parts."

Mulaney's eyes lit up. "Civics?"

"Less than ten years old."

Mulaney stood. "I know just the thing for you, chief. You keep a slot open in that garage."

He bounced out the door like a kid given permission to leave school early. Mulaney had, in the course of his career, met any number of the nastiest people to ever set foot in Texas: contract killers and arsonists, rapists and leg breakers, sociopaths of every color and creed. It was strange that one of the few who truly frightened him was, when you got right down to it, just a glorified car thief. But there were *stories* about Huey, most involving the inventive uses he had for things like hydraulic jacks and battery cables, and there was something in his eyes that made you believe all the stories were true. Just whispering his name in the presence of a DA was commonly regarded as the equivalent of putting a gun in your mouth and pulling the trigger.

He'd come here, finally, out of desperation, expecting to get tossed out on his ear, if he was allowed to leave at all. Now he was not only getting a shot, but Huey needed, of all the cars in the world, Civics. Mulaney knew where to find a Civic. Specifically, he knew where to find a Civic that happened to belong to the self-righteous bitch who destroyed his life. A chance to get paid and get payback with one popped ignition? Had to be a sign. Things were finally turning around.

"Best get used to this face, my man," he said to Rashad, reclaiming his phone and gun. "We're going to be working together a lot."

"Terrific. Can't wait to see you at the office Christmas party." Rashad turned away, jerking his head at the door. "Meantime, Mulaney, get the fuck out of here."

Luisa Serena Abbott, age twenty-nine. Hispanic mother, Anglo father, both deceased, no siblings, never married. Inherited, from her parents, a Highland Park condo. Receiving, from the insurers of the trucking company whose driver ran a red light and turned her parents into a long stain on the pavement, an annuity of $80,000, which constituted the bulk of her income. Registered owner of a 2018 Honda Civic, blue, Texas license plate BNS1433. BA in English, Harvard. MA in History, Stanford. Now studying environmental law at UT Arlington.

She didn't seem to spend much time on her studies. Over the last two years, she had become one of the most visible agitators for liberal and progressive causes in the Dallas area. She was in the news several times a month. Protests. Union drives. Voter registration. Petitions. Press conferences.

Watt studied the photos in the dossier sent to his phone. Abbott, just a shade over five feet tall, looked more like a teenager than a woman closing in on thirty. In some of the older pictures her head was shaved bald. The more recent shots showed her with a buzz cut, the tight halo of hair dyed candy-apple red.

Her condo was on the fifth floor of a six-story building with underground parking. Watt cruised by slowly in his shark-gray BMW, getting the feel of the place. Prominent cameras were mounted over every entrance. They might be dummies, but in this neighborhood, it was better to assume they were operational. There were ways around cameras. It was well past midnight now, though, and if he kept circling the block, he might attract inconvenient official attention.

He was looking for a place to park on the street when a small car came out of the condo's garage entrance, half a block up. Watt closed the distance enough to get the license plate. BNS1433. It was good he didn't have to rely on the car's color because, from the rear, it couldn't be identified. The entire back end of the Civic was covered with overlapping bumper stickers. He saw the names of the last three Democratic presidential nominees, a score of progressive political causes, a number of acronyms and symbols he didn't know. Coexist. Keep your laws off my uterus. ITMFA. Living wages now. Black Lives Matter.

It was a wonder she could park the thing anywhere in Texas and not come back to find the windows broken.

The Civic turned west. Watt settled in half a block behind, wondering where the woman was going in the wee hours of the morning.

Lyle Mulaney was feeling better than he'd felt in months.

Going to Huey was a desperation move. The next step down was going to certain people he knew and offering his services as a drug mule or working as a greeter at Walmart. The first one, he'd probably get killed. The second, he'd certainly kill himself. So far, though, the car thing was looking promising.

Mulaney lowered the window of Luisa Abbott's car and propped his elbow on the sill. "Cruisin' in the Bitchmobile," he said out loud, and winked at himself in the mirror. Okay, the door had taken him a few minutes longer than he figured but popping the cover off the steering column to get into the starter went baby-ass smooth. He'd have to send a thank-you card to the guy from the FBI who gave that long-ago seminar, walking a team of Dallas cops through the very latest in lifting cars. Hell of a lot more useful than all the sexual harassment crap HR made them sit through.

Mulaney only wished he could watch in the morning when the self-righteous bitch came down and found her parking spot empty. She was going to have a tough time finding anybody with a badge who would care much. Too many cops worked security at her protests, listening to her screech into her fucking megaphone. Too many had buddies out of work because of her demands for reform. Too many knew she was anticop, anti-troop, anti-order, just plain un-American. Some of them had even come along the night Mulaney, well past tipsy and with rumors of the firings flying, looked up Abbott's car and residence and went over to see how she liked people protesting *her*. As it turned out, she wasn't home. He hadn't forgotten, though, and when Huey mentioned Honda Civics, Mulaney knew just where to go.

He turned west on Mockingbird, planning to skirt Love Field and head straight for Huey's. He looked down for a moment to find some classic rock on Abbott's radio. When he looked back up, something tickled the back of his brain. Cop sense. He held steady on the road, scanning to figure out what was bugging him.

Those headlights in the mirror. Were they the same ones from before his last turn?

Watt kept the Civic in sight as it headed west. If Abbott went to the airport, he'd have a tough call to make. The situation would not get any simpler if Abbott was sending her demands to Nemo Shaw from New York or Chicago. Or, God forbid, Bermuda or New Zealand. He would take her in the parking garage before he let her get on a plane.

He didn't reach under his arm to check the holster. He knew it was there.

Huey. It was the only thing Mulaney could think of that made any sense. Huey had put somebody on him, somebody slick enough that Mulaney didn't pick him up until now. If he let this clown follow him back to the auto shop, Huey would say he was sloppy, too sloppy to be on the payroll. Okay. Mulaney could handle a little test. The ramp to the Dallas North Tollway was coming up. At the last moment, without using his blinker, Mulaney jerked the wheel right and goosed the gas, his eyes flicking to the mirror. The headlights wavered for a second, then followed.

So, not the airport, Watt thought. The fact that the Civic took the ramp without signaling might mean Abbott had noticed the tail, but that would be fast for a civilian. Could be she was just a bad driver. Watt let the Civic get a little farther ahead.

The headlights dropped back a bit, but at this time of night, there were few enough cars out that Mulaney could still keep track of them. Under the big halogen lamps, he could make out just enough of the body behind the headlights to see it was something higher end. Mercedes or BMW, maybe. He put the Civic in the right lane and ran two miles under the speed limit, waiting to be passed. The headlights stayed rock steady, neither gaining nor falling back.

Mulaney grinned. "Let's play."

At the 635 interchange the Civic turned east. A few miles later, it went south on 75, heading back toward downtown. Either Luisa Abbott liked driving in circles, or he'd been made. Watt closed to five or six car lengths.

The Civic abruptly cut two lanes to the left, skirting so closely in front of a semi that the night lit up for a moment with the big truck's brake lights. Watt fell back and came around the back of the truck, barely in time to see the Civic slicing back to the right. There was another semi coming up fast behind Watt, too fast for him to brake and sneak back around behind the first. He shifted one more lane to the left to let both big trucks pass, planning to come to a virtual stop to be sure he would end up back behind the Civic, but a police cruiser was riding the second truck's wake. Watt had to maintain speed. By the time he managed to drop back far enough to survey the whole road, the Civic was gone. They'd passed two exits. No way to know which one Abbott had taken, or which way she went.

Watt drove on, his hands at ten and two on the wheel, the speedometer rock steady at two miles over the limit. A passenger in the car wouldn't have guessed, from Watt's placid expression, that anything disturbing had happened. The woman was better and more careful than he expected. Next time he would know better. She wouldn't be hard to find.

Mulaney parked the Civic behind a ThriftStop that went out of business last year. Weeds outlined cracks in the disintegrating asphalt, and the back wall was a mass of illegible graffiti. It was one of the spots uniforms in this district used to catch naps, but with a shift change coming up he wasn't worried about being disturbed for a while.

By now, Huey's guy had probably called in to report losing him. Mulaney imagined driving up to the auto shop in a little while, acting all casual, like shaking a tail was no big thing. Maybe Huey would reconsider making him one of the Lamborghini guys.

Thinking about the auto shop, Mulaney remembered something he heard from Tish, the day manager, the previous year, one of the times he stopped by to pick up an envelope. Tish told him the guys cutting up a car earlier that day found $30,000 in cash hidden in a door panel. Huey took half, but it still made a nice bonus for the guys who spent all day sweating over acetylene torches.

"They find shit all the time," Tish said. "Sometimes hidden, sometimes just stuck under a seat. Cash, computers, jewelry, drugs. You'd be amazed, the shit people keep in their car without ever thinking about it."

Mulaney didn't think Luisa Abbott had bundles of cash to hide, and he sure wasn't going to fuck around with taking the doors apart. No harm taking a quick look, though, before he turned the car over. He swiveled out of the car, turned on his phone's flashlight, and crouched awkwardly to look under the seats. He was excited for a minute to see a big manila envelope, but it turned out to be full of flyers for an upcoming rent strike. He stuck one in his pocket in case he could figure another way to hassle Abbott. For the most part, the car was clean and empty. Nothing like Mulaney's own ride, with drifts of old fast-food bags almost as high as the rear bench.

Popping the trunk, Mulaney shoved aside a set of jumper cables and three umbrellas and lifted out the spare tire. There was nothing in the well underneath. He was about to put the tire back when he noticed a square of black tape on its underside. He peeled it off and a thumb drive, about half an inch long and bright yellow, fell into his hand.

Mulaney grinned. Miss Social Justice had a secret. It was just possible he really was having his first good night in a while.

Rashad told him that Huey had gone home for the night. One of the mechanics, a little Asian guy whose blue jumpsuit was so threadbare the stains seemed to be holding it together, jumped into the Civic and took it around through the razor wire to the yard behind the building. Rashad peeled four hundred-dollar bills from a roll in his pocket and held them out.

"That's it?" Mulaney said.

Rashad shrugged. "Huey decides to use you regular, we'll work something out. That's up to the man. You'll hear from us."

"How about a bonus for shaking the tail?"

Rashad looked at him sharply. "Somebody was tailing you?"

"Thought it was you guys."

"You have a serious misunderstanding of how Huey works, dude. Your bonus for not letting somebody tail you here is you get to leave with all your limbs."

"Whatever." Mulaney took the money. Maybe Huey sent somebody without letting Rashad know. Why would he tell an employee everything he did? "How do I get back to my car?"

Rashad pointed east, in the direction of block after block of warehouses and manufacturing plants. "There's a bus stop a half mile that way. If you call an Uber, do it from the hospital complex on the other side of the highway. I don't want to tell you what Huey did to the last booster who called an Uber here, but it involved a hydraulic jack."

"You give me a lousy four bills, and I have to spend part of it right away on a ride."

"Don't know what to tell you, man. There's a reason most people do this in pairs."

The Uber to the grocery store where his ancient Buick was parked cost twenty-three bucks. He supposed he should be grateful the credit card linked to the app hadn't been closed out yet. He hadn't been evicted yet, either, but his savings wouldn't last more than another couple of months. Bottom line was, no tip for the Uber guy.

He kept thinking about what Rashad had said, about working in pairs. He couldn't think of anybody who would partner with him on something like this. His old buddies who were still on the force wanted nothing to do with him. The ones who got shitcanned the same time he did had drifted away or faded into the woodwork. He was on his own.

Dawn was close by the time Mulaney finally made it back to his apartment. He ate four Pop Tarts for breakfast, looking out his window at a neighborhood that was sliding downhill fast. He remembered when there were families here, not homeless guys sleeping on every other corner. If the thing with Huey worked out, he could move somewhere better. He went into the bedroom and peeled off his clothes, and the yellow thumb drive fell out of his pocket and bounced on the floor.

He almost left it there. It had been a long damn night already.

Grunting, he picked it up and snagged his laptop off the dresser. It had fallen off a truck a couple years ago. Actually, it was in a packing crate full of laptops that didn't so much fall off the truck as get pushed off, into the bed of a waiting pickup. The gentlemen who pushed it were gracious enough to give one to Mulaney for his assistance in securing a safe place for the pushing. Mulaney mostly used it for watching porn and deleting emails from his ex-wife's lawyer.

There were two files on the thumb drive: a video, and a text file named IF I AM KILLED. He opened the text file first. It was very brief: *My name is Luisa Abbott. If I disappear or am found dead, please see that the authorities are made aware of this video.*

Huh.

He played the video.

It showed a bedroom, just about as ratty looking as his own. The big bed in the middle of the room was unmade, and clothes were scattered around the floor. A door opened and two men came in, though Mulaney was immediately inclined to think of them as boys. They couldn't have been more than twenty or so. Both slender, both with shaggy blond hair to their shoulders, both dressed only in jeans that were more hole than denim. Mulaney squinted and made the video window larger. He thought he might have once arrested the one in front. At any rate, he knew what they were as soon as he saw them. Street hustlers.

The third man, coming in behind them, wore a suit with the tie loosened. He was older, with a mane of gray hair and a neatly trimmed beard. He clutched an almost-empty bottle of whiskey and staggered a bit at the threshold. Mulaney thought he looked familiar, too, but not in a haven't-I-arrested-you kind of way. He closed the door behind him. One of the hustlers went through another door. Mulaney could only see a tiny corner of that room, but the tiled floor likely meant it was the john. The other hustler put a mirror on the dresser and deftly set out several lines of coke. He bent over and snorted, then held out a rolled bill to the older man. He said, "Get you some of this, daddy."

The older man put the bottle down and did two quick lines. He threw his head back and bellowed, thumping a chest with a clenched fist. He didn't see the hustler, behind him, roll his eyes.

Mulaney knew the old man now. Nemo Shaw. Oil and tech billionaire. He gave a speech at a police ball Mulaney was at a few years ago, something about the importance of forcefully repressing civil dissent.

The first hustler came out of the bedroom. He was nude and carried a long wooden paddle and a pair of handcuffs. He smacked

Shaw's ass with the paddle, hard enough to make the old man jump. "Okay, daddy," the hustler said. "Strip."

This time Mulaney said it out loud. "Huh."

The video was almost an hour long. It became obvious quickly that the hustlers knew the camera was there, and Shaw didn't. They frequently winked or made faces at it when he wasn't looking. It became even more obvious that Shaw enjoyed, to a rather extreme degree, being forcefully repressed himself.

Mulaney watched it all the way through. By the time he was done, he had a very different opinion of Luisa Abbott, and some very different ideas about his future career prospects.

The people! United! Can never be defeated!

Luisa led the chant, pumping her fist and holding the megaphone close to her mouth. She stood on a makeshift platform, a sheet of plywood propped between the rungs of a couple of ladders. In front of her, clustered in the middle of the open area in the middle of Dealey Plaza, a few hundred housekeepers and waiters and maintenance workers and desk clerks chanted along and waved their signs. They were hotel employees, come to one of the most popular tourist spots in the city to protest low wages and abusive working conditions. From here, they would march to the monstrously huge Marriott a few blocks away, where the police would prevent them from blockading the entrance. Protest is one thing, but inconveniencing rich tourists is something else.

Luisa was only a guest speaker for this one, not an organizer. She was still embarrassed to have arrived late, slowed by the need to report the theft of her car and slowed more by the hostile indifference of the cop who eventually showed up to take the report. She had to remind herself every few minutes to focus on the people she was talking to, the situation in front of her, the things she could actually do something about right now. Stop thinking about the damn car. Stop wondering if Nemo Shaw was involved.

Fifty yards away, Watt stood on the grassy knoll and watched the protest. Today's suit was black, the matching tie snug against his throat despite the warmth of the sun, his arms crossed, his eyes invisible behind dark prescription sunglasses. He had been standing here since an hour before the announced time for the protest. He saw Abbott arrive in an Uber, minutes before she addressed the crowd, that red hair like a neon name tag.

Sooner or later she would go somewhere alone.

An obese man in a blinding yellow shirt and bright blue shorts, with a camera slung around his neck, loomed up in front of him, blocking his view of the platform. "You secret service, mister?" The man grinned and held up his camera. "I think you're a little late, but can I get a picture anyhow?"

"You have kids?" Watt said.

"Sure." The man looked around, trying to find his family. "I think they're in the book depository."

"Get away from me," Watt said. "Or I'll kill them. I'll do it in front of you."

"The fuck you say?" The tourist took a step closer. Watt took off his glasses and looked at him and the man stopped like he'd hit a wall. He glanced around. Nobody was close enough to have heard. If anybody had, Watt knew, the man would feel obliged to do something. Instead, he swallowed, opened his mouth, closed it again, and walked away.

Watt put the glasses back on and smoothed his tie. Luisa Abbott was stepping down from the platform. There was a big man waiting for her on the ground and the two of them talked briefly. Abbott looked around, and then she and the man moved away from the crowd to an empty patch of grass.

The big man read *cop* to Watt.

"Miz Abbott," Mulaney said. "A minute of your time? It's regarding your car."

Back down on the ground, Luisa looked over at the crowd. "We're about to march over to the Marriott."

"It'll still be there when we're done." A new speaker was shouting instructions through the megaphone in an excited mix of English and Spanish, making conversation challenging. Mulaney took Abbott's arm lightly and gestured at an empty part of the plaza. "Let's go talk over there." Seeming to give her a choice without there really being a choice. Something you learned quick as a cop.

She hesitated but came along. "Did you find it already? I haven't even had a chance to call my insurance company."

"Not exactly." They were far enough away to speak privately. Mulaney fished a piece of paper from his hip pocket and handed it to her. "I thought you might want this back."

She unfolded it. It was one of the flyers about the rent strike. Her brow furrowed in confusion. "These were in the car. So, you *have* found it?"

Mulaney grinned. "What's your second guess?"

She looked at him, then back at the crowd, now forming into rough ranks for the march. For a second, he was sure she was going to bolt. "What the fuck is this? *You* stole my car?"

"We're all of us sinners at times, aren't we?"

"And now you come here to *tell* me about it? What's to stop me from going to that officer right over there?"

Mulaney had scoped out the uniforms assigned to the protest before approaching her. Most of them were rookies, so green he doubted they knew which end of the nightstick to hold. The two vets he did recognize, Lopez and Yarnell, might have been able to scrape up three working brain cells between them. They were just marking time, waiting to retire so they could climb all the way into a bottle and finish the job of pickling themselves. Yarnell nodded at Mulaney as he approached the platform during Luisa's speech. By tonight, he wouldn't remember that Mulaney had been there. The brass was not in the practice of sending their best and brightest to protect maids, especially when most of them were probably undocumented.

"Go right ahead," he told her. "We can talk to him together about the thing taped to your spare tire."

She froze. "Mother of God."

"Sounds about right."

"Did *he* send you?"

"Shaw? I guess that answers my first question. You've been in touch with him."

He relished the look on her face. This was better than being there when she found the car missing.

"All right," she finally managed. "What the fuck do you want?"

"First things first," he said. "You know who I am?"

Her eyes had been swinging wildly around the plaza, going often to the tail end of the procession, now well on its way to the hotel. Now she focused on his face. "No."

"My name is Lyle Mulaney. Mean anything to you?"

He'd give her this: she was smarter than Lopez and Yarnell. Her face hardened. "You're the dirty cop."

"Ex-cop. Thanks to you."

"Am I supposed to apologize?"

"Nah." He waggled his eyebrows. "I just thought you should know who I am, since we're going to be partners."

"You think I'm going to do anything with you? I know about you. I've read the files. You're a piece of shit."

"Let's not start calling each other names, darling," Mulaney said. "I bet I know nastier ones than you."

"Go to hell."

She turned away from him. He put his hand on her upper arm and leaned in close. "Lady," he said, "do you really need me to tell you the many, many options I have for fucking you over? We could start with me calling Nemo Shaw's security team. I bet he has a great one."

Luisa was vibrating with anger. "What do you want?"

"Let's take a ride." He started walking her east, out of the plaza. She shook off his hand but stayed with him. "My car's on the next block."

She was quiet for most of the walk. He let her stew in it, thinking about the angles. His Buick was parked by a fire hydrant a block from the plaza. He opened the passenger door and gestured her in.

She hesitated. "Where's my car?"

"The rolling billboard? What time is it?" He made a show of looking at his wrist, as if there was a watch there. "By now it's probably in about a hundred pieces. The useful ones are on shelves. Or it might be on its way to Mexico. They'll pack the panels with heroin and send some hot blonde to bat her eyes at the border and drive it back across. *Then* they'll cut it to pieces."

Her face twisted. She sat in the car. Mulaney took the parking ticket off the windshield, slid behind the wheel, and tossed the ticket over his shoulder into the mounds of trash.

"Where are we going?"

"I'll give you a ride to your place." Mulaney pulled into traffic. "Tell me about the video."

She was silent for a long moment. He thought he was going to have to ask again, more forcefully, but then she started talking. "It came in the mail last week. No return address. I have no idea who sent it."

"But you recognized Shaw."

"Of course." Iron in her voice. "Nemo Shaw is a monster. A misogynist, a racist, a xenophobe. He's been bankrolling the extreme right in this state for decades. He thinks the border should be lined with machine-gun nests. He openly advocates resegregating the schools."

"Spare me the speeches."

"You saw the video. That's a man who has said that gays and drug dealers should be executed. The hypocrisy is staggering."

"Ain't none of us perfect, sweet cheeks."

"For the love of Christ. Use my name or keep your mouth shut."

Mulaney laughed. "So, you watched the video. Then what? I can't wait to hear your master plan."

"I picked up a burner phone," she said, her voice tight.

"What the hell do you know about burner phones?"

"I have a friend who runs safe houses for abused women. She uses them all the time."

"Okay." Mulaney's eyes flicked to the mirror. He took the next right turn without signaling.

"There was a little slip of paper in the envelope with the drive. Nemo Shaw's private phone number. I sent an image from the video yesterday, with a demand."

"Which was?"

"A ten-thousand-dollar donation to Planned Parenthood of Texas, made within three days."

"Ten thousand?" Mulaney was disgusted. "That's not even pocket change to somebody like Shaw." He took a sharp left.

"This isn't the way to my place."

"Don't worry about it. Why so little?"

"It was just a test," Luisa said. "I couldn't be sure I had the right number. I couldn't be absolutely sure the video was real. If he makes the payment, I'll know I can ask for more."

"Like what?"

"I'm going to make him switch sides," she said. "Donate to progressive candidates. Bankroll progressive causes. With his money we have a good shot at turning Texas blue."

"Jesus wept," Mulaney said. "I'm partnering with Mary fucking Poppins."

"What's with this partner shit? You have the video now. What do you need me for?"

"I guessed you were already running a game on him," Mulaney said. "If he gets another demand, from some other direction, he'll assume the video is already spreading out of his control, which means it doesn't make sense to pay anybody. So, I'm going to piggyback on your play."

"That's why you need me. Why the hell should I go along with this?"

"Don't you think you owe me?" Mulaney pulled up the sleeve on his right arm. "Read that."

The tattoo on his shoulder read *If you're not cop, you're little people.*

"That's disgusting."

"It's from *Blade Runner*."

"I don't care where it's from. It's disgusting."

He dropped the sleeve. "I had that put on the day I graduated the academy. All I ever wanted to be was a cop. And you took that away from me."

"You were a bad cop."

"The tattoo doesn't say shit about being a good cop. Just being a cop." Mulaney's face was set. "For a few minutes, when I saw the video, I thought I would use it to get my job back. Shaw has the big swinging dick to make that happen, no problem."

"But that's not what you want?"

"Fuck, no. Put a target on my back just to spend another twenty years doing paperwork?" Mulaney grinned. "You can ask for whatever Pollyanna bullshit you want. I'm asking him for five million dollars."

"You think he'll pay that much?"

"I'm going to ask a more important question," Mulaney said. "You know anybody who drives a gray BMW?"

"What? No." Luisa looked around. "What are you talking about?"

"Guy's been on us since a couple blocks from Dealey." Mulaney's voice was mild, but his hands on the wheel tightened. "I think it's the same asshole who followed me last night when I was in your car."

Luisa twisted around. They were heading north on Inwood, the traffic heavy. There was a gray car one lane to the left, several car lengths back. "What does that mean?"

"Offhand, I'd say it means your friend needs to tighten up her burner phone game."

A sharp intake of breath. "You think they're from Shaw."

"Best to assume so."

"Are we in danger?"

"What's this *we* shit, white man?" Mulaney sped up, sneaking through a yellow. The BMW was close enough to make it through as well. "I just found out about this shit twelve hours ago. It has to be you they're after."

"All right," she said. "Am I in danger?"

"They're not going to try anything with this many people around. And probably not without knowing what kind of failsafe you put in place." He looked at her. "You better tell me now."

She couldn't stop looking back at the BMW. "Tell you what?"

"Tell me you had some kind of plan to protect yourself, beyond hoping that whoever inherited your car took a close look at the spare tire."

"Oh." She sat back straight. "You probably won't approve. It's something else I learned from friends who don't want official attention."

"Try me."

"Before I hid the drive in my car, I uploaded the video to a cloud site. I have to check in once every seventy-two hours and enter a password. If I don't, it automatically emails the file to half a dozen TV news divisions, ten major newspapers, the Democratic National Committee—a bunch of people."

"Not bad," he said. "Of course, it only protects you if Shaw's guys know about it."

"You think we should pull over and tell them?"

"No," he said. "I think we should lose the fuckers. Run and gun."

While they were talking, he had gotten onto the freeway, the BMW sticking close. Now he accelerated sharply into an exit, both of them leaning hard to the left as the car's tires screeched through the long curve. The Dallas Galleria was ahead of them. Barely slowing, Mulaney swung into the parking area, the car's right tires jouncing painfully over the curb.

Luisa grabbed the handle above her window. "Are we going shopping?"

"Watch and learn, kiddo."

"Don't call me kiddo."

Mulaney roared into the multilevel parking garage. It was complex, stretching around the southern end of the shopping center and encompassing several different structures of various heights and sizes, linked by a bewildering array of ramps. "When I was a rookie we used to chase each other around in squad cars here in the middle of the night," he said, his eyes darting back and forth between the windshield and the mirror.

"Great," Luisa said. "Yet again, you're a credit to the force."

They shot up two levels, Mulaney taking the tight corners faster than Luisa would have thought possible. The BMW was keeping pace. Luisa kept looking back at it. "I think there's just one guy," she said.

Mulaney grunted and slalomed around another corner. Halfway up the next ramp, a big red SUV was slowly backing out of a spot on the left. Mulaney veered to the right, punched the gas, and snuck through behind it, his right rear fender bouncing hard off one of the cars on the that side. Luisa twisted to see through the rear window again. The SUV came to a dead stop right in the middle of the lane, horn blaring. She saw the front corner of the BMW dipping toward the pavement and heard brakes screeching. Then Mulaney took the next corner, spinning the wheel hard and fast against the direction of the arrows painted overhead, and headed down a ramp designed for traffic coming up. In another minute, he was back out of the garage and heading for the 635 interchange. Luisa kept her eyes fixed on the garage exit as long as she could. No gray car emerged.

She realized she was shaking.

"I want to go home," she said.

"You absolutely cannot go home," Mulaney said. "You're burned."

"I know."

"Turn off your phone." He was already fumbling with his.

"Don't they need the police or the FBI or something to trace it?"

"Shaw can get that kind of help in a heartbeat. Turn it off."

She did it. "Where are we going?"

"Fuck if I know," Mulaney said.

Watt was vexed.

That was twice, now, in the space of less than twenty-four hours. Granted, driving was not part of his primary skill set, not one of the things he was paid for. Still. It had been a long time since anyone had gotten the better of him twice in one day. At anything.

He had no doubt that the big man, not Luisa Abbott, had been driving the Civic last night. He still thought the man looked like a cop. A boyfriend? An older brother? Someone else who needed to be taken off the board, at any rate.

After he was past the SUV, he drove to the top of the parking structure, stepped out of the car, and stretched. He walked to the waist-high concrete wall at the edge of the lot and looked out toward the main mall entrance, on the off chance the black Buick had broken down or wrecked. Nothing, of course. He took out his phone and made the call. "Black Buick," he said. "Texas license plate MBO5281. Everything you can find."

He hung up. Almost immediately, the phone buzzed in his hand with an incoming text.
BULLS. ONE HOUR.

One hour was barely enough time to get back downtown, to a spot only a few blocks from where he'd been. Watt allowed himself to feel the annoyance, then dismissed it.

The one-armed man was waiting in the midst of the life-sized cattle drive statues in Pioneer Plaza, some forty bronze longhorns, with three bronze cowboys herding them along. Workers from the surrounding office buildings and hotels ate their lunches on the grass, watching the tourists take pictures. Watt looked for the obese man from Dealey Plaza and didn't see him.

Watt had been taking orders from the one-armed man for almost a decade. He didn't speak on the phone. He didn't write anything down. He would only meet in crowded, public spaces, and he spoke so quietly that Watt, who had excellent hearing, often strained to hear him. He nodded as Watt approached. The empty right arm of his suit jacket was tucked into a pocket. "Thought you were going to be late," he murmured.

"I was at the Galleria," Watt said.

"Then you made good time. I was at City Hall."

City Hall was a block away.

The one-armed man began strolling slowly among the big bronze animals, stretching out his left hand to stroke the metal as he went by. Watt fell in beside him.

"Tell me," the man said.

"I've identified the source of the demand," Watt said. "Also a possible accomplice."

He knew the one-armed man didn't want to hear names.

"Threat assessment?"

"High. The primary source is highly intelligent and ideologically motivated. Likely to have fail-safes in place. The accomplice has some field skills."

"So, a greater danger than last time."

"Yes. The young men who made the video originally were greedy and stupid. They were eliminated within hours of their first contact."

"That should have been the end of it." By the one-armed man's standards, this was practically a shout. "We understood it was."

"As did I. Shaw assured me at the time that he had destroyed the video." Watt carefully kept his voice neutral. "Apparently he kept it for his personal viewing purposes and was careless enough to let his now ex-wife learn of it."

"Tania. Is she involved?"

"She was the source of the link. I don't believe she's involved in the extortion."

They came to the end of the line of bulls. The one-armed man turned and began walking back the other way. "What do you think of these statues?"

Watt looked at them. "I think you could impale someone on the horns."

The one-armed man tapped his teeth together. "Nemo Shaw is ideologically motivated as well," he said. "Also enormously rich, fundamentally stupid, absurdly narcissistic, and easily manipulated. A considerable asset."

Watt didn't comment.

"He could easily become an equally considerable liability."

Watt didn't see anything in that requiring comment, either.

"Well." They were back where they started. The one-armed man stopped. "We understand each other. As always."

"Yes, sir."

The one-armed man patted the neck of the lead bull. "Impressive creatures. Strong, hardy, the product of untold generations of breeding for size and power. And three inbred imbeciles on horseback can drive them easily to slaughter."

"Yes, sir."

"I won't keep you from your work any longer. Good hunting, Watt."

"You're out of your damn mind if you think I'm going into a hotel room with you."

They had passed through Irving and Arlington and most of Fort Worth. Soon the great empty expanses of the western half of Texas would be opening up in front of them. Mulaney had gotten off the interstate three times to drive in meandering circles on the surface streets, making sure they weren't being followed. His eyes were burning, and now the sun was dropping toward the horizon directly ahead.

"You have another idea, I'm listening," he said. "We can't go to your place. Or mine, now that they've seen this car. Anybody else we go to, we're putting them in danger. And I'm running on almost no sleep from last night."

"Oh, right. Because you were busy stealing my car."

"Don't think I'm not regretting it. We're past that now, lady."

"I wish you would show the minimal courtesy of using my name."

"Focus up, *Luisa*. They know who you are. They know who I am. Your old life is over now, you get that? You will never be safe, at least not in Texas. Probably not in the US."

There was a Holiday Inn sign at the next exit. Mulaney hit his blinker.

"Why should I be going anywhere with you?" she asked. "I never asked for your help."

Mulaney laughed. "Let me hear your other options. I bet it's a long list."

"I have resourceful friends. There's the woman who taught me about burner phones. She hides women."

Mulaney pulled around to the rear of the motel, parking where the car couldn't be seen from the road. "There's a big fucking difference between hiding from some drunken asshole who beats his woman in a trailer park and hiding from a billionaire who wants you dead."

"Fine, I'm stuck with you. For the moment. Why are you stuck with me? Why not just dump me here and take off?"

"I already told you," he said. "My life just burned to the ground. I have to run, and thanks to you, I don't have two fucking dimes to run with. The one and only thing I have now is the video. There's still a miniscule chance of coming out of this with some money."

"I'm not doing this for money."

"Oh, Christ, don't start telling me again about your crusade." Mulaney climbed wearily out of the car. "I'm getting a room and sleeping for the next ten hours."

She followed him around the building. "We need two rooms."

"You carrying any cash? We can't use cards."

"No. Are you?"

He still had the hundreds Rashad had given him. He held them up. "My treat. But I'm not paying for two rooms just because you're shy."

"It always comes back to money with you."

"I'll tell you a secret. It always comes back to money with Shaw, too."

The room, on the second floor at the rear, had two beds and the same internal climate as a pizza oven. Mulaney cranked the AC as high as it would go. He went to the bed farthest from the door, took his revolver from the holster at the small of his back, and put it on the bedside table.

"You're really just going to sleep?" she asked.

"Unless you want to burn off some energy," he said. "You're kind of scrawny, but it's been a while since I had a good hate fuck."

"Dream on. I wouldn't touch you without a hazmat suit on."

"What I figured." Mulaney stacked the pillows and stretched out on the bed. "You frigid, or just a dyke?"

"A woman doesn't want you, the problem must be with her, right? Sorry, Mulaney. I'm with a guy. He's just not a fucking caveman."

She realized she hadn't thought about Ty all day. She felt guilty about that, but it was way down on her current list of concerns.

"I'm sure it's a love for the ages." Mulaney rolled onto his side, facing the wall. "Be sure to invite me to the wedding so I can *not* come."

Luisa sat on the other bed. "I have to go to that website and enter the password before midnight."

Mulaney's voice was getting thick. "Try not to have your phone on for more than three minutes or so when you do it. When I wake up, we'll figure out the next move."

There was a maintenance entrance at the back of the woman's condo building. Watt approached from the side, cut the power to the camera, and made quick work of the lock. Building like this, no chance there was somebody sitting in a room watching screens. It would be days, maybe weeks, before anybody noticed the problem, even if the camera had ever worked to begin with.

The door to Luisa's condo was even easier. Watt closed the door and stood just inside for a minute, feeling the vibes of an empty home. The place was clean, but disheveled. Stacks of books and documents covered the table in the small kitchen and the coffee table in the living room and parts of the floor everywhere. Searching the place for something the size of the thumb drive would take days. Watt didn't have days, and since the file could have been copied, it was a pointless exercise anyway. The goal was to find anything that might tell him where the woman would go. If he struck out here, he'd try the ex-cop's place.

Lyle Mulaney. He received that dossier shortly after leaving Pioneer Park. Disgraced ex-cop, no known current occupation. Parents deceased, ex-wife remarried and living in Minneapolis, no kids. Abbott had been one of the leaders of the protests that led directly to Mulaney being fired. It made no sense that they were together now. Watt didn't try to figure it out. Maybe one of them would explain it before he killed them.

The back bedroom had been turned into an office. The computer was password protected. Watt had access to guys who could crack it, but that too would likely take days. He went through the drawers, without much real hope. Nobody had address books anymore. There wouldn't be a phone bill listing long-distance calls. There wouldn't be a pad of paper that would yield a vital clue if he rubbed it gently with a pencil. Most of the paperwork he found was about Abbott's various bleeding-heart causes, the rest about her academic work. He made a note of the name of her thesis advisor, knowing it was pointless. All he could really do was wait for the woman to poke her head up again.

He was in the bedroom, crouching to check the boxes in the bottom of the closet, when he heard the condo door open and close. A man's voice called out. "Lu? You here?"

Watt moved silently to the corner of the room behind the open door.

"You're not answering your phone," the voice said. The man walked into the bedroom, swiveling his head. Watt pushed the door closed. The newcomer spun to face him. He was a lanky white kid in a wifebeater and black jeans, somewhere in his mid-twenties, with a mop of brown hair and tattoos covering his bare arms. "Who the hell are you?" he said.

Watt punched him, a quick, powerful jab directly to the nose. He felt it break, and a gush of blood poured over the boy's mouth as he fell backward onto the bed. When he looked up, his hands clutched to his face, Watt was smoothing his tie with one hand. The other held a gun. "Phone. Wallet. Now."

"What the fuck, man?" The kid's voice was a squeak. Blood bubbled on his lips.

Watt took a step forward. He put the muzzle of the gun directly against the kid's knee. "Phone," he said again. "Wallet. Last chance."

The kid scrabbled to get at his pockets and passed them over. Watt stepped back to stand against the door. He put the gun away, picked up a shirt from the top of the dresser, and used it to wipe the blood off the wallet before he opened it.

"Tyrone Harris. I bet people call you Ty."

The kid was pushing himself back to the far side of the bed, holding a pillow against his bleeding nose. The eyes above the pillow were wide, terrified, and full of tears.

"Tell me, Ty," Watt said. "How long has it been, exactly, since Lu answered her phone?"

Luisa sat on her bed, listening to Mulaney snore. He sounded like a wounded walrus in an echo chamber.

After a while she stood up and did some yoga stretches. Usually a few minutes of this would put her in a meditative state. Right now, her monkey brain was continuing to insist on chattering at her. She melted into child's pose, saw a dead cockroach under Mulaney's bed, and scrambled up off the floor. She sat cross-legged against the headboard of her bed, tried again to meditate, and ended up chewing at her lips and staring at the wall. A dozen times she started to reach for her phone and remembered it was turned off. Strange feeling. She wasn't sure it had ever been turned off since she bought it.

Mulaney snored on. The light behind the curtains grew paler.

In her speeches, Luisa often talked about Archimedes. Give me a place to stand and a lever long enough, and I will move the world. When she watched the Nemo Shaw video, she thought she had her lever, the tool that would allow her to move, if not the world, then at least Texas. She still had the lever. What she didn't have, anymore, was the place to stand.

Mulaney said her life as she knew it was over. What was she supposed to do with that?

The softly glowing clock on the table between the beds said it was a little past nine when she stood up from the bed and, walking slowly, went out onto the walkway outside the hotel room door, closing it as softly as she could. The sky to the west was still lightly burnished a deep reddish orange. There were a few more cars in the lot, and she heard the buzz of TV from some room nearby, but nobody was in sight.

Luisa leaned over the railing and turned on her phone. She had about four bars of service. Plenty to go to the account she'd set up and enter the code that would hold the video back for another three days. She did it quickly and then stood, her thumb hovering over the power button.

Mulaney said three minutes. She didn't know if that specific period of time actually meant something, the space between safety and danger, or if he was just pulling a number out of his ass. She had used up about half of it.

Ty wasn't the love of her life, but he was a good guy. The specific windmill he tilted at was trying to get Texas off fossil fuels. On the weekends he trained for marathons. He was funny and good in bed and completely relaxed about not knowing where they were going, the kind of guy who, when she inevitably ended things, would actually mean it when he said they should stay friends. He deserved something from her. A warning. A goodbye.

Watt sat in the armchair in Luisa Abbott's living room, reading her copy of *The Sun Also Rises*. He assumed the many angry marginal annotations about Lady Brett were hers. Ty was lying on the couch. His hands were free, but his ankles were bound together with several layers of duct tape. Watt had satisfied himself that the kid had no idea where Luisa was, and no knowledge of the video, then permitted him to clean his face. Satisfying himself on those points had involved breaking the little finger on Ty's left hand. The hand was wrapped in a dishtowel and Ty clutched it to his chest. His face was white, his breathing rapid and shallow. The middle of his face was one enormous bruise.

Watt was honest with the kid, since there was no reason not to be. He would wait until midnight to see if Luisa called. If she didn't, Watt would kill Ty and move on to other possibilities.

He knew the kid would get frantic enough to try something. Experience suggested that it would happen when there were about twenty minutes left. Watt looked forward to it.

Ty's phone was on the coffee table between them. It rang at 9:17. Watt dogeared the page he was on and leaned forward to look at the display. Unknown number.

"Do I need to give you your instructions again?" he asked.

"No," Ty said. His voice was shaky, but clear enough.

Watt hit the button to answer and put the phone on speaker. He nodded at the kid.

"Hello," Ty said.

"Ty?" The voice had the hollow, slightly delayed quality of a poor connection. "It's Lu. Are you okay? You sound weird."

Ty tried to swing himself up into a seated position but couldn't manage it with his ankles bound and a bad hand. He fell back. "I'm at your place. There's a man here." His voice broke a little. "He's hurting me, Lu."

The connection was just good enough for Watt to hear the intake of breath.

"Ms. Abbott," he said. "You know what I want."

There was a long silence. For a moment they both thought she had hung up.

"Yes," she said finally.

"And now you know what I have."

This time her "yes" was faster.

"Let's keep this simple," Watt said. "I give you the boy, you give me the drive. In addition, of course, you will have to satisfy me that you've kept no copies, made no annoying arrangements."

"Hang on. One second." There was the sound of a door opening and closing, then she evidently muted her end of the call. Watt sat, a statue. Ty rocked back and forth, his eyes wide.

It was almost two minutes before a new voice came on the line, a man. "We're a couple hours outside town. You have to give us time."

"Mr. Mulaney, I presume," Watt said.

"Yeah. This the guy in the BMW?"

"It is. I've seen you do a couple of nice pieces of driving in the last twenty-four hours."

"Great to have fans. You want to tell me your name, so I can put you on my mailing list?"

"No," Watt said. "You have the drive?"

"Right here."

"Tell me about the fail-safe."

There was a quick burst of whispered consultation Watt couldn't make out.

"She attached the video to an email that will spread it all over hell and back. There's a password she needs to enter once a day or it goes out automatically."

"Clever," Watt said. "She'll delete it, of course. In front of me."

"Once we see the boyfriend. Then all three of us walk."

Luisa's voice broke in. "Let me hear Ty again."

Watt nodded at the boy. "Lu," he said. "I don't know what any of this is about."

"I know, Ty. I'm so sorry."

"Enough," Watt said. "What direction are you coming from?"

"West," Mulaney said.

Watt thought for a moment. "There's an abandoned truck stop on Interstate 20." He named the exit. "Can you reach it an hour?"

"Yes."

"Exactly one hour, then. Pull around behind the old truck wash."

"One hour," Mulaney said.

Watt leaned forward and ended the call. "I think I can convince her to tell me the password. What do you think, Ty?"

"Yeah," the boy said. "I bet you can. Will you tell me what this is about?"

Watt took the gun from under his arm. "No," he said, and he shot Ty in the middle of his forehead.

Watt put the gun back. He picked up the Hemingway book and put it in the breast pocket of his jacket. A mirror hung next to the front door. He stood in front of it and smoothed his tie, then turned to look at his profile. He wanted to be sure the book didn't break the line of the suit too much. He put Ty's phone in his pocket and dialed a familiar number on his own.

"Cleanup," he said when the call was answered. "One customer." He recited Luisa's address.

He left Luisa's door unlocked. It's the small, thoughtful gestures of courtesy to one's coworkers that make the modern workplace bearable.

"The kid's dead," Mulaney said, for at least the fifth time. "You have to accept that."

"I heard him talk," Luisa said.

"Yeah. You probably heard his last fucking words. They'll look great on his tombstone. *Here lies Ty. He didn't know what was going on.*"

"I'm going," she said. "None of this is worth his life. I'll give them what they want."

"Oh, I know you will," Mulaney said. "Then you'll be dead too."

"We have to leave *now*."

"Only place I'm going is to take a leak." Mulaney rolled off the bed and went into the bathroom.

When he came out, Luisa had picked up the gun from the nightstand. She was standing in the far corner of the room, pointing it at him.

"For fuck's sake," he said. "You even know how to shoot that thing?"

She lowered the gun six inches and fired into the mattress. The sound, in the small room, was an enormous flat clap. Mulaney jumped back, his eyes widening. "Are you fucking crazy?"

"I don't think this is the kind of place where people call the police," she said. She pointed the gun at him again. "You don't have to go. Just give me the keys."

Mulaney threw up his hands. "Hell with it. Let's both go. I'm not going to sit out here in this pissant town with no money and no car and nowhere to go and wait for the snipers."

"You do have the drive?"

Mulaney patted his pocket. "Right here."

Luisa didn't have a purse to hold the gun in. She took a pillow off the bed, removed the pillowcase, and wrapped it loosely around her hand to hide the gun. "All right," she said. "Let's go."

They saw nobody on their way to the car. Mulaney unlocked the doors and Luisa slid into the back seat, on the passenger side.

"Seriously?" he asked.

She shoveled garbage out onto the asphalt, making room for her feet. "You're not going to distract me and grab the gun. Damn, this car is disgusting."

"Yeah, well, you're the one fucking littering." He pulled out of the parking lot and merged onto the Interstate, pointed back at Dallas, driving five miles under the limit.

"Pick up the pace," she said. "I know where we're going, so don't try turning off somewhere else. I will shoot you, I swear it."

Mulaney accelerated.

"Why did you say one day?" she asked.

"What?"

"You told that man I have to enter the password every day. You know it's every three days. I'm asking why you lied about it."

"Because I thought you would prefer what he'll do to you if he thinks he has one day to what he would do if he thought he had three."

She didn't say anything to that.

"Have you ever been shot?" she asked after twenty minutes of silence.

Mulaney sighed theatrically. "Yeah, Luisa. I've been shot."

"Was it bad?"

"It's never good." He was quiet for a minute. "I responded to an armed stickup at a liquor store. A cop who wasn't qualified to mop floors came from the back, blasting away, and tagged me in the leg."

"What happened to him?"

"Last I knew, he was a lieutenant in Internal Affairs. Prick."

"I wish I understood you," she said. "You say you wanted to be a policeman so badly. It doesn't seem to bother you at all that you were a dirty one."

"It's not really about being a cop," Mulaney said. "It's about not being little people." He rolled his shoulders, working at getting loose. "Exit's coming up. I don't suppose you've rethought this."

"Let's get it over with."

The old truck stop sat in the middle of several acres of empty pavement. A few of the big lampposts had fallen over. Mulaney's headlights made a cone of visibility through the darkness. They could see and hear the interstate, a football field away, but the abandoned lot felt as isolated to Luisa as a lunar plane.

The truck wash was the biggest structure, five huge bays big enough to accommodate semis with 40-foot trailers. Mulaney idled around to the back and stopped in the middle of the big empty area between the wash and an empty field of scrub brush.

"Looks like we beat the asshole here," Mulaney said. "Maybe we can—"

There was a sudden booming roar of engine noise. The BMW shot out of the middle bay of the truck wash and was already doing better than thirty when it slammed directly into the middle of the passenger side of the Buick. The black car jumped and spun wildly, the world breaking up into waves of intolerable noise as Mulaney felt himself battered from all sides. It came to a tilted rest, the driver's side up on the pavement, the passenger side a foot lower in the field.

It was too soon for pain. Mulaney knew the pain would come. He had to move, he told himself. He had to move. He pawed at the seatbelt, pushing at the deflating airbag, and twisted his head to look back at Luisa. It was her side that was hit. In the weird angles of light, she was a rag doll thrown across the back seat, not moving. Mulaney's brain told him to look for the gun. He couldn't see it. Probably somewhere in all the trash on the floor.

His door was jerked open from the outside. Strong hands grabbed his shirt and pulled him out and he landed hard on the ground. He rolled to his stomach, trying to push himself up, and a hard kick came to his left ribs, sending the air out of him and rolling him onto his back.

"Mr. Mulaney," a dry voice said. "I've really enjoyed your fancy driving tricks. What did you think of mine?"

Mulaney tried to push himself away from the voice. He saw the BMW, its front crumpled. One headlight was still on, pointing off in a crazy direction, letting him see the calm man walking in slow circles around him. He was wearing a suit. He was wearing a fucking *tie*. He didn't seem at all bothered to have just been in a hard wreck.

Mulaney managed to get to his hands and knees. "You're crazy," he said. He spat blood.

"You've caused me quite a bit of aggravation," Watt said. He stepped closer and lifted his foot and brought it down hard on the fingers of Mulaney's right hand. He almost smiled at the sharp snapping noises. Mulaney howled and collapsed.

"I don't like aggravation," Watt said. He knelt on Mulaney's back. The big man bucked, trying to dislodge him, but his body wasn't answering him the way it should. Watt wrapped his hands around Mulaney's right arm, up close to the shoulder, and began pulling it backward, his knees in the small of Mulaney's back providing leverage. There was a ripping noise from the joint, and Mulaney screamed.

"Stop," a weak voice said from behind Watt.

He rose smoothly to his feet and turned. Luisa Abbott was sitting on the pavement, halfway between him and the wrecked Buick. Her legs were splayed out in front of her, and she held her right arm tight against her side. Blood trickled down the side of her face.

"Ms. Abbott," Watt said. "Please be patient. I'll be with you in just a moment."

"No," she said. "It's over." She held up her left hand so he could see the phone. "I sent the video."

"Did you," he said.

"See for yourself," she said. She put the phone on the ground and slowly, painfully, backed a few feet away from it.

Watt took out his gun. "You wouldn't by any chance be planning to shoot me, Ms. Abbott."

"I was really hoping to," she said. "But I couldn't find the fucking gun."

He glanced at Mulaney. The big man was a still lump on the ground. He hadn't moved since he screamed. Watt walked closer to Luisa, watching her carefully. He crouched and, with the gun pointed directly at her, looked at the phone, keeping her in his peripheral vision.

Luisa didn't move. She watched him absorbing the list of recipients.

"Very efficient," he said after a minute. "I don't believe that even my employers can plug this many holes in the dike." He put the phone back down on the ground. "You're too late for tonight's network news, and I suppose a lot of lawyers won't be getting to bed at all tonight, but I imagine you've given all the morning shows a new lead story."

"Where's Ty?" Luisa said.

Watt stood. He smoothed his tie. "I suppose that depends on the particular theology you subscribe to. Unless you mean physically, in which case the answer is probably a landfill somewhere."

Luisa growled. "Motherfucker. You didn't have to do that. He didn't know shit. He didn't do anything to anybody."

"Ms. Abbott," Watt said. "Given your various tiresome political obsessions, I wouldn't think you'd need to be told that the world is rarely fair."

"Now I guess you kill us," she said.

Watt shrugged. "The horse is out of the barn. You may not believe me, Ms. Abbott, but I do not kill without purpose." He looked back again at the heap that was Mulaney. "At any rate, I'll be frank in saying that I have no desire to put Mr. Mulaney out of what will be his considerable misery in the coming days. Perhaps his path will cross mine again. I don't think his tricky little moves would be as effective a third time."

"And me?"

"You?" What she could see of his face was completely expressionless. She might have been looking at an embalmed man in a coffin. "You're going to spend the rest of your life wondering what Ty would be doing if you hadn't tried to play your little game. Could I do anything worse to you?" He started walking away.

"That's it?" she said.

Watt glanced back. "That's it," he said. "Except to tell you that you have no understanding whatsoever of Lady Brett Ashley. Given your education, I'd expect better of you."

It was a pleasant night. The residual heat of the day radiated from the access road as Watt walked. He knew he'd have some pain from the wreck tomorrow, and for a few days after. That was all right. A little pain now and then is no bad thing. Lady Brett would understand that. He looked at the stars. Once in a while he heard a car coming and stepped far enough off the shoulder to stay invisible. The suit would need to be dry cleaned, if it could be salvaged at all. After a while he thought he heard a distant siren. He looked back. He couldn't see the truck stop, but there were flashing red and blue lights back in that direction.

The BMW had been provided by a local subcontractor, a very reliable man named Huey. When the police traced it, they would learn it had been stolen three years ago in New Hampshire. They would find several clean sets of his prints and discover that they appeared in no database anywhere. In time, the one-armed man would tell someone to remove them from the records of this case as well.

Five miles from the truck stop he found a feed store with a lighted parking lot. He sat on a cast-off crate in the light and called the familiar number. "New car," he said, when the call was answered. He gave his location and took out the Hemingway to read while he waited.

It was almost midnight when Nemo Shaw received the first call. Somebody from NBC, requesting comment about something he didn't understand. Shaw hung up. The phone rang again immediately. CNN. He hung up on them, too, but the calls kept coming. Shaw didn't answer again until the number of his New York lawyer showed up. For the next hour, propped up in bed, he ranted and raved, shouted and swore, telling anyone who would listen that he was going to sue the living hell out of—well, out of everyone.

It was two in the morning when CNN started showing stills from the video.

"It's not like you're going to prison, Nemo," the New York lawyer said. "Not over a little blow and some, ah, apparently consensual sexual activity."

"You're fucking fired," Nemo Shaw said. "And I'm going to sue you, too."

He stood up from the bed and put on a bathrobe and slippers. Incompetents. All of them. Never knew a lawyer who was worth his weight in gopher shit. He'd show them, by God. In a week he'd have all those smug anchors on the air begging forgiveness. That wasn't the Nemo Shaw in that disgusting video, ladies and gentlemen. It was a fake, special effects. Computer something or other. An odious attempt to smear one of the leading men of the nation. By the time he was done he would own CNN and take great pleasure in dismantling it.

He went into the big office down the hall and turned on the light. Watt was sitting in a chair in the corner. His tie was still perfect, but his suit was wrinkled, his shoes caked with dust. "Mr. Shaw," he said. "Please forgive my appearance. It's been a trying evening."

"A trying evening." Shaw gaped at the man. "I guess by that you mean a monumental fuckup. I thought you were supposed to be good at your job."

"I'll confess that I've had more successful assignments," Watt said. "Still, this could have all been avoided if you had destroyed the video."

Shaw's nostrils flared. "Don't you lecture me, boy. You know damn well who I am."

"Oh, yes. I know who you are."

"Did you even find the fuckers who did this to me?"

"Yes. I found her."

"Her, huh? Is she dead, whoever she is?"

"Not to my knowledge. She is in considerable physical discomfort."

"Jesus. You can't even kill people right anymore." Shaw sat down behind his desk. "Kill her. Fuck it, kill her whole family. And Tania. Kill her, too. Should have done that last night, saved yourself a trip."

Watt shook his head. "I apologize for any confusion, Mr. Shaw. I don't work for you, and I'm not here to take your orders."

"Oh, you're not. So, what are you here for?"

Watt took out the gun. "I'm dealing with a considerable liability."

Mulaney opened his eyes. He didn't want to, but he couldn't put it off any longer. He was propped up in a hospital bed. His right arm was in a cast that ran all the way up to his armpit and all the way down to his fingers. It was mostly numb. The rest of him hurt like hell.

Luisa Abbott sat erect in a chair by the bed. Her head was bandaged, and her right arm was also in a cast, but a much smaller one than his. When she saw he was awake, she pointed at the newspaper on the tray table in front of him. Grunting, he picked it up and found himself looking at a still from the video, the scene where Shaw was snorting cocaine. Below it was a picture of a couple of paramedics guiding a gurney, with a shrouded figure on it, out the front door of an enormous home.

NEMO SHAW DEAD, the headline said. Underneath: *Prominent local businessman, political figure commits suicide following release of sordid video.*

"Suicide," Mulaney said. His voice was raw. He cleared his throat. "I bet." He dropped the paper and looked at her. "You didn't bring flowers?"

"Ty's missing," she said. "Presumed dead."

"I told you that before we left the motel."

"He was worth a dozen of you."

"Yeah. No doubt."

"I'm not here because we're buddies now," she said. "I just thought I should remind you of a few things before you talk to the cops."

"I'm talking to the cops?"

"They're waiting outside." She scooted the chair a little closer. "You reached out to me two days ago. Said you had seen the error of your ways. Wanted to make amends. Talk about ways we could join forces to expose more corruption in the department. We went out for a drive to talk things over."

"This is quite the fairy tale."

She ignored him. "We pulled over at the old truck stop because you needed to take a leak. This other car came out of nowhere and slammed into us. By the time we pulled ourselves out, the driver was gone. We never saw them, don't know anything about them."

"Then I suppose we jumped on our pogo sticks and went to have tea with the three bears."

"They ask you anything I haven't covered, you don't remember. You do have a concussion, so that's natural enough."

"Nobody who knows either one of us will believe a word of this."

"It doesn't matter what they believe. Only what they can prove." Luisa stood up. "I don't ever want to see you again."

"Aw. Don't pretend you won't miss me, honey."

She froze. "By the way, best of luck with your finances. You owe this hospital about forty thousand dollars. Too bad we little people don't have universal health care, huh?"

Mulaney found the button for his morphine drip and hit it until it wouldn't give him anymore, wondering how much each dose was costing him. Hardly mattered. Given his nonexistent assets, owing fifty thousand wouldn't be any different than owing forty. He was going to need a new ride, too. He was looking up from the bottom of a very deep hole, and he was back to seeing only one way out.

He wasn't looking forward to convincing Huey that he could steal cars with one arm.

I met Michael Bracken in Dallas in 2019, when I went to my first Bouchercon. At the time I had sold only a handful of stories and I had more than a few attacks of imposter syndrome when I found myself in the same room with people like Lawrence Block and Joe Lansdale. Michael was pretty intimidating too. At the panel on short stories I attended, he was introduced as the author of more than 1300 short stories and the editor of a number of prominent magazines and anthologies.

A few months before, Michael had accepted a story of mine for the first time. The story was called "Riptish Reds," and it appeared in the first volume of the superlative annual anthology series Michael created at Down & Out Books, Mickey Finn: 21st Century Noir. *On the basis of that connection, I worked up the nerve to introduce myself to him after the panel. Michael couldn't have been kinder or more gracious to the tongue-tied newbie. He praised the story, expressed genuine interest in my writing goals and methods, and enthusiastically encouraged me to submit again when the second volume of* Mickey Finn *opened for submissions.*

In the years since, Michael's become a good friend (as have other folks from that panel, like John Floyd and Barb Goffman). He's published a number of my stories, and I've learned a tremendous amount about effective writing from his editing. Whatever success I've had in this field owes a great deal to him and I know a host of short story writers who would say the same.

I was delighted when Michael invited me to be one of the writers for Chop Shop, *a series of novellas centered around car thieves in Dallas. Each novella was to include at least one scene set at Huey's Auto Repair—the titular chop shop—and Michael's bible for the series offered detailed descriptions of the shop and the people who work there, but beyond that our directive was simply to "think hardboiled." My contribution, "Run and Gun," ended up being the second one published and I had a blast creating these characters and turning them loose on one another. If you enjoyed it, you can't go wrong in picking up the other* Chop Shop *novellas (there should be a total of twelve available by the time this book is published). In fact, you should snatch up any book you see with Michael's name on the cover. You won't be disappointed.*

Andrew Welsh-Huggins *writes from Columbus, Ohio, where he is the Shamus-, Derringer-, and International Thriller Writers–award nominated author of:* The Mailman, *featuring freelance courier Mercury Carter, a starred* Library Journal *pick of the month; the stand-alone crime novel* The End of The Road; *and the Andy Hayes private eye series featuring a former Ohio State and Cleveland Browns quarterback turned investigator. He is also the editor of the short story anthology,* Columbus Noir. *His stories have appeared in multiple magazines and anthologies, including* Mickey Finn 21st Century Noir; Scattered, Smothered, Covered & Chunked: Crime Fiction Inspired by Waffle House; Sleuths Just Wanna Have Fun: Private Eyes in the Materialistic Eighties; *and* The Best Mystery Stories of the Year 2021 *and* 2024.

THROUGH THICK AND THIN

Andrew Welsh-Huggins

Hayes was accustomed to the confidentiality demanded by clients, to say the least. You didn't hire a private eye in the hopes of trending on Twitter. The whole business was an oxymoron if you thought about it: revealing secrets discreetly. But even by his standards, the agreed-upon meeting place was unusual. A small picnic shelter deep inside Battelle Darby Creek Metro Park and well past Columbus city lines. Nine on a Thursday morning. As deserted a spot and as quiet a time as possible. A welcome addition to Hayes's only other job at the moment, which involved identifying who among an insurance company's employees was poisoning geese on his or her lunch break. But a head-scratcher regardless. Hayes parked his Odyssey in the shelter's adjacent parking lot, looked around, and settled for a seat on the shelter picnic table. Five minutes passed, then ten. He pulled out his phone to be sure he had the right spot. He did. At fifteen he decided to give it another five and call it a day. Getting stood up was also something Hayes was used to; cold feet were endemic among those needing his services. He was the professional equivalent of a dentist on the morning of your root canal. Three minutes later he watched a small four-door red sedan move slowly down the hill before the driver pulled into the lot beside his van. Nothing happened for a full minute. Then a man emerged, looked in the direction he'd driven from, looked in the opposite direction, shut the car door, and walked toward the shelter.

"Mr. Hayes?"

"You've got him. Call me Andy. I thought you might not be coming."

"I thought so too."

Jarrod Rodgers appeared as nervous in person as he'd sounded on the phone a day earlier. He crossed to the far corner of the shelter without shaking Hayes's hand and stood with his arms crossed over his nylon Ohio State windbreaker, all that was needed against this morning's cool April temperatures. He peered up and down the road again. He looked lost, Hayes concluded. No, more than that. He looked like a man awaiting an interview for a job he knew he'd never land.

"This is a little embarrassing," Rodgers said at last.

"Take your time."

"The thing is, I made a mistake."

"Mistakes happen. Why don't you tell me about it."

"I'm not sure where to start."

"Try the beginning. Always works for me."

The attempt to lighten the moment flew past Rodgers without recognition. Nevertheless, after some fits and starts, he told his story.

"I'm happily married. You have to understand that. This wasn't about Missy."

"Missy's your wife?"

"That's right. She's great. I don't know what I was thinking."

They usually didn't, Hayes thought. He said: "Go on."

"I was at a bar, after work. With some friends. A Friday-night thing. I'd had too much to drink. I started talking to this girl. We were, you know, flirting. Somehow, I ended up with her number.

Couple days later I texted her, just messing around. The next thing I knew I was at her apartment."

"What happened?"

The question seemed to startle Rodgers and he made eye contact with Hayes for the first time since his arrival. Neatly trimmed goatee. Fit and trim in jeans and the red golf shirt under his jacket. Early forties or so—the short-cropped hair retreating fast off his forehead the only sign of his age. Good-looking guy.

"What happened was I slept with her. Biggest mistake of my life." He laughed, short and hollow, like a man laughing by himself in an elevator car stuck between floors. "Make that second biggest. Which is why I called you."

"Second biggest?"

Rodgers looked skyward and shook his head in disgust. "I left my wedding ring in her apartment. I took it off when I got undressed. My one noble act." A count of three, and another laugh. "I need that ring back. I need—"

"Have you asked her?"

"What?" Rodgers seemed startled again.

"Have you asked her for the ring back?"

"That's the thing. I can't find her. She won't answer her phone. I snuck over to her apartment when I figured she'd be there, but no one answered. Her car's not in the lot. I'm afraid maybe she moved."

On the park road, a ranger drove past in a green Metro Parks pickup truck. Hayes waved casually, as if being in the shelter so early on a Thursday was the most natural thing in the world. The ranger waved back. Probably had seen it all, and more.

"You need me to find her? Is that it?"

"I just need to know where she is so I can get my ring back."

"I take it you haven't told your wife what happened."

"God, no. It would destroy her."

"Why?"

"Are you serious?"

"Not every affair ends a marriage. Healing is possible—hard, but possible." Except in Hayes's case, though he left that thought unspoken.

Rodgers looked taken aback by this. A moment later, as if recovering from the shock of someone's unexpected arrival at the door, he said, "Her parents split up when she was in high school after her dad had an affair. Times were tough for her and her mom, for a long time. If she found out history repeated itself? I can't even imagine."

"She hasn't realized you're not wearing the ring?"

"Not so far. I take it off occasionally when I mow the lawn. Or sometimes at work."

"Which is where?"

Rodgers explained that he worked at the YMCA on the west side. One of his jobs included regular lifeguarding stints.

"I'm afraid it might slip off and I'd never find it. Once or twice I forgot it in my locker. But the truth is I have it on most of the time. It won't be long before she notices."

"If you're being honest with me and this really was a mistake—"

"It was. I swear."

Hayes held up a hand to stop him. He said, "Assuming that's true, and assuming you're never going to see this girl again, why not tell Missy a version of the truth? You lost the ring and you can't find it. Buy another one, keep your wife in flowers and jewelry going forward, and keep your pants zipped when you're out of the house. All that's a hell of a lot cheaper than divorce." It wasn't that Hayes didn't want or need the work. But half the time it was easier just to point out the obvious, pocket a finder's fee, and move on.

Rodgers didn't say anything for a second. Hayes was left with the impression he'd thrown a stage actor for a loop by going off-script. Rodgers recovered a moment later. "It was her grandfather's wedding ring. Passed down to me. It's a family heirloom. I have to get it back. I have to."

In the end, Hayes accepted five hundred for a retainer and another five hundred to cover three days of work, with a promise of a refund if he found the girl, and the ring, quickly. Hayes had his doubts. Locating Lainey Perkins—the name of the one-night stand—was one thing. It was a lot harder to disappear nowadays because of the electronic tracks that people left, often without realizing it. Most human beings, even those who prided themselves on their independence, lived their lives trailed by a spectral cloud of ones and zeroes. It was after finding Perkins that the degree of difficulty intensified. Best-case scenario, she parked the ring at a pawn shop where chances were fifty-fifty of retrieving it in time. Worst-case—and more likely, in Hayes's experience—she was holding on to it as collateral. In which situation, separating it from her would be more or less as easy as persuading her to remove a tattoo. She would not be the first woman to turn a keepsake from her married lover into an occasional ATM machine. *Want to keep our little secret safe? Time to pony up.* Yet one more reason Hayes questioned whether he could help his new client.

He stayed in the shelter house until Rodgers, shoulders slumped, pulled away and drove out of sight. When he was alone, Hayes took out his phone and searched for his new client on Facebook. After a couple of minutes he concluded that Rodgers was the rare sane individual without a social-media presence. Missy Rodgers, it turned out, was more in line with the rest of humanity. Her profile picture showed a sunny, smiling, attractive blonde who looked, like Rodgers, to be in her early forties but with a few more lines around her eyes. Her timeline a long string of upbeat comments accompanying happy pictures of their tween-age children, a boy and girl, a golden retriever apparently called Tanner, a raft of vegetarian recipes and photos accompanied by at least one "Meat is murder" post, several memes about hardworking nurses, and a bunch of outdoor selfies of her jogging and hiking. A picture-perfect life, so far as Hayes could tell. For his part, Jarrod was a ghost on her page—a background image in the photos, rarely showing his face. Jarrod was also largely invisible on the greater Web, almost belying Hayes's belief in the ubiquity of people's e-life. The only picture Hayes found was a handout photo that a local suburban weekly used earlier in the year after Jarrod won a staff award.

Over the years, Hayes had determined that affairs were rarely about physical attraction, at least after the first spark. He confirmed this observation looking at the photos of Lainey Perkins he found next, on her far more stripped-down Facebook page.

Heavily made-up, her green eyeshadow the color of something you might skim from a pond in late summer. Hair a bright red found in nature if the nature happened to be on Mars. Not fat, but a heavy girl, as the saying went. A line of silver earrings starting in the lobes and marching up the cartilage. A nose ring to match. Pale skin with some doughy cleavage. Despite the youthful vibe she strove for, not all that much younger than Jarrod or Missy, Hayes realized. Her last post a week ago: a late-night picture of a raccoon crouched on a sidewalk, its eyes glittering from a streetlamp, a warehouse of some kind looming in the background. The caption: "Traffic blocking my commute, LOL." He could see the bad-girl affinity that might have appealed to Rodgers, but comparing Lainey to Missy gave him pause. He was reminded of something his cousin said to him years ago, after Hayes left his first wife, Kym, for Crystal, the woman who would briefly become his second bride. Thrusting Kym's wedding-day photo at Hayes, his cousin said, "Are you nuts? You traded in sirloin for hamburger."

Hayes had been nuts. Putting the beef analogy aside in deference to Missy's vegetarianism, he saw that Rodgers had been too. Lainey over Missy? Not even close. For his part he could pretend to blame domestic strife for the straying, but Rodgers hadn't hinted at any. *She's great. I don't know what I was thinking.* So, absent that, was this really a one-night stand? Or did Lainey fulfill something in him that Missy couldn't? Missy struck Hayes as a go-getter: it was possible Rodgers was just worn out and attracted by someone more willing to spend all her energy on him. But something still didn't add up. Maybe it was Hayes's own longing for life with an attractive, maternal, dog-loving vegetarian nurse that made him skeptical. Because at this point, all he had was the dog.

Lainey Perkins lived just off 3C Highway on the outskirts of Grove City, the same suburb Jarrod and Missy called home, her apartment the middle duplex in a three-unit building, one of two matching structures set back from the street and fronted by resident-only parking lots. Exterior walls a gray stucco that could have used a power washing or three; landscaping limited to a line of shaggy shrubs whose untrimmed branches crept above the lines of several front windows. Hayes considered the manicured lawn that the Rodgers's dog Tanner romped upon in Missy's Facebook photos, in front of a standard-issue suburban split-level, trimmed bushes and all. Talk about trading sirloin for hamburger. No one answered the first, second, or even third time Hayes knocked on Perkins's door. He crossed to the door to his left; no answer either. He crossed to the door on the right. After a minute, an elderly East African woman answered but shook her head politely at his questions. "No English," she said. Hayes thanked her, walked up to the donut shop on the corner, bought a small black and a Boston creme, and returned to his Odyssey. He pulled the brim of his Otterbein University ballcap over his eyes, settled back, took a sip of coffee and a bite of the donut, and pretended to study his phone.

Surveillance was a lot like foreplay, Hayes found. Occasionally, a short stint earned you a favorable outcome. But more often than not, the longer it lasted, the more likely you got what you desired. Today's vigil fell into the latter category. The complex was quiet for a Thursday morning, and for several long minutes nothing happened. Eventually, the door on the right reopened and the East African woman emerged trailed by a couple of young girls wearing bright orange dresses and jackets. They walked around the corner to a playground. Ten minutes after that, a minivan pulled in and parked in front of Hayes, momentarily blocking his view of Perkins's entryway as the driver lifted a phone to her ear. "My kids are straight-A students at Lakewood Elementary," the bumper sticker read, below one of those rear-window happy-family stick-figure decals. Screw you, Hayes thought, still smarting from the reminder of his own hamburger-over-steak failures. Fortunately for his surveillance, the driver's call ended, the van left a minute later, and his sight lines were restored. A good thing, because that's when his wait finally paid off.

He heard it before he saw it, a car with a muffler a week overdue for replacement. He watched as a man parked the beater two spaces to his left, cut the engine, and walked to the duplex to the left of Lainey's. He unlocked the door and went inside. Hayes was opening the door of his van when the man reappeared, looked out over the parking lot, approached Lainey's door, and used a key to let himself in. Interesting.

"Help you?" the man said, eyes narrowed in suspicion as he answered the door moments after Hayes's no-nonsense knock.

"Hopefully. I'm looking for Lainey Perkins."

"She's, ah, not here," the man said, unable to contain his surprise.

"Do you know where she is?"

"I'm not sure. I think she might have moved out."

"When?"

"Why are you asking?"

"Because I'm curious."

"You a cop?"

"Do you want me to be?"

"I just don't want any trouble." He seemed like the type who wouldn't. Eyes darting back and forth from Hayes to the parking lot and back. Even less hair on top than Jarrod Rodgers, and what there was would have benefited from both shampoo and conditioner. An undergrowth of facial stubble like soft, white mold spreading across leftovers. Further down, a fold of belly fat peeking out from where his Cincinnati Bengals T-shirt didn't quite meet his jeans. T-shirt so suffused with stale cigarette smoke that Hayes felt his breath catch in his throat.

"In that case, I'm not a cop and I'm going to make your wish come true." He dug out a card and handed it to him. "Back to my question."

"What's a private investigator want to do with Lainey?"

"He wants to know where she is so he can ask her a question. But you think she moved?"

The man hesitated, eyeing Hayes's card. "I'm not exactly sure, tell you the truth. I haven't seen her around the past few days."

"Why do you have a key to her apartment?"

"Listen, what's this about? Is she in trouble?"

"Not yet. How about we talk inside?"

"I'm not sure about that."

"Would you be sure if I gave you twenty bucks and promised I won't leave any marks on her carpet?" Hayes opened his wallet and removed one of the bills Rodgers had handed him.

The man didn't look sure but took the money anyway. Hayes seized the moment and pushed past him, ignoring a cry of protest. A moment later the man followed Hayes inside, shutting the door behind him.

Hayes looked around. He'd expected a place that had been cleared out, according to the man's contention a moment earlier that Perkins might have moved. Instead, he saw a cluttered living room, a dining-room table covered with papers, and a kitchen counter crowded with dishes and boxes of unopened food, as if Perkins had walked away in the midst of preparing a meal.

"This doesn't look like the apartment of someone who left."

"I know," the man said, a hint of worry in his voice.

"So, is that why you came in here just now? To check if she'd really gone?"

"I'm not sure how that's any of your business."

Hayes sighed and took out another twenty. He didn't hand this one over but let the man's eyes focus on it before placing it on the kitchen countertop and setting a not entirely clean coffee cup atop it. "Let's start from the beginning, shall we? Who are you, and why do you have a key to this apartment?"

It took a little more back-and-forth, but at last the man relented. His name was Shayne Townsley. He'd lived in the duplex next door for three years. Perkins arrived maybe six months ago.

"We got to be friends. I'd help her out from time to time, give her a ride to work if the weather was bad."

"She didn't drive?"

"Her car wasn't the most reliable. I can do some basic stuff, helped her keep it running. But Walmart's less than half a mile. She said it was just easier to walk."

"Isn't Walmart down on Stringtown Road?"

"Not a store. A distribution center. She worked the overnight shift."

Hayes recalled the photo of the raccoon on Perkins's Facebook page. The quip about the commute suddenly made sense.

"And she didn't say anything about leaving?"

"That's what's strange. I feel like she would have told me. Plus, her dog."

"Dog?"

"I'd feed it from time to time. Let it out if she had to work overtime. Then the other day I heard it barking late in the morning, even though I hadn't heard from Lainey. Her car wasn't in the lot so I figured she'd walked home as usual, then maybe gone someplace. But after a few hours, I knew something was up."

"No idea where she is?"

The man shrugged. "She's from Indy. Said this job paid more, which is why she moved here in the first place. But maybe she went home."

"Without her dog?"

"That's why I'm a little worried."

Hayes did some math in his head. "You watched her dog, gave her rides, fixed her car, and you have a key to her apartment. Sure you're just friends?"

The man looked away. "I'm sure."

"What you're describing is a boyfriend. Or am I missing something here?"

Eyes darting again, this time from Hayes to the stairway leading to the second floor and back.

"Not boyfriend, exactly."

"What then?"

"I still don't see how any of this is your business."

"Let's assume it's not. But let's assume it's weird she disappeared without telling you and left her dog here to boot, at least according to you. You and I both find that strange. The cops might too. We could get them involved if you want."

"There's no reason to do that."

"Then answer the question: Are you her boyfriend?"

"It wasn't like that, okay? I'd help her out with stuff and she'd, you know, pay me back sometimes."

"In bed?"

Townsley nodded, discomfort etching his face, which suddenly looked older and more tired, like a face seen in the full light of the sun after days inside.

"Who suggested that arrangement? You or her?"

"I don't know. It just sort of happened."

"You sure about that? Maybe her car's on the fritz, she calls, you name your price before you'll help her out?"

"It wasn't like that. You make it sound bad, like I was raping her or something."

"Were you?"

"I told you no. It was, what do you call it, consensual. That's all. I swear."

Hayes studied Townsley. The man's eyes had gone soft, and he was no longer staring furtively at the staircase. He looked lonely and confused, Hayes realized, like a man who finds himself lost in an unfamiliar city on a busy street with no idea which way to turn.

Not unlike Jarrod Rodgers, come to think of it.

"Listen up," Hayes said. He retrieved his phone and pulled up the picture of Rodgers from the suburban weekly newspaper, the one they ran after he received the YMCA staff award. "Ever see this guy?"

Townsley looked at the photo for a good five seconds without recognition. "No. Who is he?"

"Never seen him here? With Lainey?"

"Never."

"He says they had a one-night stand. Couple weeks ago. He met her at a bar and then snuck over here one day for a quickie."

Townsley looked as if he'd been physically struck. His shoulders sagged, followed by his entire body, which he folded onto Lainey Perkins's couch.

"You okay?"

"I'm not sure. It—it doesn't seem like Lainey, what you're telling me."

"You said yourself you traded sexual favors with her for household chores. What's not to believe, under those circumstances?"

Now Townsley looked as if he might burst into tears. "When was this? That they, you know, hooked up?"

"They met at a bar on a Friday night, about a month ago."

"Friday? You're sure?"

"What he said. It was an after-work kind of thing."

Townsley looked up at Hayes, curiosity momentarily replacing the misery brightening his eyes. "Like I told you, Lainey worked overnights. Wednesday through Sunday, every week. Eleven P.M. to seven A.M. She made extra, 'cause it was such an unpopular shift."

"And she always walked?"

"Unless the weather was bad. Then I might give her a ride."

"Might?"

"There were times she said she didn't want to bother me."

"Or maybe she didn't want to have to pay you back," Hayes said.

"It wasn't like that," Townsley said, slumping even further down on the couch.

Hayes took a tour of the apartment, upstairs and down. He didn't like what he found. Lainey's bed was unmade, her closet still full of clothes, her bathroom cabinet jammed with toiletries and makeup. If she'd left town, it had been a snap decision. Townsley told Hayes that Lainey drove a blue 2009 Honda Civic. It wasn't in the duplex parking lot. In the end, Hayes thanked Townsley for his help and asked him to call if he heard from Perkins. He wasn't sure he fully believed the story of consensual favor-trading. But the man's misery over Lainey's disappearance on top of her apparent betrayal of their arrangement with Jarrod Rodgers seemed real enough. After leaving the apartment, Hayes drove around the corner to the Walmart distribution center and then drove around the massive parking lot for ten minutes. No sign of Perkins's car. He parked by the entrance and approached the security booth outside the door.

"Had a question about one of your employees," Hayes said, handing the guard his card.

The man eyed Hayes's license as if it confirmed a positive COVID test.

"So?"

"So, I was hoping maybe you could help me. Her name's Lainey Perkins. She might be missing."

"From where?"

"From home. But maybe work too, which I thought might interest you."

"You'd be wrong. But it might interest my boss, which is all I care about. Okay, let me ask you this. Shopped at a Walmart recently?"

Hayes thought about it. "Bought one of my boys some mittens for a ski trip this winter. School took a bunch of kids over to Mad River."

"Close enough. I'll put it down as an inventory query. What's this girl's name again?"

Hayes waited while the guard two-finger typed Perkins's name into a tablet. The man studied the information that scrolled down the screen.

"Found her. What do you need to know?"

"Has she been to work recently?"

"Doesn't look like it. Missed three days in a row starting last week. Fired on the fourth."

"Nothing about why she missed work?"

"Zilch. But it's pretty common, actually. All the opioid stuff going on, we get a lot of dopeheads here. They work long enough for a paycheck or two and then leave and piss it into their arms. That this girl's problem?"

"I don't think so."

"Well, she's gone either way."

"I appreciate it. Oh. One other thing."

"Always is."

Hayes asked about her schedule. The guard touch-typed for a few seconds and studied the screen again. "Yup. Every Wednesday through Sunday. And I thought my schedule sucked. Actually, this girl was reliable right up until the end. No sick days or anything. We'll be lucky to replace somebody like her."

Hayes spent his lunch hour with his camera trained on suspected goose poisoners. By the end of the surveillance, he was pretty sure the round guy with the funny hair part was having an affair with the lady with the bright pink sneakers, but beyond that he was no closer to catching the culprit than when he started. He put the camera away and texted Rodgers and suggested they meet. They arranged another trip to the park, the next day, at the same shelter house as before. If anything, Rodgers looked even more nervous than the previous day. Hayes explained the little he'd learned. How he found Lainey Perkins's apartment but she was gone, though oddly she left her dog behind. That she hadn't been to work and was subsequently fired. That she appeared to already have a boyfriend, of sorts, in the form of her next-door neighbor. Examining Rodgers, he left out the Friday-night discrepancy for now. Rodgers listened, his face falling as Hayes spoke. When he was done, he unlaced his fingers and cupped his cheeks in his hands.

"So, that's it?" he said. "She's gone?"

"Looks like it."

"And there's no way to find her?"

"Could be hard, at this point. I can keep looking if you want. Though I'm not sure I see the point."

"What do you mean?"

"I mean, you having found your wedding ring and all." Hayes gestured at Rodgers's left hand, where a band of gold encircled his ring finger. A ring that hadn't been there two days earlier. Rodgers didn't say anything at first. Hayes waited for the cry of protest, the explanation about a misunderstanding, a fabricated gasp of surprised delight. Instead, after a few seconds, Rodgers said, "Shit," and placed his hands over his eyes. Hayes gave him a moment, and two more for free, and then said quietly, "So, what's really going on here?"

Through the still-greening trees, Hayes watched a pair of cyclists glide along the park's fitness trail. Startled by their approach, a white-tailed deer bobbed briefly out of the woods and onto the grass where it stood for a moment, eyeing its environs suspiciously. A couple of seconds later it faded gracefully back into the trees. It was a nice moment. Hayes wished it would have lasted longer. Slowly, Rodgers talked.

"It happened twenty-five years ago. In Indianapolis. I was fifteen. Bored and stupid. And drunk. Thanks to my buddy. No," he added quickly, shaking his head so violently Hayes was afraid his glasses might fall off. "Thanks to me. It was my decision to drink that night."

Hayes didn't say anything, wondering where this was going and if he really wanted to go along for the ride.

"There's a street running over I-65 we used to walk back and forth on. Sometimes we'd stand and watch the cars go by. Maybe pump our arms to get a truck to blast its horn."

"Sure."

"One night we found these bricks in an alley. Leftovers from some guy's patio project. Not that it matters. We grabbed a bunch and went to the bridge and started chucking them over."

"Okay," Hayes said. It sounded plausible; something similar had happened in Columbus not that long ago.

"Hitting a car's actually harder than you think. You have to calculate your throw carefully. Finally, my friend caught somebody's trunk. I realized he was hesitating a second too long. So, I timed my next one just right. I nailed a windshield. The car skidded off the road and we took off, but not without a bunch of high-fives first. It wasn't until the next day that we even heard."

"Heard?"

"She died," Rodgers said, staring into the woods where the deer had disappeared. "The passenger, I mean. Major head and brain trauma. Cheryl Stevens. She was a middle-school principal. She and her husband were on their way back from their wedding-anniversary dinner. It was all over the news. The police were everywhere in our neighborhood. My friends and I were freaking out. I made up my mind to tell my mom and get it over with, but before I could, somebody busted us. The police came to the door, hauled me away. The prosecutor wanted us tried as adults, but the judge wouldn't allow it. I ended up in juvie for six years, until I was twenty-one. I would have been out earlier, but I got in a couple fights and they kept extending my stay."

Hayes nodded, encouraging him to continue.

"I had nothing when I was released. My parents had divorced. My dad moved out of state and my mom blamed me. It wasn't hard to see her point. What I did put them through hell. The calls and the threats they got because of me. And afterward, I was useless. No one would hire me for anything. Soon as they saw the name and put it together, forget it. I was homeless for a while, it was so bad. Eventually I hired on to a construction crew as a day laborer. I met this guy who'd done time. He told me there were ways you could disappear. Taught me a few things. It took a couple of months, but the day came when I wasn't the person I used to be anymore—by name, I mean. I became Jarrod Rodgers."

"And ended up in Columbus?"

"I followed the construction crew to a job. They couldn't put up apartments and condos fast enough over here. There was so much work. I liked the money, don't get me wrong, but it was hard. I started looking around for something else. One of the guys on the crew had a brother who worked in a gym, said they were hiring. They needed a night cleaner. It was half the pay but I didn't wake up every day feeling like I'd fallen off the roof. One day the weight-room supervisor quit without any notice and they asked if I could cover his shift. I did okay and they gave me more shifts. Before I knew it, I was running classes. Next thing you know, I'm a gym guy. I had a reputation for being good with the younger crowd, and not long after that I got an offer to go work for the Y, this program they have for troubled teens." He let out a deep sigh. "Guess they picked the right guy for that, without even knowing it. Long story short, that was fifteen years ago. Been there ever since."

"So, what happened?"

He lowered his arms and dug his hands into his pants pockets. "Somebody figured out who I was."

"Somebody?"

"Lainey Perkins."

Hayes remembered what Shayne Townsley told him, about Perkins moving over from Indianapolis to take a job here at Walmart. He told Rodgers the anecdote. He nodded in confirmation.

"Who is she?" Hayes said.

"She's a nobody. Except in this case she's a somebody who recognized me from that stupid picture the paper ran after I won that award. I asked them not to put anything out, but it was too late."

"What's she want?"

"Money," he said. "Money or she'll tell the world about me. Starting with Missy."

"Your wife doesn't know about Indianapolis."

He shook his head.

"There was no one-night stand. No missing wedding ring."

Rodgers shook his head again.

"How much does Perkins want?"

"She wants more, is the problem."

"More?"

"The first time, it was a thousand dollars. She said she'd leave me alone after that. Like a fool, I believed her. It was hard as hell to find that much money without my wife knowing. Of course, that wasn't enough."

A twinge of guilt as Hayes considered the money Rodgers paid him to look for Perkins. "How much now?"

"She wanted five thousand this time. By this past Monday, or else."

"I take it she never got it?"

"Only because she disappeared. She wasn't answering her texts. I snuck over there one day after work, but like I told you, she wasn't answering her door."

"Why not just leave it be and count yourself lucky? Dodged a bullet and all that?"

"And not know if she's really gone or just planning her next move? No thanks."

"That's why you hired me. To figure out what happened to her?"

Rodgers acknowledged it with a nod.

"Here's the thing," Hayes said. "Blackmail's illegal. I'm not saying it would be easy, but why not just go to the police? Let them handle it."

Rodgers's eyes widened as if Lainey Perkins herself had appeared around the corner of the shelter. "Are you crazy? I do that and the world knows. And once my wife finds out . . ."

"What?"

"It's over. She'll be out of there. Everything I built will be gone. Everything I've tried to do, to make amends with the universe, down the toilet."

"Last time you said she'd leave because her father broke the family up with an affair. Was that a lie too?"

"No. That really happened. She's estranged from her dad and her mom died shortly after Missy graduated high school. Cancer, but she blamed her father, as irrational as that sounds. She's got trust issues, either way."

"Forgive the question, but how do you know that's what she'll do? Maybe she'd surprise you."

"I just know."

"Meaning?"

"She has a strong sense of right and wrong. Stuff she sees on her job."

"Which is?" Hayes said, though he already had a good guess from her Facebook page.

"She's an overnight ER nurse. At Grant. Eighty percent of what she sees are shootings. It's got her kind of jaded about crime."

"Is that why she's a vegetarian?"

Rodgers stared at him. "How do you know that?"

Hayes explained the social-media snooping he'd done.

Rodgers relaxed a little. "I'm not online much, for obvious reasons. And to answer your question, she's always been a vegetarian. Since she was a kid. Always hated the idea of animals being killed. It's not my thing but, you know, you adjust."

"How'd you meet?"

"She worked out at the Y a lot. We got to talking and hit it off."

"And you're sure her personality isn't the type that would forgive you for what you did?"

"For what I did, and the fact I've lied to her from the day we met? That I've hidden my entire life from her? That's one of the . . ." He trailed off.

"What?"

"That's one of the things we promised each other, when we got married. No secrets, through thick or thin."

"Admirable," Hayes said, trying not to dwell on the number of lies he told both ex-wives in the first week of marriage alone. Instead, he said, "Like I said, healing can happen."

"Maybe. I thought about it, especially after Lainey came at me the second time. But then I realized I was well and truly screwed."

"Why?"

"It happened again. Few days ago. Kid throwing rocks onto the highway—just east of downtown. The driver wasn't killed, but they're talking permanent brain damage. He was a pastor—worked with sick kids or something."

It was the story that piqued Hayes's interest earlier as Rodgers talked. He knew it was too big a coincidence.

"That triggered something?"

"We were watching the news. They did a segment on it. That's when Missy said it."

"Said what?"

"She was furious—you could see it in her eyes as she watched. When they cut to a commercial, she shook her head and looked over at me and said, 'So much good destroyed by such a vile person.' I just about ran out of the house. The way she said it. I didn't need to guess what would happen if I told her the truth. She told me then, without even realizing it."

Hayes had to admit the scenario didn't bode well for any thought of Rodgers coming clean.

"Back to Lainey Perkins. Assuming I find her, what are you going to do with that information?"

"Give her the money. And try to talk her out of asking for more."

"And that's it?"

"Yes."

"You're sure? You haven't thought about maybe shutting her up? Like for good?"

Hayes saw right away he'd struck a nerve.

"I'd be lying if I said it didn't cross my mind," Rodgers said. "I made a horrible mistake. I paid for it three times over. I rebuilt my life, tried to do some good in the world, and then along comes this loser trying to take everything away from me. What gave her the right? She was ready to crap all over twenty-five years of redemption. Would you blame me if I did what you're talking about?"

"So, the answer's yes?"

"Yes, goddammit," Rodgers said. "The answer is yes, I fantasized about putting my hands around her stupid, fat neck and squeezing until the lights went out."

He spoke so forcefully that it took Hayes aback. He thought about the sorrow he'd seen on Shayne Townsley's face as he wrestled with the fact that perhaps the one person in the world who showed him some human kindness, even if it came wrapped in a twisted sex-for-chores arrangement, was possibly out of his life and gone.

"Sure you didn't already do that?" Hayes said. "Take matters into your own hands, then hire me to cover your tracks? Who'd believe you murdered her if you paid a private eye to find her? You wouldn't be the first to try that stunt, just so you know."

"No. I swear it."

"If that's the case, how'd you know where she lives? Or what her car looks like? You said it wasn't in the lot."

"She drove the car to our first meetup."

"Which was where?"

"The parking lot at Kroger, off Hoover Road. I followed her home from there."

"And that's it?"

"Aside from going back and knocking on her door, and then sitting in the parking lot and running through that fantasy I just told you about, yes, that's it. You have to believe me."

"Why should I? You've been lying this whole time."

"I've been down that path, remember? I've already killed someone. I've lived with that pain my entire life and trust me, I wouldn't wish that hell on anyone. I know how this looks. But I'm telling the truth. I just wanted to talk to her. To see if I could explain to her what losing all this would mean to me. That's all." His last words faded into a choked-off sob.

Hayes leaned back and gave Rodgers a second. He considered the turn the case had taken. He tried to decide if he believed the story. You met a lot of prevaricators in this business. There was an old saying among private investigators. How can you tell when clients aren't telling you the whole truth? Answer: when they open their mouth. The wife looking for dirt on her cheating husband neglecting to mention she had a thing going on the side herself. And on and on. So long as the iceberg of reality below the tip of truth didn't get him killed, and he still got paid, Hayes was happy. He made a snap decision and decided Rodgers was being upfront. Sometimes a stupid reason for hiring a private eye is really just that. Plus, the need for the remote meeting place now made sense. There were secrets, and then there were secrets.

"Two choices here," Hayes said.

"Choices?"

"I can take your word for your good intentions and keep looking for Perkins. Or you can count yourself lucky that your problem's resolved itself one way or the other, forget this ever happened, and move on."

"Assume I do that. What if she calls me again?"

"Cross that bridge when you come to it?"

"So, I just spend my life waiting for the other shoe to drop?"

"No offense," Hayes said softly. "But how is that any different from the last quarter century?"

Later that morning, Hayes sat at his kitchen table staring at his laptop. Though the case was officially concluded, he needed proof that this time Jarrod Rodgers was telling the truth.

The Indy brick incident that killed Cheryl Stevens happened right before the movement to publicize juvenile names took hold, so there was less information about the guilty teens than you'd see now, including a paucity of booking photos. But eventually Hayes pieced it together. Jarrod Rodgers had been someone named Brad Hilburn. The lone picture he found of Hilburn was a skinny, sullen-looking kid angry at the world. The resemblance to his twenty-five-years-older self was there, but between Rodgers's now-muscular build, his thinning hair and goatee, and his glasses, it was hard to see. As disappearing acts went, it was nearly foolproof.

Hayes checked Lainey Perkins's Facebook page again. No change there. Her last post the same he'd seen the first time he stalked the page: the late-night picture from her walk to work. Just to satisfy himself, he found the number for Perkins that Jarrod provided him and dialed it. It went immediately to voicemail without a ring. He hesitated a moment, then left a message with his name and number, asking for her to please return the call. A moment later he texted the same request.

Finished, he flipped back to Missy Rodgers's page, still not entirely trusting Jarrod, and wondering if he'd learn something new. But all he found were updated pictures of the dog, a splash of color from front-yard tulips, and an artfully displayed plate of falafel tacos cross-posted from Instagram. He scrolled back a few posts, double-checking that Jarrod wasn't suddenly showing up in photos. He wouldn't be the first person to breathe easier with a nemesis out of the way. But he was still nowhere in sight. Hayes idly looked through the long list of Missy Rodgers's friends, just to be sure he hadn't missed anything. He felt a twinge in his stomach as he considered what a happy life Missy had for herself, at least measured by so many friends on Facebook, compared to Lainey Perkins's spare, lonely page.

He was about to click off the site and stake out the goose poisoner once again when something caught his eye. One of Missy's friends was someone named Steve Thayer. But that wasn't what captured his attention. Thayer's profile picture was a store logo. Friedmann's Meats. Hayes knew it well. An independent butcher off South High Street. An old-school business still hanging in there thanks to the loyalty of multiple longtime customers, himself included. Odd, Hayes thought, scrolling back up Missy's page, past the multiple vegetarian recipes, until he landed on one of her most recent "Meat is murder" meme postings.

On a whim, and because he was out of brats anyway, Hayes left the house and drove the mile down to the store, where it sat just north of the old Buckeye Steel complex. As he entered the shop, his regular butcher, a middle-aged man named Darnell, waved him over.

"Hey, Andy. Got a nice rump roast you might be interested in."

"Normally, you might be right. But I'm half on the clock. You got somebody named Steve Thayer working here?"

"Steve? Yeah—that's Mr. Friedmann's nephew-in-law. But he's off today."

"Maybe I'll catch him later. Well, hang on. How long have you been working here?"

"Me? Seems like forever. Almost thirty years next month."

Hayes pulled out his phone and found Missy's profile picture. "You know this lady by any chance?"

Darnell studied the phone. "Looks a little familiar. Who is she?"

Hayes told him her name and the fact she was Facebook friends with Thayer.

"Yeah, yeah. It's not Missy, though. And not Rodgers. I remember her now. Melissa Mullins. Worked here a couple summers in college, I think. Sweet girl. Good worker too. Lot of those kids, you put half a cow in front of them, tell 'em to take it apart, it's suddenly break time. Not her. She was a whiz with the knife."

"Really? She's a vegetarian now."

"That's a shame. I always feel bad for vegetarians. They think they're doing animals a favor not eating them, but all they're doing is putting a bunch of hardworking cows and pigs and chickens out of work." He crossed his arms and grinned at Hayes. "And don't even get me started on vegans."

"Maybe it's a health thing."

"Could be. Got a cousin like that. Used to smoke these killer ribs, and now all he eats is cauliflower steaks."

"I know this sounds crazy, but is it possible she didn't eat meat when she worked here? Just did it for the money?"

"Nah."

"Why do you say that?"

"It's coming back to me now, Andy. Mr. Friedmann does an employee picnic, every August. There's an eating contest goes with it. I used to be the reigning champion."

"Used to be?"

"You know that Black Men Run club I'm in?"

"Sure." Hayes had even joined him for a couple of jogs in recent years.

"You didn't know me before that. In the old days, I tipped the scales at three hundred and fifty. And man, could I eat. But this one year, that girl, Melissa, she smoked me. She was on her fifth or sixth hot dog while I was still looking for the mustard. She wasn't a vegetarian back then, tell you that much."

Hayes wasn't a betting man. He took the position that in general the odds were against him, and just lived with the consequences. He certainly wouldn't have placed a wager on the likelihood of Jarrod Rodgers and Lainey Perkins crossing paths again, one way or the other. So, he was surprised when Jarrod called him later that day to tell him the good news.

"Which is?"

"Lainey texted me. Told me to just forget it. Said she was moving on."

"Really?"

"What she said."

Hayes set his camera on the seat beside him and squeezed his eyes open and shut. He was now definitely sure that Weird Hair Part and Pink Sneakers were having an affair; he'd caught an illicit kiss by the willow on the far side of the retention pond. But still no luck on the goose poisoner, though he wondered if it really mattered. He'd decided the company probably already knew who it was and had a different reason for jettisoning the employee, one they didn't want getting out. But the size of his retainer precluded too many questions about their real motives. Plus, Hayes didn't care much for people who poisoned geese.

"Can you read it?" Hayes said.

"What?"

"Read me the text she sent."

"Hang on." A pause, and then a switch to an echoey background that told Hayes he'd been put on speaker mode.

"It says, 'Sorry I bugged you. Wasn't in a good headspace. Forget I said anything.'"

"That's it?" Hayes said after a second.

"That's it."

"When did she send it?"

"I'm not sure. There's no time on it."

"Pull the text toward you. Swipe it left, I mean."

"I didn't know you could do that."

"No charge for the tip. So, what's it say?"

"10:05 A.M."

Hayes thought about it. He thumbed over to his recent calls. Seven minutes after he'd called and texted Lainey's number after re-checking her Facebook page.

"Did you text her back?"

"Just 'Okay, thanks.' Do you think that was all right?"

"I'm sure it was fine."

So, that was it, Hayes thought, disconnecting. Lainey Perkins grew a conscience in the end. Jarrod Rodgers was scot-free. Case closed. He raised his camera and watched as an unassuming, bespectacled man reached into the right pocket of his windbreaker, pulled out a pair of blue latex gloves, snapped them on, dipped his right hand carefully into a plastic bread bag, and just as carefully lobbed a red-tinted chunk of bread toward a hissing pair of geese. Hayes clicked off a round of pictures and examined the results in the viewfinder. Bingo. Satisfied, he placed the camera down again, picked up his phone, and tried Lainey's number himself. Still nothing.

Hayes tried the number again after he returned home and transferred the photos of the goose poisoner to his computer. He compiled his report for the insurance company, embedding the photos into the document, and sent it off. The poisoner would be punished. If the company had another reason for dismissing the man, no one would be the wiser. Secrets would stay buried, along with the dead geese. He tried Lainey again to no avail, grabbed Hopalong's leash, and walked him down to Schiller Park and back, the Labrador moving slowly with age but not so slowly that he didn't alert to each and every squirrel they passed on the way. Back in the house, Hayes tried Lainey's number once more without results. Was it odd that she'd texted Jarrod not long after Hayes called and left a message, but wouldn't pick up for him? Maybe he was overthinking this. Maybe Jarrod Rodgers really had won the lottery.

But he couldn't stop thinking about the defeated, lonely look on Shayne Townsley's face; not the look of a man who'd expected his girlfriend—or whatever she was—to just up and disappear. And what to do with the lived-in apartment and the abandoned dog? Hayes thought back to Jarrod's confession in the park shelter house, and his protestations of innocence when Hayes asked what he planned to do with the information. Then he considered Jarrod's story of the night he and Missy watched the news about the pastor injured by the brick thrown over the bridge, followed by Missy's reaction. *So much good destroyed by such a vile person.* Hayes pondered the most random detail of all, sticking out like a muumuu at a formal black-tie dinner: Ardent vegetarian Missy Rodgers had worked a couple of summers at a butcher shop where many years later she was remembered for her knife-handling skills. A stint it sounded like Jarrod didn't know about. Yet what was it they promised each other on their wedding day? *No secrets, through thick and thin.* He thought again about Lainey's apologetic text message to Jarrod. Sorry I bugged you. Wasn't in a good headspace. Forget I said anything. Why send that? Why not just drop off into radio silence for good? Unless the text itself was another fabrication, part of a ruse Rodgers was maintaining to disguise the fact he really had taken matters into his own hands. And if that was the case, where was Lainey Perkins, for real?

Just past seven the next morning Hayes parked two houses down from Missy and Jarrod Rodgers's place. A mile and a quarter from Lainey Perkins's duplex, though light years in terms of per capita income. The irony: If Perkins had lived one town over, she might never have seen the photo in the suburban weekly serving the town and made the connection with Rodgers and his past.

The magnetic sign that Hayes had affixed to the outside of his van read *Dry Basement Doctor*, with an illustration of a physician pressing a stethoscope to a cinder-block wall and an accompanying 800 number. Amazing what you could have made online. Despite the hour, the neighborhood was already full of life: kids waiting for buses, dogs getting walked, joggers padding down the sidewalk. The fake business sign a must, since surveillance in a place like this was like an opened jar of mayonnaise left out in hot weather; it had a very short shelf life.

Fortunately for Hayes, Rodgers's garage door slowly rose on schedule. He watched him back out in his red sedan. Hayes prepared to start his van and follow. But then Rodgers stopped in his driveway and cut the engine. Puzzled, Hayes wondered if Rodgers had made him. But before another minute passed, a minivan approached the drive and turned in. It stopped beside Rodgers's car. Of course. His wife, Missy, home from her overnight ER shift. Ships passing in the night. Hayes watched as Missy left her car and opened the door of Rodgers's car, smiling at the children inside. Hayes watched the scene with envy. Secrets aside, the couple appeared to carry off a complicated life with compassion, respect, and love. An approach

Hayes seemed incapable of. As the couple bid each other goodbye and Rodgers slowly backed out of the drive, Hayes thought back to the window decal on the van he'd seen pulling into the parking lot the day he surveilled Lainey's place, the happy nuclear stick family, and how much that had bothered him. That and the van's bumper sticker: "My kids are straight-A students at Lakewood Elementary." But here was the problem. He'd just seen that same van again, with the stick-figure decal and the elementary-school bumper sticker. Driven by Missy Rodgers as she pulled into her driveway.

Hayes gave it five minutes, and five minutes more, and then departed his van and walked up to the Rodgers's door. He wouldn't have been surprised if Missy were on her way to bed after working an all-night shift. Instead, she answered the bell after a minute dressed in exercise clothes and wiping perspiration from her face.

"Yes?" she said, her face showing annoyance at the interruption of her workout.

"My name's Andy Hayes. I'm a private investigator. I'm here about Lainey Perkins."

Missy froze in place.

"Who?" she said a second too late.

"I think you know who I'm talking about."

"In that case, you're mistaken."

"Am I?"

"That's what I just said."

"I can always come back another time. Say when Jarrod's home?"

A skirmish of emotions briefly played out on Missy Rodgers's face before what appeared to be stoic resignation claimed victory. "Come inside, why don't you," she said.

She showed Hayes into the living room but didn't invite him to sit. Tanner, the handsome dog from Facebook, padded into the room and collapsed with a sigh beside Missy. Hayes handed her a business card. Missy examined it, folded it in half, and tucked it into the waistband of her shorts.

"So, what exactly is it that you want, Mr. Hayes? Money? Is that it?"

"I just want to know where Lainey Perkins is."

"I have no idea."

"Really? You were parked at her apartment complex two days ago, right in front of me."

"That's not true."

"We both know it is. Why were you there? Making sure no one was missing her? No one who might interfere with you and Jarrod? Or should I say, Brad Hilburn?"

She flinched as if Hayes had slapped her.

"Well?"

Missy looked down, like a person in prayer. She looked up and said, "You really don't know the extent of the damage you're causing, do you?"

"Meaning?"

"Meaning my husband's a good man."

"I can see that."

"A man who deserves to live his good life unimpeded. For his sake. And for our children's." A pause. "And for me."

"You know about Indianapolis," Hayes said.

She didn't speak, but the look on her face gave Hayes the answer anyway. In that moment, the story Jarrod told Hayes about the Columbus pastor injured by a similar prank came back to him. What was it Missy said? *So much good destroyed by such a vile person.*

Such a vile person.

No wonder Jarrod panicked. He heard the vitriol in Missy's voice and assumed the worst.

Except Jarrod got it wrong. His wife wasn't talking about the person who hurt the pastor at that moment.

She'd been talking about Lainey Perkins.

"How did you find out?" Hayes said.

"Do you have children, Mr. Hayes?"

He told her about his two boys.

"Our son is twelve. Sometimes he uses our computer for school projects. When he's finished, I always check the browser search history."

"And?"

"He likes to look at photos of women in bikinis. It's kind of cute, actually. Nothing more harmful than that."

"You found a search about Lainey Perkins."

She nodded.

"And what happened in Indianapolis," Hayes said. "Something Jarrod had been looking up."

"I'd rather have found porn, believe me. Or pretty much anything else."

"You didn't confront Jarrod?"

"Maybe I should have. Maybe I would have. But then I picked up his phone one day when he was in the other room and I saw a text, asking about money. We share each other's passcodes, in case of an emergency. It wasn't hard to track her down after that."

"Is that how you knew Jarrod hired me?"

"I saw a number I didn't recognize and looked it up on Google. When it came back to you, I knew something was up."

"And you followed me that day I went to her apartment?"

"That was a coincidence. I just went by to be sure nothing was happening, given that Jarrod had called you. I knew who you were by then. I left as soon as I realized."

A bad feeling came over Hayes. He remembered Perkins's last Facebook post. The picture of a raccoon, with a description of her "commute." The inadvertent admission on a public social-media page that she walked to work late at night. He considered for the first time the odd coincidence that both Lainey and Missy worked overnights.

"Where is Lainey Perkins, Mrs. Rodgers?" Hayes said.

She stared through him as she spoke. "I believe in justice, Mr. Hayes. Criminals should be punished. Wrongdoing shouldn't be rewarded. But I also believe in forgiveness. Retribution is meaningless if rehabilitation isn't honored. My husband paid his dues. He owes no one anything."

"He kept a secret from you."

"There are worse sins. Don't tell me you never hide things."

"I hide plenty. Everyone does. For example, a committed vegetarian disguises the fact she once worked at a butcher's shop and won hot-dog-eating contests. So much for the two of you never keeping secrets from each other." Hayes thought of Missy's carefully curated, always sunny Facebook feed; the posts cheerful and upbeat even in the days after she'd learned of Jarrod's past. How did the old saying go? The grass is greener on the other side because of all the bull crap it grows in.

Missy didn't say anything for a moment. When she spoke next, Hayes expected a note of resignation. Instead, her voice exuded defiance.

"We all make mistakes we'd rather forget."

"And keep from our loved ones?"

"It's time for you to leave, Mr. Hayes."

"Lainey Perkins," he said, not moving. "That wasn't her texting Jarrod, was it?"

"I'm begging you."

"You saw that I called her phone, which I assume you have, and figured you'd better drop one more clue. Is that right?"

"Please."

"Can you just take me to her? Or tell me where she is?"

Missy Rodgers lowered her head and didn't speak for a moment. Her shoulders drooped in defeat. When she looked up, her eyes were bright, and not with perspiration.

"I'll be just a minute," she said, slowly leaving the room and walking around the corner. Hayes heard the clink of dishes being moved. The act of a woman seeking familiarity as her life implodes before her. He felt no relief now that he knew both Jarrod's and Missy's secrets. He felt nothing less than disgust at his intrusion, regardless of its necessity. Because the problem was, he agreed with Missy. Crime needed punishing, but rehabilitation needed honoring. At what point do we stop penalizing each other for the past? Maybe it all depended on the depth one buried one's secrets.

Jarrod Rodgers's carefully constructed alternative life had evaporated thanks to Lainey Perkins's greed. Missy Rodgers's own obfuscations tripped her up as she stumbled onto the lie Jarrod had been living. But was it a lie if she never probed the life story of the man she loved? More importantly, what action had she taken to protect that love, regardless of the facade that stood behind it?

A sound interrupted Hayes's thoughts. From the kitchen, as though something heavy had fallen. Another sound followed by a woman's soft cry. He moved toward the sound. "Missy? Are you all right?"

A moment later he backed up as she rounded the corner. He stared at her face; blood trickled from a cut on her cheek, which was red and already starting to swell.

"What happened? Are you—"

"Stop," Missy said, taking a step closer. As she did Hayes watched as she raised her right hand. In it gleamed a long steel kitchen knife. "Stop."

"What are you doing?"

"You came in here, made all these accusations, then attacked me. I begged you to stop but you just kept hitting me. I barely made it to the kitchen in time. I had to defend myself."

"Put the knife down, Missy."

"I had to protect myself. For my sake, and for my family."

Faster than Hayes would have thought possible she charged him then, knife rising as she ran. He backed up but not fast enough and stumbled against a coffee table. He lost his balance and fell, hitting the carpeted floor hard and sending Tanner skittering across the room, barking loudly. Hayes raised his hands to shield himself as she came upon him. The knife rose high. Then a sound distracted her; the front door was opening. Hayes kicked hard with his right foot, striking her off-balance. Enraged, she tried to stab him but her equilibrium was off. The flat of the knife struck his arm. He tried to wrestle it away but her grip on the handle was too tight. He scooted back and kicked at her again and she raised her hand and then lost her balance for good and fell with a shriek.

"Missy?"

Hayes turned. Jarrod stood in the doorway, gaping at the scene.

"Stay where you are," Hayes said.

"Oh my God," Jarrod said.

"I said—"

"What did you do? Look at her—she's bleeding. Missy? Angie forgot her homework. I was just—"

Sentence unfinished, Jarrod ran across the room. Hayes turned and stared at Missy. The blade had buried itself deep in her abdomen as she stumbled and fell. Blood pumped from the wound around the knife, reddening the carpet. She gasped, breath coming short and shallow, her eyes moving from the knife to her husband and back.

"Jarrod," she said.

"Oh, Missy. Oh God oh God oh God."

The coroner called it a freak accident. The knife severed an artery, and the internal bleeding was worse than the exterior wound. Missy Rodgers died in the ambulance on the way to the hospital. Hayes spent the rest of the day in an interview room in the Grove City Police Department and the night in the Franklin County Jail. It wasn't until late the next afternoon that a combination of Jarrod's testimony, Hayes's own account, and grainy video obtained from the donut shop across from Lainey Perkins's apartment complex that showed Missy Rodgers moving Perkins's car in the middle of the night confirmed the truth of what happened.

The last Hayes heard, Jarrod Rodgers lost his job and had to sell his house. But he got a new job at another gym and a new house in another suburb. He kept his new name, but he was done hiding too. Hayes learned all this right around the time a fisherman's hook snagged on something big in a quarry off Trabue Road. He watched the divers like everyone else, in a clip on the six o'clock news. The body was identified as Lainey Perkins two days later. Her throat had been sliced clean through, the cut strong and true. As far as detectives could figure, Missy confronted her walking to work one night, tipped by the Facebook post of the raccoon. Jarrod none the wiser thanks to a white lie Missy told about having to work an additional overnight shift that week. The problem of Lainey Perkins resolved, permanently, Missy moved Lainey's car down the street where it sat, undetected, until news broke of Perkins's murder and police cast a dragnet for evidence.

Hayes did some research and found out about a memorial for Lainey in Indianapolis. He called Shayne Townsley to see if he wanted to go over for it, but Townsley—when he finally reached him—said he just wasn't up for it. Hayes couldn't blame him. Some things, some memories, were better left in the past.

I was thinking a lot about redemption when I drafted "Through Thick and Thin," particularly the idea of when someone has—or hasn't—paid his dues for a past crime. If justice prevailed through the legal system, is it fair to burden an ex-offender with his actions long afterward, especially if he turned his life around and now contributes positively to society? How long must someone be punished? These are questions that come to light as my fictional private eye, Andy Hayes, takes a case that focuses on adultery at first but quickly careens toward a darker reality. This story was also a departure from my usual style with the private eye series as I decided to write in the third person instead of the first, which I felt gave it a slightly more somber tone.

BONUS STORY

Very few mystery stories have been reprinted as often, or as deservedly, as "The Problem of Cell 13," the masterpiece by Jacques Futrelle (1875–1912) that introduced one of the great detectives of American literature, Professor Augustus S. F. X. Van Dusen, better known by the sobriquet given to him by admirers, The Thinking Machine.

Futrelle's reputation stands on this single story although he wrote forty-four other stories about the irascible little scientist, as well as many other stories and novels about different detectives. "The Problem of Cell 13" is the first story to be published about The Thinking Machine, but Futrelle's wife, May, also a writer, stated that Futrelle wrote the The Chase of the Golden Plate, *a short novel about the detective, a year earlier. It was published in 1906, whereas the short story made its first appearance in the pages of the* Boston American *on October 30, 1905. It is here that Van Dusen issued his challenge, declaring that he could escape from any prison merely by using his exceptional brain. This intriguing situation turned out to be a temporary frustration for readers because the story was published as a serial in six parts. It took the form of a contest with $100 in prize money offered to the reader who came up with the best solution to the apparently insoluble predicament. The contest began on a Monday and concluded on Sunday, presumably for judges to read and grade the submissions, though it is not entirely impossible that skipping an installment on Saturday was an encouragement to buy the more expensive Sunday edition. The first prize was won by a gentleman named P. C. Hosmer, who was never again heard from in the world of mystery fiction.*

"The Problem of Cell 13" was first collected in book form in The Thinking Machine *(New York: Dodd, Mead, 1906).*

THE PROBLEM OF CELL 13

Jacques Futrelle

Practically all those letters remaining in the alphabet after Augustus S. F. X. Van Dusen was named were afterward acquired by that gentleman in the course of a brilliant scientific career, and, being honorably acquired, were tacked on to the other end. His name, therefore, taken with all that belonged to it, was a wonderfully imposing structure. He was a PhD, an LLD, an FRS, an MD, and an MDS. He was also some other things—just what he himself couldn't say—through recognition of his ability by various foreign educational and scientific institutions.

In appearance he was no less striking than in nomenclature. He was slender with the droop of the student in his thin shoulders and the pallor of a close, sedentary life on his clean-shaven face. His eyes wore a perpetual, forbidding squint—the squint of a man who studies little things—and, when they could be seen at all through his thick spectacles, were mere slits of watery blue. But above his eyes was his most striking feature. This was a tall, broad brow, almost abnormal in height and width, crowned by a heavy shock of bushy, yellow hair. All these things conspired to give him a peculiar, almost grotesque, personality.

Professor Van Dusen was remotely German. For generations his ancestors had been noted in the sciences; he was the logical result, the mastermind. First and above all he was a logician. At least thirty-five years of the half century or so of his existence had been devoted exclusively to proving that two and two always equal four, except in unusual cases, where they equal three or five, as the case may be. He stood broadly on the general proposition that all things that start must go somewhere, and was able to bring the concentrated mental force of his forefathers to bear on a given problem. Incidentally it may be remarked that Professor Van Dusen wore a No. 8 hat.

The world at large had heard vaguely of Professor Van Dusen as The Thinking Machine. It was a newspaper catchphrase applied to him at the time of a remarkable exhibition at chess; he had demonstrated then that a stranger to the game might, by the force of inevitable logic, defeat a champion who had devoted a lifetime to its study. The Thinking Machine! Perhaps that more nearly described him than all his honorary initials, for he spent week after week, month after month, in the seclusion of his small laboratory from which had gone forth thoughts that staggered scientific associates and deeply stirred the world at large.

THE PROBLEM OF CELL 13

It was only occasionally that The Thinking Machine had visitors, and these were usually men who, themselves high in the sciences, dropped in to argue a point and perhaps convince themselves. Two of these men, Dr. Charles Ransome and Alfred Fielding, called one evening to discuss some theory which is not of consequence here.

"Such a thing is impossible," declared Dr. Ransome emphatically, in the course of the conversation.

"Nothing is impossible," declared The Thinking Machine with equal emphasis. He always spoke petulantly. "The mind is master of all things. When science fully recognizes that fact a great advance will have been made."

"How about the airship?" asked Dr. Ransome.

"That's not impossible at all," asserted The Thinking Machine. "It will be invented sometime. I'd do it myself, but I'm busy." Dr. Ransome laughed tolerantly.

"I've heard you say such things before," he said. "But they mean nothing. Mind may be master of matter, but it hasn't yet found a way to apply itself. There are some things that can't be *thought* out of existence, or rather which would not yield to any amount of thinking."

"What, for instance?" demanded The Thinking Machine.

Dr. Ransome was thoughtful for a moment as he smoked.

"Well, say, prison walls," he replied. "No man can *think* himself out of a cell. If he could, there would be no prisoners."

"A man can so apply his brain and ingenuity that he can leave a cell, which is the same thing," snapped The Thinking Machine.

Dr. Ransome was slightly amused.

"Let's suppose a case," he said, after a moment. "Take a cell where prisoners under sentence of death are confined—men who are desperate and, maddened by fear, would take any chance to escape—suppose you were locked in such a cell. Could you escape?"

"Certainly," declared The Thinking Machine.

"Of course," said Mr. Fielding, who entered the conversation for the first time, "you might wreck the cell with an explosive—but inside, a prisoner, you couldn't have that."

"There would be nothing of that kind," said The Thinking Machine. "You might treat me precisely as you treated prisoners under sentence of death, and I would leave the cell."

"Not unless you entered it with tools prepared to get out," said Dr. Ransome.

The Thinking Machine was visibly annoyed and his blue eyes snapped.

"Lock me in any cell in any prison anywhere at any time, wearing only what is necessary, and I'll escape in a week," he declared, sharply.

Dr. Ransome sat up straight in the chair, interested. Mr. Fielding lighted a new cigar.

"You mean you could actually *think* yourself out?" asked Dr. Ransome.

"I would get out," was the response.

"Are you serious?"

"Certainly I am serious."

Dr. Ransome and Mr. Fielding were silent for a long time.

"Would you be willing to try it?" asked Mr. Fielding, finally.

"Certainly," said Professor Van Dusen, and there was a trace of irony in his voice. "I have done more asinine things than that to convince other men of less important truths."

The tone was offensive and there was an undercurrent strongly resembling anger on both sides. Of course it was an absurd thing, but Professor Van Dusen reiterated his willingness to undertake the escape and it was decided upon.

"To begin now," added Dr. Ransome.

"I'd prefer that it begin tomorrow," said The Thinking Machine, "because—"

"No, now," said Mr. Fielding, flatly. "You are arrested, figuratively, of course, without any warning, locked in a cell with no chance to communicate with friends, and left there with identically the same care and attention that would be given to a man under sentence of death. Are you willing?"

"All right, now, then," said The Thinking Machine, and he arose.

"Say, the death cell in Chisholm Prison."

"The death cell in Chisholm Prison."

"And what will you wear?"

"As little as possible," said The Thinking Machine. "Shoes, stockings, trousers, and a shirt."

"You will permit yourself to be searched, of course?"

"I am to be treated precisely as all prisoners are treated," said The Thinking Machine. "No more attention and no less."

There were some preliminaries to be arranged in the matter of obtaining permission for the test, but all three were influential men and everything was done satisfactorily by telephone, albeit the prison commissioners, to whom the experiment was explained on purely scientific grounds, were sadly bewildered. Professor Van Dusen would be the most distinguished prisoner they had ever entertained.

When The Thinking Machine had donned those things which he was to wear during his incarceration he called the little old woman who was his housekeeper, cook, and maidservant all in one.

"Martha," he said, "it is now twenty-seven minutes past nine o'clock. I am going away. One week from tonight, at half past nine, these gentlemen and one, possibly two, others will take supper with me here. Remember Dr. Ransome is very fond of artichokes."

The three men were driven to Chisholm Prison, where the warden was awaiting them, having been informed of the matter by telephone. He understood merely that the eminent Professor Van Dusen was to be his prisoner, if he could keep him, for one week; that he had committed no crime, but that he was to be treated as all other prisoners were treated.

"Search him," instructed Dr. Ransome.

The Thinking Machine was searched. Nothing was found on him; the pockets of the trousers were empty; the white, stiff-bosomed shirt had no pocket. The shoes and stockings were removed, examined, then replaced. As he watched all these preliminaries, and noted the pitiful, childlike physical weakness of the man—the colorless face, and the thin, white hands—Dr. Ransome almost regretted his part in the affair.

"Are you sure you want to do this?" he asked.

"Would you be convinced if I did not?" inquired The Thinking Machine in turn.

"No."

"All right. I'll do it."

What sympathy Dr. Ransome had was dissipated by the tone. It nettled him, and he resolved to see the experiment to the end; it would be a stinging reproof to egotism.

"It will be impossible for him to communicate with anyone outside?" he asked.

"Absolutely impossible," replied the warden. "He will not be permitted writing materials of any sort."

"And your jailers, would they deliver a message from him?"

"Not one word, directly or indirectly," said the warden. "You may rest assured of that. They will report anything he might say or turn over to me, anything he might give them."

"That seems entirely satisfactory," said Mr. Fielding, who was frankly interested in the problem.

"Of course, in the event he fails," said Dr. Ransome, "and asks for his liberty, you understand you are to set him free?"

"I understand," replied the warden.

The Thinking Machine stood listening, but had nothing to say until this was all ended, then:

"I should like to make three small requests. You may grant them or not, as you wish."

"No special favors, now," warned Mr. Fielding.

"I am asking none," was the stiff response. "I should like to have some tooth powder—buy it yourself to see that it is tooth powder—and I should like to have one five-dollar and two ten-dollar bills."

Dr. Ransome, Mr. Fielding, and the warden exchanged astonished glances. They were not surprised at the request for tooth powder, but were at the request for money.

"Is there any man with whom our friend would come in contact that he could bribe with twenty-five dollars?"

"Not for twenty-five hundred dollars," was the positive reply.

"Well, let him have them," said Mr. Fielding. "I think they are harmless enough."

"And what is the third request?" asked Dr. Ransome.

"I should like to have my shoes polished."

Again the astonished glances were exchanged. This last request was the height of absurdity, so they agreed to it. These things all being attended to, The Thinking Machine was led back into the prison from which he had undertaken to escape.

"Here is Cell Thirteen," said the warden, stopping three doors down the steel corridor. "This is where we keep condemned murderers. No one can leave it without my permission; and no one in it can communicate with the outside. I'll stake my reputation on that. It's only three doors back of my office and I can readily hear any unusual noise."

"Will this cell do, gentlemen?" asked The Thinking Machine. There was a touch of irony in his voice.

"Admirably," was the reply.

The heavy steel door was thrown open, there was a great scurrying and scampering of tiny feet, and The Thinking Machine passed into the gloom of the cell. Then the door was closed and double locked by the warden.

"What is that noise in there?" asked Dr. Ransome, through the bars.

"Rats—dozens of them," replied The Thinking Machine, tersely.

The three men, with final good nights, were turning away when The Thinking Machine called:

"What time is it exactly, Warden?"

"Eleven seventeen," replied the warden.

"Thanks. I will join you gentlemen in your office at half past eight o'clock one week from tonight," said The Thinking Machine.

"And if you do not?"

"There is no 'if' about it."

Chisholm Prison was a great, spreading structure of granite, four stories in all, which stood in the center of acres of open space. It was surrounded by a wall of solid masonry eighteen feet high, and so smoothly finished inside and out as to offer no foothold to a climber, no matter how expert. Atop of this fence, as a further precaution, was a five-foot fence of steel rods, each terminating in a keen point. This fence in itself marked an absolute deadline between freedom and imprisonment, for, even if a man escaped from his cell, it would seem impossible for him to pass the wall.

The yard, which on all sides of the prison building was twenty-five feet wide, that being the distance from the building to the wall, was by day an exercise ground for those prisoners to whom was granted the boon of occasional semi-liberty. But that was not for those in Cell 13. At all times of the day there were armed guards in the yard, four of them, one patrolling each side of the prison building.

By night the yard was almost as brilliantly lighted as by day. On each of the four sides was a great arc light which rose above the prison wall and gave to the guards a clear sight. The lights, too, brightly illuminated the spiked top of the wall. The wires which fed the arc lights ran up the side of the prison building on insulators and from the top story led out to the poles supporting the arc lights.

All these things were seen and comprehended by The Thinking Machine, who was only enabled to see out his closely barred cell window by standing on his bed. This was on the morning following his incarceration. He gathered, too, that the river lay over there beyond the wall somewhere, because he heard faintly the pulsation of a motor boat and high up in the air saw a river bird. From that same direction came the shouts of boys at play and the occasional crack of a batted ball. He knew then that between the prison wall and the river was an open space, a playground.

Chisholm Prison was regarded as absolutely safe. No man had ever escaped from it. The Thinking Machine, from his perch on the bed, seeing what he saw, could readily understand why. The walls of the cell, though built he judged twenty years before, were perfectly solid, and the window bars of new iron had not a shadow of rust on them. The window itself, even with the bars out, would be a difficult mode of egress because it was small.

Yet, seeing these things, The Thinking Machine was not discouraged. Instead, he thoughtfully squinted at the great arc light—there was bright sunlight now—and traced with his eyes the wire which led from it to the building. That electric wire, he reasoned, must come down the side of the building not a great distance from his cell. That might be worth knowing.

Cell 13 was on the same floor with the offices of the prison—that is, not in the basement, nor yet upstairs. There were only four steps up to the office floor, therefore the level of the floor must be only three or four feet above the ground. He couldn't see the ground directly beneath his window, but he could see it further out toward the wall. It would be an easy drop from the window. Well and good.

Then The Thinking Machine fell to remembering how he had come to the cell. First, there was the outside guard's booth, a part of the wall. There were two heavily barred gates there, both of steel. At this gate was one man always on guard. He admitted persons to the prison after much clanking of keys and locks, and let them out when ordered to do so. The warden's office was in the prison building, and in order to reach that official from the prison yard one had to pass a gate of solid steel with only a peephole in it. Then coming from that inner office to Cell 13, where he was now, one must pass a heavy wooden door and two steel doors into the corridors of the prison; and always there was the double-locked door of Cell 13 to reckon with.

There were then, The Thinking Machine recalled, seven doors to be overcome before one could pass from Cell 13 into the outer world, a free man. But against this was the fact that he was rarely interrupted. A jailer appeared at his cell door at six in the morning with a breakfast of prison fare; he would come again at noon, and again at six in the afternoon. At nine o'clock at night would come the inspection tour. That would be all.

"It's admirably arranged, this prison system," was the mental tribute paid by The Thinking Machine. "I'll have to study it a little when I get out. I had no idea there was such great care exercised in the prisons."

There was nothing, positively nothing, in his cell, except his iron bed, so firmly put together that no man could tear it to pieces save with sledges or a file. He had neither of these. There was not even a chair, or a small table, or a bit of tin or crockery. Nothing!

The jailer stood by when he ate, then took away the wooden spoon and bowl which he had used.

One by one these things sank into the brain of The Thinking Machine. When the last possibility had been considered he began an examination of his cell. From the roof, down the walls on all sides, he examined the stones and the cement between them. He stamped over the floor carefully time after time, but it was cement, perfectly solid. After the examination he sat on the edge of the iron bed and was lost in thought for a long time. For Professor Augustus S. F. X. Van Dusen, The Thinking Machine, had something to think about.

He was disturbed by a rat, which ran across his foot, then scampered away into a dark corner of the cell, frightened at its own daring. After a while The Thinking Machine, squinting steadily into the darkness of the corner where the rat had gone, was able to make out in the gloom many little beady eyes staring at him. He counted six pair, and there were perhaps others; he didn't see very well.

Then The Thinking Machine, from his seat on the bed, noticed for the first time the bottom of his cell door. There was an opening there of two inches between the steel bar and the floor. Still looking steadily at this opening, The Thinking Machine backed suddenly into the corner where he had seen the beady eyes. There was a great scampering of tiny feet, several squeaks of frightened rodents, and then silence.

None of the rats had gone out the door, yet there were none in the cell. Therefore there must be another way out of the cell, however small. The Thinking Machine, on hands and knees, started a search for this spot, feeling in the darkness with his long, slender fingers.

At last his search was rewarded. He came upon a small opening in the floor, level with the cement. It was perfectly round and somewhat larger than a silver dollar. This was the way the rats had gone. He put his fingers deep into the opening; it seemed to be a disused drainage pipe and was dry and dusty.

Having satisfied himself on this point, he sat on the bed again for an hour, then made another inspection of his surroundings through the small cell window. One of the outside guards stood directly opposite, beside the wall, and happened to be looking at the window of Cell 13 when the head of The Thinking Machine appeared. But the scientist didn't notice the guard.

Noon came and the jailer appeared with the prison dinner of repulsively plain food. At home The Thinking Machine merely ate to live; here he took what was offered without comment. Occasionally he spoke to the jailer who stood outside the door watching him.

"Any improvements made here in the last few years?" he asked.

"Nothing particularly," replied the jailer. "New wall was built four years ago."

"Anything done to the prison proper?"

"Painted the woodwork outside, and I believe about seven years ago a new system of plumbing was put in."

"Ah!" said the prisoner. "How far is the river over there?"

"About three hundred feet. The boys have a baseball ground between the wall and the river."

The Thinking Machine had nothing further to say just then, but when the jailer was ready to go he asked for some water.

"I get very thirsty here," he explained. "Would it be possible for you to leave a little water in a bowl for me?"

"I'll ask the warden," replied the jailer, and he went away.

Half an hour later he returned with water in a small earthen bowl.

"The warden says you may keep this bowl," he informed the prisoner. "But you must show it to me when I ask for it. If it is broken, it will be the last."

"Thank you," said The Thinking Machine. "I shan't break it."

The jailer went on about his duties. For just the fraction of a second it seemed that The Thinking Machine wanted to ask a question, but he didn't.

Two hours later this same jailer, in passing the door of Cell No. 13, heard a noise inside and stopped. The Thinking Machine was down on his hands and knees in a corner of the cell, and from that same corner came several frightened squeaks. The jailer looked on interestedly.

"Ah, I've got you," he heard the prisoner say.

"Got what?" he asked, sharply.

"One of these rats," was the reply. "See?" And between the scientist's long fingers the jailer saw a small gray rat struggling. The prisoner brought it over to the light and looked at it closely.

"It's a water rat," he said.

"Ain't you got anything better to do than to catch rats?" asked the jailer.

"It's disgraceful that they should be here at all," was the irritated reply. "Take this one away and kill it. There are dozens more where it came from."

The jailer took the wriggling, squirmy rodent and flung it down on the floor violently. It gave one squeak and lay still. Later he reported the incident to the warden, who only smiled.

Still later that afternoon the outside armed guard on the Cell 13 side of the prison looked up again at the window and saw the prisoner looking out. He saw a hand raised to the barred window and then something white fluttered to the ground, directly under the window of Cell 13. It was a little roll of linen, evidently of white shirting material, and tied around it was a five-dollar bill. The guard looked up at the window again, but the face had disappeared.

With a grim smile he took the little linen roll and the five-dollar bill to the warden's office. There together they deciphered something which was written on it with a queer sort of ink, frequently blurred. On the outside was this:

"Finder of this please deliver to Dr. Charles Ransome."

"Ah," said the warden, with a chuckle. "Plan of escape number one has gone wrong." Then, as an afterthought: "But why did he address it to Dr. Ransome?"

"And where did he get the pen and ink to write with?" asked the guard.

The warden looked at the guard and the guard looked at the warden. There was no apparent solution of that mystery. The warden studied the writing carefully, then shook his head.

"Well, let's see what he was going to say to Dr. Ransome," he said at length, still puzzled, and he unrolled the inner piece of linen.

"Well, if that—what—what do you think of that?" he asked, dazed.

The guard took the bit of linen and read this:—
"Epa cseot d'net niiy awe htto n'si sih. T."

The warden spent an hour wondering what sort of a cipher it was, and half an hour wondering why his prisoner should attempt to communicate with Dr. Ransome, who was the cause of his being there. After this the warden devoted some thought to the question of where the prisoner got writing materials, and what sort of writing materials he had. With the idea of illuminating this point, he examined the linen again. It was a torn part of a white shirt and had ragged edges.

Now it was possible to account for the linen, but what the prisoner had used to write with was another matter. The warden knew it would have been impossible for him to have either pen or pencil, and, besides, neither pen nor pencil had been used in this writing. What, then? The warden decided to investigate personally. The Thinking Machine was his prisoner; he had orders to hold his prisoners; if this one sought to escape by sending cipher messages to persons outside, he would stop it, as he would have stopped it in the case of any other prisoner.

The warden went back to Cell 13 and found The Thinking Machine on his hands and knees on the floor, engaged in nothing more alarming than catching rats. The prisoner heard the warden's step and turned to him quickly.

"It's disgraceful," he snapped, "these rats. There are scores of them."

"Other men have been able to stand them," said the warden. "Here is another shirt for you—let me have the one you have on."

"Why?" demanded The Thinking Machine, quickly. His tone was hardly natural, his manner suggested actual perturbation.

"You have attempted to communicate with Dr. Ransome," said the warden severely. "As my prisoner, it is my duty to put a stop to it."

The Thinking Machine was silent for a moment.

"All right," he said, finally. "Do your duty."

The warden smiled grimly. The prisoner arose from the floor and removed the white shirt, putting on instead a striped convict shirt the warden had brought. The warden took the white shirt eagerly, and then and there compared the pieces of linen on which was written the cipher with certain torn places in the shirt. The Thinking Machine looked on curiously.

"The guard brought *you* those, then?" he asked.

"He certainly did," replied the warden triumphantly. "And that ends your first attempt to escape."

The Thinking Machine watched the warden as he, by comparison, established to his own satisfaction that only two pieces of linen had been torn from the white shirt.

"What did you write this with?" demanded the warden.

"I should think it a part of your duty to find out," said The Thinking Machine, irritably.

The warden started to say some harsh things, then restrained himself and made a minute search of the cell and of the prisoner instead. He found absolutely nothing; not even a match or toothpick which might have been used for a pen. The same mystery surrounded the fluid with which the cipher had been written. Although the warden left Cell 13 visibly annoyed, he took the torn shirt in triumph.

"Well, writing notes on a shirt won't get him out, that's certain," he told himself with some complacency. He put the linen scraps into his desk to await developments. "If that man escapes from that cell I'll—hang it—I'll resign."

On the third day of his incarceration The Thinking Machine openly attempted to bribe his way out. The jailer had brought his dinner and was leaning against the barred door, waiting, when The Thinking Machine began the conversation.

"The drainage pipes of the prison lead to the river, don't they?" he asked.

"Yes," said the jailer.

"I suppose they are very small."

"Too small to crawl through, if that's what you're thinking about," was the grinning response.

There was silence until The Thinking Machine finished his meal. Then:

"You know I'm not a criminal, don't you?"

"Yes."

"And that I've a perfect right to be freed if I demand it?"

"Yes."

"Well, I came here believing that I could make my escape," said the prisoner, and his squint eyes studied the face of the jailer. "Would you consider a financial reward for aiding me to escape?"

The jailer, who happened to be an honest man, looked at the slender, weak figure of the prisoner, at the large head with its mass of yellow hair, and was almost sorry.

"I guess prisons like these were not built for the likes of you to get out of," he said, at last.

"But would you consider a proposition to help me get out?" the prisoner insisted, almost beseechingly.

"No," said the jailer, shortly.

"Five hundred dollars," urged The Thinking Machine. "I am not a criminal."

"No," said the jailer.

"A thousand?"

"No," again said the jailer, and he started away hurriedly to escape further temptation. Then he turned back. "If you should give me ten thousand dollars I couldn't get you out. You'd have to pass through seven doors, and I only have the keys to two."

Then he told the warden all about it.

"Plan number two fails," said the warden, smiling grimly. "First a cipher, then bribery."

When the jailer was on his way to Cell 13 at six o'clock, again bearing food to The Thinking Machine, he paused, startled by the unmistakable scrape, scrape of steel against steel. It stopped at the sound of his steps, then craftily the jailer, who was beyond the prisoner's range of vision, resumed his tramping, the sound being apparently that of a man going away from Cell 13. As a matter of fact he was in the same spot.

After a moment there came again the steady scrape, scrape, and the jailer crept cautiously on tiptoes to the door and peered between the bars. The Thinking Machine was standing on the iron bed working at the bars of the little window. He was using a file, judging from the backward and forward swing of his arms.

Cautiously the jailer crept back to the office, summoned the warden in person, and they returned to Cell 13 on tiptoes. The steady scrape was still audible. The warden listened to satisfy himself and then suddenly appeared at the door.

"Well?" he demanded, and there was a smile on his face.

The Thinking Machine glanced back from his perch on the bed and leaped suddenly to the floor, making frantic efforts to hide something.

The warden went in, with hand extended. "Give it up," he said.

"No," said the prisoner, sharply.

"Come, give it up," urged the warden. "I don't want to have to search you again."

"No," repeated the prisoner.

"What was it—a file?" asked the warden.

The Thinking Machine was silent and stood squinting at the warden with something very nearly approaching disappointment on his face—nearly, but not quite. The warden was almost sympathetic.

"Plan number three fails, eh?" he asked, good-naturedly. "Too bad, isn't it?"

The prisoner didn't say.

"Search him," instructed the warden.

The jailer searched the prisoner carefully. At last, artfully concealed in the waistband of the trousers, he found a piece of steel about two inches long, with one side curved like a half moon.

"Ah," said the warden, as he received it from the jailer. "From your shoe heel," and he smiled pleasantly.

The jailer continued his search and on the other side of the trousers waistband found another piece of steel identical with the first. The edges showed where they had been worn against the bars of the window.

"You couldn't saw a way through those bars with these," said the warden.

"I could have," said The Thinking Machine firmly.

"In six months, perhaps," said the warden, good-naturedly.

The warden shook his head slowly as he gazed into the slightly flushed face of his prisoner.

"Ready to give it up?" he asked.

"I haven't started yet," was the prompt reply.

Then came another exhaustive search of the cell. Carefully the two men went over it, finally turning out the bed and searching that. Nothing. The warden in person climbed upon the bed and examined the bars of the window where the prisoner had been sawing. When he looked he was amused.

"Just made it a little bright by hard rubbing," he said to the prisoner, who stood looking on with a somewhat crestfallen air. The warden grasped the iron bars in his strong hands and tried to shake them. They were immovable, set firmly in the solid granite. He examined each in turn and found them all satisfactory. Finally he climbed down from the bed.

"Give it up, Professor," he advised.

The Thinking Machine shook his head and the warden and jailer passed on again. As they disappeared down the corridor The Thinking Machine sat on the edge of the bed with his head in his hands.

"He's crazy to try to get out of that cell," commented the jailer.

"Of course he can't get out," said the warden. "But he's clever. I would like to know what he wrote that cipher with."

It was four o'clock next morning when an awful, heart-racking shriek of terror resounded through the great prison. It came from a cell, somewhere about the center, and its tone told a tale of horror, agony, terrible fear. The warden heard and with three of his men rushed into the long corridor leading to Cell 13.

As they ran there came again that awful cry. It died away in a sort of wail. The white faces of prisoners appeared at cell doors upstairs and down, staring out wonderingly, frightened.

"It's that fool in Cell Thirteen," grumbled the warden.

He stopped and stared in as one of the jailers flashed a lantern. "That fool in Cell Thirteen" lay comfortably on his cot, flat on his back with his mouth open, snoring. Even as they looked there came again the piercing cry, from somewhere above. The warden's face blanched a little as he started up the stairs. There on the top floor he found a man in Cell 43, directly above Cell 13, but two floors higher, cowering in a corner of his cell.

"What's the matter?" demanded the warden.

"Thank God you've come," exclaimed the prisoner, and he cast himself against the bars of his cell.

"What is it?" demanded the warden again.

He threw open the door and went in. The prisoner dropped on his knees and clasped the warden about the body. His face was white with terror, his eyes were widely distended, and he was shuddering. His hands, icy cold, clutched at the warden's.

"Take me out of this cell, please take me out," he pleaded.

"What's the matter with you, anyhow?" insisted the warden, impatiently.

"I heard something—something," said the prisoner, and his eyes roved nervously around the cell.

"What did you hear?"

"I—I can't tell you," stammered the prisoner. Then, in a sudden burst of terror: "Take me out of this cell—put me anywhere—but take me out of here."

The warden and the three jailers exchanged glances.

"Who is this fellow? What's he accused of?" asked the warden.

"Joseph Ballard," said one of the jailers. "He's accused of throwing acid in a woman's face. She died from it."

"But they can't prove it," gasped the prisoner. "They can't prove it. Please put me in some other cell."

He was still clinging to the warden, and that official threw his arms off roughly. Then for a time he stood looking at the cowering wretch, who seemed possessed of all the wild, unreasoning terror of a child.

"Look here, Ballard," said the warden, finally, "if you heard anything, I want to know what it was. Now tell me."

"I can't, I can't," was the reply. He was sobbing.

"Where did it come from?"

"I don't know. Everywhere—nowhere. I just heard it."

"What was it—a voice?"

"Please don't make me answer," pleaded the prisoner.

"You must answer," said the warden, sharply.

"It was a voice—but—but it wasn't human," was the sobbing reply.

"Voice, but not human?" repeated the warden, puzzled.

"It sounded muffled and—and far away—and ghostly," explained the man.

"Did it come from inside or outside the prison?"

"It didn't seem to come from anywhere—it was just here, here, everywhere. I heard it. I heard it."

For an hour the warden tried to get the story, but Ballard had become suddenly obstinate and would say nothing—only pleaded to be placed in another cell, or to have one of the jailers remain near him until daylight. These requests were gruffly refused.

"And see here," said the warden, in conclusion, "if there's any more of this screaming I'll put you in the padded cell."

Then the warden went his way, a sadly puzzled man. Ballard sat at his cell door until daylight, his face, drawn and white with terror, pressed against the bars, and looked out into the prison with wide, staring eyes.

That day, the fourth since the incarceration of The Thinking Machine, was enlivened considerably by the volunteer prisoner, who spent most of his time at the little window of his cell. He began proceedings by throwing another piece of linen down to the guard, who picked it up dutifully and took it to the warden. On it was written: "Only three days more."

The warden was in no way surprised at what he read; he understood that The Thinking Machine meant only three days more of his imprisonment, and he regarded the note as a boast. But how was the thing written? Where had The Thinking Machine found this new piece of linen? Where? How? He carefully examined the linen. It was white, of fine texture, shirting material. He took the shirt which he had taken and carefully fitted the two original pieces of the linen to the torn places. This third piece was entirely superfluous; it didn't fit anywhere, and yet it was unmistakably the same goods.

"And where—where does he get anything to write with?" demanded the warden of the world at large.

Still later on the fourth day The Thinking Machine, through the window of his cell, spoke to the armed guard outside.

"What day of the month is it?" he asked.

"The fifteenth," was the answer.

The Thinking Machine made a mental astronomical calculation and satisfied himself that the moon would not rise until after nine o'clock that night. Then he asked another question: "Who attends to those arc lights?"

"Man from the company."

"You have no electricians in the building?"

"No."

"I should think you could save money if you had your own man."

"None of my business," replied the guard.

The guard noticed The Thinking Machine at the cell window frequently during that day, but always the face seemed listless and there was a certain wistfulness in the squint eyes behind the glasses. After a while he accepted the presence of the leonine head as a matter of course. He had seen other prisoners do the same thing; it was the longing for the outside world.

That afternoon, just before the day guard was relieved, the head appeared at the window again, and The Thinking Machine's hand held something out between the bars. It fluttered to the ground and the guard picked it up. It was a five-dollar bill.

"That's for you," called the prisoner.

As usual, the guard took it to the warden. That gentleman looked at it suspiciously; he looked at everything that came from Cell 13 with suspicion.

"He said it was for me," explained the guard.

"It's a sort of a tip, I suppose," said the warden. "I see no particular reason why you shouldn't accept—"

Suddenly he stopped. He had remembered that The Thinking Machine had gone into Cell 13 with one five-dollar bill and two ten-dollar bills; twenty-five dollars in all. Now a five-dollar bill had been tied around the first pieces of linen that came from the cell. The warden still had it, and to convince himself he took it out and looked at it. It was five dollars; yet here was another five dollars, and The Thinking Machine had only had ten-dollar bills.

"Perhaps somebody changed one of the bills for him," he thought at last, with a sigh of relief.

But then and there he made up his mind. He would search Cell 13 as a cell was never before searched in this world. When a man could write at will, and change money, and do other wholly inexplicable things, there was something radically wrong with his prison. He planned to enter the cell at night—three o'clock would be an excellent time. The Thinking Machine must do all the weird things he did sometime. Night seemed the most reasonable.

Thus it happened that the warden stealthily descended upon Cell 13 that night at three o'clock. He paused at the door and listened. There was no sound save the steady, regular breathing of the prisoner. The keys unfastened the double locks with scarcely a clank, and the warden entered, locking the door behind him. Suddenly he flashed his dark lantern in the face of the recumbent figure.

If the warden had planned to startle The Thinking Machine he was mistaken, for that individual merely opened his eyes quietly, reached for his glasses and inquired, in a most matter-of-fact tone: "Who is it?"

It would be useless to describe the search that the warden made. It was minute. Not one inch of the cell or the bed was overlooked. He found the round hole in the floor, and with a flash of inspiration thrust his thick fingers into it. After a moment of fumbling there he drew up something and looked at it in the light of his lantern.

"Ugh!" he exclaimed.

The thing he had taken out was a rat—a dead rat. His inspiration fled as a mist before the sun. But he continued the search. The Thinking Machine, without a word, arose and kicked the rat out of the cell into the corridor.

The warden climbed on the bed and tried the steel bars in the tiny window. They were perfectly rigid; every bar of the door was the same.

Then the warden searched the prisoner's clothing, beginning at the shoes. Nothing hidden in them! Then the trousers' waistband. Still nothing! Then the pockets of the trousers. From one side he drew out some paper money and examined it.

"Five one-dollar bills," he gasped.

"That's right," said the prisoner.

"But the—you had two tens and a five—what the—how do you do it?"

"That's my business," said The Thinking Machine.

"Did any of my men change this money for you—on your word of honor?"

The Thinking Machine paused just a fraction of a second. "No," he said.

"Well, do you make it?" asked the warden. He was prepared to believe anything.

"That's my business," again said the prisoner.

The warden glared at the eminent scientist fiercely. He felt—he knew—that this man was making a fool of him, yet he didn't know how. If he were a real prisoner he would get the truth—but, then, perhaps, those inexplicable things which had happened would not have been brought before him so sharply. Neither of the men spoke for a long time, then suddenly the warden turned fiercely and left the cell, slamming the door behind him. He didn't dare to speak, then.

He glanced at the clock. It was ten minutes to four. He had hardly settled himself in bed when again came that heart-breaking shriek through the prison. With a few muttered words, which, while not elegant, were highly expressive, he relighted his lantern and rushed through the prison again to the cell on the upper floor.

Again Ballard was crushing himself against the steel door, shrieking, shrieking at the top of his voice. He stopped only when the warden flashed his lamp in the cell.

"Take me out, take me out," he screamed. "I did it, I did it, I killed her. Take it away."

"Take what away?" asked the warden.

"I threw the acid in her face—I did it—I confess. Take me out of here."

Ballard's condition was pitiable; it was only an act of mercy to let him out into the corridor. There he crouched in a corner, like an animal at bay, and clasped his hands to his ears. It took half an hour to calm him sufficiently for him to speak. Then he told incoherently what had happened. On the night before at four o'clock he had heard a voice—a sepulchral voice, muffled and wailing in tone.

"What did it say?" asked the warden, curiously.

"Acid—acid—acid!" gasped the prisoner. "It accused me. Acid! I threw the acid, and the woman died. Oh!" It was a long, shuddering, wail of terror.

"Acid?" echoed the warden, puzzled. The case was beyond him.

"Acid. That's all I heard—that one word, repeated several times. There were other things, too, but I didn't hear them."

"That was last night, eh?" asked the warden. "What happened tonight—what frightened you just now?"

"It was the same thing," gasped the prisoner. "Acid—acid—acid!" He covered his face with his hands and sat shivering. "It was acid I used on her, but I didn't mean to kill her. I just heard the words. It was something accusing me—accusing me." He mumbled, and was silent.

"Did you hear anything else?"

"Yes—but I couldn't understand—only a little bit—just a word or two."

"Well, what was it?"

"I heard 'acid' three times, then I heard a long, moaning sound, then—then—I heard 'number eight hat.' I heard that twice."

"Number eight hat," repeated the warden. "What the devil—number eight hat? Accusing voices of conscience have never talked about number eight hats, so far as I ever heard."

"He's insane," said one of the jailers, with an air of finality.

"I believe you," said the warden. "He must be. He probably heard something and got frightened. He's trembling now. Number eight hat! What the—"

When the fifth day of The Thinking Machine's imprisonment rolled around the warden was wearing a haunted look. He was anxious for the end of the thing. He could not help but feel that his distinguished prisoner had been amusing himself. And if this were so, The Thinking Machine had lost none of his sense of humor. For on this fifth day he flung down another linen note to the outside guard, bearing the words: "Only two days more." Also he flung down half a dollar.

Now the warden knew—he *knew*—that the man in Cell 13 didn't have any half-dollars—he *couldn't* have any half-dollars, no more than he could have pen and ink and linen, and yet he did have them. It was a condition, not a theory; that is one reason why the warden was wearing a hunted look.

That ghastly, uncanny thing, too, about "acid" and "number eight hat" clung to him tenaciously. They didn't mean anything, of course, merely the ravings of an insane murderer who had been driven by fear to confess his crime, still there were so many things that "didn't mean anything" happening in the prison now since The Thinking Machine was there.

On the sixth day the warden received a postal stating that Dr. Ransome and Mr. Fielding would be at Chisholm Prison on the following evening, Thursday, and in the event Professor Van Dusen had not yet escaped—and they presumed he had not because they had not heard from him—they would meet him there.

"In the event he had not yet escaped!" The warden smiled grimly. Escaped!

The Thinking Machine enlivened this day for the warden with three notes. They were on the usual linen and bore generally on the appointment at half past eight o'clock Thursday night, which appointment the scientist had made at the time of his imprisonment.

On the afternoon of the seventh day the warden passed Cell 13 and glanced in. The Thinking Machine was lying on the iron bed, apparently sleeping lightly. The cell appeared precisely as it always did from a casual glance. The warden would swear that no man was going to leave it between that hour—it was then four o'clock—and half past eight o'clock that evening.

On his way back past the cell the warden heard the steady breathing again, and coming close to the door looked in. He wouldn't have done so if The Thinking Machine had been looking, but now—well, it was different.

A ray of light came through the high window and fell on the face of the sleeping man. It occurred to the warden for the first time that his prisoner appeared haggard and weary. Just then The Thinking Machine stirred slightly and the warden hurried on up the corridor guiltily. That evening after six o'clock he saw the jailer. "Everything all right in Cell Thirteen?" he asked.

"Yes, sir," replied the jailer. "He didn't eat much, though."

It was with a feeling of having done his duty that the warden received Dr. Ransome and Mr. Fielding shortly after seven o'clock. He intended to show them the linen notes and lay before them the full story of his woes, which was a long one. But before this came to pass the guard from the river side of the prison yard entered the office.

"The arc light in my side of the yard won't light," he informed the warden.

"Confound it, that man's a hoodoo," thundered the official. "Everything has happened since he's been here."

The guard went back to his post in the darkness, and the warden phoned to the electric light company.

"This is Chisholm Prison," he said through the phone. "Send three or four men down here quick, to fix an arc light."

The reply was evidently satisfactory, for the warden hung up the receiver and passed out into the yard. While Dr. Ransome and Mr. Fielding sat waiting, the guard at the outer gate came in with a special delivery letter. Dr. Ransome happened to notice the address, and, when the guard went out, looked at the letter more closely.

"By George!" he exclaimed.

"What is it?" asked Mr. Fielding.

Silently the doctor offered the letter. Mr. Fielding examined it closely.

"Coincidence," he said. "It must be."

It was nearly eight o'clock when the warden returned to his office. The electricians had arrived in a wagon, and were now at work. The warden pressed the buzz-button communicating with the man at the outer gate in the wall.

"How many electricians came in?" he asked, over the short phone. "Four? Three workmen in jumpers and overalls and the manager? Frock coat and silk hat? All right. Be certain that only four go out. That's all."

He turned to Dr. Ransome and Mr. Fielding.

"We have to be careful here—particularly," and there was broad sarcasm in his tone, "since we have scientists locked up."

The warden picked up the special delivery letter carelessly, and then began to open it.

"When I read this I want to tell you gentlemen something about how—Great Caesar!" he ended, suddenly, as he glanced at the letter. He sat with mouth open, motionless, from astonishment.

"What is it?" asked Mr. Fielding.

"A special delivery letter from Cell Thirteen," gasped the warden. "An invitation to supper."

"What?" and the two others arose, unanimously.

The warden sat dazed, staring at the letter for a moment, then called sharply to a guard outside in the corridor.

"Run down to Cell Thirteen and see if that man's in there."

The guard went as directed, while Dr. Ransome and Mr. Fielding examined the letter.

"It's Van Dusen's handwriting; there's no question of that," said Dr. Ransome. "I've seen too much of it."

Just then the buzz on the telephone from the outer gate sounded, and the warden, in a semi-trance, picked up the receiver.

"Hello! Two reporters, eh? Let 'em come in." He turned suddenly to the doctor and Mr. Fielding. "Why, the man *can't* be out. He must be in his cell."

Just at that moment the guard returned.

"He's still in his cell, sir," he reported. "I saw him. He's lying down."

"There, I told you so," said the warden, and he breathed freely again. "But how did he mail that letter?"

There was a rap on the steel door which led from the jail yard into the warden's office.

"It's the reporters," said the warden. "Let them in," he instructed the guard; then to the two other gentlemen: "Don't say anything about this before them, because I'd never hear the last of it."

The door opened, and the two men from the front gate entered.

"Good-evening, gentlemen," said one. That was Hutchinson Hatch; the warden knew him well.

"Well?" demanded the other, irritably. "I'm here." That was The Thinking Machine.

He squinted belligerently at the warden, who sat with mouth agape. For the moment that official had nothing to say. Dr. Ransome and Mr. Fielding were amazed, but they didn't know what the warden knew. They were only amazed; he was paralyzed. Hutchinson Hatch, the reporter, took in the scene with greedy eyes.

"How—how—how did you do it?" gasped the warden, finally.

"Come back to the cell," said The Thinking Machine, in the irritated voice which his scientific associates knew so well.

The warden, still in a condition bordering on trance, led the way.

"Flash your light in there," directed The Thinking Machine.

The warden did so. There was nothing unusual in the appearance of the cell, and there—there on the bed lay the figure of The Thinking Machine. Certainly! There was the yellow hair! Again the warden looked at the man beside him and wondered at the strangeness of his own dreams.

With trembling hands he unlocked the cell door and The Thinking Machine passed inside.

"See here," he said.

He kicked at the steel bars in the bottom of the cell door and three of them were pushed out of place. A fourth broke off and rolled away in the corridor.

"And here, too," directed the erstwhile prisoner as he stood on the bed to reach the small window. He swept his hand across the opening and every bar came out.

"What's this in bed?" demanded the warden, who was slowly recovering.

"A wig," was the reply. "Turn down the cover."

The warden did so. Beneath it lay a large coil of strong rope, thirty feet or more, a dagger, three files, ten feet of electric wire, a thin, powerful pair of steel pliers, a small tack hammer with its handle, and—and a derringer pistol.

"How did you do it?" demanded the warden.

"You gentlemen have an engagement to supper with me at half past nine o'clock," said The Thinking Machine. "Come on, or we shall be late."

"But how did you do it?" insisted the warden.

"Don't ever think you can hold any man who can use his brain," said The Thinking Machine. "Come on; we shall be late."

It was an impatient supper party in the rooms of Professor Van Dusen and a somewhat silent one. The guests were Dr. Ransome, Alfred Fielding, the warden, and Hutchinson Hatch, reporter. The meal was served to the minute, in accordance with Professor Van Dusen's instructions of one week before; Dr. Ransome found the artichokes delicious. At last the supper was finished and The Thinking Machine turned full on Dr. Ransome and squinted at him fiercely.

"Do you believe it now?" he demanded.

"I do," replied Dr. Ransome.

"Do you admit that it was a fair test?"

"I do."

With the others, particularly the warden, he was waiting anxiously for the explanation. "Suppose you tell us how—" began Mr. Fielding.

"Yes, tell us how," said the warden.

The Thinking Machine readjusted his glasses, took a couple of preparatory squints at his audience, and began the story. He told it from the beginning logically; and no man ever talked to more interested listeners.

"My agreement was," he began, "to go into a cell, carrying nothing except what was necessary to wear, and to leave that cell within a week. I had never seen Chisholm Prison. When I went into the cell I asked for tooth powder, two ten and one five-dollar bills, and also to have my shoes blacked. Even if these requests had been refused it would not have mattered seriously. But you agreed to them.

"I knew there would be nothing in the cell which you thought I might use to advantage. So when the warden locked the door on me I was apparently helpless, unless I could turn three seemingly innocent things to use. They were things which would have been permitted any prisoner under sentence of death, were they not, warden?"

"Tooth powder and polished shoes, yes, but not money," replied the warden.

"Anything is dangerous in the hands of a man who knows how to use it," went on The Thinking Machine. "I did nothing that first night but sleep and chase rats." He glared at the warden. "When the matter was broached I knew I could do nothing that night, so suggested next day. You gentlemen thought I wanted time to arrange an escape with outside assistance, but this was not true. I knew I could communicate with whom I pleased, when I pleased."

The warden stared at him a moment, then went on smoking solemnly.

"I was aroused next morning at six o'clock by the jailer with my breakfast," continued the scientist. "He told me dinner was at twelve and supper at six. Between these times, I gathered, I would be pretty much to myself. So immediately after breakfast I examined my outside surroundings from my cell window. One look told me it would be useless to try to scale the wall, even should I decide to leave my cell by the window, for my purpose was to leave not only the cell, but the prison. Of course, I could have gone over the wall, but it would have taken me longer to lay my plans that way. Therefore, for the moment, I dismissed all idea of that.

"From this first observation I knew the river was on that side of the prison, and that there was also a playground there. Subsequently these surmises were verified by a keeper. I knew then one important thing—that anyone might approach the prison wall from that side if necessary without attracting any particular attention. That was well to remember. I remembered it.

"But the outside thing which most attracted my attention was the feed wire to the arc light which ran within a few feet—probably three or four—of my cell window. I knew that would be valuable in the event I found it necessary to cut off that arc light."

"Oh, you shut it off tonight, then?" asked the warden.

"Having learned all I could from that window," resumed The Thinking Machine, without heeding the interruption, "I considered the idea of escaping through the prison proper. I recalled just how I had come into the cell, which I knew would be the only way. Seven doors lay between me and the outside. So, also for the time being, I gave up the idea of escaping that way. And I couldn't go through the solid granite walls of the cell."

The Thinking Machine paused for a moment and Dr. Ransome lighted a new cigar. For several minutes there was silence, then the scientific jailbreaker went on:

"While I was thinking about these things a rat ran across my foot. It suggested a new line of thought. There were at least half a dozen rats in the cell—I could see their beady eyes. Yet I had noticed none come under the cell door. I frightened them purposely and watched the cell door to see if they went out that way. They did not, but they were gone. Obviously they went another way. Another way meant another opening.

"I searched for this opening and found it. It was an old drain pipe, long unused and partly choked with dirt and dust. But this was the way the rats had come. They came from somewhere. Where? Drain pipes usually lead outside prison grounds. This one probably led to the river, or near it. The rats must therefore come from that direction. If they came a part of the way, I reasoned that they came all the way, because it was extremely unlikely that a solid iron or lead pipe would have any hole in it except at the exit.

"When the jailer came with my luncheon he told me two important things, although he didn't know it. One was that a new system of plumbing had been put in the prison seven years before; another that the river was only three hundred feet away. Then I knew positively that the pipe was a part of an old system; I knew, too, that it slanted generally toward the river. But did the pipe end in the water or on land?

"This was the next question to be decided. I decided it by catching several of the rats in the cell. My jailer was surprised to see me engaged in this work. I examined at least a dozen of them. They were perfectly dry; they had come through the pipe, and, most important of all, they were *not house rats, but field rats*. The other end of the pipe was on land, then, outside the prison walls. So far, so good.

"Then, I knew that if I worked freely from this point I must attract the warden's attention in another direction. You see, by telling the warden that I had come there to escape you made the test more severe, because I had to trick him by false scents."

The warden looked up with a sad expression in his eyes.

"The first thing was to make him think I was trying to communicate with you, Dr. Ransome. So I wrote a note on a piece of linen I tore from my shirt, addressed it to Dr. Ransome, tied a five-dollar bill around it and threw it out the window. I knew the guard would take it to the warden, but I rather hoped the warden would send it as addressed. Have you that first linen note, Warden?"

The warden produced the cipher.

"What the deuce does it mean, anyhow?" he asked.

"Read it backward, beginning with the *T* signature and disregard the division into words," instructed The Thinking Machine.

The warden did so.

"*T-h-i-s*, this," he spelled, studied it a moment, then read it off, grinning: "This is not the way I intend to escape.

"Well, now what do you think o' that?" he demanded, still grinning.

"I knew that would attract your attention, just as it did," said The Thinking Machine, "and if you really found out what it was it would be a sort of gentle rebuke."

"What did you write it with?" asked Dr. Ransome, after he had examined the linen and passed it to Mr. Fielding.

"This," said the erstwhile prisoner, and he extended his foot. On it was the shoe he had worn in prison, though the polish was gone—scraped off clean. "The shoe blacking, moistened with water, was my ink; the metal tip of the shoe lace made a fairly good pen."

The warden looked up and suddenly burst into a laugh, half of relief, half of amusement.

"You're a wonder," he said, admiringly. "Go on."

"That precipitated a search of my cell by the warden, as I had intended," continued The Thinking Machine. "I was anxious to get the warden into the habit of searching my cell, so that finally, constantly finding nothing, he would get disgusted and quit. This at last happened, practically."

The warden blushed.

"He then took my white shirt away and gave me a prison shirt. He was satisfied that those two pieces of the shirt were all that was missing. But while he was searching my cell I had another piece of that same shirt, about nine inches square, rolled into a small ball in my mouth."

"Nine inches of that shirt?" demanded the warden. "Where did it come from?"

"The bosoms of all stiff white shirts are of triple thickness," was the explanation. "I tore out the inside thickness, leaving the bosom only two thicknesses. I knew you wouldn't see it. So much for that."

There was a little pause, and the warden looked from one to another of the men with a sheepish grin.

"Having disposed of the warden for the time being by giving him something else to think about, I took my first serious step toward freedom," said Professor Van Dusen. "I knew, within reason, that the pipe led somewhere to the playground outside; I knew a great many boys played there; I knew that rats came into my cell from out there. Could I communicate with someone outside with these things at hand?

"First was necessary, I saw, a long and fairly reliable thread, so—but here," he pulled up his trousers legs and showed that the tops of both stockings, of fine, strong lisle, were gone. "I unraveled those—after I got them started it wasn't difficult—and I had easily a quarter of a mile of thread that I could depend on.

"Then on half of my remaining linen I wrote, laboriously enough I assure you, a letter explaining my situation to this gentleman here," and he indicated Hutchinson Hatch. "I knew he would assist me—for the value of the newspaper story. I tied firmly to this linen letter a ten-dollar bill—there is no surer way of attracting the eye of anyone—and wrote on the linen: 'Finder of this deliver to Hutchinson Hatch, *Daily American*, who will give another ten dollars for the information.'

"The next thing was to get this note outside on that playground where a boy might find it. There were two ways, but I chose the best. I took one of the rats—I became adept in catching them—tied the linen and money firmly to one leg, fastened my lisle thread to another, and turned him loose in the drain pipe. I reasoned that the natural fright of the rodent would make him run until he was outside the pipe and then out on earth he would probably stop to gnaw off the linen and money.

"From the moment the rat disappeared into that dusty pipe I became anxious. I was taking so many chances. The rat might gnaw the string, of which I held one end; other rats might gnaw it; the rat might run out of the pipe and leave the linen and money where they would never be found; a thousand other things might have happened. So began some nervous hours, but the fact that the rat ran on until only a few feet of the string remained in my cell made me think he was outside the pipe. I had carefully instructed Mr. Hatch what to do in case the note reached him. The question was: Would it reach him?

"This done, I could only wait and make other plans in case this one failed. I openly attempted to bribe my jailer, and learned from him that he held the keys to only two of seven doors between me and freedom. Then I did something else to make the warden nervous. I took the steel supports out of the heels of my shoes and made a pretense of sawing the bars of my cell window. The warden raised a pretty row about that. He developed, too, the habit of shaking the bars of my cell window to see if they were solid. They were—then."

Again the warden grinned. He had ceased being astonished.

"With this one plan I had done all I could and could only wait to see what happened," the scientist went on. "I couldn't know whether my note had been delivered or even found, or whether the rat had gnawed it up. And I didn't dare to draw back through the pipe that one slender thread which connected me with the outside.

"When I went to bed that night I didn't sleep, for fear there would come the slight signal twitch at the thread which was to tell me that Mr. Hatch had received the note. At half past three o'clock, I judge, I felt this twitch, and no prisoner actually under sentence of death ever welcomed a thing more heartily."

The Thinking Machine stopped and turned to the reporter.

"You'd better explain just what you did," he said.

"The linen note was brought to me by a small boy who had been playing baseball," said Mr. Hatch. "I immediately saw a big story in it, so I gave the boy another ten dollars, and got several spools of silk, some twine, and a roll of light, pliable wire. The professor's note suggested that I have the finder of the note show me just where it was picked up, and told me to make my search from there, beginning at two o'clock in the morning. If I found the other end of the thread I was to twitch it gently three times, then a fourth.

"I began the search with a small-bulb electric light. It was an hour and twenty minutes before I found the end of the drainpipe, half hidden in weeds. The pipe was very large there, say twelve inches across. Then I found the end of the lisle thread, twitched it as directed and immediately I got an answering twitch.

"Then I fastened the silk to this and Professor Van Dusen began to pull it into his cell. I nearly had heart disease for fear the string would break. To the end of the silk I fastened the twine, and when that had been pulled in I tied on the wire. Then that was drawn into the pipe and we had a substantial line, which rats couldn't gnaw, from the mouth of the drain into the cell."

The Thinking Machine raised his hand and Hatch stopped.

"All this was done in absolute silence," said the scientist. "But when the wire reached my hand I could have shouted. Then we tried another experiment, which Mr. Hatch was prepared for. I tested the pipe as a speaking tube. Neither of us could hear very clearly, but I dared not speak loud for fear of attracting attention in the prison. At last I made him understand what I wanted immediately. He seemed to have great difficulty in understanding when I asked for nitric acid, and I repeated the word 'acid' several times.

"Then I heard a shriek from a cell above me. I knew instantly that someone had overheard, and when I heard you coming, Mr. Warden, I feigned sleep. If you had entered my cell at that moment that whole plan of escape would have ended there. But you passed on. That was the nearest I ever came to being caught.

"Having established this improvised trolley it is easy to see how I got things in the cell and made them disappear at will. I merely dropped them back into the pipe. You, Mr. Warden, could not have reached the connecting wire with your fingers; they are too large. My fingers, you see, are longer and more slender. In addition I guarded the top of that pipe with a rat—you remember how."

"I remember," said the warden, with a grimace.

"I thought that if anyone were tempted to investigate that hole the rat would dampen his ardor. Mr. Hatch could not send me anything useful through the pipe until the next night, although he did send me change for ten dollars as a test, so I proceeded with other parts of my plan. Then I evolved the method of escape which I finally employed.

"In order to carry this out successfully it was necessary for the guard in the yard to get accustomed to seeing me at the cell window. I arranged this by dropping linen notes to him, boastful in tone, to make the warden believe, if possible, one of his assistants was communicating with the outside for me. I would stand at my window for hours gazing out, so the guard could see, and occasionally I spoke to him. In that way I learned that the prison had no electricians of its own, but was dependent upon the lighting company if anything should go wrong.

"That cleared the way to freedom perfectly. Early in the evening of the last day of my imprisonment, when it was dark, I planned to cut the feed wire which was only a few feet from my window, reaching it with an acid-tipped wire I had. That would make that side of the prison perfectly dark while the electricians were searching for the break. That would also bring Mr. Hatch into the prison yard.

"There was only one more thing to do before I actually began the work of setting myself free. This was to arrange final details with Mr. Hatch through our speaking tube. I did this within half an hour after the warden left my cell on the fourth night of my imprisonment. Mr. Hatch again had serious difficulty in understanding me, and I repeated the word 'acid' to him several times, and later on the words: 'number eight hat'—that's my size—and these were the things which made a prisoner upstairs confess to murder, so one of the jailers told me next day. This prisoner heard our voices, confused of course, through the pipe, which also went to his cell. The cell directly over me was not occupied, hence no one else heard.

"Of course the actual work of cutting the steel bars out of the window and door was comparatively easy with nitric acid, which I got through the pipe in tin bottles, but it took time. Hour after hour on the fifth and sixth and seventh days the guard below was looking at me as I worked on the bars of the window with the acid on a piece of wire. I used the tooth powder to prevent the acid spreading. I looked away abstractedly as I worked and each minute the acid cut deeper into the metal. I noticed that the jailers always tried the door by shaking the upper part, never the lower bars, therefore I cut the lower bars, leaving them hanging in place by thin strips of metal. But that was a bit of dare-deviltry. I could not have gone that way so easily."

The Thinking Machine sat silent for several minutes.

"I think that makes everything clear," he went on. "Whatever points I have not explained were merely to confuse the warden and jailers. These things in my bed I brought in to please Mr. Hatch, who wanted to improve the story. Of course, the wig was necessary in my plan. The special delivery letter I wrote and directed in my cell with Mr. Hatch's fountain pen, then sent it out to him and he mailed it. That's all, I think."

"But your actually leaving the prison grounds and then coming in through the outer gate to my office?" asked the warden.

"Perfectly simple," said the scientist. "I cut the electric light wire with acid, as I said, when the current was off. Therefore when the current was turned on the arc didn't light. I knew it would take some time to find out what was the matter and make repairs. When the guard went to report to you the yard was dark. I crept out the window—it was a tight fit, too—replaced the bars by standing on a narrow ledge and remained in a shadow until the force of electricians arrived. Mr. Hatch was one of them.

"When I saw him I spoke and he handed me a cap, a jumper and overalls, which I put on within ten feet of you, Mr. Warden, while you were in the yard. Later Mr. Hatch called me, presumably as a workman, and together we went out the gate to get something out of the wagon. The gate guard let us pass out readily as two workmen who had just passed in. We changed our clothing and reappeared, asking to see you. We saw you. That's all."

There was silence for several minutes. Dr. Ransome was first to speak.

"Wonderful!" he exclaimed. "Perfectly amazing."

"How did Mr. Hatch happen to come with the electricians?" asked Mr. Fielding.

"His father is manager of the company," replied The Thinking Machine.

"But what if there had been no Mr. Hatch outside to help?"

"Every prisoner has one friend outside who would help him escape if he could."

"Suppose—just suppose—there had been no old plumbing system there?" asked the warden, curiously.

"There were two other ways out," said The Thinking Machine, enigmatically.

Ten minutes later the telephone bell rang. It was a request for the warden.

"Light all right, eh?" the warden asked, through the phone. "Good. Wire cut beside Cell Thirteen? Yes, I know. One electrician too many? What's that? Two came out?"

The warden turned to the others with a puzzled expression.

"He only let in four electricians, he has let out two and says there are three left."

"I was the odd one," said The Thinking Machine.

"Oh," said the warden. "I see." Then through the phone: "Let the fifth man go. He's all right."

THE BEST MYSTERY STORIES
2025
HONOR ROLL

Additional outstanding stories published in 2024

Tyson Blue, Promises to Keep
About That Snowy Evening: Stories Inspired by Classic Poems from Emily Dickinson to Walt Whitman & More, ed. by Stephen Spignesi, Andy Rausch, and Keith Lansdale (Stephen John)

Jacqueline Freimor, Cruel to Be Kind
Dark Waters, Vol. 2, ed. by Kirstyn Petras & N. B. Turner

Nick Kolakowski, One Year in the Life of Marilyn
Rock and a Hard Place (Issue #12)

Linda Landrigan, Born Cross-Eyed
Friend of the Devil: Crime Fiction Inspired by the Songs of the Grateful Dead, ed. by Josh Pachter (Down & Out)

Leigh Lundin, Razing the Bar
Murder, Neat: A SleuthSlayers Anthology, ed. by Michael Bracken & Barb Goffman (Level Short)

Tom Mead, The Velvet Mask
The Indian Rope Trick and Other Violent Entertainments by Tom Mead (Crippen & Landru)

Joyce Carol Oates, The Heiress. The Hireling.
Ellery Queen Mystery Magazine (September/October)

M. E. Proctor, A Redhead and a Green Car
Motel: An Anthology, ed. by Barbara Byar (Cowboy Jamboree)

Emily Ross, Let the Chips Fall
Devil's Snare: Best New England Crime Stories, ed. by Susan Oleksiw, Ang Pompano, and Leslie Wheeler (Crime Spell)

dbschlosser, The Barnum Doctrine
The Killing Rain: Left Coast Crime Anthology 2024 (Down & Out)